ANGEL
OF
DESTRUCTION

Susan R. Matthews

A ROC BOOK

ROC
Published by New American Library, a division of
Penguin Putnam Inc., 375 Hudson Street,
New York, New York 10014, U.S.A.
Penguin Books Ltd, 27 Wrights Lane,
London W8 5TZ, England
Penguin Books Australia Ltd, Ringwood,
Victoria, Australia
Penguin Books Canada Ltd, 10 Alcorn Avenue,
Toronto, Ontario, Canada M4V 3B2
Penguin Books (N.Z.) Ltd, 182–190 Wairau Road,
Auckland 10, New Zealand

Penguin Books Ltd, Registered Offices:
Harmondsworth, Middlesex, England

First published by Roc, an imprint of New American Library,
a division of Penguin Putnam Inc.

First Printing, October 2001
10 9 8 7 6 5 4 3 2 1

Cover art by Matt Stawicki
Cover design by Ray Lundgren

 REGISTERED TRADEMARK—MARCA REGISTRADA

Printed in the United States of America

PUBLISHER'S NOTE
This is a work of fiction. Names, characters, places, and incidents either
are the product of the author's imagination or are used fictitiously,
and any resemblance to actual persons, living or dead, business
establishments, events, or locales is entirely coincidental.

Look for these other great works by Susan R. Matthews

An Exchange of Hostages

"A riveting character study of a conflicted young man . . . the book [has] a dark energy that, coupled with Matthews's intelligent prose, her genius for the unexpected, and her keen sense of atmosphere, produces an extremely compelling read."
—*New York Review of Science Fiction*

"Powerful, insidious, and insightful—a singular accomplishment for a tenth novel, let alone a first."
—Melanie Rawn

Prisoner of Conscience

"A brilliant author. A wonderful book. A new SF star has risen."   —David Feintuch

"Matthews has the ability to translate the ugliness of human society into highly readable prose. One of the most original and enjoyable works to be found in the genre in quite a while."   —*Starlog*

Hour of Judgment

"The series remains a mix of compelling storytelling, frighteningly intense depictions of evil, sentimental portraits of loyalty and courage, and some strangely reimagined conventions and stereotypes." —*Locus*

"[Matthews] brilliantly uses science fiction's freedom of creation to make a world in which she can explore deep moral conflicts."   —*The Denver Post*

Avalanche Soldier

"Matthews will stand out in a field dominated (in numbers if not in stature) by mediocre imitators."
—*Analog*

To absent friends

Prologue

Garol Vogel stood in the wheelhouse of the flagship as the Langsarik fleet came off the exit vector and dropped to subtractical speed. The Langsarik commander stood beside him; together they watched the massed ships of the Jurisdiction's Second Fleet come to position, flanking the Langsariks as they progressed toward Port Charid and their new home.

Their prison.

The Langsarik commander—Flag Captain Walton Agenis—stared impassively, her expression so flatly neutral that Garol knew it was a struggle for her to contain her emotion. The Langsarik fleet surrendered under escort with full military honors, true enough, but surrender was surrender nonetheless, and now they were wards of Jurisdiction.

The terms of their probation were not punitively strict. Port Charid was a small tightly knit community dominated by the Dolgorukij Combine, people among whom the Langsariks would stand out by virtue of their accent and their non-Combine blood. The Bench was counting on Port Charid to deny the Langsariks access to space transport and to provide a certain basic level of population monitoring—roll call, head count, attendance reconciliation.

In return Port Charid received the Langsariks, a population of five thousand souls with sophisticated technical skills, proven adaptability, and nowhere for them to work but as cheap labor to fuel Port Charid's

commercial expansion in cargo management and
freight handling.

"Are we clear?" Agenis asked; and one of her lieu-
tenants stood to answer. Hilton Shires was actually
her nephew as well as her lieutenant, though Garol
didn't think there was more than twelve years between
them; and Agenis had yet to see forty years, Standard.
She and Ga ol himself were almost the same age.

"Reports are complete, Captain, the fleet has
cleared the vector. Standing by."

Walton Agenis had been a lieutenant herself when
the Jurisdiction had annexed the Langsariks' home
system. She had risen to command over the fifteen
years of the Langsarik fleet's stubborn if futile resistance, forging what had been a local commerce patrol
fleet into mercantile raiders whose continued evasion
of Fleet's best efforts to locate and contain them had
become a scandal from one end of the Bench to the
other.

She'd seen her family either ostracized on her home
world—where it was no longer expedient to admit to
having kin with the Langsarik fleet—or lost in battle;
and now she stood witness to the final loss of the
fleet itself.

Still, it was only the ships that they were losing.

The Langsariks themselves—people who had made
the Langsarik fleet a challenge and a reproach to Jurisdiction—would live; and someday yet be free. Eight
years of probation as Port Charid's labor pool was not
so terrible a price to pay for reconciliation with the
Bench; and once eight years had passed the Langsariks
could go home.

"Specialist Vogel," Flag Captain Agenis said, not
looking at him. Garol bowed in salute at her side.

"Ma'am."

"The fleet is assembled in good order and ready to
surrender the controls as agreed. Your action, Bench
specialist."

Langsariks didn't salute. It wasn't the Langsarik way.

"Thank you, Flag Captain. Lieutenant Shires, if you would hail the *Margitov*, please."

Jils Ivers was on the Jurisdiction Fleet Flagship *Margitov*, waiting. She had worked as hard as Garol himself to see this happen: a peaceful solution to the Langsarik problem, one that avoided the crying waste that simple annihilation would have been. Lieutenant Shires made the call; and piped Jils Ivers's voice over the public address in the wheelhouse.

"Jurisdiction Fleet Flagship *Margitov*, standing by. Prepared to assume direction."

It was tactful of Jils to say "direction," and not "command" or "control." The reality of it was hard enough for those proud people to accept. They were under no illusions as to the impact of the change in status waiting for them. It was to their credit that they went forward into a sort of bondage as bravely as they ever had confronted the Bench in sortie.

"By direction from Flag Captain Walton Agenis," Garol said, choosing his words carefully. "Properly delegated by the Langsarik fleet to do so on its behalf. The Langsarik fleet surrenders the motivational controls to remote direction. Now."

Lieutenant Shires sat back at his post and folded his arms.

The images on the panoramic screens that lined the wheelhouse walls, the picture of space on monitor, faltered; then steadied again.

"The ship is on remote direction," Lieutenant Shires said, looking over his shoulder at Flag Captain Agenis. "They've got us, Captain."

I hope we're doing the right thing.

Shires didn't have to say it for the message to be clear, and Agenis didn't need to answer.

The Langsariks had made their decision.

They had agreed to accept amnesty and terms.

Not all of the Langsariks had agreed that it was their last best chance for survival under Jurisdiction: but the entire Langsarik fleet had sworn to be honor-bound by the majority vote, and Langsariks kept their promises. Sometimes all too well.

"Your ship, Bench specialist." Captain Agenis bowed her head and stepped back half a pace. "What are they going to do with it, may I ask?"

After the obvious, of course, repossession, disarmament, and evacuation of all Langsarik personnel on arrival at Port Charid. The Bench had hired transport from the mercantile resources in port to ferry the Langsariks from orbit to Port and from there to the nearby settlement that had been prepared for them.

Under the terms of the amnesty no Langsarik was to own, lease, direct, or appropriate space transport for the duration of the probationary period, unless under immediate and direct supervision by non-Langsarik employers. And these ships, the ships of the Langsarik fleet, the ships whose computing systems had just been surrendered to remote control, these ships had been home to the Langsariks for more than fifteen years.

"I believe they're to be taken back to Palaam." The Langsarik system of origin had a technical claim on the ships. Once the planetary government—the puppet government—of Palaam had formally repudiated them, the Langsariks had become pirates in the eyes of the law, and the hulls they fought with and lived on belonged to Palaam. "I don't know what the Palaamese government will do with them."

Agenis made a sour face, but it was gone almost as quickly as it had appeared. In a sense it was no hardship for the Langsariks to be forbidden to return to Palaam for eight years, Garol knew. As far as the Langsariks were concerned they had been betrayed by their own government, their families, their communities all turning their backs under pressure from the Bench. Maybe after eight years the Langsariks would come to forgive their home world for bowing to pressure. They were about to gain firsthand knowledge of how dispiriting life under Jurisdiction could be.

"Well. I hope they get some good maintenance people in. The condition of quarters, really, Bench specialist. It's shocking."

But her forced humor could not cover up her grief; and Garol could offer no help. He had already done everything he could for the Langsariks, not only to get the amnesty approved, but to structure the amnesty so that it would not become intolerable to the Langsariks. He felt responsible for them now; it was his doing that they were to accept probation here, his and Jils's. It had to work. Criminals by Bench definition, no question, but they were brave, smart, stubborn, strong-willed people, and the Bench could not afford to waste the resource they represented for the sake of mere vengeance, or ego gratification on the part of Palaam's Bench-appointed puppet government.

Since he could not change the hard facts of the matter, Garol attempted to provide reassurance of another sort, instead.

"I've inspected the settlement, Flag Captain. All new construction." Put up in a hurry, and not the best quality. Fleet contracting, let to the lowest bidder, but Garol had been given the authority to demand some of the less satisfactory elements be upgraded and improved.

It wasn't luxury.

But it would keep weather out and heat in; and the Langsariks would be able to make changes themselves, as time went on. "Paint job all one color, more or less, but at least it's clean. Funny thing, though. Not a trace of rose gold to be seen in the entire settlement."

She smiled, as if despite herself, and glanced down at the front of the uniform that she wore. Rose gold. The colors of the Langsarik fleet. "Do we surrender our clothing as well, then, Garol?"

Negotiations had gone on for months, and they'd been intense. In all that time, she'd never used his personal name. Garol was pleased and honored by her grant of intimacy, formal though it was, and at the same time grieved by the depth of her personal distress.

"You'll remove all rank and insignia on the ferry shuttle between the ships in orbit and Port Charid. But no. You keep your clothing." The Langsariks didn't have any other clothing, not after fifteen years. For all Garol knew they slept in uniform. "There'll be a concession store to serve your needs at the settlement, but they haven't selected a vendor yet. Food service and clinic and utilities, yes."

There were five thousand people in the Langsarik fleet, men, women, and even children born to a people at war with the civilized worlds and the Bench that governed them.

There were many logistical details yet unresolved, but Chilleau Judiciary would do the best it could for the Langsariks.

Chilleau Judiciary had no choice.

The First Judge—the single most powerful individual under Jurisdiction, the woman who held the tie-breaking vote on the Bench—was old; the Second Judge at Chilleau Judiciary was ambitious, and well placed to mount a bid for the First Judge's position when it became vacant. But there were nine Judges in all, several with their own ambitions with respect to the ultimate position of influence under Jurisdiction, and the Second Judge had suffered a staggering humiliation within the past year.

Chilleau Judiciary's political rivals had made full use of the lurid details of torture, murder, and waste of lives and property that had been taken into evidence during the trial of the Domitt Prison's administration for failure to uphold the rule of Law.

If the Second Judge was to reclaim her honor from the blow it had received in the court of public opinion after the scandals at the Domitt Prison, the Langsarik settlement could not be allowed to fail.

Chapter One

"Okidan Yards, this is the freighter *Sevior* requesting docking protocol. Please respond."

In the year since the Bench had settled the Langsariks at Port Charid, Port Charid itself had prospered, through its unequal partnership with its captive labor pool. Traffic was up more than 35 percent overall, and the arrival of a freighter at a warehouse yards excited much less notice these days than it might have done a year and a half gone by.

Fisner Feraltz stood in the dockmaster's office on the asteroid warehouse complex of the Okidan Yards, watching the freighter's approach on monitor.

He could remember.

He'd been fifteen years old, interning on a Combine ship carrying a shipment of garments from the manufactory in Berin, in Givrodnye—where he'd been born—to the clearinghouse at Corcorum, outside Combine space. They'd been attacked by Langsariks, ordered to stand by for boarding and prepare to surrender goods on demand. Someone—no one had ever claimed to know who it might have been—had fired the ship's signal guns, which weren't designed for offensive purposes.

So it hadn't even been Langsarik fire that had destroyed the ship. It had been an accident. The signal guns had never been used before, and somebody under the stress of the event hadn't unshipped the barrel shunts. Or had used the wrong rounds. Or something; and it didn't really matter, in the end. The entire crew but one had been lost in the explosion.

The Langsariks had never hinted at suspecting him, and no one else who might have accused him had survived.

But he lived with shame that never ended.

The dockmaster spoke from her post at her masterboard. "We have you, freighter *Sevior*, Okidan Yards confirms. Stand by for transmission of docking protocol."

The Langsariks had boarded the crippled freighter and found him barricaded in the cargo holds, trembling in terror. They'd taken him with them, because the ship had been too badly damaged to hold its atmosphere for long enough for rescuers to reach him from any other source.

He had been the only survivor.

And how could he have gone home to his family, after that? How could he explain the fact that he was alive while his brothers, uncles, cousins were dead? How could he have hoped to tell the truth—that the Langsariks had offered threats, but no violence; and had cared for him with creditable charity until they could see him safely on neutral ground—without raising questions in people's minds that he could not bear to face?

No.

There was no hope of any such homecoming, not for him, not forever.

He had stayed with the Langsariks for almost a full year, Standard, until they found a way to smuggle him back into friendly hands. That had been at Markov, as it had happened, and Fisner had never gone home.

The freighter on-screen, *Sevior,* turned its great bulk slowly to sink down between the signal markers on Okidan's flat side and come to ground. The Shawl of Rikavie was full of asteroids like Okidan; large enough to site warehouses and docks, small enough to maneuver out of the way of other asteroids in orbit if need arose. There was plenty of room to maneuver in the Shawl—the asteroid belt halfway between the planet Rikavie and the Sillume vector, entry and exit, the space-lane terminals that give Rikavie system its place in the web of transport under Jurisdiction.

The Jurisdiction had failed to take revenge for Fisner's family. After fruitless attempts to bring the pirates to account, the Bench had cravenly made peace with them instead, and left the crime unpunished to burn in Fisner's heart.

He had found work where he could, ending up at last within the Combine's mercantile authority, the oversight agency that coordinated trade on behalf of Combine interests within Jurisdiction as a whole.

It had been chance that had brought him to Port Charid, to work in the warehouses on-planet and oversee the Combine's yards on its own asteroid base in the Shawl.

But once the Jurisdiction had brought the Langsariks to settle at Port Charid and be its labor pool, Fisner Feraltz had understood the hand of the Holy Mother in his life, and known what he had to do.

If there had been no Langsariks, there would have been no accident.

It was their fault his family was dead, and he was exiled. No amount of self-serving charity on their part could wash away their guilt, or ease his suffering. Blood called for blood. Nor could he afford to forgive and forget in his heart, whatever the requirements of social discourse. The Holy Mother herself expected vengeance of him: The Angel had told him so.

On-screen, Fisner could see that the freighter *Sevior* had settled into its berth. Its umbilicus had completed its initial handshake, pressurized environment to pressurized environment. It was bright on the surface where the freighter lay, and the small sun of Rikavie shone like a beacon over the shoulder of the beast. The dockmaster sat at her station, however, her fingers drumming the console absentmindedly.

"Funny," she said, and Fisner thought it was maybe only to herself—idle curiosity, but no alarm. "That doesn't look like the specs it sent. Didn't they say it was a dray? That looks like a distance carrier, to me."

"Hard to say," Fisner replied politely, just in case she was talking to him. "But it does seem a little other than one would expect. Maybe we could ask the captain about it. Get a tour. You never know what's coming out of shipyards these days."

He was lying, in a way, because he knew quite well that it was a heavy transport freighter. It hadn't come to deliver stores to Okidan. It was here to take the Okidan Yards for everything it could plunder.

The dockmaster clearly didn't have a clue, not yet—just the germ of a suspicion. She pivoted slowly around in her seat and stood up, frowning slightly. "Good manners to go say something, either way. Coming?"

"No, thanks. I've got finishing up to do."

Inventory validation was a chore, but it had to be done. Since the Combine Yards were the largest in system, it had quite naturally fallen to the Combine Yards to oversee and facilitate, to manage all of the administrative details required to keep the flow of traffic moving, to provide insurers and contract holders alike with assurances as to the quality and condition of goods, to collect and remit fees and taxes, and generally to act as the Bench proxy in Port Charid.

The dockmaster left Fisner to his task. He was alone; and after a moment he locked the office door, secure in the knowledge that the observation ports—which were proof against unplanned decompression—would not be easy to break in, should someone on staff try to find shelter in the office from what was to come.

On the station's master monitor screens Fisner could see the dockmaster cross the loading apron to where the freighter's cargo umbilicus debouched into the loading docks. No one had appeared from the freighter yet. Abandoning his task for more pressing concerns, Fisner moved to the dockmaster's masterboard to cut the video feeds between the docks and the rest of the warehouse complex.

The dockmaster's chair was still warm from her body heat. Fisner hefted it to test the weight, and smashed it down across the master communications nexus board. The auxiliary fail-safe panel was on a subsidiary board some paces removed, and he left that intact. He had no intention of dying here.

There were people coming out of the freighter's umbilicus now, the cheerful color of their Langsarik blouses clearly visible even at a distance. They had the dockmaster, but she had yet to panic—at least to judge by appearances. Was it his imagination, or was she looking up into the monitor, up into the screens?

She knew he was in the office. She might be hoping for some quick-witted action on his part.

Fisner bore her no ill will. It wasn't her fault. It was the fault of the Bench, the Jurisdiction's fault for suffering Langsarik predation to go unpunished. Fisner set off the station alarms: standard emergency procedure, and it would bring everyone on station running to the loading docks. The freighter's crew had had enough time to get themselves into position by now, and were lying in wait.

The Bench had said that he had no claim against Bench or Langsariks for damages, that the loss he had suffered had been through misadventure. An accident.

The Angel of Destruction said differently.

The Angel of Destruction said that it was an offense against the Holy Mother herself that an ungodly and alien hand had been permitted to steal from Dolgorukij, and with impunity; an amnesty was no punishment for such a crime. The Angel of Destruction had sought him out and recruited him, sounded him out and tested him, tried his mettle and his faith—but at the end of it all the Angel had opened its arms to him and welcomed him, granted him membership in its sacred fellowship and made him the agent of the vengeance of the Holy Mother against the Langsariks at Port Charid.

The warehouse staff were unarmed; the slaughter was quick and efficient, over almost as soon as it had begun. Fisner scanned the loading docks outside the dockmaster's office with the remote monitors, counting the bodies.

Everyone seemed to be accounted for.

The dockmaster was to be shot over her boards, as if in the act of trying to call for help. She was still alive, standing under guard with two raiders in Langsarik dress as the plunder of the warehouse commenced. The hand of the Holy Mother was clearly discernible in the fortunate circumstance that had brought the Langsariks to Port Charid. They were a perfect cover for the Angel's fund-raising activities, and once they were shown guilty—too guilty for the Bench to overlook their faults and let them live free, this time—Port Charid would go begging for labor once more.

Labor that the Combine was in a position to provide, at a premium, of course.

Labor that would only solidify the hold the Holy Mother held over trade at Port Charid and access to the Sillume vector alike.

Meanwhile the Angel stood in need of goods to convert into funds, because the righteous were not welcome in the debased Church of the Autocrat's court. The Angel of Destruction had been outlawed through the malice of its enemies and the weak-spirited failings of the Autocrat himself octaves ago, when even Chuvishka Kospodar—the man who more than any other had nurtured their holy order, and welcomed it as the hand of the Holy Mother on Sarvaw— had been forced publicly to repudiate the Angel and its fearless defense of Her honor.

The money had to come from somewhere.

Just now it was coming out of the Okidan Yards,

and the Langsariks would be blamed—two blessings in one devotion.

After a while the raiders in Langsarik dress came to the door of the dockmaster's office, and Fisner opened the door. They had the dockmaster with them, and her eyes brightened with sudden hope when she saw him.

Hadn't she figured it out yet?

No, for they had been coached very carefully, Langsarik phrases, Langsarik swear words, Langsarik songs. Langsariks were responsible for the slaughter here, not honest Dolgorukij.

"Here?" raid leader Dalmoss asked Fisner, gesturing toward the broken master console with a tilt of his chin. A shot could serve to disguise the previous damage that had been deliberately inflicted on the communications console; with enough blood, people would be discouraged from looking very closely. It wouldn't be a problem. There were good reasons for the Langsariks to have first smashed the console and then shot the dockmaster, if anyone felt honor-bound to establish a precise sequence of events.

Fisner nodded.

Dalmoss bowed his head and glanced toward his people. They pulled the dockmaster over to her console and turned her so that she faced Fisner and the raid leader alike; but the venom in her expression, the hatred in her eyes, the acid in her voice was all for Fisner.

"You. I should have known better."

It was as if she no longer even saw the others, staring at Fisner with baffled rage. "Sharing spit with Langsariks, you might as well have been one of them all along. Imagine you working for the Combine. I guess you must have grown to like the life, is that what happened?"

He could snatch Dalmoss's weapon and kill her himself.

But that would have been a gesture of anger, an act

of violence done with a resentful heart. The Angel killed without mercy, but without malice. The Angel was only the humble tool of the Holy Mother, blessed by Her toward the furtherance of Her sacred plan; and therefore when the Angel killed it was without anger, without fear, without hatred or joy in cruelty.

It was for that reason that the Angel could kill, and not sin in doing so.

Therefore, Fisner simply nodded to Dalmoss. The raiders in Langsarik dress who had brought the dockmaster to her console backed away; she was so focused on Fisner that there was no need to watch for any sudden moves on her part. She was paralyzed with hatred as surely as though it had been fear.

Dalmoss shot her in the middle of her body, and her shoulders and head fell backwards over the top edge of the communications console while her legs fell in opposite directions, to each side of her shattered pelvis, as her arms flew wide.

What a mess, Fisner thought. And Dalmoss had prudently used his sidearm. Had he used one of the others' more powerful weapons—it didn't bear thinking on.

Just as well that the false Langsarik colors didn't have to be particularly clean to be recognizable for what they were.

"And now you, firstborn and eldest brother," Dalmoss said respectfully.

This was the most challenging part of this raid; but Fisner almost welcomed it. He would put any lingering doubts about his courage to rest, he would bear witness to his devotion to the Holy Mother with his body. And not least of all, he would bear witness with his words as well, damning witness against the Langsariks—so long as he survived, and his testimony was properly handled.

"I'm going over here to the auxiliary call," Fisner explained, setting the scene, proud of himself for being able to speak so calmly. He was afraid. But he would not falter. "You shoot me down, I fall, you leave. Near miss, but there must be enough damage to make it convincing." They'd been over all that already. They'd carefully chosen the angle of the shot, and where Dalmoss should aim. "Here I go—to reach the auxiliary call, and give the alarm—"

He had his back turned, so he didn't have to see Dalmoss raise his weapon.

And when the blow came it was so huge and shocking that he completely lost track of what he was doing.

People were dragging him along the ground, why was that?

Lifting, pressing his hands against the console.

Something was wrong with him.

The right side of his body seemed to have disappeared, and yet he could see it well enough—arm, leg, foot, hand.

He was bleeding, and his clothing was torn. Something in his mind noticed that no blood gushed, though it seeped quickly, and took that for an encouraging sign.

He lay against the auxiliary communications console with his face to the panel. Someone moved his hand; and there was a light, there, very close to his eyes. Green. Communication. Sending.

"Help me," Fisner croaked. He was supposed to say something. What was he supposed to say? He needed help. Yes. Langsariks had attacked the Okidan Yards. "This is Okidan. Feraltz. We're raided. Dying. Help."

His hand dropped away from the toggle, then his body followed, sliding slowly to the floor.

He didn't feel the impact as he fell.

He lay on the floor and stared at the wall stupidly until the room went black on him.

Langsariks.

Langsariks had done this.

It was all the Langsariks' fault that this had happened.

*　　*　　*

Standing at the aide's station in the small Combine hospital, Garol Vogel scanned the status report. *Fisner Feraltz, Combine citizen, Givrodnye national. Injuries sustained at the hands of armed pirates at the Okidan Yards in the Shawl of Rikavie, Rikavie system.*—

Rikavie system: port of departure, Charid—where the Langsariks had been settled by the Bench, just over a year ago, now. Checking the date on the status report Garol made a quick calculation. Twenty days. They'd brought Feraltz here as soon as he could be stabilized for distance transport; Port Charid had a small clinic of its own, and they could handle just about anything there, but Feraltz was Dolgorukij, and Dolgorukij suspected that nobody else really understood the intricacies of a Dolgorukij physique.

And perhaps they were right.

Injuries including but not limited to mass soft tissue laceration, especially of the right portion of the body. Knee joint requiring replacement, ankle may require fusing, biomedical netting wrap on long bones of thigh and lower leg, silica glazing therapy in effect over 85 percent of rightmost surface of hip.

"Lucky to be alive," Garol said to the patient's advocate who was serving as his guide and escort. The advocate nodded.

"That's what the staff says as well, Bench specialist. But since he is alive, the surgical board felt it best to postpone any interviews until he had regained at least some of his mobility. Since his basic evidence had already been read into the record at Port Charid."

Well, there wasn't a Record at Port Charid, not in the formal sense. For a Record to be official a Judicial officer qualified for custody was required, and Port Charid didn't rate any on-site staff, let alone a Record of its own. It was on circuit, yes, but that was it.

So far.

Once traffic started to pick up at Port Charid the Bench would site Chambers there—as well as a fleet detachment, to monitor attempts at unauthorized communication across the Sillume vector with Free Government insurrectionaries outside the pale of Jurisdiction, out in Gonebeyond space.

But first Port Charid had to grow its traffic. It took an on-site tax base to support Chambers and Fleet detachments, and so far Port Charid's tax base simply did not qualify.

"Langsariks, I heard." Garol frowned down at the closed medical record. "In fact I'm told there's been more than one disturbance at Port Charid recently."

The patient's advocate shrugged, looking almost bored. "If that's what they say, Bench specialist. Nothing to me one way or the other, except of course when they start shooting at honest Dolgorukij. No aspersion on the Bench umbrella, of course."

Of course not. Equal respect in theory for all hominid species under Jurisdiction was an important aspect of good Bench citizenship. And sensible acknowledgment of the fact that people would always favor their own was just common sense, and no offense to it.

"Very properly so, Advocate. Can we go in now?"

The patient's advocate looked to the medical aide who waited in the doorway; the medical aide nodded, and opened the door. It was a hinged door, here, in a hospital. Dolgorukij knew what was proper: at least what they believed to be proper. This little hospital smelled of money all the way out to the street. And Fisner Feraltz, the patient Garol had come to see, was here at his employer's expense, heroically wounded in a cowardly attack.

Garol had a notion that they'd made Feraltz very comfortable indeed, here.

The patient was in plain clothes, resting on an incline-board and doing a slow lift with his right leg. Physical therapy; Garol recognized the apparatus, and he could sympathize deeply with the look of carefully screened pain and concentration on Feraltz's face.

Even with the brace, it wasn't fun.

Feraltz wore bracing all over his right side, but

Garol knew how little of the load the bracing really took off injured limbs and joints—not nearly enough. Feraltz would be wearing pieces of that body-bracing for months, if not years.

Personally Garol had always preferred to discard such aids as quickly as possible and pay the price of mobility in pain.

Garol stopped a pace or two from where Fisner Feraltz pursued his physical rehabilitation with grim determination and nodded a polite greeting.

"Thank you for seeing me, Feraltz. I'm Vogel, Bench specialist Garol Aphon Vogel. Doing your exercises I see."

Feraltz was middling tall but well made, to look at him, more bone than flesh but adequately muscled by his hands and shoulders, fair-skinned and blue-eyed and very nearly blond. It was a type more general than some Dolgorukij Garol had met, who could have never been mistaken for Dynad or Jekrab, Nurail, or any other similar ethnicity; still, it was a type. Garol was a mixed category hominid himself, and his family generally tended toward a muddier complexion and less lithely limber a frame.

Feraltz lowered his eyes in acknowledgment. "Yes, thank you, Bench specialist. —Not at all, my pleasure, sir, as well as my duty." Well-spoken young man, and no trace of an accent that Garol could detect offhand. He noticed that. Dolgorukij generally had an accent, in part because of the basic conviction of the superiority of their blood and culture, in part because as a result of that conviction Dolgorukij who spoke Standard had very seldom learned to do so as children.

Nor had they taken it quite seriously as adults.

There almost wasn't any such thing as an unaccented Standard. The only people who spoke Standard as their native tongue were wards of the Bench raised at public expense; those, or the crèche-bred Command Branch officers the Bench was experimenting with, the orphaned children of the Bench's enemies raised by the Bench in strict indoctrination to serve the Bench and uphold the rule of Law.

"I'm concerned that the evidence I gave the Clerk of Court could be too liberally interpreted," Feraltz added, while Garol mused, distracted, on Feraltz's lack of an accent. "So I hope you haven't come on a misunderstanding, Bench specialist. But I'm glad to answer any questions you might have, sir."

Polite, as well as a well-spoken man. "How do you mean, 'liberally interpreted'?" It was an interesting thing to say, and could serve to ease in to the questions Garol had come to ask. "If you would care to elaborate."

The statements that had been forwarded to him said Langsariks. If there was going to be any trouble with the Langsarik settlement at Port Charid, Garol needed to cut it out quickly and quietly, before Chilleau Judiciary got any creative ideas about revising the amnesty.

Feraltz was very willing to elaborate, apparently. "If I can say so without reproach, Bench specialist, the Clerk of Court who came to see me seemed to be determined that she already knew exactly what had happened. She kept on helping me out, you know the kind of thing I mean, and I think she recorded things I didn't actually say. I really think she did. There's no real reason to blame the Langsariks for that raid, it's just circumstantial evidence, from start to finish."

Well, that was a start on what Garol wanted to hear; so it was that much more important to be careful about it, accordingly. "I've reviewed the evidence certified by the Clerk of Court who interviewed you, but it's been a few days since then. I do seem to recall a positive identification attributed to you. Langsariks, in the raiding party."

Difficult to tell whether Feraltz's pained expression resulted from psychological distress over a potentially serious misunderstanding, or just reflected physical pain. "I never made any such assertion, Bench specialist, I'd swear to it. I might not have been as coherent as I would have liked to be, though."

The statement had been taken only days after the Okidan Yards had been raided and its crew left for dead. Feraltz's statement had been taken at Port Charid while Feraltz had been waiting for transport to the private hospital here at Nisherre, and thus given while Feraltz had been surrounded by Langsariks—figuratively if not literally, the Langsarik labor force having relatively few technically proficient medical practitioners to spare from the clinic in the settlement for hire out to the port.

So in a sense Feraltz's continued survival argued against any Langsarik involvement in the Okidan raid: if Feraltz had been in a position to give credible evidence against Langsariks, to positively implicate Langsariks, the Langsariks in danger had had perfectly good opportunities to silence him before his evidence went anywhere.

And they hadn't.

So Feraltz wasn't and couldn't, and therefore hadn't needed to be silenced. Unless Feraltz's prior association with Langsariks, a detail Garol had found buried in the intelligence analysis, hinted at collusion; but if there was collusion, surely they would have managed a way to arrange Feraltz's survival without the risky cover of the physical injuries Feraltz had sustained?

"Without reference to your earlier testimony." Garol knew he could challenge that testimony, which had not been taken under appropriate controls, potential drug interactions compromising quality of evidence, and so forth. And he would, if he needed to; but first he needed to be sure of the facts. To the extent that there were facts. To the extent that objective truths even existed. "How about telling me what you remember that could be used to identify the raiders. Don't worry about anything you said before, for now. Just talk to me."

Feraltz let his leg rest, frowning. "That's probably

the problem right there, Bench specialist. I don't have much to offer. I was in the dockmaster's office doing inventory audit for the tax assessment, and I heard her talking to them on the comms, but I don't remember anything the least unusual about the conversation. I only barely remember hearing her talking to them at all."

He probably hadn't been paying attention. Dockmasters talked to inbound freighters all the time. A Langsarik accent was one of the more subtle ones—as if a Langsarik wouldn't have disguised his or her voice anyway. As if any pirate wouldn't have done that, out of baseline prudence.

As if Langsariks could have come up with a ship to mount a raid in the first place: unfortunately fifteen years of successful commerce raiding had created a belief in the public mind that the Langsariks could work miracles before breakfast, when it came to their ships.

"She went out, she shut the door; I remember thinking she might have some unrecorded transaction going with the freighter. And it's none of my business; I audit to the record, there are specialists who audit for unrecorded transactions. So I minded my own business."

It had just been bad luck for Feraltz that he'd even been there in the first place. But inventory audit was supposed to be unannounced, and the raiders wouldn't have expected him to be in the dockmaster's office.

"I heard the door, it was pushed open with a crash. Startled me. There were three men, and the dockmaster. She made a break for the master communications panel. They shot her. Into pieces."

The surprise of finding the dockmaster's office occupied would explain it; otherwise, it would have been hard to understand the dockmaster getting away from her escort, even for a short dash across the room. They'd probably meant to force her to open her safe room. If so, the death she'd won by resisting might well have been one infinitely to be preferred to the manner in which she might have died—except that Langsariks had never gone for torture in any big way. Nor massacre, come to that.

"And I think they were wearing that color, the yellow-pink. Langsarik colors. What is it called? Rose gold. It's a familiar color, Bench specialist, I should tell you that I spent some time as the guest of the Langsarik fleet, when I was younger." Garol made a mental note; Feraltz's candid confession simplified things a bit. "But that doesn't make them Langsariks. I could wear a Bench intelligence specialist's uniform if I wanted, but it wouldn't make me a Bench intelligence specialist."

No, it would make him a criminal. It was against the law to wear a uniform to which one was not legally entitled—or bound, in the case of the bond-involuntaries. The point was well taken, all the same.

"What do you remember about their appearance apart from the color of their clothing?" Garol prompted. "Anybody you may have thought you recognized, for instance. Cut of the garment. Hair color. Size and shape. Accent."

But Feraltz frowned, with apparent perplexity. "I'm sorry, Bench specialist. I didn't recognize anybody. They were all men, I think. I remember the color very vividly. But about the people themselves—not much."

Disappointing; but predictable. Feraltz had only seen them moments before he was shot, and then only under conditions of deep emotional shock and horror.

The Bench couldn't pin a Langsarik crime on the settlement on the basis of this evidence. Feraltz knew Langsariks, had lived with Langsariks, and refused to say that they were Langsariks; but the strength of the evidence went both ways. Maybe he was protecting someone.

And yet Garol couldn't discount the implications.

Maybe the raiders wore Langsarik colors in order to divert suspicion to a visible target in the event that they were seen. It would be a coup for Langsariks to manage a raid from quarantine; unfortunately, the Langsariks had proved—time and again—that they were capable of almost anything.

And therefore maybe the raiders wore Langsarik colors because they were Langsariks, and that was the only clothing they had.

That was the simplest—and therefore most obvious, if unlikely—explanation; and Garol did not look forward to taking this intelligence to Chilleau Judiciary.

It was his duty. He didn't have to like it.

The only way he was going to be able to determine whether or not there was a problem with the amnesty agreement was to go to Port Charid and see for himself. If nothing else, the public-relations angle had to be carefully managed, and he could best decide how to handle that on-site.

"Are you willing to do a pharmaceutical investigation?" Garol asked, because he had a duty to ask. Sometimes the right drugs could pull up a previously unretrieved detail from memory; but drugs were also frequently responsible for the spontaneous generation of false memories, or for complete misinterpretation of imperfectly understood information.

It took a real expert to hope to tell the difference, especially in circumstances where the subject witness might have ulterior motives that affected what and how much he remembered.

Garol wasn't particularly interested in risking the survival of the Langsarik settlement on a point of interpretation; so he was just as glad when Feraltz shook his head, rejecting the suggestion. Reluctantly. But absolutely.

"I'm sworn to Abstain, Bench specialist, and it's hard enough that I have to take all of this medicine, even though the priest insists on it. I'll do a drug inquiry if you come back with an Ecclesiastical Exception, of course I will. But I really don't want to. I'm sure I've already told you everything I remember."

The Dolgorukij church administration would make

allowances for the requirements of Bench process, even for zealots like Abstainers. But zealots hated to compromise, on Ecclesiastical Exception or any other grounds. This young man had already suffered; Garol was quite willing to forgo a step that might only produce ambiguous or flawed evidence for which there was no pressing immediate need—at least for the time being.

If there were problems on Charid, he would find out about them his own way; too much potentially ambiguous information too soon would only seriously constrain his freedom of action.

"Let's not worry about that for now. Time enough later if we need corroborative evidence," Garol reassured Feraltz, who seemed to relax gratefully. "I'll be going, Feraltz. Thanks for your time. And keep up with your therapy. It's the best thing for a complete recovery."

He should talk.

But maybe giving lip service to the acknowledged but disregarded truth would balance out his own personal and admittedly flamboyant disobedience of doctor's orders, and help even everything out in the end.

He was going to have to go to Chilleau Judiciary and talk to the Second Judge's First Secretary, Sindha Verlaine; that could be as unpleasant as rehabilitation therapy, so maybe that would count on the credit side of his personal register, too.

It was worth hoping for.

Garol set his mind firmly on that encouraging but unlikely idea and left Feraltz to exercise in peace.

Kazmer Daigule strolled casually through the narrow lanes of Port Charid's warehouse district with his hands deep in the worn pockets of his old coat, trying to guess how long it would take for the early-morning sun to warm the air at street level. It would be midmorning before the shadows began to lift, as far as he could tell; these lanes were only wide enough to admit

a small transport mover, and the warehouses themselves towered to the skies.

At least that was the impression from ground level,
and the effect seemed to have a discouraging impact
on the relatively few people Kazmer could see coming
and going in the streets. Maybe they were all just
minding their business; Kazmer could approve of that.

Then something caught his eye.

Didn't he know that man—

Kazmer had seen the familiar figure approach, but
so far as he could tell he hadn't been remarked upon
for his own part. This could be good. Looking around
him quickly, Kazmer located the nearest doorway and
ducked into the shallow alcove the doorway offered
for concealment, then waited.

Moments passed.

Then the man crossed in front of him, and Kazmer
knew him all right. Tall and thin, big-boned, almost
gangly, with a fine sharp expression of quick intelligence and lively wit—and big ears that stood out from
his head, though perhaps it took a friend to notice.
Frowning, just now, and apparently sunk so deep in
thought that he didn't so much as look up until
Kazmer spoke.

"Hilton Shires, as I live and breathe. What brings
you into Port Charid, Hilton?"

Kazmer stepped out of the alcove and extended his
hand in greeting, but it seemed that the surprise he'd
given Hilton was unpleasantly complete. It took Hilton a moment to respond.

"Kazmer. Hey. Long time, how've you been?"

Well, it hadn't been all that very long a time. Not
really. He'd taken his leave of the Langsariks well
ahead of their rendezvous with the Jurisdiction fleet,
and he hadn't seen hide nor hair of a Langsarik since.
Two years, maybe.

"I've got no complaints." Kazmer took a step or
two down the street, to encourage Hilton to walk with
him; but Hilton wasn't moving. Maybe Hilton was an-

noyed at Kazmer for getting the drop on him, which would be a little oversensitive on Hilton's part. It was Kazmer who owed his life to Hilton, and not the other way around. "You?"

"Life is changed." Hilton made the obvious point so blandly that it was almost as though the fact had just occurred to him. "Not like old times at all, Kazmer. What brings you to Port Charid?"

"I've been called in on a transport job." By Hilton's people, as a matter of fact. As if he didn't know, him with his Langsarik colors showing beneath the sober collar of a new if inexpensive work shirt. But maybe he had gotten cautious, in his old age; or it could as easily be that Hilton felt they were too vulnerable to eavesdropping, out in the street like this. They'd be a lot less obvious if they were walking together, Kazmer told himself; but Hilton had a stubborn streak. "From what I've heard there's been more than one of that sort of thing through Port Charid lately."

But what could Langsariks need cargo transport for? The Langsariks' property had been impounded by the Bench, along with the Langsarik hulls—as a very practical means of assuring good behavior by removing the means of any independent behaviors at all.

The only transport a Langsarik could get would be illegal and surreptitious by definition. So the only need that Langsariks could have for a mercantile pilot to transport cargo was to move contraband, and Kazmer and Hilton both knew it.

Which only made Hilton's resolute play at oblivious ignorance all the more irritating. "Well, traffic is picking up. That's true. Plenty of work to go around." And Hilton actually leaned his back up against the external wall of the warehouse that fronted on the street, folding his arms across his chest as he did so. Those were his racing thermals that Hilton was wearing with his new work shirt, Kazmer noted. Somewhat the worse for wear, too, but Hilton had always been hard on his racing thermals. A demon for speed, land-borne, airborne, spaceborne. "Still. Isn't this a little out of the way for you?"

Yes, it was. I'm a free agent, and I thought it sounded interesting." He wouldn't have come so far on a job offer for anyone but Hilton's people—let alone for a job offer that involved contraband. He was trying to get away from contraband. The least Hilton could do was acknowledge the debt, even if it was obliquely. "Are you on your way to anywhere in particular yourself?"

Of course he was. Hilton was there for the same reason Kazmer was; Kazmer was sure of it. Hilton, however, shook his head, and lied.

"Not really. There isn't much to do out in the settlement, though, and I got a pass. So I thought I'd come down to watch the shuttle traffic, kind of get away from it all for a bit."

Now Kazmer was annoyed, and beginning to think about being insulted. Prudence was one thing, but Hilton was taking this whole secrecy bit a little too far. And if that was the way Hilton was going to be, Kazmer would not keep him any longer.

"I see. Well, enjoy yourself, Hilton. Give my regards to your family, all right?"

Hilton's family.

There was a thought.

So long as Hilton was here in Port Charid maybe Kazmer would have a chance to get out to the settlement and see sweet little Cousin Modice.

Hilton had warned him—if only half-seriously—never to let him catch Kazmer in bed with his little girl-cousin ever again; and him knowing what the joke was, because it had been Hilton's idea. It hadn't taken Kazmer long to develop a crush on Modice, true, but he'd known from the start that there was no real future in it.

Modice's guardian—the Flag Captain of the Langsarik fleet herself—had let him know that Sarvaw mercantile pilots didn't figure into any Langsarik domestic equations that she was willing to consider for her niece. She'd done it gently and with humor, but the message had been clear enough.

Fine.

Hilton wouldn't catch him.

Modice was a grown girl, or close enough to it to make up her own mind. By now, anyway. It had been three years since the bed incident.

"Sure thing," said Hilton. "Maybe I'll see you around. Before you go. Where are you staying?"

Kazmer was tired of the game. "Just in, actually, I don't know yet. I'll be in touch. Nice to see you, Hilton."

He was on his way to meet with Hilton's people in a common mealroom two streets over, right now.

But if Hilton genuinely didn't know where he was, there was no danger of Hilton guessing that he had gone out afterward to see Modice.

That would pay Hilton out for being so excessively cagey with him in the street. Pleased with this thought, Kazmer went on to his meeting with his prospective employers in good humor once again.

Hilton Shires lingered on the pavement, leaning as casually as he could manage against the exterior wall of a featureless warehouse building, watching Kazmer Daigule's back as he lumbered out of sight.

Of all the bad luck, rotten luck, disgusting luck, unfair luck.

No, he had nothing against Sarvaw mercantile pilots, not in so many words. Kazmer was his friend; he'd saved Kazmer's life—or at least it had been his stratagem that had saved Kazmer's life—and there was little that endeared one man to another quite so strongly as the sense of being benefactor to a peer.

It was true that Kazmer had shown signs of getting sweet on Modice, but that was hardly Kazmer's fault; Modice had that sort of effect on a lot of people. And the provocation had been more extreme than usual, what with their first meeting being in such potentially compromising circumstances.

But mercantile pilot Kazmer Daigule was one of the last people Hilton had expected to see in Port Charid that morning, and the surprise rendered the awkwardness all the more unpleasant.

He'd made up his mind to take action. They were a displaced people on probation; and while the Bench provided well enough for them to evade public outrage and avoid creating discord from extremes of want, the Bench did not provide for them generously, in any sense.

Hilton's parents had grown old at war, serving with the Langsarik fleet. The cold season was coming on in the settlement, and the weary bones of retired warriors creaked in the chill wind that blew from the south-southwest. He was young and fit and could labor; and also he had destroyed the latest in a long line of speed machines, and needed the wherewithal to buy another.

But he wasn't about to admit to Kazmer, of all people, that Hilton Shires was looking for a job. Kazmer knew him as a lieutenant in the Langsarik fleet, a man of acknowledged capability, authority, daring. Kazmer still had space transport, and no Fleet directive to restrict him from using it. Hilton was grounded and flightless, emasculated, powerless.

He had swallowed a good deal of humiliation over the past two years, as the necessary price of purchasing their lives and eventual freedom from a vengeful Bench; but there were limits to how low he could tolerate forcing himself to bend, and confessing his sorry estate to Kazmer was right down there near rock bottom.

It was almost enough to put him off his enterprise altogether: But Kazmer was gone, and the weather was still slowly but surely on its way toward wintertime. The Combine Factor in Port Charid—a big, brash, bearded man named Shiron Madlev—had been a friend to the Langsarik settlement in too many quiet subtle ways to deserve rude behavior from Hilton. Accepting Madlev's offer of a job interview and then canceling at a moment's notice would be an entirely gratuitous slap in the face.

And without a speed machine to remind him, howsoever briefly, of the freedom of the stars, Hilton was not sure he could survive; so he took a deep breath and composed himself, and walked on.

It was easy enough to find the Factor's front office, even though Hilton hadn't been there before. There was a man behind a desk with a high counter, and another man sitting by the beverage server having a flask of the leaf-based beverage that Combine people drank by preference—rhyti, that was right. It smelled like flowers to Hilton, but his aunt liked the stuff.

"Good-greeting. My name is Hilton Shires." The man at the desk had watched him come in; clearly the doorkeeper, so Hilton spoke to him first. "I have an appointment for an interview."

Out of the corner of his eye Hilton saw the other man present put down his flask of rhyti and stand up. The doorkeeper nodded at the second man, but he was speaking to Hilton.

"Yes, Shires, you're expected. This is floor manager Dalmoss. Factor Madlev has asked the warehouse foreman to interview you, you're to go with Dalmoss to find him, if you please."

Well, Hilton had found the prospect of talking to Factor Madlev himself about a job a bit awkward. He was just as glad he would be talking to a foreman; the less overall power the foreman had in the organizational structure of the Combine Yards, the less keenly Hilton expected to feel the gap between what the foreman had the power to dole out and what he himself could expect or hope to be offered.

Something like that.

"Dalmoss Chzagul," the floor manager said, coming up to Hilton. Then, unexpectedly, Dalmoss offered his

hand to clasp in the Langsarik fashion. Hilton didn't
particularly need to clasp hands with any non-Langsarik,
but it was a nice gesture and would be rude of him
to ignore it, so he took Dalmoss's hand and clasped
it politely.

"Pleased. Hilton Shires. Thank you for seeing me."

Dalmoss seemed as willing as Hilton to call the gesture complete and break contact, but that was entirely
fair as far as Hilton was concerned. "I'll be honest with
you, Shires, it's not my idea." But the admission was
merely frank, and not challenging; Hilton could find
no cause to take offense. "Still, we need help. I can
grant you that, without hesitation. Let's go find the
foreman; he said he might be in the mealroom this
time of the morning. We'll check there first."

It was a way of giving him a tour of the facility,
maybe. Hilton looked around him with interest as Dalmoss led him through the administrative offices, across
a loading dock, past the great hulls of not one but
three freighter tenders being off-loaded, and finally
out into the street and down a half a block to a subsi-
dized mealroom, where Dalmoss paused in the foyer
to scan the crowded hall.

"Look at all these people," Dalmoss suggested.
"You can see our problem. We keep on picking up
freight. We're running out of capacity to handle it."

Hilton followed Dalmoss's lead in looking around
him politely. It was very candid of Dalmoss to make
such remarks when they both knew that the reason
the Combine Yards were picking up freight was that
the Okidan Yards and other yards before it had lost
capacity, and the freight had to be handled somewhere. The Okidan Yards hadn't merely lost capacity,
of course. The Okidan Yards had lost its staff and
its plant, and there was a lot of gossip that blamed
Langsariks. Hilton knew the gossip was baseless. It
was still an awkward situation to be in.

Who was that over there by the far wall?

Kazmer Daigule, sitting at table with some people

Hilton didn't recognize—discussing terms and conditions of hire, clearly enough, public mealrooms being convenient meeting spaces for people without offices to call their own. Such as Sarvaw mercantile pilots.

So Kazmer was here to run a Combine cargo.

That would explain his refusal to come right out and say what he was doing here. Kazmer was Sarvaw. Hilton knew what Kazmer thought of the rest of the Dolgorukij Combine—or at least he knew what Kazmer had to say about other Dolgorukij.

"I don't see him here," Damoss said. "Something you need to know about the foreman, Shires. He was at the Okidan Yards when the—when it was hit. He's only been back at Charid for two days, still in med-assist; so it's hard for him to get around, or he'd have met you himself. You can thank him for your job. He saw your name on the resource list and grabbed for you."

Dalmoss had started to move again; Hilton had to keep up. "That's flattering. If confusing. What's one Langsarik among others? You know what I'm saying."

Dalmoss grinned. Hilton was beginning to think he liked the man. "I wondered myself. Feraltz insisted. Said you had the leadership skills we were going to need in the remote warehouse. You were an officer? If you don't mind me asking."

" 'Was' being the pertinent word. Yes. Junior officer. But these days I'm just another unemployed Langsarik, like the rest of us."

That was unfair, maybe. There were plenty of jobs for Langsariks at Port Charid; that was one of the reasons the Bench had settled them there, after all, to be Port Charid's very own captive labor pool. There were all the nasty, difficult, soul-wearing, low-paying jobs anyone could want available.

"A cut above the rank and file, even so. We're expanding. Fisner will tell you all about it—he said to try Receiving if he wasn't having firstmeal."

Fisner Feraltz.

The name seemed familiar, somehow.

Dalmoss moved quickly, and there was a lot of territory between the mealroom and the receiving floor. A man could clearly get his exercise, working here.

Hilton had heard about warehouse operations, and he had an idea of their size from living near Port Charid; but he'd never been so deep inside of a major mercantile complex before. The receiving floor was the size of an asteroid warehouse, it seemed, and there were more freighter tenders there, four of them.

Four.

Hilton let his eyes rest on the great beasts that Port Charid used to ferry cargo between the surface and the freighters in orbit, the ships that were too large to land and lift except from the yards in the Shawl of Rikavie, where the gravitational pull was minimal.

Four freighter tenders.

He'd seen passenger shuttles that would carry maybe a thousand souls, at least for two days or so, and these freighter tenders were even bigger than a mass passenger ferry. He slowed to a stop without noticing what he was doing and stared at the ships hungrily; then Dalmoss's voice called him back to where he was.

"There's the boss," Dalmoss said. "Over there. On the crate, by that mover. Come on."

Those freighter tenders might as well be crates themselves. He'd not be allowed to so much as move them into orbit, if he was allowed onto them at all. Hilton pushed his wild fantasies firmly into a corner of his mind and followed Dalmoss to where a man of Hilton's approximate age was sitting on a crate, waiting for them.

Fisner Feraltz only half sat on the crate, his right leg stretched out straight and resting on the floor, covered in bracing. A little more to the fleshy side than Hilton himself was, perhaps, but then it wasn't as if the food in settlement encouraged overindulgence.

"Hilton Shires, Foreman," Dalmoss called. "We missed you in the mealroom, sorry."

Feraltz waved the apology off with his left hand. The right hand was braced stiff. "My fault, Dal, I didn't make it to firstmeal. Too much effort. Hilton Shires? Fisner Feraltz. Excuse me if I don't offer my hand."

He was a lot more informal than Hilton had expected, which came as a relief. "Quite all right. When in Combine Yards do as Combine does, after all. Thanks for the opportunity to interview."

Feraltz beckoned him closer, so that he could speak more quietly Hilton supposed. "My pleasure, Shires. I owe a debt of gratitude to your family, but I'm keeping quiet about it. Sentiment isn't very supportive of Langsariks in Port Charid just now, I'm afraid."

Feraltz.

Of course.

Dalmoss wasn't looking surprised, so it apparently wasn't a particular secret; but Hilton could certainly understand why Feraltz might want to avoid calling attention to his personal history, just at the moment. To have spent a year with Langsariks was probably about the same as having been raised by wolves, as far as Feraltz's fellow Dolgorukij were concerned.

"So. Look at this, Shires." Feraltz's gesture took in the entire sweep of the receiving area, the tenders, the work crews, the loading cranes. The crates. "The Combine Yards are picking up the slack for lost capacity elsewhere in system. We're going to have to make some pretty significant increases to accommodate the overflow. There's new facilities under construction—"

Hilton knew that. The Combine's new warehouse project had been one of the first things Port Charid had drawn on its new Langsarik labor pool to get started.

"—but we're not staffed for it, and I need someone with prior management experience to help us grow. I'll need to start you on the entry levels, of course, so you can familiarize yourself with the administration of this kind of an operation."

It sounded good.

"I don't have any prior management experience." It sounded a little too good. All right, Feraltz felt he owed something to Aunt Agenis's extended family for saving his life and getting him safely back to his own people, even though it had taken them a while. Hilton still wanted to be sure that Feraltz wasn't overestimating his ability, in his desire to be accommodating. "I was a lieutenant. It's people like my aunt who actually ran things."

He'd commanded raids, successful ones, but he wasn't about to make a point of that. Not here. Very poor taste.

Feraltz shook his head, rejecting Hilton's disclaimer. "I know what your position was, and I think the skills are transferable. I'd like you to accept an entry-level position in order to train for assistant floor manager, looking forward to the time when the new facility comes up to capacity. I can't promise anything, but I'm confident you'll demonstrate the qualities we need. Will you consider my offer?"

It really wasn't an option. He needed the job.

"I'll be happy to accept your offer, Foreman. I appreciate the opportunity to come work for the Combine Yards and learn about warehouse management. I see it as a long-term investment. And I'm not going anywhere."

Maybe he shouldn't have said that last bit. It sounded a little bitter, a little petty. He'd only make things worse if he made a fuss about it by qualifying or rephrasing, though, so he bit his tongue firmly to shut himself up, and waited.

Feraltz smiled sympathetically, while Dalmoss—his arms folded across his chest—looked at the floor, smiling as well, and scuffing his foot against some unseen object by way of making a show of going along with the joke.

"I understand perfectly," Feraltz said. "Dockman's wages to start, Shires; you'll report to Dalmoss here, you can discuss your shift with him once you've done your in-processing. Do we have a contract?"

Dockman's wages were better than the day laborer's rates usually offered to Langsariks. Maybe Feraltz was serious about his plans; one way or the other he was certainly making it much easier for Hilton to commit himself to regular employment than Hilton had expected.

"Contract," Hilton agreed. "Thank you, Foreman. Floor manager."

Dalmoss had waved someone over, and the man approached them with a look of genial curiosity on his face. "This is Ippolit," Dalmoss said. "Ippolit, Shires is coming on to join receiving and inventory. Would you take him out to personnel, please, they're expecting him."

Were they, indeed.

But the prospect of dockman's wages went a long way toward sweetening any residual difficulties Hilton might have experienced on that account; and he followed the man called Ippolit away to the personnel office, not so much happy as relieved enough to feel almost as though he were.

Fisner Feraltz watched Shires leave with Ippolit. Dalmoss was unhappy; Fisner knew it. He could tell.

"Was it prudent to remind him, firstborn and eldest?" Dalmoss asked, his voice pitched low enough to guard against anyone eavesdropping by accident. "He may speculate."

"He may." Fisner could afford to accept a portion of the rebuke from Dalmoss; it was no challenge to his authority. "But he's the Flag Captain's nephew. To not have at least mentioned it would look like ingratitude. He might have wondered why I'd not allowed the obligation."

Dalmoss thought about it for a moment, time Feraltz used to adjust his position on the crate. The bracing was awkward. He was having a hard time adjusting to it.

"I understand. Yes," Dalmoss said. Fisner knew that what Dalmoss understood about Fisner's history with Langsariks was not the whole truth, but that was the way it had to be. No one could know the true depths of his shame: That was between him, and the Angel of Destruction, and the Holy Mother. "Does the bracing trouble you, firstborn and eldest?"

Well, yes, it did. But Dalmoss's anxiety could be traced at least in part to the fact that it had been Dalmoss who had fired the round that had injured him.

"It's an annoyance, I admit." And there were drugs for annoyance, as there were drugs for pain. He'd told the Bench Specialist that he was an Abstainer, but he'd had reason for that deception that did not extend so far as actually to abstain from medication required to heal flesh, knit bone, and ease one's way through life generally. "But a minor one. And it puts our purpose forward."

It was very convenient if others thought him to be Abstaining, of course.

It could only increase the effectiveness of his deception if people who saw him at all only ever saw him obviously crippled, dependent upon the medical brace to support a clearly only slowly healing frame.

Dalmoss nodded. "I'll go arrange for a team meeting, Foreman. To introduce our new employee. We start him on inventory, I believe."

Yes, so that it would be creditable to claim that Shires had learned to manipulate the inventory systems. Not only to learn the location of cargo to be appropriated, but also to hide stolen goods within the Combine Yards themselves, so that when the Bench finally sent troops to Port Charid to search, the evidence of Langsarik predation would be utterly damning. Unchallengeable.

"You have nothing with which to reproach yourself, Dalmoss." Since they both knew what they needed to do with Shires, Fisner decided to address the other issue instead. The one that had been there, unspoken but near palpable, hanging in the air between them since Fisner had returned from the hospital in Nisherre. "All went as expected, as hoped. As planned. Believe me, next born and second eldest. From my heart."

Dalmoss could not but accept his superior's assurances, whether or not he seemed fully convinced by them. "Just as you say, then, eldest and firstborn. I'll be going to call my crew meeting, with your permission."

Fisner was not concerned. Dalmoss would learn that Fisner spoke only plain truth.

Dalmoss had not done him any injury, even though Dalmoss's shot had injured him.

Dalmoss had made it possible for the plan to go forward: and Fisner had nothing but gratitude to him, for that.

Chapter Two

The rendezvous had been set for a public cafeteria deep in the warehouse district—a fine anonymous place for a plot, Kazmer told himself, pausing on the threshold to take in the scene. The morning meal line was beginning to slow down, and the room was neither so full that people could not sit apart without drawing attention to themselves nor so empty that individuals stood out against the general void. There was too much ambient noise to fear a directional sensor, but not so much that a man would need to raise his voice to make himself heard.

It was near perfect.

Kazmer paid for a breakfast tray and carried it over to one of the tables at the far wall. Third from the left, he'd been told. There were people there already; but none of them looked like Langsariks to Kazmer.

He sat down with his back to the wall, facing the entrance to the meal line. The woman who had moved over on the bench to make room for him eyed him with mild curiosity; then she spoke.

"It'd be Kazmer Daigule. Mercantile pilot. Didn't you carry some kennels of Clement's spotty dogs to Julerich, last year?"

Maybe he had, and maybe he hadn't. He took a drink of his morning brew and grimaced, reaching for the syrup packet on his tray. Sometimes the only thing to do was to syrup the stuff up and get it down somehow. A man needed his morning drink to help him get started on his day's work.

"What's your interest in spotty dogs?" he retorted, but mildly. "There are worse cargoes. And I know, because I've carried them."

There was an older man seated across from Kazmer; that would be the ship's master, Kazmer guessed. He had an accent that Kazmer couldn't place, but it wasn't any of his business.

"You can do better than spotty dogs, pilot. There's a chance of a cargo to leave from the Shawl soon, and a good market even for goods whose documentation might not be quite perfect."

So far, so good, but there was no sense letting down his guard before he was sure of his surroundings. "That's as may be. But it takes more than a pilot to move cargo."

The completely undistinguished person on the other side of the woman to Kazmer's left leaned forward, and looked directly at him. "Not too many more, if someone else does the load-out. There'll be resources on-site to transfer cargo, and I can get a ship packed and ready in three hours or less. Guaranteed."

"I can vouch for it," the man on the other side of that man said. "I've seen it happen." And Kazmer—looking down to the end of the table—got confirmatory, conspiratorial nods from the three other people at the foot of the table besides. All right.

"Navigator?" he asked, and the woman coughed discreetly.

"Ship's master," the man facing Kazmer said, the one who'd made the remark about goods and documentation. "So think of me as Engineer. To my right, your left, transmission specialist. To my left, your right, cargo disposition manager."

The fence, in so many words. The man who would be responsible for getting rid of stolen goods and paying them all off.

"And that's just cargo management," Fence emphasized, quietly, but with a solid sort of determination in his voice and his serious expression. "No wet goods.

Or I'm not even playing. Anybody have any different ideas? There've been assurances given me, no squishy stuff."

Kazmer felt a little offended. "Come on. These people don't waste energy. It's not going to be a problem, I've seen them in action. I wouldn't touch a cargo with moisture on it."

That wasn't exactly true. He'd handled cargoes with blood on them before: just not life's-blood. He'd been prudish or he'd been lucky, or possibly both, but he'd stayed clear of blood-guilt since he'd taken his pilot's license, and he meant to keep it that way.

"You've been out of system, pilot," the woman—Navigator—said. Suggested, explained? "You haven't heard. The latest raid at Okidan, only one survivor."

She was right. He hadn't heard. Was there a problem? Kazmer tucked into his bowl of porridge, hoping to get most of it down before it congealed in the dish.

"I was promised different this time," Engineer said. "But I won't pretend it really matters. There's a job. I need one. Someone's going to do it, and I may as well collect the fee as any other man. Worth taking just to see how it's being managed, to my mind."

At least the engineer was honest. That didn't mean Kazmer had to respect the man's point of view. Still, he was curious about the logistics himself; and was there any sense in pretending to keep to high moral ground? Cargoes all came from someplace. People got in the way of live fire from time to time, without anyone meaning any harm. Accidents happened. Carrying contraband goods was against the law whether or not anyone had gotten hurt in the initial cargo-acquisition phase of the transaction.

But he'd never done more than economic harm to any man. He wasn't about to start now, not even to help Langsariks. Not even to help Hilton.

"I'm not getting paid to risk a capital charge," one of the crew said, her voice low enough to keep her words carefully within the limited area of the table without attracting attention by whispering. "They claimed you'd worked with this outfit before, pilot."

And so he had. "Where are they, by the way? Does anybody know?" He could tell them where one of the members of the group that had hired them was, or near to it, at least. Hilton had to be somewhere close.

The navigator shook her head. "The man who contacted me said that any direct contact would be too risky for all of us, especially so soon after Okidan. Said you could answer any questions we might have. We disperse, we get a call, we load and leave."

Oh, he'd disperse, all right. He'd disperse straight out to the Langsarik settlement to see Modice. The Langsariks were keeping a low profile? He'd be sure no one caught him on his way there or back. Hilton wouldn't be able to accuse him of any underhanded subterfuge; he would merely be taking prudent measures to avoid attracting any attention to himself.

"Well, it's true what they told you. About prior association," Kazmer added hastily. Hilton had a wickedly dry sense of humor; there was no telling what he might have said to these people. "I've always found them to be efficient. Conservative. No unnecessary effort." Meaning, by implication, no unnecessary violence. "I'd expect them to be especially careful to keep the noise level down. Frankly, I'm a little surprised they're risking any noise at all."

And maybe "they" weren't. Maybe this whole setup wasn't Langsariks at all, or at least not fully sanctioned. Maybe Hilton and some of his peers were just blowing off a little steam. It had to be hard on people like Hilton to settle down on dirt and look for mundane, lawful employment after having spent nearly sixteen years as a law unto themselves, answerable to none, taking what they needed when they needed it from wherever they could find it.

That could be.

The fence shrugged. "Who knows if what the authorities say about the other procurement is even true? Maybe there wasn't any broken furniture."

A good point, that, what with public propaganda being what it was. Maybe the events associated with this Okidan raid were being exaggerated for effect.

Just then something caught Kazmer's eye for the second time this morning, and it was the same something, too. Hilton, in the entryway that led to the meal line, standing in the entrance with someone, discussing something. Hilton looked across the room, looked right at him, but gave no sign of recognition; and moved on.

Kazmer decided.

Accidents happened and people changed, and Hilton was a Langsarik pirate; but Hilton would not involve himself with murder. If this was a Langsarik gig, and Hilton was in on it, it was a straightforward grab-and-run operation. And Hilton was in on it; there could be no question. There was no other reasonable explanation for his presence here, for his behavior earlier.

"I'm in." He'd had all the porridge he could stomach. Pushing the bowl away from him, he started to leave. "I'll see you all later."

The engineer nodded, and then the navigator. The fence stared at his hands, picking at the ragged cuticle of his left thumb, and finally nodded at the table in turn. "All right," the fence said. "I'll see you later, too."

The others had apparently already decided. So they were a crew.

What had happened at Okidan?

It might call unwelcome attention to himself if he started asking questions. Maybe he'd hear some gossip in Port Charid. He could always get the details from the more well informed members of this crew, once they were safely on their way to wherever it was they were going.

So there would be plenty of time to hear all of the

news, public, private, rumored, and invented. At the moment Modice Agenis was waiting to see him, though she didn't know it yet.

Garol Vogel turned his shuttle over to the transport pool for maintenance and refueling. He never spent much time at Chilleau Judiciary's administrative center; he didn't intend to spend much time there now.

Chilleau Judiciary was within Garol's orb of assignment, so he had an office in Chambers—along with Jils Ivers, and whoever else was on rotation this cycle. It was nice to have someplace to come back to, even if it was at an administrative center. Nice to have a corner to himself, dark and cool and quiet, where he could be sure that things would be where he had left them and nobody would have tried to tidy up.

People might have been in to have a look at what he was doing, yes, that was something that happened from time to time; but sensitive information was always either secured or otherwise protected, and people who were after information they had no business being interested in could be relied upon to put things back carefully, as exactly as found as possible.

Garol walked through the great gates and into the administrative center of Chilleau Judiciary's Chambers in the middle of the night. Traffic on campus was relatively light, the corridors comparatively empty. He let himself into his office—three levels down from the senior administrative complex, fully five floors down from the Second Judge's personal quarters—and put his cloth pack down to one side of the door, pulling off the jacket he wore when he wasn't being official. Old campaign jacket, and from a really obscure planetary fleet; the cut and color offered few clues as to the identity of the wearer.

No clues whatever, in fact. Any branch-of-service markers that might once have decorated that old worn jacket had long since eroded with wear to the point of indecipherability, and Garol liked it that way.

He locked the door and turned on the desk lights, started some bean tea, sent the courtesy notifications to First Secretary Verlaine—the Second Judge's senior administrative official—and another message down to the media watch in Intelligence Analysis asking for the current situation report from Port Charid.

There were dockets on his desk he hadn't looked at, but he was in no hurry. He was here to brief the Second Judge about Port Charid and the Langsariks. Anything else Chilleau Judiciary got out of him this visit would be gravy for them, and since Jils had sent him a briefing packet on some of Verlaine's recent moves, Garol was not in a particularly gravy-ladling mood.

Putting his feet up on the dockets stacked on the desk, Garol meditated over a cup of hot bean tea, waiting for the runner from Intelligence Analysis.

He was halfway through the cup of tea when the signal came, and he had to get up and open the door. He could have left it unlocked, he supposed, but he didn't like being interrupted by well-wishers poking their heads in to attempt to cultivate his acquaintance.

Unlatching the door, Garol pulled it open. "Oh, hello. You've got the report I asked for? Thanks."

He knew the Clerk of Court who'd brought the report down, though.

Mergau Noycannir.

The rabid Inquisitor-without-portfolio that Verlaine had made as an experiment in shifting control of Inquiry from Fleet to the Bench—an experiment which had failed with Noycannir. The whole point of Inquiry was the use of judicial torture as an instrument of statecraft, and for torture to have the looked-for deterrent effect, it had to be perceived as something to be afraid of, something that could be used to obtain evidence against one's friends and family, something that could be used to render entire communities vulnerable to sanctions at the discretion of the Judge.

Noycannir just killed people.

That wasn't an enjoyable experience, at least not from any near-miss accounts that Garol had heard and fully acknowledging the lack of any real firsthand recitation from the dead concerning their feelings about the whole thing. But a threat that only endangered one's own self had nothing like the emotional impact of one that could be used to condemn one's near and dear based on one's own testimony.

Other Inquisitors could obtain incriminating evidence, and some of them actually found things out— Andrej Koscuisko, for one, the rash young Inquisitor who had cried Failure of Writ at the Domitt Prison, and set the wheels in motion of a scandal from which Chilleau Judiciary still reeled.

But not Noycannir.

Nor was she wearing the uniform of an Inquisitor, but the more plain and humble dress of a senior Clerk of Court; and she had come from Intelligence Analysis?

Garol took an almost involuntary step backward; he hadn't been prepared for this apparition at all, let alone its mind-boggling implications.

It was a mistake.

Noycannir lowered her head and followed him, as though she'd been invited in.

"I've been reviewing this information since word came you were in, Specialist Vogel," Noycannir said, and walked right past him to open the documents case she'd brought and lay it out flat on the desk surface. "You'll find this interesting, I'm sure. Here. Have a look at these transport minutes."

Garol could only stand and stare in genuine admiration. She had nerve. No longer functioning as an Inquisitor, that much was obvious, but playacting the role of the peer of a Bench intelligence specialist when not even an Inquisitor was that, presuming responsibility and influence that were no longer hers—had never been hers.

She was a piece of work, was Noycannir.

But he wasn't interested in playing her game and

declined her invitation to join her in review at his own desk. "I intend to do just that, but all in good time, Dame Noycannir."

If she was a senior Clerk of Court, she could still claim the courtesy title she had demanded as hers by right when she had held the Writ to Inquire. Garol wondered what the formal status of that Writ was. It was probably more than Verlaine's pride would allow actually to return the credentials to Fleet with an apology, or return them at all, though they could only be executed by Noycannir. No, he'd probably simply dispensed with Noycannir's services, started to send his witness interrogations to a qualified Fleet practitioner, and given her something else to do.

Noycannir didn't respond, standing at his desk with her back to him, leafing through the sections of the report he'd called for. "Taken together with the movement of goods through Sillume, I think you'll agree that a very interesting pattern emerges. I've been looking forward to sharing this with you."

But she wasn't sharing anything with him, when she had brought the report he'd requested.

She was running an errand.

Verlaine had apparently put her off to one side in Intelligence Analysis, a secure job, a comfortable placement, where he could keep an eye on her. Intelligence Analysis was strictly support. They had no authority, made no recommendations, controlled no data.

He'd never liked Noycannir.

He had reasons, too.

And now—though he could fully sympathize with the keen sense of lost status that had to be behind her pathetically desperate pretense—he was getting annoyed.

He didn't believe in gratuitous rudeness, but if she was going to ignore polite hints—

Garol opened his mouth to say something pointed,

but a voice from the still-open doorway did the trick for him.

"Thank you, Mergau. Would you excuse us now, please."

That was the voice of the First Secretary, deep and powerful and utterly implacable. Noycannir stiffened when she heard it, and closed up the documents case with almost fearful care.

"Of course, First Secretary. I'll be at my post should you wish to call for a tertiary analysis, good-greeting."

Bench Intelligence specialists did their own tertiary analyses, and they all knew it.

Noycannir left the room with her head meekly lowered, her eyes carefully fixed on the floor. Verlaine stood aside to let her pass, watching her as she went with an expression that spoke volumes to Garol of the First Secretary's disappointment, disgust, and a guilty sort of forbearance. Well, the First Secretary had a reason to blame himself if Noycannir had failed. It had been his wish that she make the trial in the first place, and as much his failure as hers.

It couldn't be pleasant for Verlaine to be reminded of his responsibility for the unfortunate experience Noycannir had had with her Writ, rendering it almost admirable on Verlaine's part that he kept her close—protected her from the enemies she had made in plenty—and paid her salary, even if it was only that of a Clerk of Court.

Verlaine closed the door. "Excuse the intrusion, Bench specialist," Verlaine said. "Can I have a few moments?"

If Verlaine had called Garol to his office, Garol would have gone; it was a concession on Verlaine's part to come down to Garol instead—a concession, or a mark of the importance Verlaine put on the current health of the Langsarik settlement. Garol could respect that.

"Not at all, First Secretary. I've only just gotten in,

though; I haven't had a chance to review the intelligence reports. Have a seat'"

Verlaine was staring at the documents case that Noycannir had left on Garol's desk; Garol didn't think Verlaine was really listening. "But you've just come from Nisherre, talking to that survivor. The eyewitness. How bad is it? Can you tell me?"

Garol didn't have to. In point of law a Bench intelligence specialist was answerable to the Bench, not to any administrative officer. But Garol respected the working relationships Verlaine maintained with the Second Judge, and he wanted to keep Verlaine on his side, if possible. For protection against Mergau Noycannir's intrusions, among other things.

"Declines to state that Langsariks shot the crew. Declines to deny that they were Langsariks. My reasoned evaluation? They could have been Langsariks. Or at least Feraltz, that's the survivor, believes they could have been. There is circumstantial evidence as well."

Not what Verlaine wanted to hear, but that was all right—it wasn't what Garol wanted to tell him. Verlaine folded his arms across his chest and nodded, rolling his lower lip against his teeth. It gave him the appearance of an animal who was still deciding whether or not a physical attack would be required to assure his safety.

"I'm surprised at your acceptance, Specialist. The amnesty agreement was in large part a personal accomplishment on your part. A very significant one, at that."

Garol sat down at his desk and tilted his chair back a bit. "I don't like it, but I'm not going to ignore the trends. There could be mitigating factors. I don't know. I came here to tell you that there appears to be a problem. You may wish to brief the Judge."

A real problem, that was to say, and not the product of idle rumor or frivolous gossip. Verlaine nodded again. "Your approach then, Bench specialist?"

"I'm going back to Port Charid. If Langsariks are up to something, I'd like to see how it's done, and the Flag Captain has a right to be given an opportunity to explain her perspective on things. I'll take it from there." He didn't know what his approach was going to be. He wouldn't know that until he got there. "Maybe it's still salvageable. I don't know."

Verlaine unfolded his arms, turning to go. "Well. I don't need to tell you how badly the Second Judge needs the Langsarik settlement to work. We're under fire on all sides, it seems. But we can't afford to shield any scofflaws either. The mercantile interests are very vocal. Anything else?"

Well, yes, as a matter of fact there was. "So long as you mention it. I heard about the assignment you arranged for Koscuisko. Can't say I understand your motivations there particularly well, First Secretary."

Jils had told him all about it. There was something about Koscuisko that interested her, the subtle tension between sanity and psychosis, perhaps. Verlaine blushed angrily, the red blossoming across his cheekbones visible even in the low light in Garol's office. But Verlaine was exceptionally fair-skinned, like many red-haired people in his class of hominid.

"Resource management is not in your brief, Bench specialist." But that was rude, as well as untrue, and Verlaine backed down fractionally from the claim as soon as he'd made it. "We filled the vacancy with the highest priority, no more, no less. The *Ragnarok* had been without a Ship's Surgeon for longer than any other ship in its own, or any equivalent, class."

The *Ragnarok* had no equivalent class. It was an experimental ship, black-hull technology, and commanded by a man who had become incapable of exercising battle command, by reason of a critical failure in the command relationship. "Because Captain Lowden goes through Ship's Surgeons at a pretty good clip. Uses them up, and not in trauma surgery; the *Ragnarok* is still in test status. Proving cruise. No live fire, no active engagements. It's a waste of medical resources to post Koscuisko to the *Ragnarok*."

Garol heard himself getting disgusted as he spoke. He hadn't realized he'd cared one way or the other, not really.

"Yes," Verlaine said; and his tone of voice was flat, unemotional, and completely implacable. "But we must look at the larger environment. The *Ragnarok* is on a proving cruise, so it tours, and the Judicial resources it carries are more frequently tapped than any other active-duty ship. What is the single most efficient use for a man like Koscuisko, Bench specialist?"

There were too many ways to answer that question, so Garol didn't try; and Verlaine had clearly not exhausted his thought.

"Ship's Surgeon, you impact the welfare of a ship's complement, a single ship's complement. Ship's Inquisitor, you materially reinforce the executive power of the Bench by expertly demonstrating the negative consequences of violating the rule of Law. You saw Koscuisko at Rudistal, Bench specialist, you were there—before and after. You tell me. Where does Koscuisko best serve the Judicial order?"

And Verlaine had a point. Koscuisko was a perfectly adequate surgeon, but a brilliant torturer; and after his highly publicized execution of the once-administrator of the Domitt Prison, Koscuisko was well known as someone to fear. Garol wasn't impressed, even so. It was all just rationalization on Verlaine's part. Andrej Koscuisko had embarrassed Chilleau Judiciary; Andrej Koscuisko was to be punished.

"You could serve the Judicial order even better by putting Lowden on ice." Because the *Ragnarok*'s notorious commander did no good at all for the public trust and confidence in the fairness and objectivity of the Bench and its officers. "And maybe Koscuisko would live to see forty, if you did. Not like the last Ship's Surgeon we sent to the *Ragnarok*."

Suicide was wasteful, and waste was offensive in

principle. Ship's Surgeons were expensive, Ship's Inquisitors even more so.

"You have more urgent concerns than any Fleet
officer's health and welfare, Bench specialist. If you
don't mind my saying so." Verlaine had apparently
decided to end a conversation whose subject was distasteful. "I'll hold the mercantile interests off Port
Charid for as long as possible. Let me know how it
goes and if I can help out in any way."

Garol took a deep breath, centering himself.

Verlaine had committed an act of petty revenge in
Koscuisko's case, revenge that would be executed at
the expense of whoever was unlucky enough to be in
Bench custody when Captain Griers Verigson Lowden
of the Jurisdiction Fleet Ship *Ragnarok* came looking
for diversion and material with which to create an
object lesson.

But it was Verlaine's call, and Verlaine's responsibility. Nobody had asked Garol's opinion. He'd said
his bit, Verlaine had tolerated the impertinence; it was
time to move on.

Garol stood up.

"Thank you for your support, First Secretary." He
could say it without hypocrisy. First Secretary Verlaine
had always been an honest player; it was just some of
his game that Garol didn't like. Nothing personal. "I'll
be leaving once I have a chance to review the intelligence reports. Specialist Ivers has agreed to accompany me. We'll keep you informed."

Verlaine closed the door behind him, firmly but quietly. Garol latched the door and settled in to work.

The sooner he got out of there the happier he'd be.

He had real problems waiting for him at Port
Charid.

Walton Agenis sat bolt upright in her bed, her fingers tingling with adrenaline.

Something was wrong.

Stilling her breath with the self-discipline that had

yet to desert her even in times of enforced placidity, she listened to the small sounds that the settlement house made in the night. The settlement housing had been built quickly and not overcarefully, and talked to itself as the outside temperature rose and fell and the wind shifted; she had learned to sleep through the creaks and moans and cracks and chirps of the structure that sheltered her family.

Why was she awake?

It was dead black outside; no light shone into the room through the chinks in the shutters. The local utility plant was obviously off-line for the night, and the predawn deliveries had apparently not started rounds; by that token, it was two to four hours before the little yellow sun of Rikavie rose to warm and wake the settlement.

The pounding of her own heart in her ears faded quickly as the energy surge that had jolted her awake subsided.

Walton began to hear things.

There was something clattering at the outside of the house, not loudly, but with too much deliberation for it to be the normal cooling of the plain metalweave shutters, and it came with a scratching sound so faint she almost doubted she heard it at all.

Turning the bedclothes back, layer upon layer upon themselves, Walton stood up. The floor was cold beneath her bare and bony feet, rug or no rug.

But she knew she heard something.

There were sounds of movement from inside the house as well, the small noise muffled behind the closed door of one of the bedrooms. Walton slept with her door open. She could not bear not to hear what was happening in her own house.

She was beginning to think she might know what was going on. She picked up the truncheon she kept on the floor beside her bed for self-defense; she didn't like weapons that could be deployed at distance, not for protection of her own hearth. Accidents happened.

Anyone close enough to hit with a truncheon was too close to be mistaken for an enemy rather than simply some imprudent young person who had made a mistake.

The shrill squeak of a shutter being raised on its track sounded clearly in the dark stillness: Walton grinned to herself.

Modice's room.

And there was conversation. The hissing sounds of whispered sibilants was clear enough; there was the pattern of language, but the sounds themselves could not be parsed into meaning.

Silent on bare feet, Walton crept down the hall to where her older sister's only daughter had her narrow bed. She heard no alarm in the drift of whispered words, no threat—no particular passion of any kind.

This sort of thing had happened more than once before. Was it Modice's fault? She was an utterly unspoiled beauty, and so sweet-spirited that she seemed to arouse as much fraternal as any other passion in the hearts of her admirers.

Here.

If Walton paused and listened very carefully, she could almost locate the source of the whispering as at the window; so maybe Modice hadn't let him in, whoever he was. Yet. This time.

The door was not quite latched. None of the doors hung true on their cheap hinges. Walton eased down on the lever carefully and pushed, wondering whether those very hinges would betray her before she could make a really dramatic entrance.

Who was at the window?

Walton could hear Modice, though she still couldn't quite make out the words. Modice's tone of voice was all surprise and perplexed joy; there was no alarm nor any uncertainty there. Whoever it was inspired no fear of any sort in Modice's nineteen-year-old heart. But Modice was fearless.

"—for a cargo. Of course I agreed. I haven't seen you in more than two years."

Walton frowned.

On the resource side of the status sheet, to judge by the sound of the voice the man who was explaining—excusing—his presence so blithely to Modice was *at* the window, yes, but on the other side of it yet. He was not in the room with her sister's daughter. Modice was in no danger of finding herself overcome by instinct, let alone violence, or at least not yet.

On the draw-down side was the fact that Walton thought she recognized that voice.

Modice said something, and stifled a giggle. Walton listened carefully to the man's reply, her suspicions mounting moment by moment.

"Forget you, never, Modice. There isn't anyone like you under Jurisdiction, and I've never been to Gone-beyond space. I'd have come to see you sooner if I'd had a decent chance."

That Sarvaw mercantile pilot.

What had his name been?

Kazmer. Kazmer Daigule.

The friend of her older brother's oldest son, Hilton, a big lumbering barge of a man with sufficient calm quiet charisma to have almost seriously disturbed Modice's psychological equilibrium, not too many years ago.

Modice was clearly not very disturbed right now; her voice had strengthened from a whisper to a murmur, and Walton could hear what she was saying even though Modice clearly had her back to the room, talking out the window.

"If you had the interest, you'd have come sooner. But it's nice to see you. And Hilton will be sorry he missed you. Hilton likes you, Kaz."

There was no venom to her scolding, but no childish uncertainty, either. Walton listened to her with pride and wonder: if only Modice's mother was alive, to hear how her daughter had grown. Modice seemed clearly confident of her ability to hold her own with a man several years her elder. She had learned well, during the years that the Langsariks had lived as a fleet-borne community. She took after Walton herself a bit, maybe; or maybe it was just the result of having been beautiful all her life, Walton admitted to herself, reluctantly. Modice couldn't have learned that from her aunt Walton.

"Oh, there are those in your family who don't like me at all, Modice." Daigule seemed to be teasing, but his tone of voice was ambiguous—was that genuine regret that she heard? "Your aunt doesn't care for me a bit. She told me so. Well, she told Hilton."

She would have to see his expression and his body language to decide for sure. For that she would have to be able to see into the room, to spy as well as eavesdrop.

"Aunt Walton is just a little overprotective. That's all."

Walton didn't know if she wanted to hear this. Raising Modice hadn't been her idea; she had neither expected nor been prepared to take responsibility for the child that Modice had been when her parents had been killed. She knew she hadn't done as good a job as a real mother could have, would have done. But if she withdrew—to avoid hearing scornful words from Modice—she would be leaving the situation unresolved; and she would not be able to close the door quietly enough to avoid alerting Modice to the fact that someone had been listening.

"She's no such thing." Given her suspicions about Daigule's designs on Modice, it certainly felt odd to hear him, of all people, come to her defense. "She just means to see you properly married to someone who shares your own culture. Sometimes I think she forgets that you and I have already been to bed together."

Walton tightened her grip on her truncheon. Been to bed together, was it? She'd give him "been to bed together," all over his foolish skull. *Been to bed to-gether.* How dare he?

"Kazmer, no joking. That was serious. You know very well it was the only way to hide you. Shame on you."

That Sarvaw had been fully clothed at the time. At least from the waist down, a certain degree of bareness being necessary to carry the deception off. The soldiers had been too busy trying not to stare at the blinding perfection of Modice's flawless shoulders to think too deeply on the potential correspondences between the person of interest they were hunting for and the apparently naked young man in her niece's bed.

Or if they had made up their own minds about what was going on, their insufferable tyrant of a junior officer had arrived at no such conclusion, and nobody had bothered to disabuse him of a notion that he had clearly felt to be near sacred on account of having been his.

"Come on, Derchie, I'm only joking, it's just you and me. I didn't mean any harm by it, who else can I talk to? And I'm here to tell you that any man who got to share a bed with you, and didn't want to talk it up, would have to be crazy."

"No jokes!" Modice sounded exasperated; she had raised her voice, but quickly dropped it again. "We're in settlement now. We have to maintain appearances. If my aunt so much as caught you here, she'd call my cousins to beat you. And if you can't at least respect my feelings, I'll call for her, I'm warning you."

That was a good idea, too, Walton thought. The one about calling Modice's cousins to run Daigule off. How had he gotten past the perimeter watch? She'd have something to say to the night security tomorrow morning at debriefing.

Still, Daigule hadn't done anything to deserve a beating—yet. And cousins could get overenthusiastic where they thought the honor of a girl-cousin was involved.

"I'm sorry, Derchie. I didn't come to quarrel." It seemed that Daigule finally realized that he'd overstepped the boundaries of Modice's maidenly modesty. It had been three years. Modice had been much younger, so much so that Walton doubted Daigule had fully realized the potential damage his lighthearted flirting might inflict. Modice had always looked older than she actually was; her beauty surrounded her with an aura of knowledge and power that was easy to mistake for that of an adult woman.

"It's all right, Kazmer, we're friends. But it hurts my feelings when you make fun of me. Nobody knows about that but family." No, they'd kept the secret of Kazmer's escape, to avoid compromise. And to spare Modice the teasing. "Still. You should go now. Come in the daytime if you want to visit me. Bring a present for my aunt."

Walton held her breath.

Was Modice giving Daigule permission to court her?

Or was she just pointing out the awkwardness of coming to a young woman's window in the middle of the night?

"I did bring a present for you," Daigule said. "Don't worry, it's nothing that might embarrass you. Unless you have some bizarre objection to really tasteless patterns."

Modice almost succeeded in stifling an apparently involuntary shriek of thrilled horror, so that it came out a squeak. "Kazmer. It's awful. What is it?"

Walton listened eagerly for the answer.

"For your hair, Modice. Head scarf. Or a handkerchief. Rolled for a fabric belt, I don't know. Can be used to dust small and not easily breakable objects. Put this on first thing in the morning and nothing worse will happen to you for the rest of the day."

Well, it clearly wasn't an intimate garment, or something that would have been otherwise improper between friends. Walton relaxed a bit.

"Go away, Kazmer," Modice said, her voice soft with what sounded like affection. "And don't come back unless it's to the front door. In the daytime."

Where Walton could be waiting—with reinforcements, if necessary. Now that she knew that there was the possibility that Daigule would visit.

"By your command, beautiful Modice. Give my regards to your family. My respects to your aunt. No. Wait. Better hold off on that for a day or two. Give me time to get out of system. Good night."

Walton had to smile.

It was a shame Daigule was so unsuitable for a Langsarik household. He already knew them so well.

But he wasn't suitable for a Langsarik household—because he wasn't a Langsarik.

Walton heard the shutters click against one another as Modice closed her window. She pulled the bedroom door back shut, carefully matching her movements to the sounds Modice was making in order to mask anything that might draw attention to herself.

Modice had carried the mission on her own, and hadn't needed backup after all.

How long would it be before Modice told her about Daigule's visit?

Would Modice tell her?

The only way to find that out was to wait and see; and that could be done just as well or better from the comfort of one's own bed as standing barefoot in a dark hall.

Her feet were cold.

Modice might decide to visit the bathroom before she went back to sleep. The hall had to be empty in case that happened.

Satisfied with Modice's handling of her midnight suitor, Walton Agenis went back to bed.

Chapter Three

Kazmer Daigule stood close behind the Langsarik raid leader in the dockmaster's office at the Tyrell Yards, keeping his head down and his eyes lowered. Between the visored cap pulled low over his brow and the artificial beard that covered most of the rest of his face there was little chance of anybody being able to recognize him later; but he was taking no chances.

"Sorry to make you wait," the Tyrell Yards' dockmaster said to the raid leader, keying her transmit. "We just can't be too careful these days. Have you heard about what happened at Okidan?"

If Kazmer tilted his head just a bit and squinted hard he could see the message the dockmaster sent scrolling across the capture unit. *Request confirmation, freighter on scheduled load-out from Port Charid to receiving office in Tweniva. Tyrell Yards. Please authenticate as follows.*

This was the tricky part.

There was a small courier shuttle in the vehicle transport bay of the freighter Kazmer had piloted from Port Charid to the Tyrell Yards, here in the Shawl of Rikavie. On board that shuttle was an illegal communications intercept board, and the woman working that board had to intercept the dockmaster's signal and match it with precision and delicacy in order to ensure that it was fully damped—effectively canceled out—before it could reach Charid.

Then it was just a question of waiting for the right

interval to pass before transmitting a false response with the right security characteristics to pass scrutiny.

"Okidan. Yes." The raid leader had given his name as Noman, a transparent but perfectly acceptable label under the circumstances. "And everybody has their own theory of how it was managed, too. Which they'll tell you all about, if you don't get away in time."

Noman wasn't anyone that Kazmer recognized; not that he'd really expected to—Noman had taken prudent steps of his own to disguise his identity. A beard, a little transparent gum at the corners of his eyes to change their size and shape, all the tricks—and so well done that Kazmer had to really look closely to realize the deception.

Noman's voice was casual, even light; Kazmer envied his composure. Kazmer did his best to stay calm as the moments passed; finally, the dockmaster's board chirped its receipt announcement. Kazmer already knew what this one was supposed to read, but he couldn't help being nervous about it.

We authenticate, Tyrell. Freighter Sansifer *en route to Tweniva with authorization to carry manifest as follows. You may proceed with assurance.*

Kazmer rubbed the back of his neck irritably as if scratching a sudden itch, just to cover the relief he felt.

The dockmaster closed the transmission with a casual gesture; clearly, she hadn't been genuinely concerned—just prudent, in unsettled times. Nor was there any particular reason for her to be suspicious; there hadn't been a raid in weeks, and unannounced traffic was apparently not unusual.

"Right," the dockmaster said. Turning around, she started toward the door to her office that would lead back out onto the loading docks, beckoning for Noman and Kazmer to come with her. "Let's load cargo."

Time to get started, then.

Noman nodded to Kazmer, who acknowledged the unspoken command with a crisp nod of his own before breaking into a quick jog-trot, heading out toward the freighter, where it waited with its loading ramp unshipped and ready. They had cargo to unload and cargo to load, and then just before they left they'd off-load the courier so that the raiding party could make a separate escape.

That way the freighter's cargo stayed clean, with no stray weapons or unexplained extra crew to cause suspicions in anyone's mind when they came to pass inspection by the Port Authority at Anglace. Kazmer was just as happy to be rid of the courier. The presence of the illegal communications equipment would be a dead giveaway to any inspector, and there was no sense in risk for risk's sake.

By the time the freighter's crew had the cargo crates ready to move, the dockmaster had called up some station resources to help; the work went quickly. There were seven large cargo crates tagged for offload at Tyrell, and once they were on the dock the engineer took charge of getting them lined up—at right angles to the back of the freighter—as Kazmer went to let Noman know that they were ready to start the load-in.

The freighter's crew all wore caps and gloves, but dockworkers frequently wore protective gear when loading and unloading cargo; it was nothing to remark upon. Meaning in turn very little danger of being recognized: final reassurance that there was to be no killing on this raid. The raid leader would hardly have gone to all the trouble he had to ensure their anonymity if he'd been planning on simply murdering any potential witnesses, after all.

The dockmaster was reviewing the manifest with Noman. "This is an odd lot," she said; and there was a little hint of discomfort in her voice. Was she beginning to suspect something? "Here, Pettiche, take a look. This could take a while, there doesn't seem to be much coherence to the pull list."

If he looked behind him, Kazmer could see the engineer and the fence standing with the off-loaded crates, waiting for the next phase. Freighter to the left of them, the long wall of the dockmaster's office to their right, they had a good view of the entire docking bay.

One of the people who had been helping them off-load joined Noman and the dockmaster at the foot of the freighter's loading ramp; Kazmer thought for a moment that he recognized the man.

"Er, well." Noman's voice was vibrant with slightly embarrassed apology. "The fact is, we're already late. My fault, not my crew's fault, so I owe them considerably. But we'll all lose our promptness bonus if we don't deliver in good time. Is there any way to hurry this along?"

The third person looked the manifest over, then handed it back to the dockmaster. "We don't have to take all of that long." No, Kazmer realized, hearing the man speak. He didn't actually recognize the third person. He only recognized who the third person was, in a general sense. "If we called all available hands. They'll complain about losing their sleepshifts, some of them, but I imagine the cargomaster here—" nodding at Noman— "could find some way to make it up to them, am I right?"

Kazmer was Sarvaw. He knew Dolgorukij when he saw one. The accent was as good as a star chart, and the face more so, familiar in the indefinable way that people of one's own blood were familiar. Veesliya Dolgorukij, or Kazmer missed his guess, and he didn't think he did. Sarvaw knew from Dolgorukij. A beaten dog never forgot the face of its tormentor.

"Oh, you can be sure of that," Noman replied with grateful enthusiasm. "If we can get our load-out done in time to meet the schedule, you won't be sorry. I know I've got something on board worth missing a sleepshift for, I guarantee it'll be a memorable occasion."

The dockmaster shrugged and smiled. An older woman, she had a professional smile, one of the kind that involved lips and teeth but no real feeling. It didn't seem to be anything personal, though; it seemed clearly to be her habit to be a little reticent. Because she sounded positive about the whole idea. "Well, all right. See it done, Pettiche. The sooner we get cargo off, the sooner we can all relax and enjoy a little well-earned treat."

Up into the freighter for the special crate, then. Kazmer and the navigator moved it down the ramp to the front of the loading ramp, just to one side of Noman and the dockmaster. By the time they got it into position cargo pallets were starting to arrive on the docks, and people with them.

Raising his head to get a good view, Kazmer scanned the busy scene quickly before adjusting his visor. There were a lot of people here, fifteen, twenty perhaps. A lot of cargo. Tyrell Yards was holding luxury fabrics and botanicals, and the freighter would carry a full load to Anglace.

With the station crew on hand to help, the load-in went as smoothly as anyone could wish. Kazmer watched the freighter's cargo bays fill with a mixture of satisfaction and anxiety. On the one hand a load-in was just a load-in, like any other; and loading was unexciting drudgery by its very nature.

On the other hand, he'd never been so intimately involved in a raid before. He'd moved illegal cargo, and he'd participated in the illegal disposition of somebody else's goods, but this was the first time he'd ever participated in an actual raid. And yet what was there to worry about? These were Langsariks. They knew what they were doing.

When the load-in was finished Kazmer joined the freighter's crew gathered around the special crate at the side of the freighter while Noman and the dock-master reviewed the cargo manifest, checking for completeness.

The seven cargo crates they'd off-loaded first were big standard prepack units, each just less wide than a standard freighter corridor was wide, just less tall than a standard freighter's cargo bay overhead clearance.

The special crate was much smaller, tabletop-square, the sort of thing that usually held luxury goods. Specialty meats. Bulk confections and delicacies. Small containers of liquor or recreational drugs. The station crew had started to collect in the now-empty space between the freighter and the dockmaster's office, clearly waiting for the promised reward that the special crate represented; endorsing the manifest with a satisfied chop of his personal handseal, Noman handed the documents board back to the dockmaster, assessing the assembly with a measuring eye.

"This must be everybody on base," Noman said to the dockmaster, but a little too loudly for just the casual remark that it seemed to be. "Can there be anyone at all who isn't here?"

Looking up from the completed manifest, the dockmaster went from face to face, counting bodies against the backdrop of the seven cargo crates Kazmer had helped to unload earlier. One of the men Kazmer saw there was wearing the Langsarik colors, the uniform denuded of any identification markers but unmistakably Langsarik by its cut and shade. One of the people supposedly called in from sleepshift, obviously, or he'd be wearing a station work suit instead of his personal clothing.

"That's everybody, all right," the Dolgorukij at the dockmaster's side—Pettiche—answered.

Noman nodded.

"Very well, then. Ladies and gentlemen, I'm announcing a small change in plan."

It was the signal.

The fronts of the seven cargo crates exploded with sudden shocking violence, scattering chips of structural board across the loading bay floor.

Startled and stunned like the rest of her crew, the dockmaster took an involuntary step forward, trying to see what was going on. Raiders. The crates were full of raiders, two Langsariks to a crate, moving out quickly to form a tight-curved line with weapons trained on the station crew gathered in the loading bay.

The engineer broke into the special crate and handed out the weapons that were there. Some of the station crew were starting to step back, looking to the belly of the freighter to take cover; but Kazmer and the other freighter crew had that escape route in their line of fire, now.

No escape.

The fence nudged the dockmaster in the ribs with the muzzle of an assault weapon; and slowly—with visible reluctance, her face showing her confused shock and helpless rage—the dockmaster raised her open hands away from her body, with her palms flat in a gesture of surrender.

"Let's everyone just sit down where you are," Noman suggested. "We don't want anybody getting hurt."

If anybody made a break for cover beneath the freighter, they could lose control of the situation. There would be shooting. Kazmer waited, holding his breath.

Nobody moved.

Then—slowly, and with evident reluctance—Pettiche the Dolgorukij bent his knees awkwardly and sank down slowly to sit cross-legged on the floor.

"Everybody sit down," Noman repeated. "Dockmaster. We'd appreciate your cooperation. With a little luck and some common sense, nobody needs to be the worse for this. Except maybe the owners, and they're insured anyway, aren't they?"

Kazmer still didn't dare relax.

But the situation did seem unquestionably weighted in the Langsariks' favor; and nobody wanted trouble, after all.

The dockmaster spoke, finally. "You heard the

man." Her disgust was clear, but so was her evident
realization that they were at the mercy of the raiders.
"I'm making this an official direction, one you promised to obey when you endorsed your contract documentation. Everybody sits down. Slowly. No sudden
moves. Two by two. We'll start with Gerig and Elsing,
sit down on the floor and keep your hands where they
can see them. Let's go, people. Move."

Kazmer could breathe again.

No bloodshed.

Once everyone was sitting down and under guard
in the middle of the room, Noman spoke.

"Right, unship the courier and get out of here.
Dockmaster. New manifest. This will be easy to load.
Everything's right through there, on the other side of
the security door in your office. All we need are your
security codes, and we can be out of your way in no
time."

One of the Langsarik crate-raiders came around the
outside of the perimeter to relieve Kazmer and his
crew. Kazmer surrendered his weapon gratefully. As
soon as the courier ship was unloaded they could
leave.

Things were going as smoothly as any Langsarik
raid should; but Kazmer didn't like what Noman had
just said about the dockmaster's secures.

And still, nothing bad had happened, at least not
yet.

Why should anything bad happen at all?

It wasn't the most welcome experience for the staff
here at the Tyrell Yards, perhaps, but it was just cargo.
Not even their cargo. Someone else's cargo. And the
Langsariks had been careful to leave them no choice
in the matter, no choice at all.

With the courier on the floor and the freighter secured, Kazmer joined the navigator in the wheelhouse,
and settled himself into the seat beside her. He was
still tense; he couldn't shake a feeling of residual apprehension, and it apparently showed. The navigator

took one look at him and grinned with what seemed to be sympathy, giving his shoulder a friendly shake.

"Almost ready to load-out," she said, reassuringly. "I just saw the boss Langsarik heading for Central Dispatch. He had another Langsarik with him. One from the Tyrell crew. There was an inside man."

Of course. There had to be.

Noman's talk about secures would be just talk, after all. They'd placed a man on-site; they already had the secures.

Kazmer was astonished at the depth of his relief.

The engineer came forward to give Kazmer the word, his face flushed with effort and his expression full of a grim sort of satisfaction.

"We're off," the engineer said. "Let's get out of here."

Kazmer toggled his comm. "Docking bay clear?" he asked the dockmaster, or whoever was in Central Dispatch; but he wasn't too surprised when the voice that answered him had a distinctly Langsarik lilt to it.

"Docking bay clear and sealed for depressurization, all personnel safe and secure. Launch dome opening sequence."

The Langsarik crew he had brought with him in the decoy cargo stacks would secure the crews, destroy the station's communications to prevent a premature alarm, and ensure that nothing incriminating was left behind.

"Freighter initiating primary launch sequence. Issue warning order."

There were no Fleet patrols between him and the Sillume entry vector. Once they had reached the vector they would be safe, because there was no technology that could track a ship across a vector. The authorities would assume that they'd made for the sanctuary of Gonebeyond space.

The ship was fully pressurized; the docking-bay launch dome lay open. Kazmer fired his positioning jets, carefully maneuvering the freighter into the precise angle he wanted for the best—fastest—cleanest departure from Tyrell. They couldn't actually fire the main thrust until they were far enough from Tyrell to avoid perturbing its orbit, or risk someone at Port Charid noticing and sending up an alarm. That would be a dead giveaway. Whether or not there were any Fleet patrols in the neighborhood, it was idiocy to borrow trouble.

The freighter eased clear of the docking station and began to gain space between it and the Tyrell Yards.

Kazmer watched his power profiles as the freighter slowly picked up speed.

He'd learned that Langsarik raiding was something he simply wasn't comfortable doing. Not even with Langsariks. Not even with the best—most decent— people he knew, and Hilton Shires was way up toward the top of that list. It had been too tense. It could have gone wrong too easily.

He brought the fuel lines up to maximum feed carefully, gradually, slowly; and the freighter began to really move.

He was never going to get so close to a potential disaster ever again so long as he lived, if he had anything to say about it.

Raid leader Dalmoss Chzagul stood in the doorway of the dockmaster's office within the sealed confines of Central Dispatch, rubbing the cleargum from his face absent mindedly as he watched the freighter lifting away from the Tyrell Yards on monitor.

It was three days over the Sillume vector to the nearest Fleet detachment, so the freighter was in no danger from Fleet.

Port Charid had some police resources available, three swift cruisers with just enough firepower to stop the freighter short of the exit vector; but so long as no alarm reached Port Charid from Tyrell, the freighter was in no danger from Charid's own limited police either. No alarm would reach Port Charid until

Dalmoss was finished here. He had complete confidence in the effectiveness of his communications intercepts, and for good reason—they had insider information, after all.

So the freighter was free and clear. They had plenty of time to finish up and make their escape.

"All quiet?" Dalmoss asked Pettiche, who sat outside the dockmaster's office, monitoring the master communications board. Pettiche nodded.

"The freighter lifted away during a black slice on the sweeps, 'Noman.' Just as you planned. The most we have to watch for is a routine query if anyone at Port notices."

"Well done, Brother Charil." The alien name came strangely to his mouth, but they all used Langsarik names during a raid. Attention to detail was an important part of their success: even as it had been for the Langsariks themselves. "Thank you."

Now that the freighter was gone it was time to move to the next stage in the exercise, and Dalmoss stepped back into the relative privacy of the dockmaster's office, calling to one of the men nearby. "Efons, take over on the panels, I need Charil's help. Brother Charil?"

The dockmaster's office in Central Dispatch was glassed in along the side that fronted on the main room, so that the dockmaster could keep an eye on her employees. Which was humorous, in a sense, because Dalmoss was using the dockmaster's vantage point to keep an eye on the dockmaster herself. She was sitting on the floor against the far wall of Central Dispatch with the rest of the station's crew, with her hands bound behind her back to encourage docility.

Pettiche stopped a respectful half a pace behind his superior, and bent his head in token of salute. A gesture small enough to avoid drawing attention to itself—Langsariks didn't salute—but Dalmoss knew that the respectful submission was genuine and heartfelt.

"Yes, Noman."

Dalmoss nodded in the direction of the station's crew, in turn. "This is everybody, Brother Charil? We need to be sure." That was Pettiche's job: to be sure. Pettiche had been placed here at Tyrell for months, just waiting for the time to come when he would be needed.

"I've cross-verified with Sumner, Noman. Everyone is here. No soul has been overlooked."

Good. "We'd best get on with it, then, Charil. Start with the dockmaster. We had to get her security codes, after all."

It was therefore necessary that her corpse present clear evidence of the extraction process through which the station's security codes had been presumably obtained from her assumedly reluctant lips. Pettiche bent his head once more, a swift gesture of acknowledgment; but he didn't turn immediately to leave. What? Something was wrong? "Talk to me, Charil."

"Out of respect for hospitality, Noman. I have taken bread from her hands. I ask to be excused the letting of her blood."

Well, of course. Hospitality was Holy ordinance; it could not be set aside. The moment Pettiche said it Dalmoss realized the propriety of the objection, and was ashamed of himself for not taking it into account. "Truly I deserve rebuke, Charil. Tell Sumner, then. You take Parken and secure him on board the courier, yes?"

It was necessary for Tyrell's one Langsarik employee, Parken, to leave the station alive. There would be more than enough physical evidence to indict the Langsariks for this raid; but a bloodstain of the wrong type, if they were unfortunate enough to have it come to someone's attention, could conceivably raise questions in someone's mind. So the Langsarik would walk out. They'd dump his body somewhere it could be used to further incriminate the Langsariks. Later.

Pettiche's body wouldn't be found here either.

But they'd find a way to cover for that: and negative evidence was always so much less obvious and persuasive than the positive evidence that they meant to provide.

Once Charil had left Central Dispatch, Silves—whom they called Efons when they were raiding—spoke from his station on monitor. "Noman. In the name."

Silves did not complete the formula, maintaining discipline as Pettiche had. Dalmoss watched Pettiche walk across the warehouse floor to give Sumner his orders.

"I'm listening."

The formula was the one they used when someone wanted to gain a deeper understanding of a senior's orders, and as such it was Dalmoss's duty to submit to questioning.

"It soils the soul, Noman. Is this really necessary?"

Silves's voice certainly held only respectful desire for understanding. There was no challenge there; and it was a reasonable question.

"The dockmaster at least must suffer before she dies, Efons." They could expect an autopsy, to support Charges; the Bench made a clear distinction between the unlawful physical abuse of a living being and the much lesser crime of incidental mutilation of a corpse. "We can expect the most attention to be focused on her. The others—well. We'll see how the timing goes."

They might not have to torture more than three or four of the others to convince the Bench that an atrocity exceeding mere murder had taken place. But it was truly necessary to convince the Bench that murder had been wantonly committed in full knowledge of the crime as it was being done. The Angel would settle for nothing less than the destruction of the Langsariks as a people, for the insult they had given the Holy Mother in preying on Dolgorukij shipping and to take the blame for a systematic destruction of the physical assets of other trading interests at Port Charid.

Sumner came into Central Dispatch with the dock-master and two of Dalmoss's other men; Dalmoss pointed them through to the safe room, the place inside Central Dispatch where the smallheavies had been. Sumner closed the door. Sound would not carry far from inside the room.

He could start to compose his after-action report—in his head, of course, it was never to be written or recorded.

They were very near their goal.

After just a few more Langsarik raids there would be no mercantile interests left in Port Charid with the resources to contest with the Dolgorukij Combine for primacy.

The Dolgorukij Combine could afford to rebuild infrastructure. The Dolgorukij Combine could afford to purchase and rebuild the damaged warehouses of its fellow mercantile interests, leasing them back at a reasonable premium to cover its expenses.

And the Holy Mother would grant Her blessings to Her faithful servitors forever, after they made Her Queen in Port Charid.

Chilleau Judiciary sat at the node of one of the most powerful vectors under Jurisdiction. The Chilleau vector gave access and egress to dozens of systems, but Port Charid wasn't one of them.

The easiest way from Chilleau Judiciary to Port Charid was through Renicks via Omot, but Garol was in a hurry, and the easy way took a good two days Standard more than the transit in through Garsite. Garsite was small and relatively out of the way, as vector nodes went, so there was a risk—if something went wrong in flight, the wait at Garsite for replacement parts could be tedious.

So nothing would go wrong in flight: and that was all there was to it.

The Chilleau vector was one that Garol traveled all the time. But if he'd ever jumped Garsite, it had been so long that he'd forgotten; and that meant taking advantage of Jils's presence to cross-check his setup stats, just for extra assurance. Once he was clear of the exit vector from Chilleau to Garsite and on arc toward the Garsite entry vector, Garol called back from the wheelhouse of the courier ship to the aft compartment for her.

"Hey, Jils." She was in the rear compartment of the courier, reviewing, he assumed, the intelligence reports they'd brought with them from Port Charid. She probably wouldn't mind a break. "Would you come give me your once-over on this?"

The angle of approach, rate of acceleration, and path of the courier had to be calculated to create a transit funnel that would drop them out of the figurative flume of the vector at the desired destination.

People made mistakes in vector calculations.

Some of those mistakes led to the discovery of new termini on a previously identified vector; but most of the time ships and crews simply vanished, leaving no sign of what might ultimately have happened to them.

Garol wasn't interested in finding out.

Garol wanted to go to Port Charid, not off into the unknown on an adventure.

Jils came forward slowly, rubbing her forehead. "Sure, Garol, let's have a look."

He hadn't been surprised when she'd expressed an interest in going to Rikavie with him; the Langsarik settlement was too important to the Second Judge's prestige and public opinion to take any chances. He didn't mind having her present, either, for moral support if for nothing else.

He angled the navigation calculation screen carefully toward her to minimize any glare, but Jils wasn't looking at his calculations, she was staring at the forward observation screens instead. Some things Garol didn't mind obtaining by virtue of rank. This courier had full-sweep screens. It was a new model out of the Arakcheyek shipyards—Dolgorukij Combine, absolutely state-of-the-art, and priced accordingly. All in support of the rule of Law.

"Hey," Jils said. "Space is pretty, out here."

Garsite space was pretty. She was right. The light bent softly around the flat almond-shaped boundaries of the vector, creating a subtle sort of back lighting. The vector had a halo.

"Yeah, and I'd like to be reasonably sure of seeing it again someday. So would you check the vector calculations please."

Jils shook herself slightly. "Oh. Right. Sorry, Garol. I'll do a scan on them. You go stow for vector transit, why don't you."

Undivided attention on vector calculations was a good thing. Garol was all in favor of enabling it on Jils's part, so he went off to lock things down. It wasn't that a ship risked losing its gravity during a vector transit, or at least not usually; but it was easier to recover from an accidental lapse in gravity if a person had taken measures to minimize the potential mess beforehand.

Jils had documents strewn from one end of the aft cabin to the other. Incident reports on raids at Sonder, Penyff, Tershid, Okidan, Tyrell. Forensic manifests, where available. Cause of death. Body counts.

Garol didn't like the picture that was forming. It didn't fit the Langsarik pattern; and how could the Langsariks have managed?

He'd have to get Jils's thoughts about it. Once they had the vector, maybe.

After the aft cabin was as thoroughly stowed as it could get, Garol went back forward. Jils was finishing a countercheck reconciliation, but everything looked pretty stable. He didn't see where she'd had to correct anything he'd done.

He waited until she'd completed the countercheck before speaking to her. "How's it look?"

Scanning the calculation set from start to finish one last time, Jils nodded. "You're solid, Garol, you can calculate vector transits for me anytime. Good to go. Let's do it."

And Jils was good. Methodical, precise, and much better at details of a certain sort than he was. If Jils said the calculation set was solid, it was solid.

"Strap yourself in, then, and let's go."

No time like the present.

He had set the ship's environmentals to low normal, so there were no artificially generated somatic signals that would indicate a change in their rate of speed; but the forward visual screens were in working order. Excellent working order. Really rather amazingly good working order, and worth almost the entire price the Bench had paid to get them from Combine ship-yards.

Garol hit the sequence initiate instruction, and space on the forward visual screens started to spin, the status markers on the ship's vital signs creeping upward as the ship gained speed.

The courier ran for the vector like a child's playing sphere fired along the lip of a great funnel, gathering momentum as it got closer and closer to the funnel's mouth. Garol closed his eyes: Looking at the forward screens was dizzying. He thought Jils looked a little green, as well, but he was in no shape to mention it.

With the ship's gravities set as low as they were, he could begin to feel the approach as pressure in his ears, like the sensation of spinning around in a chair until his head swam. He opened his eyes, swallowing back the sharp acid taste of bile that rose from his stomach as the nausea born of perturbations in the vestibular apparatus in his ears threatened to over-whelm him.

It was a clear, short approach to the vector transit for Rikavie. It was. Clean, sweet, easy, and nearly overdue, and Garol was anxious in spite of his faith in Jils's evaluation.

Anytime now, Garol told the courier ship in his mind, trying not to focus on the unnatural whirling of light objects on the screens in front of him. *You can make the vector anytime you'd like. In fact the sooner the better, for my money at least.*

The mad rotation of stars on-screen tightened and condensed to one bright spot of light that vibrated ever more quickly as the intensity of the light increased. They were close now. The glowing center of the visual display tightened and brightened and tightened moment by moment, gaining in intensity of brilliance as it shrank in size until it was almost too bright to bear; and then the screens blanked.

There would be nothing more to see until they reached Rikavie, and dropped out of the vector like a stone.

"We have the Garsite vector." Garol made the announcement with relief he didn't mind sharing with Jils. Vector transit was certain and secure enough to move ships by the hundreds of thousands from one end of Jurisdiction space to the other; and yet it was never completely, absolutely, entirely, eight-and-eighty-and-another-eight certain. "Next stop Rikavie. Port Charid. Warehouse asteroids; Langsariks."

"Spectacularly beautiful and very young women," Jils added, unfastening the secures of her harness. "Or at least one spectacularly beautiful and very young woman. Girl. How old would she be by now? Probably married, Garol, she *was* a looker."

What was she talking about?

Oh.

Modice Agenis.

Walton Agenis's niece.

All right, so he had noticed Modice—how could anyone have failed to? But it had been so long that Garol could laugh, without resentment. Without much resentment. "Old enough to know her own mind, Jils, now as then. You're on the wrong process branch about that. The girl was just a really sweet girl." A really sweet and astonishingly beautiful young girl, but

there'd been no mistaking her for a serious prospect
of any kind.

Not really.

It had been enough of a pleasure just to sit in her
company and listen to her voice, and feel fellowship
with all the other men who had noticed that she filled
the world with her presence and validated their entire
lives by just breathing.

"That's why you want me to go make the contacts
with the Port Authority while you go straight out to
the settlement. Right." But she was just teasing him.
He knew it. Wasn't she?

"It's the Flag Captain I really want to see. Agenis
the Deep-Minded. Before everybody in Port Charid
knows we're there. She deserves to know right up
front about the problem. And I want the straight
story, direct from her."

He had made the treaty with the Langsariks, and
Walton Agenis was their leader, then as now. They
had come to terms of mutual understanding, founded
on a necessarily qualified degree of trust. She had ad-
vised her people to accept the strict terms of the amnesty that the Bench offered through Garol in part on
the basis of her evaluation of his personal integrity.

It had made him uncomfortable at the time, even
while the personal if unspoken understanding between
them had been what made the amnesty possible. If there
was a problem, she would tell him. And if something
had really gone wrong, he had to let her know that
amnesty violation could mean an end to the amnesty,
and slavery—death, and dispersal—for the Langsariks.

"Yeah, yeah." Jils's singsong rejection of his claims
of disinterestedness was not entirely serious, if admittedly sharp. Not because she didn't believe him, but
because if she admitted to understanding his motives,
she'd have nothing to tease him about. "I'll take the
first watch, Garol. You go catch up on your fantasy
life."

He was a Bench intelligence specialist.

He didn't even have a fantasy life.

But if he had—

If he had a fantasy, it was that the Langsarik amnesty would work. That the Langsariks would prove their merit to the Bench in Port Charid and survive the test of years to be fully integrated as respected citizens of a benevolent Bench. That Modice Agenis would marry and be happy and secure . . . and that Walton Agenis would never have cause to decide that she'd been wrong when she'd trusted him with the future of the people who looked to her for leadership.

That was his fantasy. He could never admit it, though.

If he admitted that it was a fantasy, even to himself, he would have to acknowledge the fact that he was deeply worried about them all—the brave, proud, honorable people that he, himself, Garol Vogel, had essentially forced into settlement at Port Charid.

Kazmer Daigule stood in front of the receiving officer's desk at Anglace Port Authority, doing everything in his power to keep calm as she examined his forged cargo documentation. The contraband from the Tyrell Yards was fully accounted for, of course; the cargo manifest was one of the most beautiful works of art Kazmer could remember having seen.

It would have been much easier for him to feel confident about the validity of the counterendorsements on his documentation if there hadn't been four fully armed representatives from Fleet's shore patrol with him in the office, along with the receiving officer; but there was no reason to fear that this unusually aggressive presence was in any way related to the potential weaknesses in his documentation.

No reason.

He had to stay calm.

"Grain, medicinal botanicals, and luxury fabrics from Shilling," the receiving officer read aloud. "Interesting mix, pilot."

Kazmer bowed. "Yes, ma'am. We had to piece a cargo together from odd lots to get a full load." Otherwise, grain and luxury textiles wouldn't normally be traveling together—the margins were all off. Without the grain they'd carried with them from Port Charid, however, it would have been too easy for a suspicious mind to match their cargo to a list of goods misappropriated in a raid on a warehouse at Rikavie.

There was obvious risk of arousing suspicion even with the camouflage the grain provided the cargo, but that was what they were being paid for—to run the risk of getting caught with stolen merchandise.

It went without saying that there was nothing in the documentation to indicate that the freighter had been anywhere near Rikavie recently.

"H'mm." She handed the documentation back to him, but she hadn't stopped to seal it for release. Maybe she'd just forgotten. Yes. Surely she'd just forgotten. It would be so embarrassing to be caught with irregular documentation. It had never happened to him. "Well, everything looks unobjectionable, pilot. But Fleet wants every freighter in your gross weight category off-loaded and searched. It'll be half a day, and Port Anglace apologizes for the inconvenience. Quarantine. These people will escort you."

It didn't have to be a problem. It didn't have to be. Ships were off-loaded from time to time as a check on blatant cargo fraud, but the ports resisted it, because it was a time-consuming inconvenience and discouraged traffic. Kazmer stalled, hoping for reassurance.

"Of course, receiving officer. I hadn't realized there was a new policy in place at Anglace, though. I have to admit I'd have gone to Isener, I'd have been able to pay the crew off that much sooner."

And since the chartering company he was claiming to represent was responsible for wages until the crew was released, and since Kazmer was representing himself as a joint owner of the small cargo-carrying venture, it was a direct hit to his very own personal profits.

The receiving officer's mouth twisted in a sour grimace. "So would everybody. But it wouldn't have done you any good."

Of course not, Kazmer thought. The fence's contact was here, and he was responsible for getting the goods to the drop site, and that meant Anglace. Not Isener. But the receiving officer didn't know that. What she apparently did know provided no particular comfort, unfortunately.

"This is systemwide, but only for ships of your weight class. There's been more trouble at Port Charid, and the mercantile corporations are screaming for Fleet support."

Bad. Very bad. "I heard some gossip at Shilling," Kazmer admitted, speaking slowly, hoping to encourage the receiving officer to talk. "A lot of inventory wastage going on at Port Charid. Some words about Langsariks, but that doesn't make sense—where would they even get ships?"

The shore patrol didn't seem to be in any particular hurry to rush him to quarantine, so it couldn't be an issue of any real urgency. He might have to pay off the Port Authority; that was going to be hard to manage with Fleet personnel on the premises. But he could still get through this all right.

The receiving officer shook her head with evident relish for her role as the source of sensational information. "It's not inventory wastage they're yelling about. There was a raid at Port Charid a few days ago; they tortured half the crew and merely murdered the rest. Trashed the station's warehouse storage with high-energy impact rounds. Battle cannon. Where they've been hiding *those* all this time is anyone's guess."

Kazmer stood silent, stunned.

They'd only been on vector for a few days. Had someone mounted another raid after the Tyrell job?

Because she couldn't be talking about the Tyrell

Yards. She couldn't be. There had been an inside man. Nobody had been tortured, that was why the Langsariks had planted an inside man, to get the information without resorting to uncertain and excessive means. They had all been alive when the freighter had left.

"That's, er, not common knowledge, pilot," one of the shore patrol troops said, a little apologetically. "We'd appreciate it if you didn't disclose any of the details to your people. Let's get you to quarantine; there's cots and food, and it'll only be half a day."

It couldn't have been the Tyrell raid.

And if they suspected him, what point would there be in asking for his cooperative silence?

Nodding politely to take leave of the receiving officer, Kazmer turned from her desk and went with two of the armed troops.

Were they actually covering him?

Or were they armed for show?

It made no real difference. He couldn't afford to try for a break. They'd have him within moments; and an attempt to flee was as good as a sworn admission of wrongdoing, whether it was theft or killing.

He'd done nothing wrong . . . or nothing so wrong as that.

He was innocent of any act of murder.

And it was entirely beyond belief that Hilton Shires could be responsible for the torture, let alone the murder, of disarmed and helpless warehouse staff.

Impossible.

But if Fleet started to ask questions . . . if they were implicated, howsoever unfairly, in murder, and the Bench authorized preliminary inquiry, and there was enough incriminating evidence to convince someone to implement the Question—

He couldn't protect Hilton under torture.

Kazmer had no illusions about the power of his own will in opposition to all of the tools and tricks that a Fleet Inquisitor had at command, and everyone had heard about the range of atrocity permitted an Inquisitor; there had been that Tenth Level Command Termination. Koscuisko. Kazmer had remembered the name of the Inquisitor, because a Sarvaw had good reason to be mindful of all of the descendants of Chuvishka Kospodar.

He had to do something.

But the first thing that he had to do was wait, because this would all pass over. It had to. There was no connection between the freighter's cargo and any murders. Fleet would let them go.

There could be some penalty for the contraband they'd carried from Tyrell, but no more than that, and a good chance of getting off lightly even on that heading, since Fleet's interests were focused on the search for murderers. Not mere pirates.

Yes.

That was right.

Fleet had much more immediate concerns than one small-time operator from Port Charid, if there were murderers at large.

Chapter Four

Walton Agenis woke to the sounds of conversation in the house, an unfamiliar sensation—she was accustomed to quiet—and an unfamiliar voice. No, a familiar voice, but distantly so; coming from the kitchen, coupled with that of her niece.

What, had Kazmer Daigule come to the front door, as Modice had admonished him to do?

It wasn't Daigule's voice. It was deeper and lighter at the same time, lacking the reedy note of resigned weariness that gave everything the Sarvaw said its own characteristic wry humor. So Modice had another gentleman caller.

Walton sighed and rose, belting her robe around her, working her bare toes into her scuffs while she waited for her head to clear of sleep. She couldn't belt her robe around her waist, not really; because she'd never had much of a waist to belt anything around, being more or less all of one line from her shoulders to her hips with a miscellaneous diversion or two.

She secured the robe's ties around her middle instead and went out to find out who was courting Modice now, at this early hour of the morning.

The voices were coming from the kitchen, and Walton could smell the grain soup cooking—Langsarik breakfast, grain soup with shaved meat. Once it had been a fighting ration, easy to cook, easy to eat, easy to digest; now it was just daily fare. They'd lost so much: Or they'd given it away, and they'd given it away on persuasion from the man who was sitting in the kitchen with Modice, peeling a dish of gourds for a porridge.

Garol Vogel.

Jurisdiction Bench intelligence specialist, and the negotiator who had secured the amnesty responsible for the Langsarik settlement at Port Charid.

Vogel rose hastily to his feet as Walton entered the room, snatching his old campaign hat off his knee to make a precise salute. Hat in hand. Well, of course, hat on head was impossibly incorrect, in a kitchen. For a moment Walton felt embarrassment on account of her rather worn robe; but Vogel's own jacket had seen better days, too, so she put it out of her mind.

"Flag Captain Agenis." It was oddly formal of him to call her that; she had no fleet to command, and she didn't know what the land-based equivalent of a space fleet commander might be. Militarization had come late to the Langsariks, their fleet originally nothing more than a well-ordered commercial enterprise with government oversight. She'd always thought that helped to explain their success as commerce raiders: their strong commercial foundation. "I'm sorry to come unannounced, Captain, and so early in the morning. It's important that I meet with you. Should I come back later?"

Her nightdress embarrassed him, robe and all. That was funny. If he was embarrassed by her nightdress, the sight of the kerchief that Daigule had given Modice would probably make him faint outright. It was worth a try.

"Be seated, Specialist, it's all right. Has Modice given you soup?"

Probably not, because the grain soup was still cooking. Vogel declined to sit down. "With respect, ma'am. I wouldn't have come this early at all if it hadn't been business. You might want to hear what I have to say before you extend your hospitality, and I don't want to share your meal under false pretenses."

He was a queer duck, was Vogel; she'd learned that

much about him during the negotiation of the amnesty settlement. He slept on floors, ate when he remembered that he was hungry, and at one memorable meeting she had seen him rinse a drafting brush in his tea—and then drink his tea, having apparently forgotten that he'd rinsed his drafting brush in it.

And yet on certain forms and protocols he was absolutely formal and excruciatingly diffident.

"Vogel, we have a past relationship with you, and I accept that you speak for the Bench and not for yourself. Therefore, sit down and take grain soup on your behalf, and not that of the Bench. I grant hospitality to you, not to your Brief."

Now it would be rude of him to decline, so he accepted. He rolled his cap into a cylinder and thrust it deep into the left-hand pocket of his jacket before he sat back down to resume peeling gourds for Modice.

"Thank you, ma'am. Most gracious."

Modice set the morning tea on the table, with syrup and ground spice-bark to sprinkle on top. She could be a discreet little soul, Modice. Now that Walton was awake and on-line Modice concentrated on breakfast, quiet, efficient, and as much in the background as she could manage.

Walton let her morning tea sharpen her consciousness, drinking in silence as Vogel peeled vegetables. She thought she could guess why he might have come. He'd wait for her to open the talks, though, his tact as much personal as professional; so once Walton felt a little more alert she fired the opening round.

"What business brings you out to the settlement, then? Periodic status check, maybe."

But probably not. Vogel shook his head. He seemed a little more bald on top than he had been the last time she'd seen him, but his moustache was still thick and iron gray and showed no signs of thinning.

"Special embassy, Flag Captain. Chilleau Judiciary sent me. Local area mercantile predation, concerns about the robustness of the amnesty."

Since this was what she'd suspected once she'd recovered from the surprise of seeing him, Walton had an answer at the ready. "As if Langsariks could raid warehouses in the Shawl from a settlement on Rikavie. We'd need transport, for a start. We haven't got any."

She was almost glad he'd come with the issue; she'd been pondering the news and dreading the inevitable questions. No one had come right out and accused her of breaking faith—yet. Probably because people who were the least bit familiar with the Langsarik settlement had to realize how improbable the logistics were.

Vogel tilted his head a bit to one side, presenting his case. "They're small raids, but well mounted. Transport was stolen for the Okidan raid at least, so it could come from anywhere but has been coming from Port Charid. Never been more than two ships involved. So the thinking tends to be that if anybody could manage it, it'd be Langsariks, quarantine or no."

Walton frowned, and Modice set a dish of grain soup down in front of her. Plenty of pepper. It smelled very appetizing; Modice was a good cook.

"I couldn't so much as lay hands on a single freighter, Specialist. Not without someone noticing." She'd only ever heard about single ships; where did "two ships" come from? "I could see a possibility that some of our young people might sneak into the occasional warehouse here at Port Charid. For creature comforts."

Vogel thanked Modice in a murmured aside for the dish she gave him. Modice smiled at him and took the dish of peeled vegetables and waste peelings away. Gazing at the surface of his dish of grain soup, Vogel replied to the food, with his eyes resolutely focused on the dish. Polite. Nonconfrontational.

"Freighters. And battle cannon. The pattern doesn't exactly fit the Langsarik model, that's clear from intelligence sources. But the Bench is responsible for the protection of property and the maintenance of good order, and the rule of Law."

"Battle cannon? That's a good one." Walton ate grain soup, thinking. Vogel had information she hadn't heard yet, that much was now clear. "Where would I get battle cannon? Where would I hide battle cannon? If I had battle cannon, I certainly wouldn't blow my cover on any given raid; I'd keep them safe until I decided I really needed them."

Vogel seemed to remember, suddenly, that it would be rude to leave his meal uneaten, and attacked the problem with his spoon, with a strange sort of convulsive thoughtfulness. Walton didn't know whether Vogel's focus was a strictly personal characteristic or one common to Bench intelligence specialists; she was just glad he'd remembered his soup before it got cold.

If he'd come to court Modice, he would have tucked into it right away, in order to have the opportunity to compliment her cooking. So he had clearly gotten past the abstract sort of a crush he'd had on her.

"Um. Good soup. Thank you, Modice." But there was no particular weight to the phrase. Confirmed, then, Walton told herself: Vogel was polite as always, but he clearly had other things than her niece's beauty on his mind. "I can't answer that question, Flag Captain."

Question? Oh. About the battle cannon. Walton waited; Vogel spoke on.

"But I'm not sure it matters. We have three issues here. There's the apparent violation of amnesty."

He put a very careful weight on that word, *apparent*. Just enough to stress the hypothetical nature of the allegation without discounting the weight of the damning appearance.

"Then there's the Bench being pressured by the various big commercial interests with warehouses in the Shawl, along with other interests reluctant to invest, even at Chilleau Judiciary's very persuasively phrased invitation, so long as the area is not secure. The Bench wants the commercial investment. Finally, somebody is out there robbing warehouses. Killing people."

All three issues were intimately related. She didn't need Vogel to tell her that. "We may have been raiders, Bench specialist. We may have been good at it. But we were never murderers."

Had people been killed during Langsarik raids? Yes. She wasn't going to deny it; she also didn't need to explain to Vogel. They carried blood guilt, because people had died as a result of Langsarik actions; but it was not guilt for murders either premeditated or accepted as any sort of an acceptable concomitant to raiding. It had always been an unfortunate accident when it happened. They'd always done what they could to minimize the chances that people would get hurt, because it had never been blood that they'd wanted, but freedom. And survival.

Now Vogel put the spoon down and met her gaze very directly. There was no accusation or deception in Vogel's sharp gray-green eyes. "That's as may be, Flag Captain. People are getting killed. There are capital crimes to account for. We don't have very much free-board here."

Always set his documents on reader, Vogel had. Shared information, full disclosure, no hidden agenda. Asking her to engage with him in partnership for the accomplishment of mutually beneficial goals: pacification, survival.

Port Charid's administration treated her very much like the only marginally trustworthy representative of a defeated and criminal people. They were forced to rely on her for head-count reports and policing the settlement, but it was strictly for lack of any other resources.

Vogel was still negotiating with her as Flag Captain. "What do you need from me, Garol?"

"Couple things. Thank you for asking."

Coming from almost anyone else, she would have sneered at the courtesy or simply ignored it. Anyone else, and it would have been meaningless; but Vogel meant it. Vogel was for real.

Vogel was talking; Modice was washing dishes, quietly, in the background. "Not to be insulting, Flag Captain. But are we clear on what happens if Langsariks are found to be violating the terms of the amnesty agreement?"

Yes. They were very clear. "Violation in substance of the amnesty agreement nullifies the Bench's suspension of prosecution. Execution for some of us. The Bond for any of our young people who test out." And Langsariks would test out well for enslavement under governor, Walton was uncomfortably sure of it.

It took a person with character, ability, and unusual psychological resilience to qualify for the Bench's most horrible punishment, the living death of enslavement as a Security bond-involuntary, conditioned to obey or suffer hugely disproportionate punishment from an internal governor, condemned to execute the orders of a Ship's Inquisitor as the hands of a torturer.

Langsariks could survive even that. Langsariks had what it took to make whatever sacrifices they had to make, in order to survive. "Penal colonies for everyone else. Dispersal and death. Dissolution as a people and disenfranchisement for next of kin still living on Palaam."

The Langsarik pirates per se were not a large community; there were only about five thousand of them in total.

But it was her community.

Vogel nodded grimly. "The stakes are too high to risk any stratagems on either of our parts, Flag Captain. Before I go any further with this issue I'd like permission to ask you up front, man to man. Just between us."

"Man to man," was it? Walton knew what was coming. "All right. Ask away."

"Are you personally aware of anything going on within the Langsarik community that we need to know about that might have a bearing on the recent warehouse invasions. And have you any unexplained anomalies with your head-count and reconciliation reports."

Incriminate her own?

Yes. If that was what it took to protect the community as a whole.

Luckily for her she didn't have to face sacrificing any of her people. "If I knew anything that would link any Langsarik to warehouse predation, I'd tell you, Vogel."

He would know that she was telling the truth; he'd as much as told her that her word was as good as her oath when he'd asked permission to ask the question. "But I don't. So far as I know there isn't anything going on. We've had the occasional anomaly"—the Sarvaw mercantile pilot who had slipped through the firewatch perimeter, for instance—"but nothing that might enable any plots. And I have no idea where we could lay hands on a freighter, let alone a battle cannon, not with what we have to work with here."

Modice had left the kitchen as Walton spoke; now she came back again, standing beside Walton where she sat, with her hands folded underneath the apron she'd put on to do the dishes. Modice was very white in the face.

Vogel noticed.

"Are you all right, pretty lady?" Vogel asked, gently; and Modice drew her hands out from underneath her apron. She had something in one hand.

It was the scarf that Kazmer Daigule had given her, the night he'd turned up at Modice's window.

"The Bench specialist might want to talk to Hilton, Aunt Walton," Modice said, her voice a little quavery, but determined. "Hilton will know what his friends are up to, even if we don't. So the Bench specialist could give this to Hilton to give back to Kazmer. If you wouldn't mind, Specialist Vogel."

Thinking on her feet, was Modice. And clearly frightened.

Daigule had come to Port Charid, and probably not just to see her; it was logical to suppose that he had business, and—in the absence of any concrete knowledge of what that business was—not too far-fetched for Modice to wonder if there was something that Daigule had gotten himself tangled up with that he shouldn't have. Because Daigule was a man of immoderate enthusiasms and uncertain discretion.

Did Hilton know about Daigule's business?

Had Hilton been part of whatever had called Daigule to Port Charid in the first place?

Sending Daigule's scarf back through Hilton was as good as a warning to everybody, one way or the other. If Hilton didn't know that Daigule had been in Charid, sending the scarf to Daigule through Hilton would tip off her nephew and warn him of potential trouble.

If Hilton had called Daigule in on a raid, letting the Bench Specialist return the scarf would put Hilton on notice that the authorities were close to him, and—since Modice had entrusted Vogel with the errand, with Walton's knowledge to be assumed—that he would not be protected if he endangered his people.

If Daigule was involved with something that Hilton didn't know about, getting the scarf returned to him by Hilton via Vogel would let Daigule know that the authorities were closing in on him, and that his activities were a danger to Modice as well as to himself.

And giving the scarf to Vogel was as much as telling Vogel that the Langsarik authorities were genuinely ignorant of the fact if it was a fact, with an entire sheaf of corollaries besides.

Walton couldn't believe that Hilton would be engaged in anything he knew could jeopardize his entire community.

If she thought about it, she couldn't really believe that Daigule was involved in murder, either.

She was still impressed with Modice for having the

moral strength to admit the possibility and take action on the margin of the odds.

Vogel didn't know who Daigule was; obviously enough Vogel had no knowledge of Daigule's night visit. Modice had only told Walton herself about it within the past few days, and it had been twice that long since it had occurred. Vogel simply accepted the scarf at its face value and folded it into another pocket of his jacket. "To be returned by Modice Agenis to Kazmer Daigule through Hilton Shires. Glad to oblige. Where do I find the lieutenant these days, Flag Captain?"

Modice left the kitchen again, and Walton knew that she fled in her heart even while she walked with casual care in the flesh. If Modice liked Daigule, it would be torture to her to think that he might be involved.

If Modice liked Daigule, she would have to know whether he was involved or not, so that she could cut him out of her heart as soon as possible—should it be necessary.

There would be much to digest after this breakfast.

"Hilton is in Port Charid. Doing orientation in the warehouses there." Vogel clearly remembered him from the negotiations; there was no need for anxious concern that the name and the relationship might be firm in Vogel's mind because Hilton was suspect. "He's gone to work for the Combine Yards. There's a new warehouse complex under construction."

Vogel nodded. "Well. I'll be going. I hope you won't hesitate to call on me if you think of anything or learn something. Is there anything I can send you from Port Charid?"

There was an unusual softness to his voice, and something in his expression that seemed almost tender. Caught by surprise, Walton felt a blush coming on like steam rising into her face from a cup of freshly boiled water for hot tea.

"Ah. No. Thank you. We're fine." Noodles. She

wanted noodles. She liked noodles, especially with snap-spice broth, and poultry. They weren't expensive, but a person had to have a supplier, and the local concession hadn't stocked any as long as they'd been here. "Send me the news, Garol, when you can. I want to know what develops."

He stood in the middle of the kitchen with his cap in his hand for a moment, looking around the room as though he had forgotten something.

"And thanks for coming, Bench specialist. I'll let you know if I find out anything."

He seemed to give himself a mental shake. "Yes, of course. You're welcome, only due respect, and so forth. Good-greeting, Flag Captain, I'll show myself out."

Her grain soup had gotten cold, but she finished it anyway.

Modice, Daigule, Hilton. Vogel.

Battle cannon.

There could be no connection.

But if there was—

She was Flag Captain Walton Agenis; and it was up to her to protect the Langsariks.

Against her own family. If that was what it took.

Kazmer Daigule could hear the voice through the open doorway, clear and resonant and cold, like the penitence bell on the Day of Atonement. During the days he had been held in Fleet custody here at Anglace he had played this coming confrontation over and over and over in his mind, testing each link in the fearful chain, hoping in vain to find a weak spot somewhere. During hour after hour of restless solitude he had written and rewritten the story in his mind, the train of events, the best interpretation he could put on them; and hour after hour of restless solitude had led him ever and again to despair, in the bleak conviction that things could not possibly be worse for him.

And it was worse.

The Holy Mother loved her Sarvaw stepchildren: Kazmer had been catechized with care, during his short childhood. She cared for and nurtured the Sarvaw almost as tenderly as if they had been her own children, and not the offspring of bondservants. But the Holy Mother was a vicious bitch for all that.

This Inquisitor was Dolgorukij.

And of all the Inquisitors who could have been called off a routine cruise to take legal and binding testimony on Record, there was only one that Kazmer had ever heard of who was Dolgorukij; because after the Domitt Prison—and the execution of its master—everyone had heard of Andrej Koscuisko.

Someone came to the door of the interrogation room, someone in Fleet colors. Big. Very ugly. The officer's doorkeeper, perhaps; his narrow yellow eyes rested briefly on Kazmer's face without changing expression. Then he tilted his head with a decisive gesture.

"The officer is ready for you," the man said. His voice was as wrecked as his face was, so unlovely that Kazmer could almost pity him. Almost. "This is the pilot? Let's go."

They would question each of the crew members separately, and then check their stories against each other to decide who would go on to further interrogation. Kazmer had thought it all through. Contact with the Langsariks had been through anonymous drops, third-party relay, double-blind exchanges. None of the crew knew any more about who had hired them than the absolute minimum, unless, of course there was a Langsarik plant among them. He couldn't afford to postulate the presence of a Langsarik plant; it was too uncertain.

He had to proceed under the assumption that he was the only one among them who could point a finger and name a name.

His guards started him forward with a shove; he kept his balance, but not gracefully. He was tired, and he was hungry, and he'd been sleeping in his clothes for days. It demoralized a man. He knew very well that he stank; but was the subtle expression of disdain that crossed the Inquisitor's face a reflection of his all-too-powerful odor?

Or did Koscuisko recognize him as Sarvaw?

"Thank you, Mister Stildyne." Yes, it had been Koscuisko's voice he'd heard from outside the room. Tenor, and strangely feral. "Be seated, pilot, there is nothing to fear. For the moment. My name is Andrej Koscuisko, and I hold the Writ to which you must answer for questions that exist pertaining to the potential involvement of your ship and crew in murder and theft in the Shawl of Rikavie."

He'd heard some of the details by now, before the guards from the local port authority had realized that their gossip might contaminate his evidence. He still couldn't believe it. Either murder had not been done, or Hilton wasn't involved in it: But all the Bench would hear from him was the name, not his insistence on Hilton's innocence.

Kazmer had no confidence in his ability to withhold the name.

One of Koscuisko's people set a glass of water down on the table in front of Kazmer, where he could reach it with his hands chained at his waist. Kazmer stared at the man's sleeve as he placed the glass: a uniform blouse with green piping at the cuff.

Greensleeves.

Bond-involuntary.

That was what they would do to Hilton, to all of his family; plant a governor in his brain and set him to serve a torturer, or suffer torture himself. And Modice? Modice was so beautiful. They would prostitute her less horribly, perhaps, because it was more traditional a fate for a woman in the hands of her enemies; but they would put a meter on her body and vend the private secrets of her flesh to any bully who could come up with the price.

It made him sick just to think of it.

And he would be the cause of it, because he had seen Hilton in the street.

He took a drink of water to steady his resolve; and the Inquisitor sitting across the table from him, with a tidy little rhyti-set at one elbow and a pair of black leather dress gloves laid casually to one side—nodded at him, as if approvingly. Kazmer could smell the perfume of hot sweet rhyti, and it made his mouth water with longing. He hadn't had a decent cup of rhyti since—

What did it matter?

He couldn't afford the quality of leaf that Koscuisko used anyway.

"Let us begin, then," the Inquisitor said. "State for me your name, pilot. And your cargo, your point of origin, and the identification of the ship on which you traveled here to Anglace."

Koscuisko knew his name.

The Inquisitor had the information there in front of him, the printed copy of the Port Authority's report in a neat and damning stack.

But there were rituals to all of one's interactions with the Bench: and Kazmer could not afford to permit this one to go any further.

"I declare myself Sarvaw, your Excellency, Kazmer Daigule, from Peritrallneya near Sivan. I throw myself upon the mercy of the Malcontent, to answer to him or none. Sir."

The Inquisitor froze where he sat, staring, his pale eyes blank and unreadable. None of the others would know; it was lucky, in a way, that Koscuisko was here, because otherwise the declaration might not be read into Record until it was reviewed prior to logging at the end of the session. And there might have been unpleasantness, upcoming.

The ugly man spoke, from the post he'd taken at the officer's right hand. "Sir—"

Koscuisko silenced the ugly man with an upraised

hand. "You will leave us, Mister Stildyne," Koscuisko said. "Robert may stay, and Lek. I place the Record in suspense, now excuse us please. Immediately."

The ugly man wasn't happy.

But the Inquisitor was senior, and rank apparently prevailed. Were they afraid he might assault the Inquisitor?

What physical damage could he do, with his hands chained and his feet shackled?

When the room held only the four of them— Kazmer, and the Inquisitor, and two bond-involuntary troops—the Inquisitor spoke.

"You have placed your election on record, Daigule, no one will defraud you of your choice. But consider. Is the penalty you face truly worth the sacrifice required to avoid it? You have spoken the name of the Malcontent, and your mother will wonder forever after how she failed you in your upbringing."

As if Koscuisko's own mother had no such doubts, and him a noble and upright pillar of the Judicial order.

"I have nothing further to say, your Excellency. To you or anybody." He had already said that he would answer to the Malcontent. But even the Malcontent would refrain from asking one question; that was the foundation of the contract. A man who elected the Malcontent gave over to the Saint his name, his freedom, his body, his mind and heart and soul; his all, in return for one thing: whatever it was that he wanted.

Would the Malcontent accept his contract?

The Malcontent turned no man away.

Koscuisko rose to his feet, with a decisive gesture of disgust. "Then you are guilty. You cannot be otherwise. It is the counsel of a coward, to seek the Saint to evade deserved punishment."

But Kazmer knew what he had to do. He had fought it out during those long hours of waiting and wondering what would happen. He could implicate Langsariks by name. So far as he knew he was the only one of the freighter's crew who could do that.

They gave him no option for any other escape; so the Malcontent was his only hope, and Hilton's only hope as well.

"I neither affirm nor deny your statements, your Excellency, but submit myself to the mercy of the Saint. In reverence. And silence."

Koscuisko wasn't looking at him.

Koscuisko was looking at one of the troops he'd kept with him in the room; and Kazmer remembered what the Inquisitor had said to the ugly man, as he sent the ugly man away. Robert and Lek, he'd said. Kazmer hadn't paid much attention to the bond-involuntaries, he'd been too wrapped up in his own issues to have energy to spare: but Lek was Sarvaw, too. Sarvaw with an Arakcheyek in his mother's nightmares, by his height; but Sarvaw nonetheless.

"Who am I to say?" Koscuisko asked Lek, with a little shrug that looked almost embarrassed. "It could be that there are worse things, whether guilty of greater or lesser crimes."

The bond-involuntary Sarvaw bowed his head in response, and Koscuisko nodded. Then shook his head, but apparently at some strictly personal regret or disappointment. Kazmer stared at the glass of water on the table in front of him. There were worse things than to elect the Malcontent. One of them was to be enslaved under Bond.

Let Koscuisko believe that that was what Kazmer feared.

Or let Koscuisko believe whatever he liked, just so long as Kazmer could protect the Langsariks from the fate that had been visited upon Lek, the fate worse even than the election of the Malcontent.

"Open the door, Robert," the Inquisitor said; then called out to the ugly man, who apparently stood waiting outside. "Mister Stildync. It will be necessary to go and see the Consul, to obtain the representative of the Malcontent. Present my excuses to the Port Authority, and let us go directly."

The guards who had brought Kazmer in took Kazmer out, surprised enough by these developments that they forgot to shove, and let him walk at a normal pace. They went back to his cell. When he was alone again Kazmer put his face down between the palms of his chained hands, fighting to quiet his mind.

He had done it.

He had elected the Malcontent. Soon he would be damned as all Malcontents were damned, despised, disenfranchised, disdained, and disregarded.

He would be alive; and if an evil fortune should call Hilton's name up before that Dolgorukij Inquisitor, at least it would not be from Kazmer's mouth that it would go on Record. Or maybe not at all.

And Modice Agenis?

He could not even think of little Modice.

He would be Malcontent. He did not have the right.

Knowing that he had had no choice if he was to hope to protect his friend gave him no comfort, in the horrible certainty that even the hope of Modice was lost to him forever.

When he got back to Port Charid Garol Vogel stopped at the yards where the courier was berthed, but Jils wasn't on board; there weren't any messages. There was news on the reader from Chilleau Judiciary, but Garol wasn't interested. He sat down at the scheduler instead, keying a line for Shiron Madlev, the Combine Factor at Port Charid.

He needed to pay a courtesy call.

The Bench recognized Factor Madlev as the spokesman for the local mercantile council, which made Madlev something close to the civilian authority here. The port's only secured communications with Chilleau Judiciary were held in Factor Madlev's office. It was politic to go and make appropriate noises expressive of profound concern on the part of the Bench, pledges of speedy resolution, promises of action—all of those things.

Therefore, Madlev was the obvious place to start, if Jils hadn't done the honors already. Madlev might well expect a call either way, after Garol's previous meeting with his foreman—what had the name been? Fisner Feraltz—at the hospital at Nisherre.

There was also an errand to run, for Walton Agenis.

When the access tone cleared, Garol identified himself, his voice a little strange in his own ears in the silence of the courier.

"Bench intelligence specialist Garol Vogel. I've been detailed by the Second Judge at Chilleau Judiciary to solve the piracy problem at Port Charid. Requesting an entrance interview with Factor Madlev, at his earliest convenience."

There were clicks and hushes on the line as the screener on the other end scrambled to take the message line. Garol could appreciate the humor in the situation. He was sitting in a quiet ship with his clothing in moderate disarray and what hair he had left in an emphatically uncombed condition from his journey to the Langsarik settlement and back on a speed machine; but a Bench intelligence specialist was a Bench intelligence specialist—and the line wasn't video. Just audio.

"—Excuse me, Bench specialist." A live body, at the other end. "If you would care to nominate a time when Factor Madlev could look forward to receiving you."

The sooner he got his duty calls out of the way the better. Jils had already gone to tie in with local Judicial resources, such as they were in a mercantile port.

"I can be there inside of an hour, if that's convenient. And say, I heard there's someone I need to speak to, working in the Combine warehouses somewhere in Charid. Maybe someone could show me where to find him, after I meet with Factor Madlev. Hilton Shires. Langsarik."

The voice at the other end sounded a little surprised, but seemed to be recovering. "He's a new man, Bench specialist, here this morning I believe. It shall be done. When may I tell the Factor to expect you, sir?"

Don't. It's better if he doesn't expect me. Garol resisted the temptation. He'd already lost the advantage of surprise anyway. As if he needed surprise when he was just giving an in-briefing, not probing for information.

Madlev would be expecting some questions.

Best to get them out of the way up front.

"Give me an hour. I'll be seeing you. Thanks for making the time."

When Garol Vogel walked into Factor Madlev's office—shaven and suited in uniform dress, and exact to the hour—he was not entirely surprised to find Jils Ivers waiting for him, with a documents case in one hand and a face that spoke code. She had something interesting, then. She was a fast worker.

Garol was surprised to see Fisner Feraltz there as well—the sole survivor of the raid on the Okidan Yards, the man he'd interviewed in the private hospital at Nisherre. Feraltz didn't look much recovered to Garol; he was still braced from head to foot on his right side. Hadn't been doing his physical therapy, Garol concluded. Feraltz bowed a little stiffly in response to Garol's nod of greeting, but there was no other way to move in all that bracing but stiffly.

Factor Madlev was a big man whose face seemed fractionally too large for his head, even with his very full beard taken into account; but there was no faulting his enthusiasm, or his manners. Now that Garol had given Feraltz the nod, Madlev came forward to meet Garol with hearty goodwill, offering a greeting that seemed perfectly genuine.

"Bench specialist Vogel. An honor, sir. I'm Shiron Madlev, Factor Madlev, people call me Uncle. Or, er,

Factor. You've met my foreman, I think? Welcome to Port Charid; we are very glad to see you."

"Pleasure to be here. Yes, in fact, I had a talk with Feraltz before he was released from hospital. Good to see you on the road to recovery, Feraltz."

Garol returned the Factor's eager embrace with one of moderate warmth, not entirely comfortable with Madlev's effusions of joy. "The Bench is deeply concerned about recent events in Rikavie, Factor Madlev, and we'll do our best to get to the bottom of the problem. I see my second has anticipated me, however."

No, she'd come because she knew he'd come here as soon as he got back from the settlement. The rental company's locator on the speed machine would have told her when that had happened. She wasn't supposed to be able to read the machine's locator, it was private information, after all. Proprietary to the rental company. But rank had its privileges; also its problems, inconveniences, headaches, warts, and the occasional lethal surprise.

"Yes, honored by two such visits, and on the same morning. Please. Be seated. Can I offer?"

Offer what? Offer anything. It was a subtle lure, equally receptive to requests for money or drugs as bean tea or cavene. Garol discarded the cynical reflection as uncalled-for, and settled himself. Feraltz simply leaned up against the Factor's desk, keeping to the background, resting his right leg; no sitting down in that medical web, or at least no sitting down in any chair with arms. No room.

"You're very kind." Garol had eaten breakfast already, a big bowl full of Modice Agenis's grain soup. Not that it was anyone's business. "Nothing for me, thanks. Just a moment or two of your time. The intelligence reports contain no anomalies in the head-count and reconciliation reports, yet rumor insists that Langsariks are responsible for recent raids in the Shawl of Rikavic."

Madlev shrugged with a smile, as impervious to Garol's lure as Garol to his. "Bench specialist. We have so few resources. What can I tell you? We have no choice but to rely on the Langsariks themselves, for self-policing."

Madlev was a little too big for his chair, which could barely contain the span of his broad thighs. Broad powerful, not broad fleshy, but the effect was a little ludicrous all the same; it reminded Garol of a grown man trying to make use of a child's seat, for want of anything more appropriately sized.

"Quite so. Very true." Madlev wasn't in a very expansive mood, it seemed; but it was hard to believe that Port security wouldn't have caught on by now, if something was going on. If. "But you do periodic spot checks, I understand. And there haven't been any problems there?"

The Bench had put the Langsariks here at Port Charid, but hadn't stationed any police resources to monitor them—that was up to the Port Authority. As far as the Bench was concerned the ban on transport was all that had been needed to ensure that Langsariks stayed here. Port Charid was responsible for overseeing that ban; how did Port Charid explain the apparent access of Langsarik raiders to hulls on which to raid?

Madlev nodded. "That's right, Specialist Vogel. We do unannounced spot checks three times a week, and we haven't found anyone missing yet." Madlev's response was ready and complete enough, but Garol thought there was a hint of defensiveness there all the same. "There have been one or two minor discrepancies, but all explained to my complete satisfaction. No transport gone missing from Port Charid either, and I think we'd notice, Bench specialist. They're good. If it's true what they say, of course, and there's no proof. Is there?"

No help there, in other words. Walton Agenis had claimed she didn't know where she'd find a freighter;

Factor Madlev apparently had no insight on the question—none that he was willing to share, at least.

"The public word is very much Langsarik," Jils said, in a tone of mild—very mild—reproof. "It seems unnecessarily complicated to speculate on some unknown responsible party. They *are* Langsariks. And they are dangerous."

She was feeling Madlev out, Garol knew; repeating only what she'd heard said. Garol found her remarks a little distasteful, even so. Jils hadn't forgiven the Langsariks for having been as successful as they were. She seemed to have no room in her heart for admiration for the discipline and sacrifice of a worthy foe; or she felt it as keenly as he did, but would not acknowledge any foe worthy that challenged the rule of Law, let alone as profitably as the Langsarik fleet had done.

Madlev shrugged with his palms upturned in a gesture of conciliatory petition. "Of course everyone says Langsariks. They're a defenseless target. When were Langsariks ever stupid, though? And what would endangering the settlement be, if not sheer idiocy? No. I don't believe it."

It was interesting for Madlev to be so definite, with his foreman still visibly marked by injuries sustained in the Okidan raid. Feraltz didn't seem to find Madlev's insistence distasteful, even so. That was right: Feraltz's story had been that the raiders couldn't be proved to be Langsariks. Feraltz was on the Langsarik side, at least as far as sympathy went.

"We'll get it straightened out, Factor Madlev. That's what we're here for. Though I do have a personal request to make, as well."

"Yes, anything." Factor Madlev didn't really have much room to lean forward in his chair; his legs were too long for its height, so that leaning forward looked more awkward than sincere. He seemed to know that. "Office space. Local transport. Communications links; dinner. Anything."

All of which Garol could arrange just as well or

better for himself, but there was no advantage to be gained by gratuitous rudeness. "You have a Langsarik in the warehouse. Hilton Shires." He had mentioned wanting to see Hilton when he'd made this appointment; had Madlev been told? "I have a message from his aunt; I promised I'd pass it on."

That, and he wanted access to Shires.

Garol was ready to believe that Agenis had told him the truth when she'd said that her hands were clean; she had more sense than to try to shield any guilty parties at the expense of the entire Langsarik settlement. That made the problem more complicated, but less stressful to Garol personally.

The scarf was a signal of some sort, and Agenis had chosen to let Garol deliver it. Agenis wanted Hilton to cooperate, in other words. Garol didn't need to know the ins and outs of it. All he needed to know was who was raiding, where they were, and how to stop them before they brought horror and destruction down on the heads of innocent people.

"Yes, of course. Immediately. Fisner?" Madlev pushed himself out of his too-small chair with evident relief; and Feraltz straightened up, clearly ready to receive instruction. Why didn't Madlev have all of his chairs done large enough to suit his size? Garol wondered. Was it because of the negotiating advantage Madlev gained, when people were foolish enough to read physical awkwardness for a relative dullness of wit and failed to shield their strategies or secrets accordingly?

Jils stood up, too

Feraltz moved awkwardly toward the door, talking as he went. "I'm still at a bit of a disadvantage, Bench specialist, so I've taken the liberty of asking Dalmoss to come and escort you. He's one of our floor managers." There was a man waiting in the Factor's front room, newly arrived since Garol had gotten here; the man came forward at a signal from Feraltz.

"Dalmoss will take you to Shires's workstation, so

you can talk privately if you like. Without publicity. And here's Dalmoss. Dalmoss, these are Bench intelligence specialists Vogel and Ivers, looking for Hilton Shires."

Perhaps not exactly "looking for," Garol thought. Wasn't there an implied accusation or assumption of guilt of some sort there? He'd asked to see Shires, he hadn't come looking for Shires to question him. And yet that could be what the foreman thought he was going to do; the foreman didn't seem to like the idea, either.

"If you'll come with me, gentles. I'll take it from here, sir. Shires? He'll be in receiving reconciliation this morning, we can run him to earth there. As it were."

Maybe he was being oversensitive, Garol decided. To consistently decline to identify the Langsariks as guilty, and then imply howsoever indirectly that Shires was a person of interest for a Bench investigation—it would mean that Feraltz was a hypocrite, or seriously ambivalent, or so secure in his conviction of Langsarik innocence that he hadn't given the phrase a second thought.

Overreacting.

Yes.

As an Abstainer, Feraltz was probably avoiding the drugs he needed to manage his pain. That would more than cover any apparent inconsistencies in his communications. He was probably exhausted, and almost certainly distracted by the trouble his still-healing injuries were undoubtedly giving him.

Yet something was ever so slightly off-kilter; and Garol didn't know what it was.

Oversensitive.

He'd talk it all out with Jils, as soon as he'd concluded his errand for Walton Agenis.

Hilton Shires set his mark to another line of audit code on the receiving report with a sense of accomplishment too thoroughly mixed with a sense of the ridiculous to be completely enjoyable.

He was learning to do receiving reconciliation and inventory management. The acquisition of new skills was an intrinsic good. There was no telling when it might turn up suddenly useful to be able to audit a cargo in record time and present a fair report on wastage and dilapidation.

But he was also Hilton Shires, a once-lieutenant in the Langsarik fleet that had exercised its own particular if not inimitable brand of wastage and dilapidations against cargoes permanently diverted from warehouses much like this one and absorbed directly against the bottom line of somebody else's books.

The contrast made for meditation that was not free from bitterness. It wasn't because he was ungrateful. The warehouse crew didn't go out of their way to be friendly, no, but he'd known Dolgorukij kept to themselves when he'd accepted the job. He'd been glad to accept the job. He'd wanted the money, and moldering in settlement without anything constructive to do could only lead to trouble.

He was glad to see the foreman coming toward him from the direction of the administrative offices; he could take a break from congratulating himself on learning how to count cargo crates. A little self-admiration went a long way. He had little enough he could admire in himself these days. Who was that with the foreman?

He watched them come.

Middling-sized man, square-shouldered and light on his feet, where had he seen that uniform before? Bench standard trousers, overblouse, cap, footgear; but the color was a peculiar gray, and there was no rank that Hilton could see.

Bench intelligence specialist.

The woman, too, a little on the short side but as sturdy as a chisel. Once Hilton identified the uniform in his mind he remembered where he'd seen those people before, or at least the man. Garol Vogel. The man who had made it all possible, the settlement, the amnesty, Hilton's job, everything. He had a lot to thank Vogel for, but in his heart he knew that genuine thanks were owing.

So he would be polite.

His foreman waved to him, having obviously realized that Hilton had noticed them; so Hilton signed off on the counter—never leave a counter unsecured and open, he'd been told; otherwise, it was vulnerable to unauthorized emendation that would invalidate the count—to join the foreman and the people he had with him. He hadn't heard there were Bench intelligence specialists in Port Charid. Bench intelligence specialists were devious that way.

"Hilton Shires," the foreman said to Vogel, as Hilton approached. "This is the man you want? The Bench specialists are asking after you, Shires. Don't be too long, though, there's a lot to be done before we can load-out that shipment for storage, and our freighter's due to dock in less than two days."

Right.

The foreman walked on. Hilton stopped short and waited for Vogel to open the discussion.

"Garol Vogel," Vogel said, politely, in case Hilton hadn't recognized him, Hilton supposed. "I've just been out to see your aunt. There's a problem with raiding in the Shawl, I expect you've heard all about it."

As indeed he had. "Not since the hit on the Tyrell Yards." If there had been anything since then, it was news to Hilton. "Disgusting waste of time and energy. Not to mention the vandalism."

Vogel shook his head. "Nope, that's the last one. Till the next one. The Bench is worried, Shires; people are talking about Langsariks."

As if he didn't know, Hilton told himself, indignantly. The crew here in the warehouse were good about it—they seemed genuinely to admire the Langsarik fleet's history of successful, if ultimately futile, resistance to assimilation within the embrace of the Jurisdiction. The Combine itself hadn't been all that eager to make treaty, if he remembered his history correctly.

"Target of opportunity, Specialist Vogel. Specialist Ivers? Good to see you again. You were at the talks, weren't you?"

She wasn't giving him much of a reaction one way or the other, listening politely but without response. It didn't matter. He was just making his point. "You'll remember the terms, I expect. The Langsarik fleet to yield all transport and articles of war or aggression, including such weapons that might otherwise be granted for defensive purposes. The Bench to decline to exercise judgment on condition that behavioral guarantees are met. Yes, people talk, Specialist Vogel. But not even my aunt could manage to attack a warehouse in the Shawl from a shack on Rikavie. And if she had, she wouldn't have made such a sloppy botch of it."

People had been murdered. The authorities were keeping the details close in order to avoid compromising evidence; a person didn't need much imagination to guess at the general outlines of the crime. Langsariks had been commerce raiders. The Bench had called it piracy, but there was a world of difference between assisting the creative redistribution of material resources and killing people while one was at it.

"Even so." Vogel's voice was reasonable, even sympathetic. He had an open manner that invited confidence; it seemed to indicate an honest heart—as far as that went. "The Bench isn't always as careful as we'd like about politically volatile situations. Primary value is the rule of Law and the maintenance of the Judicial order, which means that the appearance of an issue can be an issue. The Flag Captain says she doesn't know of anything going on in-house. Suggested that we see if you had heard anything."

Hilton felt himself redden in the face with vexation. Aunt Walton had said that? Sent Vogel here to get his assurances? Maybe she'd been thinking about speed machines. It was true he'd succumbed to temptation and borrowed one without having had the opportunity to ask permission. He'd paid for the repairs, hadn't he? That machine had been better than new once the work had been finished, too. He had even been invited to wreck another of old Phiser's speed machines anytime.

"What Walton Agenis doesn't know about what's going on in settlement isn't worth knowing. If she says there's nothing, then there's nothing, Bench specialist. But since she told you to ask me. No. I haven't heard any hints of raids or thievery from any Langsariks I know. People are depressed, not stupid."

Vogel nodded. "Good enough for me, Shires. Your aunt is a woman of her word. In fact, the Bench granted amnesty on the strength of that word, pretty significant sign of respect there."

So don't embarrass her, Vogel was saying. What made Vogel think he was involved in anything? Vogel was an intelligence specialist. He surely knew exactly how much weight it was appropriate to give the gossip of idle minds.

"And well placed, Bench specialist." His response sounded a little stiff and offended to himself, but Vogel didn't seem to take offense. He just reached into the front of his uniform blouse for a packet of some kind.

"I agree. Well, we'll be going, Shires; if you hear anything that might help us discover who's responsible for the Tyrell murders, I hope you'll let us know. Here. The Flag Captain asked me to give this to you."

It was a scarf, and a hideous one, an incredibly garish length of cloth patterned in great gouts of completely incompatible colors. Even the color tones themselves were mismatched.

"I don't understand." It was beyond belief that his

aunt would send something so horrible as a gift. "Is there an explanation that goes with this thing?"

Vogel folded his hands together in front of him, his fingers loosely interlaced. "Not much explanation, I'm afraid. Modice gave it to me to give to you, to be returned to someone named Kazmer Daigule, the next time you saw him. Does that mean anything to you?"

Ivers had been staring at the scarf in Hilton's grasp with horrified fascination. When Vogel said Kazmer's name she glanced up quickly at Vogel, though, as if she'd been taken by surprise.

Was this a setup, to see if they could get a guilty reaction out of him by surprising him with the name of a possible accomplice? It could be. But it wasn't.

If Vogel and Ivers had set a trap, Ivers would have watched his face, not looked at Vogel. So there was something going on that they hadn't worked out between themselves, yet.

"Kazmer Daigule is a friend of mine. He courts Modice to annoy me." What Kazmer had been doing in Port Charid the morning of Hilton's interview with Factor Madlev Hilton could only guess. He would rather Kazmer had not come into any conversation with Bench intelligence specialists, on principle; Kazmer had ferried the odd illegal cargo.

But Kazmer would never be party to murder.

Now that it was clear that the Bench specialists knew of Kazmer's visit, the best thing to do was make full disclosure and trust in truth. Hilton didn't like it, though.

"He was in port not long ago to move a cargo. I saw him, but we both had places to go. I guess he went out to the settlement. Aunt Walton doesn't approve of his suit for Modice's affections." Hilton refolded the scarf as he spoke, putting it away in the side pocket of his warehouseman's coveralls. "And with taste in scarves like this, I guess you can see why. Anything else?"

He was unhappy about the turn this talk had taken,

and it showed—he could hear it in his own voice. Vogel shook his head.

"No, that about covers everything for now. Thank you for your time, Shires. Factor Madlev will know where to find us if you need to reach us about anything."

Good.

He could go back to receiving reconciliation, with the single worst pattern in known Space radiating great waves of sheer unadulterated tastelessness from his pocket. He probably glowed in the dark with it. He hoped it wouldn't alter his genetic structure; he would probably be lucky if it merely scarred him for life.

He wished more than ever that he hadn't seen Kazmer in the street that day, but now it was more for Kazmer's sake than that of his self-pride.

He knew Kazmer wasn't a killer.

But he didn't trust the Bench to display equivalent perceptiveness; and not even Aunt Walton could wish the Bench on Kazmer Daigule, whether or not she thought he had any business courting Hilton's cousin Modice.

Walking in companionable silence out of the warehouse, Garol waited for Jils to make the first move. She had something on her mind; so much had been obvious by virtue of her presence at his interview with Factor Madlev. And he was interested in whatever it had been that caught her attention in his talk with Shires.

He found the speed machine where he had left it, parked outside of the warehouse's administrative offices. Jils stopped short of the machine while Garol straddled it with a certain degree of self-conscious bravado. He only had one safety helmet; but Jils liked to live dangerously.

At least any woman who voluntarily surrendered her body to the ministrations of bone-benders—dubious professionals at best, outright charlatans at worst—had nothing to say to anybody about merely riding a speed machine without a helmet. That would be his line, anyway.

"Hey, pretty lady, wanna ride? For you, no charge."

But she knew him too well to rise to the bait. She pulled a tab on one of the panniers behind the pillion seat, and there was a safety helmet. Damn. Perfectly good tease, shot to hell.

Fastening the helmet strap beneath her chin, Jils mounted the pillion seat behind him, passing him a piece of documentation as she settled herself. "Drive, you smooth-talking seducer of innocent young women," Jils suggested—in part because of the line he'd started to run, yes, but it would serve just as well to cover them from casual observation. "We have much to do, and time flies like youth itself."

What, had she been reading the Poetic Classics again?

The documentation was a receiving report from the Port Authority at Anglace, where the bulk cargo from the Tyrell raid had apparently turned up. Part of it, at least. There'd been an anonymous tip. Those were always interesting—anonymous tips almost never had anything to do with concern for law and order, and everything to do with personal malice of one sort or another.

But that wasn't the really interesting part.

The pilot of the impounded freighter was a Combine national named Kazmer Daigule.

Garol passed the documentation back to Jils and started his motor. "Say," he suggested, calling back to her over the sound of the speed machine's engine. "There isn't really a whole lot to do in Port Charid. Let's go find some action, shall we?"

Port Anglace.

Public opinion blamed the Langsariks for recent predation at Okidan, Tyrell, and several earlier targets.

Hilton Shires had been a lieutenant in the Langsarik fleet, and it couldn't be very easy for him—or any of his fellows—to adjust to their reduced expectations and meekly take direction from people who had been prey.

Kazmer Daigule had been in Port Charid recently, and was personally acquainted with both Hilton Shires and the lovely young Modice Agenis.

Walton Agenis said there was no Langsarik involvement that she knew of, but Modice had let Garol know that there was a connection between Daigule and Shires, so either the women were genuinely unaware of any deeper implications of Daigule's visit—or they were giving Garol the keys he'd need—or they just didn't know, but felt that Shires and Garol should be equally warned.

It was enough to make a person think very hard about starting a melon patch and abandoning the whole Bench intelligence specialist thing for a quiet life of preserves, jams, jellies. Compost. Maybe a pond, with salamanders.

"Talked me into it," Jils responded, only Jils used the communications link built in to the safety helmet, rather than trying to make herself heard over the noise of the engine. The sound of her voice reminded Garol that he was the one who was supposed to be driving, instead of just sitting there brooding.

Garol nodded.

Slipping the neutral on the speed machine, Garol pulled away from the parking apron, heading back to the docks, where their courier was waiting.

This news from Anglace gave him the perfect excuse to depart Port Charid immediately and leave Hilton Shires alone with his thoughts.

If Shires was guilty, he had all the time he needed to make a run for it. Somewhere. Anywhere. Gone-beyond space, maybe, across the Sillume vector.

If Shires was innocent, he'd stay right where he was, oblivious to implications or standing on his integrity as a matter of principle, maintaining his honor in the face of adverse situational elements.

And if Shires were guilty, but didn't run, using his behavior to signal his innocence, intent on playing the game at its highest level—then Hilton Shires was Walton Agenis's own blood kin.

No help there.

Maybe they'd know more once they could talk with the Sarvaw pilot Kazmer Daigule, in Anglace.

Chapter Five

Three days of waiting after his interview with the Inquisitor had driven Kazmer almost to the point of distraction, torn between his relief in having found a way to protect Hilton, his sense of loss, and his shuddering horror of what he had done.

The Malcontent.

To elect the Malcontent meant to become one of them.

That meant doing anything they wanted him to do; and there were stories about what Malcontents were like behind the impenetrable walls of their safe houses.

He knew what his motives had been, but any casual acquaintance could only assume the most obvious explanation: that Kazmer had failed to reconcile his sexuality with the ordinance of the Holy Mother and the expectations of decency and morally upright behavior; that he had been forced to elect the Malcontent at last or face ostracism even more profound and absolute than simple criminality could ever have meant for him.

They'd think he wanted boys.

Modice would think that, if she ever heard. Maybe she wouldn't even hear. Maybe as far as Modice was concerned he would simply disappear and never be heard of or from again, ever. Aunt Agenis and Hilton himself would surely keep the truth of his fate to themselves, if they ever found out.

Boys.

It was almost more than Kazmer could bear, even

knowing as he did what the Bench would do to Hilton—and Modice, and the rest of the Langsariks—if Kazmer had been referred to interrogation and implicated them all by virtue of simply knowing their names.

He'd visited Modice in Port Charid.

The Bench would be sure to see conspiracy there.

But boys?

To be a Malcontent could mean becoming the chartered agent of reconciliation for other Malcontents, people whose pain had forced them to take such drastic measures because they did like boys, or men; because their desire was not for the ocean within the sacred cradle of a woman's womb but for the succulent and inviting waters of an atoll, or even the narrow constrained channel of a dry wash.

Three days.

After three days, two guards came to the door of the holding cell to which the Inquisitor had returned Kazmer, calling him out to go back to the room in which he had had his fateful interview. There was someone waiting for him there, now as before.

For one confused moment Kazmer thought that the Inquisitor had come back—but why in plain clothes?

No, Koscuisko had pale eyes, and this man had not. The man who sat waiting for Kazmer was about Koscuisko's height, perhaps, and there were similarities in the face and in the expression. But this man had dark eyes, and hair that shaded several degrees further toward the tan side than Koscuisko's had done; and, most tellingly of all, this man was wearing a necklace made of bright red ribbon that showed clearly beneath his collar before disappearing beneath his shirt.

This man was Malcontent.

One of the slaves of the Saint, set apart by the halter he wore around his neck, collared with a necklace that marked him as a slave without any legal identity of his own.

Kazmer had sought that bondage of his own free

will, because questions that one wished to ask of the Malcontent had to be addressed to the legal person of the Malcontent rather than to any mere slave; and the legal person of the Malcontent had been dead for octave upon octave—ever since the Malcontent's revolt against the autocrat's court, for excess tax impositions—rendering the entire issue a little problematic.

There was a legal entity to serve as the proxy of the Saint, of course—empowered to enter into contracts and to transact business on the Saint's behalf—but any particular question or demand could lawfully be referred to Saint Andrej Malcontent himself for a decision.

Some of the questions thus put before the Malcontent had been waiting for three or four lifetimes for a response, without notable success.

The Malcontent might or might not be actually and truly and traditionally dead, being a Saint. But it was certain that the Malcontent wasn't talking, at least not to answer claims that the Saint felt to be impertinent.

Kazmer sat down, not because he meant to presume the privilege without being asked, but because with every added notice of the reality of his election, the enormity of what he had done weighed more heavily upon him, so that he could not find the strength to stand.

"How fragrant are the little blue-and-yellow flowers that line the pathway to the kitchen-midden," the Malcontent said, his voice as deep as damnation for all the note of humor it might have contained.

He meant that Kazmer stank.

It had been more than a week, now, with no change of clothing or any chance to bathe—

The folkish homeliness of the old adage was too much for Kazmer. Sorrow and fear and grief overwhelmed him, and he was too deep in pain even to care any longer when he began to cry.

Too much.

It was all too much.

The Malcontent let the storm pass without comment, waiting in compassionate silence for the moments it took for Kazmer to bring his emotions to heel once more.

Then the Malcontent pulled a whitesquare out of a pocket somewhere and passed it to Kazmer across the table. "Here. Wipe your face. The Bench expects you to suffer, Daigule, but you don't have anything to prove to me."

They were alone in the room. The Malcontent must have sent the guards away. Kazmer blew his nose, blotting his eyes with the residual clean portion of the whitesquare. His face was dirty; the whitesquare came away soiled. It was an offense against human dignity to deny a man the chance to wash. Kazmer supposed he was lucky enough that they'd fed him.

"Sorry." He handed the dirty whitesquare back, and the Malcontent accepted it without comment. Or recoiling, which was charity on his part. "This has all been a challenge. Maybe more than I'm really up to."

Yes, the Bench expected him to suffer. That was the only reason a Combine national was allowed to call for the Malcontent—to escape from the Judicial process—in the first place: because the Malcontent had successfully convinced the Bench that the life of a Malcontent was a comparable experience to whatever sanctions the Bench was likely to impose.

There were exceptions, of course; for certain classes of crimes—those against the Judicial order—not even the Malcontent could stay the hand of the Bench. That was what had happened to the Sarvaw bond-involuntary that Kazmer had seen with the Inquisitor, he supposed.

Kazmer was luckier.

The most his potential crime would have amounted to was an offense against private property and the lives of citizens under Jurisdiction, not a crime against the Judicial order itself.

There were so many gray areas, even so.

Kazmer knew he should count himself fortunate that the Inquisitor had not challenged the issue: Or if the Inquisitor had, it had been after Kazmer had made the call, and if the Inquisitor had objected, the Inquisitor had obviously lost. Or the Malcontent would not be here.

"Well." The Malcontent leaned back in his chair, hooking one arm over the chair back and crossing his legs. "You called for the Malcontent, and I'm here. But before I lead you out of this place we need to talk. My name is Stanoczk, feel free to call me 'Cousin.'"

The Malcontent used a Dolgorukij word for the title that gave Kazmer a profound appreciation for the shakiness of the ground on which he stood. Religious professionals were all "Cousin," but Malcontents were usually addressed as the kind of cousin that was the barely legitimate offspring of the unfilial daughter of a younger son of a collateral branch of the family who had made an inappropriate liaison with a social inferior—possibly Sarvaw.

The "Cousin" that the Malcontent offered to permit Kazmer to call him was the older son of the older son of the direct lineage of a family to which one belonged only as the younger son of a younger son of a cadet line. There was no hope of truly expressing the nuances of such a thing in Standard; but Kazmer and the Malcontent would know.

"Thank you, Cousin Stanoczk." Kazmer used the Dolgorukij word back with humility in his voice and a determined submissiveness in his heart. "What do you need from me?"

Cousin Stanoczk nodded. "When a soul born of the Holy Mother's creation calls the name of my Patron, may he wander in bliss forever, they must do so in full knowledge of the price to be paid. And my Patron, he also must know what is required of him in exchange for what he will exact from you."

The first part was easy. Kazmer knew the answer to the first part. " 'Who calls the name of the Malcontent becomes no-soul with no name, no family, no feeling but the will of the Saint.' Yes, Cousin Stanoczk. I understand what duty I owe."

Straightening up in his chair, Cousin Stanoczk leaned forward over the table, so close that Kazmer could smell his breath. Stanoczk smoked lefrols. What was going on? "Then kiss me," Stanoczk said. "Convincingly, if you please. Demonstrate to me the depth of your commitment to the irreversible step that you propose to take."

Oh, Holy Mother.

Kazmer's stomach pitched at the very thought.

But he had said it. He needed the protection that he could only get from the Malcontent, protection not for himself, but for Hilton and Modice. For the Langsariks.

He reached forward slowly to put a hand to the side of Cousin Stanoczk's neck, sliding his fingers caressingly around to bend Stanoczk's head toward him. Maybe if he pretended. Maybe if he thought about Modice. But Stanoczk was not Modice, and could never be Modice; Stanoczk smelled of lefrols and musk, the scent of a man's sweat and a man's skin. Kazmer tilted his head to Cousin Stanoczk's mouth, shuddering in his heart, trembling like a man gripped deep in terror.

At the last possible moment Cousin Stanoczk spoke. "Well, that'll do. For now." Kazmer opened his eyes, astonished, and found the Malcontent looking at him with a wry and moderately amused expression. "There is no need for you to turn your stomach inside out, it is a bad precedent for a first meeting."

Kazmer sat back down.

Had he passed the test?

Or failed it?

"I can do this thing, Cousin Stanoczk." He could take no chances with ambiguous signals. "I can do what I'm told. I will. No price is too great to pay for what only the Saint can grant me."

Cousin Stanoczk had settled back sidewise in his chair, and quirked his dark eyebrows at Kazmer skeptically. "It remains to be seen. The spirit is willing, but the flesh rebels, and to elect the Malcontent is to surrender body and soul. Yet there will be time to negotiate on some issues later."

It made no sense for the Malcontent to demand performance of a duty too strongly repugnant to him to be borne with a willing heart. The Malcontent was all about freedom from pain, even if it came at a high cost. Kazmer sat in his place, confused, feeling a little as though he was in shock.

"We move on. What is it that you of my Patron require?" Cousin Stanoczk asked. Did that mean that his failure to approach Stanoczk like a lover on demand was to be excused him, overlooked?

And exactly how was he to explain?

"Protect me from the Bench, Cousin Stanoczk. The Bench wants to ask me questions that I can't afford to answer. And I know I won't have any choice except to answer; I've heard the stories. Stand between me and the Inquisitor, and let me keep my answers to myself."

How much could he say without giving up the information he sought to protect?

If he told Stanoczk that he didn't want to give evidence, Stanoczk might guess that there was someone to be protected. From there it was a very short span to the obvious implication that the people Kazmer had to protect were Langsariks, so that electing the Malcontent was just another way of implicating Hilton, indirectly.

Implication was not evidence actionable under law. Kazmer waited.

Langsarik predation was not an issue that could possibly interest the Malcontent—not unless and until Combine shipping became involved. By the time that happened Kazmer would not be in a position to implicate anybody, so maybe the Malcontent wouldn't care.

"That which the Malcontent directs, you must unfailingly perform," Stanoczk warned. "It may be that the information you wish to protect comes out through avenues other than a Bench claim against you. it may be that the mission upon which you will be sent will have as result exactly what you wish to avoid, revelation of information pertinent to whatever issue by another. Your duty to the Malcontent could require that you comply with your instructions, in such a case."

This helped. This clarified things. This gave Kazmer his mission, his pledge, the prize he was willing to trade his hope and future for. "Let me not incriminate people who may be guiltless by my testimony, Cousin Stanoczk, because testimony can be interpreted so wrongly. If there are guilty, let me find them. Only— if a friend of mine is to face the Bench on Charges, let it be on evidence independent of any confidences between us."

Not as if there had been any.

Hilton had been very annoying about that, as Kazmer remembered.

Cousin Stanoczk stood up.

"Here's what we'll do, then."

Did that mean Kazmer had won? Or lost? Because to win was to lose, but to lose—would be to lose more than Kazmer could bear to contemplate . . .

"You are no longer Kazmer Daigule, and therefore you no longer have any information potentially of interest to the Bench. And yet the problem of the Langsariks may not be ignored, and if our holy patron deprives the Bench of information, it may be that we owe the Bench a decent story in return."

Kazmer hadn't said anything about Langsariks.

But Cousin Stanoczk had probably been fully briefed, as his next words proved.

"So we will go to Port Charid, where the Holy Mother cherishes many mercantile interests which are deserving of our Patron's protection accordingly. You will pledge your faith as one of the Saint's children to do your utmost to find who has been responsible for the raid on Tyrell Yards; and if the trail leads back to people you love—we will negotiate."

Kazmer thought about this.

The first and critically important thing was to ensure that Hilton Shires would not be named in evidence, that the Langsariks not face sanctions from the Bench for breach of amnesty on account of any testimony from Kazmer Daigule.

But the larger problem would not be solved thereby. Someone had raided Tyrell. Kazmer needed to know if the stories of torture and murder he'd heard were true. One way or the other the Langsariks had to be warned of the danger they were in.

If it had been Hilton Shires behind that raid, and people had been killed, then shielding Hilton further would no longer be the act of a friend, but that of an accomplice.

Slowly, Kazmer nodded his head. "Just give me the chance, Cousin Stanoczk, and I will find out what is at the bottom of all this. I know I can, if I have time, and the Saint's blessing on the enterprise."

It felt awkward using such language. "The Saint's blessing," indeed.

"Right. Put this on, then," Stanoczk said, tossing a small packet to him. Kazmer caught it by pure reflex, startled. A packet of ribbon: red ribbon, a band of ribbed silk ribbon as broad as the tip of his index finger was wide, and with a slip-noose in it. The halter of the Malcontent, the symbol of his self-elected slavery. "Only be sure of what you do, Daigule, because once I have led you on tether out from this place and into the street, there is no going back for you. Do you wish to take a moment to consider?"

Kazmer slipped the noose over his head and pulled it snug around his throat. "Get me out of here, Cousin Stanoczk," he said, holding the tag end of the ribbon-halter out in the open palm of his left hand. The hand for giving things away. "I will requite the Saint faithfully, in wholehearted fulfillment of my duty."

Cousin Stanoczk stood silent for a moment, as if making a final evaluation of Kazmer's sincerity.

Then he took the ribbon end from Kazmer's waiting hand. "Right. Let's go, then." Raising his voice, Stanoczk called out for the guards. "Security. Open the door, we're leaving."

The door to the interview room opened, and an orderly came in with a packet of documentation that she opened across the table.

Stanoczk pulled the ident-code that hung at the end of his own halter out from underneath his blouse and set his mark to the paperwork.

Kazmer felt his hope diminish with every emphatic strike of seal to document.

This was real.

It was official.

Stanoczk kept his hand low to obscure his grasp of the ribbon end, and Kazmer kept close behind to keep the halter slack so that it would draw as little attention to itself as possible; but he was being led out of the building at the end of the leash of the Malcontent, and once they reached the street—once he stepped clear of the Port Authority—it would be final.

Well, he had gotten what he'd needed.

The conflict between what he'd wanted out of his life, and what he had to accept as his life going forward, was no longer other than an empty issue for idle hypothetical debate.

Scowling, Garol tossed a data cube into the jumble of cubes on the table that formed the focus of the courier's small common room. "Okay. That's it for the interrogatories we have." They were good interrogatories, too, well developed, thorough, reasoned, and carrying the unmistakable stamp of a judicious mind. "But where is Kazmer Daigule in all this?"

Jils reached forward and tipped the data cube flat

to the table's surface, marshaling the several records into a tidy array. "Well, he's the pilot," Jils said, but she didn't mean it. They both knew perfectly well that Daigule had been the pilot of the impounded freighter that Anglace had intercepted before the crew had had a chance to dump its incriminating cargo. She was just being provoking.

Garol suppressed a sigh. It wore on a man to be in transit, even when he could get information on transmit. The courier's address systems were robust, they could receive even priority transmission; but all they had seen during the past two days' time spent in vector transit were the files on other crew. All the other crew. Everybody who had been associated with that freighter, except Daigule.

"What in particular do you want from Daigule, anyway?" Jils asked, apparently by way of a conciliatory gesture. "These are all consistent. What can Daigule tell us that these people couldn't?"

Of course their stories were internally consistent. They'd had days in vector transit to themselves, time enough to practice a cover story. The freighter's crew had not apparently done so, however; the inquiring officer was on record with his assessment of that, and Koscuisko knew his stuff. So much was obvious from the interrogatories he was producing.

But if the crew of Daigule's freighter had not coordinated a cover story amongst themselves, they were either stupid, arrogant, or truly unaware of the critical importance of a good explanation for their role in the murders at the Tyrell Yards. As though they had all been genuinely unaware of any such murders.

The inquiring officer was on record about that, too.

Koscuisko had logged a formal and judicial opinion that the crew members of the freighter that he had interrogated had been unaware of the carnage at Tyrell. That they were therefore liable to civil penalties for conspiracy to misappropriate private property, and for receiving stolen property with intent to intercept any proceeds for gain, but not liable for criminal penalties, as persons knowingly and willfully engaged in robbery by use of lethal force with intent to commit collateral murder—to the detriment of the rule of Law and the Judicial order.

"Daigule knows Shires. Shires is Flag Captain Agenis's nephew, and former Lieutenant. Daigule knows things about Langsariks that other people probably don't."

The interrogatories had established the pattern of recruitment, anonymous transmission of direction, care taken at every step to maintain a safe separation between the crew and the people who had chartered it. Maybe the crew should have guessed that such prudent people would not risk leaving any living witnesses.

But if whatever steps the raiders had taken to disguise themselves were good enough to protect them from incriminating testimony on the part of the crew, why had the raiders felt it necessary to murder those people at Tyrell?

"Well, it's got to be coming." Jils keyed the receiver on the table console, checking for any new information. "We have everybody but. Queue's still empty. Saving the best for last, maybe."

Maybe the interrogating officer had simply saved Daigule for the last of the series, waiting until a full picture of the pilot's exact role developed through the testimony of the other crew. Except that none of the other crew apparently believed that Daigule really knew any more about specific individuals than anybody else, even while reporting Daigule's apparent conviction that they'd been hired by Langsariks. There was no reason for the interrogating officer to have known beforehand that Daigule was to be the key to the affair.

Koscuisko's intuition was apparently well developed, but he wasn't psychic, at least not from any evidence in the interrogatories Garol had reviewed.

Garol wanted Daigule's interrogatory.

He wanted it now.

He was going to have to talk to Chilleau Judiciary when he got to Anglace. He wanted a head start on analyzing what Daigule had to say.

"Go ahead, why don't you. Check." She was on line with the courier's link; she could just have a look. "At least find out how much longer we're going to have to wait. We're still a day out from Anglace. I've done all the word puzzles I can stand."

Jils frowned.

It wasn't an encouraging expression.

"There's nothing in the process queue at Anglace, Garol," Jils said. But she'd just said that. Hadn't she?

Garol waited. Jils addressed the courier's interface, and there was silence in the small cabin broken only by the shifting of a half-empty cup of bean tea atop a stack of pullsheets. Garol caught it before it had a chance to tip. Jils was concentrating.

"Nothing in the queue. Nothing in holding." Leaning back in her chair, Jils ran one small square hand up across her flat forehead and through the thick black strands of her hair fringe. "He's not in the system, Garol; Anglace isn't holding any Kazmer Daigule. But he was there."

Garol had seen the receiving report she'd brought to Factor Madlev's office two days ago now. He knew Daigule had been there. "Incomplete inquiry?" Garol suggested, but even as he spoke he doubted the possibility that Daigule had died under interrogation. These interrogations weren't any more than drug-assist, not at this point; the Bench wanted information, not merely confession to a crime. They hadn't determined exactly what crime it was to be, yet. And Koscuisko didn't lose people in mid-inquiry, not from what Garol had seen of his work at Rudistal.

"There isn't even any session initiate on record. Nothing. Am I going out of my mind, or what?"

Garol had an idea, and it was an unpleasant one. "What," he agreed. "It would be too frustrating. Jils.

Daigule's the only one who might really be able to implicate the Langsariks, at least specifically enough to stand scrutiny on the Bench. And Kazmer sounds Dolgorukij to me, what do you think?"

She stared, but she caught on almost immediately, and her reaction was disgusted. "Damn. That's not fair. Are you sure? This is contrary to the maintenance of the common weal, we can protest."

Garol knew how she felt.

But there could be only one reason Garol could think of that would explain how a man who had been taken into custody could be suddenly no longer in custody, with no notation in the record about death or escape to cover the discrepancy.

Kazmer had got out somehow.

Dolgorukij could claim religious exception and go off to join the Dolgorukij church's secret service, penitents—or operatives—who identified themselves with an obscure parochial saint who had been dissatisfied with his life. No. Not dissatisfied.

Malcontent.

They couldn't afford to let Daigule escape so easily. Murder had been done at the Tyrell Yards, murder and torture. Langsariks were suspected. Daigule might be able to tell them, if not who had been the planning committee behind the raid, then perhaps at least for certain who had not.

Daigule's friend Hilton Shires, for instance.

"See if you can raise the local Combine consulate." There was nothing they could do until they reached Anglace, no physical action they could take. It was maddening, but there was no help for it. "Try to get an appointment. See if they'll admit to having a Malcontent on the premises."

Maybe it was just as well. They had a day to think about this, to decide what to do. How to approach the problem. What to say to gain cooperation from a government agency exempt by formal pact from many of the checks and balances otherwise imposed on organizations representing civil governments. How to get through to the Malcontent.

This unexpected setback only strengthened Garol's growing conviction—irrational though it was—that somehow Kazmer Daigule held a crucial piece of information that would lead him to the truth about what was going on at Port Charid.

He would get access to Kazmer Daigule, no matter what he had to do to get it.

Fisner Feraltz stood with his floor manager in the basket of a construction crane, surveying progress on the new warehouse complex west of Port Charid.

There were Langsarik work crews busy across the entire span of the foundation clearing, from the dormitory buildings—still under construction, and meant to house the workers themselves now, the warehouse staff later—out to the old launch site that was being upgraded, hardened to withstand more frequent freighter-tender traffic than the six or seven a week that the port's main facility could handle.

A warehouse to store their loot, a dormitory to concentrate them, plenty of overlooked corners in which to hide illicit equipment, freighter tenders to be borrowed for illegal use—it was a brilliant trap.

He only hoped he would see it fully baited, before it was sprung.

"Another raid, eldest and firstborn?" There was a note of reluctant uncertainty in Dalmoss's voice. Dalmoss was frowning at the sun on the western horizon as it set. "It seems so soon. With humility I offer the words, eldest and firstborn—it seems precipitous."

It was unusual for Dalmoss to question direction from his superior at all. Fisner expected better of him. "We have been unfortunate in our intelligence, next born. There was no warning about the Bench intelligence specialist, and he was the one who won the settlement from the Bench for the Langsariks. It will take more to move him, if in fact he can be moved."

The evening breeze blew past the crane's basket, eights and eights above the ground. Dalmoss tightened his hold on the guardrail with a convulsive movement; Fisner noted that the knuckles of Dalmoss's hand had whitened, where Dalmoss gripped the rail. Maybe Dalmoss wasn't questioning his orders, Fisner realized. Maybe Dalmoss was simply afraid of heights.

It would be kindest not to notice, if it was nerves. If it was defiance, there would be time enough to raise the issue as a formal criticism once the Angel's work at Charid had been completed. One way or the other there was no profit to be gained from creating a confrontation now.

"So you force his hand, eldest and firstborn. As suits the agent of our divine Patron."

It would be almost vainglorious, foolhardy to mount a raid with Bench intelligence specialists actually at Port Charid. The Bench expected to receive its due respect, even if it was only to keep up appearances.

That Chilleau Judiciary would control public access to the news of raids and atrocities at Port Charid had been an accepted fact of the Angel's plan from its inception, but the personal involvement of one of the Bench's agents-outside-of-Bench-administration had the effect of flattening public outcry further than originally anticipated.

Bench resources at that level were more valuable than battlewagons and carried more of the Bench's prestige with them—there were three times as many cruiserkiller warships in Fleet than there were Bench intelligence specialists under Jurisdiction. So long as there were Bench intelligence specialists involved, no planetary government or mercantile interest could seriously accuse the Bench of failing to treat the problems at Port Charid with the appropriate degree of gravity.

Something needed to be done to increase the pressure on Chilleau Judiciary, so that the temper of the Second Judge could be reliably manipulated when the evidence that the Angel planned to reveal became public knowledge—or at least knowledge revealed to the Bench and related mercantile interests, which was as public as the disgraceful treachery of the Langsariks was likely ever to become.

"You have me precisely, second eldest and next born. What target would you guess I mean to take?" Fisner asked the question in a friendly tone. He had nearly decided that he was being oversensitive, in wondering if Dalmoss cherished defiance or resentment in his heart.

His own sense of cringing inadequacy could as easily be to blame. Just because he wondered if Dalmoss ever questioned the orders that had made Fisner his superior didn't mean that Dalmoss ever had any such thoughts. Fisner had come to the Angel later in life, in his twenties. Dalmoss had been the Angel's soldier in faith for longer than that.

Dalmoss didn't answer immediately; it was both polite and prudent of him to pretend that he'd had no thoughts of second-guessing his superior. Or maybe he was just thinking. "I would very much like to take Finiury, we know that there are armaments there. But the body count wouldn't make much of a splash. And the Bench couldn't afford publicity; we wouldn't get any noise out of it at all."

The Angel knew something about Finiury that wasn't in the public sphere: Finiury was managing illegal arms shipments for parties to civil unrest in Perk sector. Any publicity about a raid on the Finiury stores would have to gloss over the illegal armaments being stored there.

Nor could Maperna system—Finiury's sponsor—put much real pressure on Chilleau Judiciary for justice and revenge, once Finiury's illegal arms trade was uncovered: So all in all Finiury was as safe as though it had been truly warehousing no more than industrial ceramics in quarantine. Dalmoss's reasoning was sound.

Fisner waited.

The sun was going down. They would have to return the crane's basket to ground level soon, and they would not be able to talk as openly on the surface. It was getting cold as well. The medical bracing Fisner continued to wear took the chill with annoying keenness.

"I can't pretend to have the same insight as you, eldest and firstborn." Meaning, Fisner supposed, to excuse his analysis if it turned out to conflict with Fisner's own. "But on the face of it. I would take Honan-gung. Some of its traffic is in cultural artifacts, which are therefore irreplaceable. And the casualty list will carry adequate weight."

The Combine Yards in the Shawl were out of the question, of course—at least for the immediate future. But Fisner had not thought seriously about Honan-gung. Baltovane had a much more tempting inventory.

Still, Baltovane's parent government would not make the noise that the planetary government of Yeshiwan system could be relied upon to make at the loss not only of innocent lives—that should be avenged by the Bench that had failed to protect them—but also of cultural artifacts. Historically priceless examples of Yeshivi art. Irreplaceable icons of the spirit of the Yeshivi people, destroyed with impunity by vandals the Bench itself had put in place and provided with opportunity.

Honan-gung was a much better choice, and there was an inside man there, as well as at Baltovane. Dalmoss need never know that he'd changed Fisner's mind.

"I could hardly have said it better."

Fisner set the crane in motion to lower the basket. The floodlights were blooming to life on the field below; soon the second shift would come on. They were still months from bringing the new facility completely on-line; but it could be ready well before then.

It only had to be far enough along to shelter the cargo pallets he had reserved for his purpose, and absorb three full shifts of Langsariks on-site. Once it was that far along it would be ready. They were already moving freighter tenders from its improved airfield.

Once they had reached that point, he would destroy the Langsariks.

Garol Vogel locked off the courier's communications systems and opened the maintenance codes to the Port Authority's computers. There were probably messages waiting for him, but he wasn't interested in any of them.

"Jils, come on. Let's go. There's things we need to do." He was in a hurry to leave the courier clear for maintenance and refueling, because he was heartily tired of it. It had been a long day span between finding out about Daigule and arriving at Anglace. Now he wanted to know whether it had done him any good to bother to come at all.

"No hurry." Jils was forward, doing some final something or another before she was ready to leave. "You're a Bench intelligence specialist, business will come to you. We have a visitor. Are you expecting anyone?"

What was she talking about? He didn't want to go forward to see. He was sick of going forward. He'd been doing nothing but going forward, then going back, then going forward again, for hours.

He went forward.

Jils had the docking bay on the forward screens. There was someone out on the loading apron under the bright lights of the Port Authority's docks, someone in civilian dress who stood there with his hands clasped behind his back looking at the courier with what seemed to be genial curiosity. At least that was what it looked like from a distance.

Garol could guess who that was.

"Shut it down and let's go," he insisted, killing the display with an impatient gesture. "I'm telling you, the air in this courier is all used up. I've got to get out of here."

Jils had one of her tolerant faces on. She let his ill-tempered ranting wash over her without generating a similar impatience in her. He didn't know how she could be so calm.

Yes he did.

She didn't care.

The Langsarik settlement had been one successful negotiation among many, to Jils. If the Langsariks fell foul of the Bench after all the work they'd done to make a positive solution of howsoever imperfect a sort, she would feel regret, but mostly for the waste of time and energy.

It wasn't Jils that Walton Agenis had trusted to come to a fair agreement with the Bench.

"Coming, Garol. What are you waiting for? Let's go."

The man on the docks hadn't moved between the time Jils had pointed him out and the time Garol finally got her clear of the courier; he was still standing there, watching. He had to know they'd seen him, wasn't that the whole point of standing there out in the middle of a busy loading apron doing nothing? Garol considered walking right past the man, just to be difficult. It would just put the progress of his investigation back if he did, though, so Garol made straight for the man, stopping when he was within speaking range.

Brown-eyed and blond, or maybe not quite blond; solid as a battering ram, and reminded Garol vaguely of Andrej Koscuisko. So he was Dolgorukij. It meant nothing. There were plenty of Dolgorukij.

From time to time Garol had found himself wondering whether there weren't perhaps possibly just one or two or several hundred thousand too many.

The man inclined his head politely.

"Cousin Stanoczk," he said in a voice as deep as an engine's subharmonics. Garol already knew that *he* wasn't anybody's Cousin Stanoczk and would have been surprised if Jils turned out to be somebody's Cousin Stanoczk. So he said nothing, and waited.

Cousin Stanoczk didn't seem to notice. "You have queried the Combine's administrative offices here at Anglace, looking for me—or for someone for whom I am responsible. I thought I would save you an unnecessary trip by meeting you, because I am certain there is not much to hold you in Anglace. You will wish to return to Port Charid immediately."

People generally didn't make assumptions about what Bench intelligence specialists did or didn't want, were or weren't going to do; or when they did they were usually wrong. Garol considered his options: *What makes you say that; who asked you; do you know something I don't know; who died and made you First Secretary?*

"I'm looking for Kazmer Daigule."

All of the other things that he could say would provide some emotional satisfaction, perhaps, but were unlikely to yield any real information. He could always fantasize about being gratuitously, flamboyantly, insanely rude at some other time. Personal feeling had no place where Bench business was concerned. "Am I correct in concluding that religious exception is to blame for the loss of his testimony?"

"Religious exception" was the formal legal term for it, when the Bench released a person of interest or an accused to the tender mercies of the Dolgorukij church. The interplay of concession and adjustment the Bench's relationships with all of its subject systems required in the interest of peace and good order created significant injustices, from time to time.

There was no telling whether Daigule's escape from questioning and prosecution was one such injustice. There would be no telling for Daigule at all, without the cooperation of the Malcontent.

Cousin Stanoczk nodded once more. "Religious exception is certainly the cause of his departure from incarceration at the Port Authority. It need not go so far as loss of testimony, Bench specialists. Excuse me, but which of you is Vogel and which Ivers? If I may ask."

Maybe Cousin Stanoczk didn't know, and maybe he was just being polite. "I'm Vogel." And Garol was frustrated. "What exactly do you want, Cousin Stanoczk. There are five thousand people at Port Charid whose lives may depend on my access to Kazmer Daigule. I need to talk to him."

"I want to take him back to the Tyrell Yards." Cousin Stanoczk's answer was straightforward, if confusing. "I don't care about five thousand Langsarik outlanders, Specialist Vogel, but I do care about one beloved son of the Holy Mother shot and left for dead at Okidan, and another as yet unidentified at the Tyrell Yards. I mean to go there with Daigule. You can grant access to the site."

Twenty-seven people dead at Tyrell, and Cousin Stanoczk only cared whether one of them might be Dolgorukij. Garol let go of his feeling of reflexive disgust: That *was* Cousin Stanoczk's job, he supposed. Look out for Combine interests, and only Combine interests, and never mind who else might suffer unjust death by violence. There was no sense in getting emotional about it. The Malcontent was a Combine operation, not a Bench resource.

"I clear you to Tyrell, you give me access to Daigule. Is that it?" Because it sounded too simple.

Sure enough, the Dolgorukij shook his head.

"Daigule kneels beneath the shield of my holy Patron, Specialist Vogel, I have no power to grant you access to him. But it may be that there is something he can tell us, about Tyrell. What he can tell us that I can share, I will share willingly. I am looking for one of the Holy Mother's children, you are looking for evidence. Perhaps we can help each other out."

Garol thought about it.

The forensics team was probably just getting started

at Tyrell. The site had been secured, its atmosphere sealed to preserve evidence and inerted to avoid deterioration of the bodies prior to examination and autopsy. No identifications had been released, but any good intelligence agency would have been able to come up with the assignment list: So the Malcontent might have a valid interest in the site.

If Cousin Stanoczk wanted to take Daigule to Tyrell for whatever obscure purpose, it was possible that Daigule would say something under the stress of returning to the scene of his crime. Garol might be able to get somewhere with some incautiously blurted phrase or implication.

He had five thousand Langsariks to worry about, and no apparent chance of getting to talk to Daigule except through Cousin Stanoczk.

He was going to have to visit the Tyrell Yards sooner or later anyway. The only reason he'd not gone direct to Tyrell after checking in at Port Charid was that Jils had gotten news of the freighter impound here at Anglace. So now that Daigule was out of his official reach for purposes of formal interrogation, Tyrell was his next move anyway.

"I object in principle." In a perfect world he could violate religious exception if he had reasons of state for doing so. He was a Bench intelligence specialist. He had reasons of state by definition.

The Bench would not be well served by such an arbitrary action on his part, though, no matter how well justified Garol himself might feel it to be. A mere five thousand Langsarik lives—disposable, dispossessed, stateless, and criminal lives—were not as important as keeping the peace between the Dolgorukij Combine and the Bench.

There were potentially many more lives at stake than just five thousand if he violated the Combine's sense of entitlement. It had been luck and hard negotiating that had brought the Dolgorukij under Jurisdiction in the first place, one hundred and several years ago. The Combine was in a position to create major disruptions of the lawful conduct of trade to the detriment of the rule of Law if they were provoked to it.

So he would go along with Cousin Stanoczk's proposal and keep his hands off Kazmer Daigule.

He would also try every trick he could think of to work around Cousin Stanoczk and shake the truth out of the Malcontent's newest refugee, on the way from Anglace to Tyrell.

Garol inclined his head. "Still, you have me at a disadvantage. Very well, Cousin Stanoczk, I accept. Let's go to the Tyrell Yards. Let's go right now."

What questions Garol had to refer back to the other members of the freighter crew he could transmit en route.

What questions he could ask Kazmer Daigule—if he only once found a chance—he could consider as they returned to Rikavie.

"If you would care to accept the use of my courier. I have a suitable vehicle placed on alert status." Cousin Stanoczk neither paused to savor Garol's concession or even note it as such, sensitivity that Garol could appreciate. So the man was a diplomat. Well, the Malcontent had not become the secret service of the Dolgorukij church—and of the Autocrat herself, by extension—by mismanaging its relationships.

Still, Cousin Stanoczk's tact took much of the sting out of being on the wrong side of the balance of power for Garol as Stanoczk spoke on. "Secured transmission will be available, of course. So that you may report to the Bench, as you like. Or not."

If they turned around and went back to Rikavie on Cousin Stanoczk's offered transport, First Secretary Verlaine would not know where he was and could not query him for progress or status.

It was a tempting proposition.

He could always appropriate the vehicle on emergency loan if he had to. Knowing that was a portion of revenge in and of itself, but it was a real satisfaction for all its petty nature.

"Let's go."

He'd report back to Verlaine from Port Charid.

He wouldn't have anything real to report until he'd seen what had happened at Tyrell for himself anyway.

Chapter Six

Without prior knowledge of what to listen for from which precise direction, with all of space to monitor the odds of any single short data-pulse being intercepted or observed was slim to the point of functional impossibility. It was the great distance between worlds that made transmission secure, not codes and ciphers per se. The Bench made use of every tool science had to offer to keep its sensitive information to itself; the Angel of Destruction put its faith in the Holy Mother and the huge background noise of random signals, and had never been betrayed in its trust.

The message was minute and modest.

Vogel leaves on arrival for Tyrell, with Malcontent. Daigule wears red.

Fisner Feraltz stared at the pulse on his screen, his gut gripped in the acid-sharp talons of a familiar anguish.

It would go wrong. He was worthless. He had failed in everything he had ever put his hand to; he had not even been raised by decent people, but was tainted beyond redemption by his life among the Langsariks.

Vogel leaves on arrival for Tyrell, with Malcontent. Daigule wears red.

It was a disaster.

After all that he had done, and all that he had planned, and all he had arranged so carefully and cleverly, Daigule had failed him. Daigule had not done as he was expected, intended, meant to do, had not told the Bench everything he knew about the Langsarik raid on the Tyrell Yards. Who would have guessed that a Sarvaw, of all people, would do so base a thing?

To protect his friend.

They had gone too far when they had made sure that Daigule would see Shires in the mealroom that morning. It had been a mistake. It had been his mistake. He was responsible for this disaster. But who would have thought it, of a Sarvaw?

Fisner toggled his transmit. "Send to me Dalmoss, Ippolit, if you please."

The Malcontent.

The greatest enemy that the Angel had, the bastard pervert among the Saints under canopy, not even a saint at all except by popular acclaim—he had no theological claim to the honorific. So what if there were healings, miraculous events, apparently divine interventions? It was all fraud and lies, like everything else about the Malcontent.

Perhaps the Saint himself had been Sarvaw, all along. There was a thought. No decent Dolgorukij could ever have tolerated such perversions as the Malcontent had during his life, and he had been near heretic as well—at least there were stories to that effect.

Health and happiness greater goods than loyalty and piety.

To feed the hungry more blessed than to rule them, schooling them to submission; alleviating suffering more pleasing in the eyes of the Holy Mother than teaching devout acceptance of all the lessons suffering had to offer—even that it was not blasphemy to think of the Holy Mother as a father, as well as mother, and that the Child of the Canopy might have an equal divinity with his Parent.

"You sent for me, Foreman?"

Dalmoss was at the door to the small office Fisner used while he was here at the new construction site. Fisner beckoned for Dalmoss to come in and close the door. It was tiresome to sit behind a desk, in bracing; but the illusion of bodily infirmity had to be maintained to minimize any chance that someone who might happen to see him late at night would make the connection between a dimly glimpsed, but able-bodied stranger going amongst the crates, and the still-disabled foreman Fisner Feraltz.

"The Sarvaw freighter pilot returns to Rikavie, next born and second eldest. To Tyrell, and will almost certainly come back to Port Charid." It was the clear implication of the message. The Malcontent would go to Tyrell with the Bench intelligence specialist and had the Sarvaw with him; from there they would quite naturally return to Port Charid to make a report, think, discuss, strategize. Investigate. "We can't risk him realizing that he has seen you before. This was not planned."

He had no allowances for any such setback in any of his contingency plans.

He had been sure of the Sarvaw.

Dalmoss stood humbly waiting for direction, saying only, "What do you want me to do, firstborn and eldest?"

A test of his faith in Divine providence, perhaps, a gentle reminder that it was through the will of the Holy Mother—and through Her will alone—that the Angel triumphed over the enemies of the Church. A mark of loving admonition.

If only he could be secure in that.

"Go tell Hilton Shires that you have been called to the factory at Geraint for a few days. Tell him you have asked that he step up to supervise the work crews on construction in your absence. As a temporary duty, and in light of his previous experience, Langsarik supervising Langsariks."

Fisner spoke slowly, but gained confidence as he spoke. Yes. Something was coming together. "We'll think of something to plant the seed of Honan-gung in his mind. We'll let him think that he has stumbled on information. Let him warn the Bench specialist."

The Honan-gung raid had been intended to force the Bench's hand, to ensure that the momentum they were building up would not flag. Shires could help. He could warn Vogel about a raid, send Vogel into an ambush. If they took Vogel out, there would be no one for Chilleau Judiciary to send as a trouble-shooter, and no further question about Langsarik involvement. The Bench would have no choice but to send troops to arrest the Langsariks instead. No more hesitations, qualifications, cautious investigation.

It could work.

The Holy Mother was merciful. She had sent this to show him the way. He was not a failure. He was the Angel of Destruction in Port Charid. She had as much as reached out Her hand to shadow his forehead in benediction. Fisner's relief as he realized it was so immense that Dalmoss—looking at him with a quizzical if very small frown—would wonder about it, unless he distracted Dalmoss. Opening his heart to a subordinate was out of the question.

"Come up with a pretext, and speak to Shires. We will send Pettiche to Geraint in your place." He couldn't afford to let Dalmoss actually leave; Dalmoss was his raid leader. Dalmoss had to remain on-site, if hidden; and they needed to get Pettiche out of the way, as well. Though there was only a relatively small, if real, danger of the Sarvaw recognizing Dalmoss if he saw him, there was a much greater danger that the Sarvaw would realize that he had seen Pettiche before, at Tyrell. "You will have to stay out of sight, after that. It will be tedious. But it should not be for long."

Brilliant.

Dalmoss was right to salute him with undisguised admiration. "It shall be done, firstborn and eldest. I'll send you my formal request for Shires's temporary promotion within the day."

His mind had never worked so well, so quickly.

Surely the hand of the Holy Mother Herself was

guiding him, to the complete fulfillment of Her purpose.

Kazmer Daigule stood at the side of Cousin Stanoczk in mute misery, his eyes fixed to the ground. The main docking bay at Tyrell Yards was splashed and stained with blood; he should have realized that it would still stink.

It had been nearly two weeks.

But the site had been secured and its atmosphere inerted, so that the bodies would be as fresh—their evidence as bald and horrible—when the autopsy specialists arrived as when they had been discovered, and they had been discovered a scant twelve hours after the killing had begun. Kazmer knew that, though he had not been told—the forensics people would fix the time well enough for Bench purposes.

Still, Kazmer knew. Twelve hours.

Three hours from Port Charid to the Shawl of Rikavie, traveling slowly in a freighter meant to present the appearance of being already almost fully loaded. Three hours on station. These people had all been alive when he had left, the alarm had been planned for ten hours after that, so the rescue party had arrived within two hours of the alarm and secured the site. He knew. Fourteen hours, at the absolute maximum.

"Complete jumble," one of the forensics people was saying to Cousin Stanoczk. "Here, have a look. At least five individuals, though we haven't really bothered with the detail, at least not yet. One percussion grenade. Result, meat paste, with bone and bits of clothing. Sorry, had you eaten?"

Forensics people saw horrors day to day, or at least they had too often in the Shawl of Rikavie. There had been Okidan, and one survivor. Kazmer thought he could remember hearing stories of at least two, possibly three raids, prior to that. He'd ignored the horror stories at the time, his mind full of Modice Agenis and his heart sure of Langsarik innocence—or had it been the other way around?

"But you can type for hominid at a gross level," Cousin Stanoczk insisted, after mastering an apparent wave of nausea. Of revulsion. "And I am responsible to the Church for it. Dolgorukij. Class two hominid. No?"

Kazmer could not stop himself.

He had to look around.

There was the dockmaster's office, where torture had been done. Why? They'd had the security keys. There had been an inside man. Why had torture been done?

"No Dolgorukij." The forensics worker shook her head with emphatic conviction. "Nothing like anywhere near a Combine genotype, and the way the tissue got blended by that grenade we'd catch it if there had been any. Any at all. Maybe your Dolgorukij got away. There was a survivor at Okidan, wasn't there?"

She knew perfectly well that there had been no survivors here. She was just making conversation. Cousin Stanoczk shook his head in turn.

"I don't know what to say. Pilot. Let's go have a look at the others, he must be here. The rosters all confirm his presence."

Cousin Stanoczk had called him only "pilot" since the Bench intelligence specialists had come on board the courier Cousin Stanoczk had secured for this trip. Kazmer didn't think the Bench specialists were misled in the least, or that Cousin Stanoczk even cared if they were. Kazmer was grateful enough to be mere "pilot," even so. As horrible as it was to be there, to see these brutalized and murdered bodies, and know that he had had a hand in it—howsoever indirectly— Kazmer could not imagine being able to stand if the others knew that he had been part of the raid. Part of the murders.

He hadn't really been able to believe it before. He hadn't wanted to believe it. The Bench's propaganda was as reliable as the word of a Dolgorukij; they could have been making it all up.

He knew better now.

These people had been done to death cruelly, atrociously, and for absolutely no good purpose. He shared the blame for it, because whether or not it had been his idea, he had been part of the raid. If he hadn't been so sure that it was a Langsarik raid when he'd met the others at Port Charid, he might not have convinced them to go along with it. So he was more to blame than they.

They'd believed him when he'd said it was Langsariks and that there would be no murder.

He, and not any of them, was to blame for their guilt by association. It was just and judicious that he become the slave of the Malcontent, fit and fair that he give up his life to the Saint in partial atonement for his crime.

He followed Cousin Stanoczk in silent anguish as his mentor, guide, master crossed the loading dock around the corner behind the dockmaster's office. There were bodies there that had been checked and cataloged, laid out and arrayed for transport as evidence once the on-site processing was done; Cousin Stanoczk paced the long row thoughtfully, looking at the faces.

Fourteen people.

None of them the man Cousin Stanoczk was looking for.

None of them Langsarik either, and Kazmer clearly remembered seeing a Langsarik on staff—the inside man. It had been part of why he hadn't minded leaving with the raiding party still there. There had been a Langsarik. Kazmer had seen him. That meant that there could have been no cause for any force to be used to get at secure codes—any inside man worth his wages would have that information at the ready.

No Langsarik.

No Dolgorukij.

Kazmer had seen the Dolgorukij, as well. Had recognized the man's ethnicity. He wasn't there.

There was only one more place to look.

Cousin Stanoczk looked up into Kazmer's face. His expression was sympathetic and supportive, but not sympathetic enough. Kazmer heard no "You stay here and wait for me," no "I'll just go have a look by myself" from Cousin Stanoczk. That meant that he was going with Cousin Stanoczk to look at the last of the dead.

It was part of his punishment, perhaps.

Kazmer hadn't elected the Malcontent to escape punishment—merely to escape becoming the instrument of unjust punishment of innocent parties. He couldn't quarrel with Cousin Stanoczk about that.

The Langsariks were innocent of any involvement in this raid, whether or not they'd found any Langsarik dead. These were brutalities possible only for hardened criminals to commit. The Langsariks had been pirates and commerce raiders and thieves, but never so criminal as to be capable of this. Whatever else Kazmer didn't understand, he knew that one thing to be the truth.

Kazmer followed Cousin Stanoczk into the dockmaster's office, where the bodies of the people who had been slowly murdered were segregated. Where they could be hidden safely away from any chance glance or encounter.

The dockmaster was there.

He could not tear his eyes away from her face for a long moment. She had been so unwary. She had been confident, comfortable with her crew, in control.

And had died so horribly—

"No," Cousin Stanoczk said, from the other side of the grim line of bodies. "I don't see any Dolgorukij. Do you, pilot? Do you recognize any of these people?"

He was to look at each and every one. There was no particular note of gloating or sadistic pleasure in Cousin Stanoczk's voice, but Cousin Stanoczk clearly meant for Kazmer to see each element of this atrocity as individual and plumb the depths of his indirect guilt as part of the price for the protection that the Malcontent had granted to him. Cousin Stanoczk himself did not tarry; he had turned away to engage the Bench specialists in the outer office, with his back to the torture room with its plundered safe and mutilated corpses.

Fourteen people simply shot, five people tortured, at least five killed who knew how and then blown up with a percussion grenade—Kazmer hoped they had been killed and then blown up, and not been killed by the grenade itself—

That brought the total up to twenty-four.

There had been twenty-seven people. He remembered counting them. Three were unaccounted for. One of those three Kazmer could understand not being there, at least if he didn't think too hard about it; if it had been a Langsarik raid the inside man—the Langsarik—would naturally have left, and not been murdered.

It hadn't been a Langsarik raid, so where was the Langsarik?

But he had thought it was a Langsarik raid. Everything he'd heard or seen had only supported that assumption. They'd worn Langsarik colors. They'd used Langsarik names. Langsarik habits. Someone had gone to a bit of trouble to make it look like a Langsarik raid: So the Langsarik was dead, even if he wasn't among the bodies.

Kazmer hadn't been mistaken.

He'd been set up.

Where was the Dolgorukij?

Kazmer stared helplessly at the bodies of tortured dead, half-blind with confusion. It simply didn't add up. It made no sense. And they could not find the body of their countryman. Or of Cousin Stanoczk's countryman, because Kazmer himself was Sarvaw, and no Dolgorukij would claim kinship with a Sarvaw except in opposition to other people of even more alien blood.

What kind of monster committed such crimes?

Killing could be clean, when done by luck against an armed opponent in active resistance. Murder could be swift and simple, a quick knifing, a shot to the head, the snap of a neck.

These killings had been done against people already disarmed, already helpless to protest against atrocity. Twisted rope. The slow cut. Blows from a club, a stick, a weighted baton. The mutilation of a living body, making grotesque sport with a man's own gizzard and guts—

Kazmer stared.

There was no earthly explanation for such horror.

And yet he knew where he'd seen it before, very exact, very precise.

There was no Dolgorukij body.

He opened his mouth to scream; but what came out was an animal sound, a wordless roar of outrage and blind fury.

"Naturally it is of concern, who is responsible," the Malcontent Cousin Stanoczk was saying. Garol and the Malcontent stood together with Jils Ivers in the dockmaster's office; Stanoczk had left Kazmer Daigule to consider the tortured dead. "But first one must find one's countryman, and set his family's anxiety at rest. Who knows? If he cannot be found, perhaps he's still alive somewhere."

A slim enough chance, Garol thought, given what they were seeing. It was not merely grotesque. It was thorough. He never would have dreamed Langsariks could be capable of mass atrocity, but who was he to say?

Could something have gone this wrong, this quickly,

in a population trapped and despairing? Was he ultimately to blame for having trapped the Langsariks
into an amnesty settlement at Port Charid?

Then Kazmer Daigule, the Malcontent pilot who
had brought them there, came roaring out of the inner
chamber where the torture victims were; and flung
himself headlong at Cousin Stanoczk, knocking him to
the ground. Screaming.

Shock froze Garol in his place for just long enough
to hear some of what Daigule was saying—he thought.
His Dolgorukij was passable, but his Sarvaw was
shaky. Though the Dolgorukij dialect he'd been taught
had been High Aznir, the swear words were less dis-
similar than some of the other elements of the dialects
might be. Kazmer Daigule was howling about a bitch
and a mad dog; then Cousin Stanoczk—who had struggled onto his back on the floor in the moments it took
Garol to react—planted his boot in Daigule's belly
and pushed, hard.

Garol stepped out of the way and Daigule went up
and then back down again. Cousin Stanoczk was up
and on the pilot in one swift predatory lunge, shaking
Daigule ferociously with his hands gripping Daigule's
shirt at the throat and shouting in turn. Cousin Stanoczk spoke High Aznir in his fury. Garol could tell
exactly what Cousin Stanoczk was saying.

*Profane as well as mad, shit-eating Sarvaw, no one
protects the blasphemer. Shut your filthy mouth.*

Daigule wasn't shutting up.

He had his hands up to Stanoczk's hands now,
though he wasn't trying to get up. There was a wrench-
ing note in his tone of voice that told Garol that Daigule wasn't raving, as Cousin Stanoczk's curse had
seemed to imply; just insisting on something. There
was the mad dog again, though Garol heard no more
about bitches. Mad dogs, murderers, and a missal or
devotional book of some sort. Maybe a counting
string, it was hard to tell.

Cousin Stanoczk seemed to be in control of the situation.

Garol waited, to see what would happen.

Slowly the Malcontent straightened up, releasing his grip on Daigule's collar with what seemed to be a stern effort of will. It was hard to tell with Dolgorukij, but Garol thought that Stanoczk had paled. Turning his back on Daigule, Stanoczk raised his eyes to some point located halfway across the top of the doorway out into the loading area; and when he spoke again, it was in plain Standard.

"You allow your imagination to run away with you, pilot. The mad dog of which you speak has been dead for more than one hundred years. You are grasping at smoke, to divert suspicion."

This was interesting. Garol sat down, deliberately drawing attention to himself with the action, just to be sure that they realized he was listening. He and Jils. He wanted to get through to Daigule very badly, but he wasn't about to steal access after having made a deal—howsoever unsatisfactory—with Cousin Stanoczk.

Daigule gathered himself to sit cross-legged, slumped at the floor and staring at the ground. "You say. But we know. They just went underground, Cousin Stanoczk, they've always been there. Waiting. Grant me at least the expert's eye in the matter."

The story was beginning to sort itself out to Garol's satisfaction. Whether or not he believed it was another matter.

"Nobody is going to take such a thing the least bit seriously." Oddly enough it seemed that Daigule had gotten through to Cousin Stanoczk, at least in some sense; Stanoczk sounded genuinely shaken. "You are afraid it was Langsariks, you wish to divert suspicion, you invent. What would the Angel be doing in Port Charid, what reason imaginable could there be? It's too forced, pilot, it won't do."

Daigule was shaking his head, though, rocking gently back and forth where he sat on the floor as if to give his insistence additional emphasis. "No Langsarik in the history of Langsariks ever did such a thing, but the mad dog was always accustomed to. For piety. This was not a Langsarik raid. This was a raid done by people wishing to be taken for Langsariks but betrayed by habit. Let me talk to the Bench specialists, Cousin Stanoczk. I can tell them things they need to know."

All of the time in transit between Anglace and Tyrell Yards the pilot had kept strictly to himself, neither speaking nor responding when spoken to by anyone but Cousin Stanoczk, but it had been perfectly obvious to Garol that the pilot was Kazmer Daigule. He'd even felt a little sorry for the man; it had to be an awkward position to be in.

"Out of the question," Cousin Stanoczk snapped, angrily. "You have your oath taken on it already. I will not allow it. Still." He seemed to run out of irate energy as he spoke, as if forced to entertain an alien and unpleasant concept. "Still. It doesn't fit the Langsarik model. There is the bracelet, I saw it. Why invoke the Angel, though, pilot?"

Bracelet, bracelet—what bracelet? Garol traded glances with Jils, momentarily confused. He saw realization in her eyes even as he grasped the meaning of the phrase himself. Torture victims, mutilations, bodies cut open before the victim was dead. All right. He could understand "bracelet."

"Because there was a Dolgorukij here, and we can't find him. There was a Dolgorukij at Okidan, wasn't there? Who survived."

"If you mean to accuse—" Cousin Stanoczk started to say. He was obviously angry again. Kazmer Daigule stood up and held his hands out, petitioning.

"No accusations, Cousin Stanoczk. Just an observation. But this"—Daigule spread both hands and opened his arms, to include all of the carnage at the Tyrell Yards—"this is the very type and pattern of the mad dog. Admit it. Why would Langsariks go crazy, in such specific ways?"

"Not just one Dolgorukij is missing." Cousin Stanoczk seemed determined to resist whatever conclusion it was that Daigule was trying to communicate. "A Sarvaw also survived, pilot. I grant you that no Sarvaw ever joined those ranks, that my holy Patron knows of."

The suggestion seemed to stagger Daigule, almost literally. It was a moment before he could respond.

"If you were not my cousin," Daigule said, only he used one of the dozens of words that Dolgorukij had for cousin, and Garol thought this one was a particularly extreme form of the relationship from a power standpoint. "And I didn't owe you. You'd take that back, Stanoczk. And beg my mother's pardon, and her mother's pardon, and the pardon of my mother's mother's mother, sincerely. I would see to it."

Mad dogs and bitches. Angels. Dolgorukij and Sarvaw.

Nobody said anything for a moment or two, as Daigule stared at Stanoczk, who stared back.

"We're being rude," Cousin Stanoczk said finally. "Bench specialists. We are finished here, Kazmer Daigule and I. Let's please leave this place. I will explain, but I warn you that I do not believe it."

It was an admirably restrained sort of thing to say after the fireworks Daigule had just set off. Garol could not bring himself to tarnish its perfection by elaborating or insisting on it.

"Your ship, Cousin Stanoczk." And therefore up to Cousin Stanoczk to decide when to leave, by implication. "Your pilot. Yes, we'd be happy to accept transportation to Port Charid, kind of you to offer."

Garol's own courier would be waiting there soon, freighter-ferried from Anglace. It had been relatively easy to arrange ferry transport; there seemed to be a surplus of available freight heading into Port Charid. Wholesalers weren't feeling very comfortable about the security of goods warehoused in the Shawl of Rikavie, it seemed; the business base at Charid was bound to be suffering. Chilleau Judiciary was going to want to talk to him about that.

Chilleau Judiciary was going to want to talk to him about a lot of things. An uneasy conviction that things just weren't adding up was going to answer questions the Bench had a right to ask him about piracy and murder.

The floor manager, Dalmoss, was standing behind his desk as Hilton stepped into the open doorway. It looked as though he were packing. Hilton rapped sharply at the doorjamb with the curled knuckles of his left hand, to alert Dalmoss to his presence.

"You sent for me, floor manager?"

Dalmoss raised his head sharply, looking a little startled, then seemed to relax. "Shires. Don't creep up on a man like that. Come in, close the door."

The floor manager's office was just inside the small administrative area at one end of the new warehouse. Things were still unfinished. There was nobody else in the administrative complex—reception desk, foreman's office, storeroom and toilet all unoccupied; maybe it was just the draft Dalmoss wanted to shut out. Hilton shrugged mental shoulders and closed the door behind him.

"Are you leaving, floor manager?" Hilton started to ask the question, but it didn't quite come out the way he'd thought it might. The situation did seem obvious.

Nor did Dalmoss seem to take offense at any presumption on Hilton's part. "I have to go to Geraint for a few days, Shires, something's come up. I've asked the foreman to let you fill in on temporary assignment, and he's agreed. He's been very pleased at your progress so far."

That was a compliment, Hilton supposed, or at least it seemed that Dalmoss intended it as such. "Very kind. I'm sure." He wasn't sure, not really, what progress there was to impress anybody. He'd learned to tick boxes in array. That didn't take much progress.

Dalmoss grinned. "Not doing you any favors, really, Shires. You get to skip roll call because we expect you to be working early and late, but that's about it. Corporate practice. We'll work you for months under pretext of training before we get around to actually paying you for the job you're doing. Here, take this."

Dalmoss tossed something at Hilton, something small and light. Hilton caught it, curious: cylindrical, metallic, and the spider-brain that lived inside of it made its status lights sparkle. An identity chop.

"What's it for?"

It couldn't be Dalmoss's chop. Dalmoss was going to Geraint and would probably be needing his signature key. Even if he didn't, Dalmoss's chop was no good to anyone but Dalmoss; identity chops were tuned to the genetic markers in a person's sweat and skin, so that no one but Dalmoss could use his chop, not and get a seal. So it wasn't Dalmoss's chop.

"Backup release marker," Dalmoss explained. He'd dropped his voice, and was looking past Hilton to the door of his office—to make sure it was closed, Hilton supposed. "I don't like taking it off-site. Just hang on to it, Shires; you won't be asked to use it for anything, just make sure you keep track of where it is until I get back."

Backup release marker? "I don't want to be difficult," Hilton protested. "But I'm a little uncomfortable. My status, and all that. Are you sure it's a good idea to leave it with me? Why not the foreman?"

It wasn't an identity chop, it was a corporate marker, used to sign off on documents releasing ships and cargo. Authorizing movement of freighter tenders from surface to orbit. Clearing a pilot to take a ship and go.

Langsariks weren't to have access to such things.

Dalmoss came around from behind his desk to stand

close to Hilton, speaking quietly and quickly. "We had to have the second one made when the foreman was injured at Okidan. But we got busy, I never got around to the documentation, you know how it's been around here. And the foreman doesn't want to know about it."

Oh, good.

Not only was it a violation of the amnesty for Hilton to be in possession of a backup release chop.

It was contraband in its own right, as well.

"Listen, floor manager, I appreciate the trust reposed and all that, but I really don't know if I can be comfortable holding on to this."

Undocumented backup release marker.

Black-market value, one full freighter load of dried confer wood, great thick fragrant bales of the stuff. A fortune for any man, let alone a disenfranchised Langsarik.

"It'll be all right." Dalmoss gave Hilton's shoulder a friendly reassuring shake and turned him toward the door. "The administrative stuff is in process, it's just a little behind, is all. I'll make it right with the foreman when I get back. And it's not a problem for you to have it, so long as you don't use it, that's all."

Feraltz didn't want to know about it, Dalmoss said.

Did that imply that Feraltz knew, and was politely ignoring the whole thing till the documentation was completed?

Maybe it was all right.

It wasn't as if there was any real danger of Hilton using the chop to lay hands on unauthorized transport, after all. And what did the terms of the amnesty say? Not that Langsariks were absolutely forbidden potential access; just that they were not to take advantage.

At least that was one way to interpret it.

"Well." If the foreman knew, Hilton felt it would be unnecessarily prudish of him to insist on the letter of the administrative regulations. "So long as the documentation is in work. I suppose." It couldn't be a real secret, then, not if the covering documentation was in process. A little irregular, maybe, but trade seldom ran precise to specification. "I'll hang on to it for you till you get back. What else, floor manager?"

The whole issue of the backup release marker was apparently so negligible to Dalmoss that Hilton's agreement was taken in stride, as only natural. Hilton felt himself relax a little bit more. Yes. It was all right. There was no cause for concern, it was just one of those administrative mismatches, that was all.

"I need you to take the floor meeting at second shift, the assignment matrix is posted to your reader, and I'm loading some notes. They'll be ready for you by the time you get back from the floor meeting, we can do final tie-in then. You'd better hurry."

It wouldn't do to be late for his first official acting-floor-manager assignment. No.

Tucking the little token into a shirt pocket absent-mindedly, Hilton hurried out for his meeting, focusing his mind on the new challenges that had just been laid before him.

Once Cousin Stanoczk's sleek little courier had cleared the Tyrell Yards for Port Charid, Cousin Stanoczk sent his relief pilot forward and called for Kazmer Daigule. There were two to three hours of travel time between the Shawl of Rikavie and Port Charid from the Tyrell Yards, at this time of year. Garol supposed Stanoczk wanted to talk in a secure environment.

When they were all assembled in the courier's salon Cousin Stanoczk took a deep breath, and started to speak. "To your mother I apologize very humbly, Kazmer. And also to her mother, and her mother's mother; to the mother of your father, and her father's mother, as sincerely as I am able. I had no cause to suggest such a thing, but you made me angry, suggesting what you did. I tell you to explain, not to excuse the insult, for which I place myself in humility before your antecedents."

"Suggesting what? The Angel of Destruction?" Jils asked. She'd been quiet and self-contained since Daigule's outburst at Tyrell; Garol was surprised to hear her speak. Jils wasn't one to open her mouth unless she had something to say, though: and it sounded like she was ahead of him on this one. "I heard horror stories from the forensics team at the Domitt Prison in Port Rudistal. They were Sarvaw, too."

Now that she put it into context for him Garol began to make sense of it all. Sarvaw, terrorism, atrocity, the Angel of Destruction. Right.

"It is an outlaw, and has been for several lives."

Cousin Stanoczk was clearly not at all eager to talk about it. He could hardly refuse to discuss the issue once it was raised, however, not unless he wanted to focus their attention on the subject by so doing.

"Since the time of Chuvishka Kospodar, who was the grandfather of my grandfather's father. I have the family shame. Yet even at the time of its outlawry, there were questions, within privileged circles, about whether the monster were truly dead, or merely feigning."

"Start at the beginning," Garol suggested. It generally helped him make sense of things. "What's your angle in all of this, Stanoczk?"

Stanoczk had started to pace. The Malcontent's courier ship was considerably more commodious than Garol's usual transport. There was much more room in which to move.

"We were as skeptical of the Langsarik settlement as any, Garol Aphon." Stanoczk used two of his three names, Garol noted. Showing off that he knew them, perhaps? Stanoczk was obviously upset; maybe he was just reverting unconsciously to his natal syntax. Garol hoped Stanoczk regained control of his emotions soon. He'd never cared for his middle name.

"Therefore, someone was tagged to keep a watch

on the progress of the experiment. The Langsariks were efficient predators, you may remember. We had no desire to see them continue to feed off Combine shipping."

Old news. Garol settled himself back in his chair, resigned to a long siege. Comfortable chair. The pilot didn't look very comfortable, though. Pity.

"Then there were problems, and it could have been youthful high spirits. Perhaps it was at first. The first of the raids where there was killing concerned us."

Hit-and-run raids were one thing, characteristic of Langsarik battle tactics. Warehouse invasion was not, nor had killing ever characterized a Langsarik operation. So far, so good.

"The Combine is in contention with other local interests for commercial ascendancy, here at Port Charid. Was it too convenient that the Combine's competition has been raided in series? And yet if there was a secret plot on the part of my government, I would know about it. I wouldn't tell you, of course. But I would know about it."

Interesting. Cousin Stanoczk might be a more highly placed player than Garol had realized; or he might be making this part up.

"Thus if there was no plan that we knew of, and yet events did seem to follow a plan to strengthen Combine interests at the expense of any others, who could be responsible? Raiding takes organization. And in this case murder."

"The Bench likes to consider itself responsible for that sort of problem," Jils noted, in a mild and dispassionate tone of voice. As if she was simply making an abstract and objective observation, not pointing out that the Bench saw no functional difference between lawbreaking and the unauthorized upholding of the Law, the upholding of the Law by persons not properly deputized to do so. "It has Bench intelligence specialists to work issues like raiding at Port Charid."

Cousin Stanoczk seemed to be trying to nod and

shake his head at the same time, and ended up describing a sort of a figure eight with his chin. "But if this was Combine business, Bench specialist, it is our responsibility. We can't ask the Bench to intervene in family discipline."

Begging the question rather neatly. "Go on," Garol said. Maybe Jils had drawn her conclusions and filed her mental report, but he still wanted to hear Stanoczk's take. "Responsible."

"We are not so familiar as you with the Langsariks, Specialist Vogel. It could be that their styles had changed. What reason could Langsariks have to promote Combine interests, though, especially at the risk of their own lives and freedom? And then there were more raids. We began to see a pattern. One with potential historical precedent."

At that the pilot raised his head, staring at Cousin Stanoczk with black despair in his brown eyes.

"You knew all along it wasn't Langsariks." Daigule's claim was not so much an accusation as a flat statement. "And you let me give it all away. Knowing all along."

He seemed to hit a nerve with Cousin Stanoczk, even so. "We knew no such thing. I still don't know. There is potential evidence. Is it good enough for the Bench? Certainly not. What would have happened had I denied you, in violation of my sacred duty?"

Good question, Garol thought. "That's what I'd like to know." With Stanoczk here, it couldn't be said that he was going behind anyone's back. "If your evidence could divert suspicion, pilot, you logically would have wanted to give it." Which could presumably be exactly what Kazmer Daigule was doing even now, his utmost to divert attention from the Langsariks. "Apart from any personal vulnerability, your only likely reason for bolting has to be that your evidence would have indicted Langsariks."

"Because I thought it was Langsariks," Daigule said flatly.

Cousin Stanoczk started to raise his hand, as if to silence Daigule.

Lowering his head—so that he would be unable to see any such signal, Garol supposed—Daigule forged on. "I didn't know what to make of the rumors of killing; but I knew that if anyone got serious with questions, I was bound to mention Langsariks sooner or later. And I'd seen a friend of mine in the street the day I arrived to meet with the rest of the crew. If it really was a Langsarik raid, he almost had to be part of it, whether or not I ever saw him after that. If it wasn't a Langsarik raid, it was that much more vital to keep his name out of it. His, and that of any other Langsarik, including the name 'Langsarik.'"

Hilton Shires had known that Daigule had been in Port Charid, though he'd not wanted to say so. Garol understood. "And now you're sure it wasn't. Your evidence, please. If Cousin Stanoczk permits, of course."

Cousin Stanoczk had ceased his pacing to lean up against the bulkhead behind Daigule, folding his arms. Stanoczk said nothing, so Daigule answered, with evident eagerness.

"Everything points to Langsariks, don't you see? I was recruited anonymously, but there were hints. At every step, clues and indications. The raid party all wore pieces of Langsarik colors, nothing too obvious or overdone, just what you would expect. The Langsarik body is missing. But so is another body, and there's no sense in the murders. Especially not in torture."

Daigule's point presumably being that nobody could have so consistently given signs of being Langsarik and not been Langsarik unless they had been deliberately intent on presenting the impression that they were Langsariks.

First Secretary Verlaine was not likely to be convinced.

"It isn't evidence." Jils said the unpleasant truth for him, and Garol thanked her with a grateful glance.

"As it stands it's just a coincidence. We can't even say if it's a real coincidence. The missing Dolgorukij may turn up somewhere alive and healthy. We need more to go on."

Garol didn't know exactly what would do it. But he agreed with Jils that what they had was not enough.

"If you blame Langsariks for these raids, the public may be appeased." Straightening, Cousin Stanoczk stood with his hands on his hips and a very determined expression on his face. "But it will neither effect the punishment of the guilty nor necessarily put a stop to the criminal activity if we do not correctly identify the criminals."

All right, they could all agree on that. "So what's your plan?" Garol asked. There had to be a plan. This Cousin Stanoczk was too devious not to have something already up his sleeve; so Garol wasn't surprised at Stanoczk's response.

"Work with me, Bench specialist, and every resource I command is at your disposal. It cannot be the Angel of Destruction. It must not be the Angel of Destruction. But if it is the Angel of Destruction, it must be stopped, and decisively."

Whether or not such action would place Cousin Stanoczk in violation of Bench direction.

Maybe the rule of Law could be stretched to cover an extrajudicial punitive transaction on neutral ground, in light of the fact that it was to be Combine against Combine . . . maybe.

"Can I get Daigule?"

Garol put his question to Cousin Stanoczk, careful to observe the appropriate protocol. "Bearing in mind that so far as I know this is still all just an elaborate ruse to protect Langsariks. Making no promises."

He had to be careful.

He wanted it not to be Langsariks.

He wanted it not to be Langsariks so badly that he could halfway convince himself that Cousin Stanoczk's wild talk about Dolgorukij terrorists made sense. It would comprise an explanation of sorts; but he'd have to review the elements with Jils in private before he could be sure that his own personal investment in the success of the Langsarik settlement wasn't adversely affecting his ability to weigh and judge.

Daigule started to speak, but Cousin Stanoczk spoke over him. Daigule shut up, looking surprised and a little sheepish.

"Daigule will offer you every cooperation at his command, so long as you respect his confidence. You may not ask him to name names. You must not use any part of his effort to incriminate the Langsariks. If the Langsariks are to be incriminated, you must find other means than Kazmer Daigule through which to do so. Kazmer, you will answer to these conditions, and say yes or no."

Who did Cousin Stanoczk think he was, to set limits on the rules of evidence?

A Malcontent.

It was galling to have to operate under such constraints, offensive in principle even if they made no functional difference.

Daigule nodded, looking first to Cousin Stanoczk and then to Garol. "If it's Langsariks, they know what they're risking," Daigule agreed, firmly. "But if it isn't, I'm not going to be the man who makes the case, just to cover the Bench. Yes, Cousin Stanoczk."

If they'd had this conversation at Anglace, they could have gotten Kazmer to do an interrogatory, saving themselves several awkward and unproductive days in transit.

But if they hadn't come to Tyrell Yards, he would still be struggling to gain access to Daigule, and Daigule's cooperation.

Maybe he didn't need an interrogatory.

Garol had a notion that he was going to want to stick close to Port Charid until he had an answer that he could be satisfied with.

"We'll start by retracing your steps in Port Charid,

then." Now that Daigule had agreed, Garol didn't have to worry about going through Stanoczk, and addressed himself to Daigule directly. "Where you met with the rest of the crew, where you got transport, how you found your freighter. Be thinking about those things. Do your best to remember every detail."

They would be making planetfall at Port Charid very soon.

Hilton Shires had a scarf in his possession to be returned to Daigule; maybe a confrontation between the two men would shake something loose that would prove useful.

He was going to have to get back to Walton Agenis, to let her know the status of the threat to the settlement; and in the meantime he had damage control to conduct, with First Secretary Verlaine.

He wished more than anything that he had something more reassuring to transmit to the Flag Captain: But she trusted him, because he had been honest with her.

Whether or not the truth was something either of them wanted to face, he had to be honest with her.

Walton Agenis was weeding in her kitchen-garden when her nephew Hilton Shires peered over the short fence into the enclosure to hail her in the Standard fashion.

"Good-greeting, Aunt, how does the day find you?"

She'd been expecting to see Hilton. Sitting back on her heels, Walton wiped the sweat out of her eyes with the back of her hand, contemplating the tidy rows of tuber greens as she formulated her response.

"I'm well and doing tolerably, young Shires." It was a joke between them to emphasize the distance between nephew and aunt, though his father was her older brother. Her brother had gotten to be an old man, and could no longer weed tuber greens. It was a shame, because weeding in a garden had been one of the things she'd missed most, during the years of the Langsarik fleet's outlawry. "How's by you?"

Apparently encouraged, Hilton slipped the latch on the garden gate and let himself in. He had new clothes, she noticed; the collar of the undershirt that showed its crescent of fabric beneath his jacket was a generic white. Not rose gold. Going native. She wasn't exactly sure how she felt about that, though. Fitting in was good. Forgetting who you were and where you'd come from was not good.

"I've just come home with my wages for my folks. It's a decent job, Aunt Walton. They're talking about management."

He squatted down in the garden as he spoke, gathering the weeds into the wastebasket that lay at the head of the row. Hilton had always been good at making himself useful. "There'll be a lot of opportunity when the Combine's new warehouse complex opens. I heard Modice has gone to work for the administration out at the contractor site?"

His intelligence net was working. That was always a good thing. Walton smiled at the weeds, almost despite herself; she was as proud of Hilton—tall and whipcord-wiry and beautiful, intelligent and goodhearted—as though he had been her son, rather than her nephew.

"Shift scheduler, nights. They're keeping her busy."

Modice's new job had created some interesting byproducts as well. For one, there were fewer night prowlers and day callers. For another, some of the young people who had not quite nerved themselves up to go to work for outlanders had suddenly realized the dignity of honest toil—particularly at construction sites—shortly after Modice had gotten a job at the construction site. Modice had needed the distraction. Walton thought she was worrying about Kazmer Daigule.

"Um. I saw that Bench specialist in town the other day, by the way. What's his name. Garol Vogel."

Walton dug around the base of a sapweed with her fingers. One needed to get as good a grip on the root as possible in order to pull it out. If you let the root break, the weed just came back, and seemed to be stronger than ever. Weed management was a near-forgotten art among her fleet's crew, but the principle hadn't changed.

"Brought you a scarf, I expect. Were you able to return it? Because I'm absolutely not having that thing back. Not under my roof."

Reaching casually back toward a pocket on the back side of his work pants Hilton seemed to pause, hearing her warning, and think twice. Teasing her.

"Well. All right. I'm not sure it's safe for me to be carrying around, though. But seriously."

He'd picked up all the weeds that were there, so he joined her at the edge of the tuber bed to help her work. "Which ones? These? No. These. All right. I'm worried about Kaz, Aunt Walton."

He was worried, Modice was worried, why should Langsariks worry about any seventeen Sarvaw pilots? Daigule was a good-hearted man, and Hilton was fond of him. That was one thing. Modice being fond of him was something else altogether. "He was out here one night, courting your cousin. We haven't seen him since. You?"

Shaking his head, Hilton pulled a plant up out of the ground with a stern effort, only then seeming to notice that he'd pulled the wrong thing. Replanting it hastily, Hilton scowled at the dirt while Walton did what she could to avoid noticing the error.

"Once, in port. Days ago. Going on weeks. He had something on his mind, and I didn't want to talk to him. Pride. I was nervous about my job interview."

The tuber was back in the ground. It would survive. Now that Hilton knew by experience which plant not to pull he would be that much more efficient, and that was all to the good.

"What do you mean, something on his mind. Worried?"

Hilton seemed to think about this, pulling weeds. The right ones. He had a good grip on things when it came to roots, Walton noticed.

"Not so much worried. He was dropping hints about his job. I didn't care, and he got irritated at me and left. Now I wish I knew more about what he was doing here."

Or, maybe not. Of course that was the whole problem, right there. "I can't see that man mixed up in the sort of trade they've been talking about lately." Hilton would know what she meant. As hard as it was for her to say something nice about a brash young outlander, she had to be fair. "He's not a killer. Still less a murderer."

Brushing the dirt away from the roots of his latest conquest, Hilton held the weed up to the sky and squinted at it. "Here's my worry, though. Suppose he thought I was bald-facing him. Suppose he thought I'd hired him."

Yes, it was in fact a weed. Hilton tossed it over his left shoulder and rocked forward onto his hands and knees to seek out his next target. "Because if if if, we might have learned something. Something that might be important for a person to know."

Or, maybe not, as before. The dirt around one of her tubers had gotten kicked up as she pulled a weed; Walton patted the earth back down around its roots, thinking.

"What did you tell Vogel?"

Hilton shook his head. "I didn't have anything to tell Vogel. All right, I know about the problem Cheff's had with the bottling plant, but that's just hooliganism. There isn't anything to tell Vogel. You?"

His job had been keeping him very busy; he'd probably had to delegate some of the intelligence work. But he was a good intelligence officer, was her nephew. He would still have heard anything that might be important.

"About the same." So they both knew there was a problem. The Bench might lie to the public about raids on warehouses for obscure Bench purposes of its own. But Vogel would not come and ask her about it if it hadn't happened. "There's gossip, I expect."

Hilton nodded, grinning. "Oh, yes. We're much more dangerous people than we ever realized, Aunt Walton. But people do half believe murder of us, and I don't care for that."

Nor did any of them.

Vogel would figure it out.

If Vogel didn't figure something out—they had more than just a problem; they had a potential crisis on their hands. That meant that she needed to think of some way, somehow, that they could protect themselves.

It was not going to be easy. The Bench had their transport, their weapons, their star charts, their communications equipment, their everything.

All they had was Langsariks.

It would have to do.

"There's this row left to finish, then you can start in on the next."

Walton dusted off her hands and stood up, thinking. "I'll send someone out with a drink of water in a bit. Come into the house when you're finished here, and I'll tell you what you can do next."

The muster net had been set up upon their arrival, and tested periodically since. It was time to make sure that the communications network was absolutely up-to-date. Just in case they needed to pass information in a hurry.

If they waited until they needed it, it would be too late.

"Aunt Walton, I'm on my day off. I was going to have a nap," Hilton protested. But it wasn't a serious complaint.

Leaving Hilton to the garden, Walton Agenis went into the house, to set the cultivation of the Langsarik self-defense communication network into order and get the weeding done while there was time.

Chapter Seven

Fisner Feraltz had gotten the word as soon as the Bench intelligence specialists docked in Port Charid. He'd hurried to Factor Madlev's office immediately. The priority transmit equipment the Bench specialists would be wanting was secured in Factor Madlev's office—safe within the jurisdiction of the Combine Yards, where Factor Madlev could provide oversight and regulation.

He barely had time to get settled and launch the report he'd brought to cover his errand when his quarry arrived: Bench intelligence specialist Garol Vogel, all right, coming into the room with a kind of focused determination that seemed to give him more momentum than mere mass and velocity could impart.

"Excuse me, Factor Madlev," Vogel said. "Feraltz. If you would be so kind. I'd like to engage priority transmit, I'll have to ask you to step outside for a moment or two."

Vogel hadn't called ahead; his visit was unannounced, and Factor Madlev was inclined to stand on his dignity a little. Fisner started to gather his documents up immediately, taking care to drop the odd document to the floor as he did so; nothing too obvious, of course, but Factor Madlev took the hint as though it had truly been his idea.

"I protest, Bench specialist," Factor Madlev said mildly—but he had not stood up when Vogel entered the room. "My foreman is my second-in-command, as it were, my proxy. I need hardly point out his very personal interest in your investigation; surely he can be trusted to keep a confidence?"

Fisner said nothing, continuing to collect himself. He didn't have to overact to make the point about how awkward it was for him to get around in the medical bracing. The awkwardness was genuine enough; the challenge was precisely how to avoid overplaying it.

"It's rather difficult for him to get out from the new warehouse to see me, I'd rather he were allowed to stay," Factor Madlev added, in a rather more ingratiating tone of voice. Vogel seemed to consider, watching Fisner packing, chewing on the left corner of his lower lip.

His decision when made was expressed abruptly and ungraciously, but Fisner didn't take it personally. Vogel was clearly absorbed in his own issues, and meant no particular offense. "Very well. Feraltz, this communication is Bench-restricted, not to be discussed. Factor Madlev, if you would do the honors, please?"

Bench-restricted. Fisner felt a little thrill go through him at the phrase. He wouldn't be hearing anything truly sensitive; if Vogel had had something important to say he would have summarily excused Factor Madlev as well as Fisner. But Fisner would get to hear the status of Vogel's investigation up front. It would save time and effort as he analyzed the movements of his antagonist.

Factor Madlev engaged the security web that shielded the walls and coded his secures into the priority-transmit apparatus. Then he gave Vogel the nod; and Vogel spoke clearly and carefully, so that the encoders could perform their voice confirms and clear his signal.

"Bench intelligence specialist Garol Vogel, for the First Secretary. Chilleau Judiciary. Priority transmit."

First Secretary Verlaine. Chilleau Judiciary would act as the Angel's weapon against the Langsariks. The

Bench specialist would be the man to set the wave of destruction in motion.

"Stand by for Chilleau Judiciary, Specialist Vogel. Signal is clearing."

It was getting dark in Factor Madlev's office. The lights were still running on summer-cycle; though the sun was going down, the lights had not come on yet. The weather was turning as well. It was getting colder day by day, and the stiffness of his medical bracing was an increasing source of annoyance to him—one he welcomed for such use as he could make of that annoyance, as in this present instance.

"Signal is cleared. Specialist Vogel, I have the First Secretary, Chilleau Judiciary. Bench concern security in effect, go ahead please."

"First Secretary? Bench specialist Garol Vogel here. We've just come from the Tyrell Yards."

"Do you have a status report, Specialist Vogel?"

That would be the voice of First Secretary Sindha Verlaine. Fisner felt a thrill go up his spine: this was his man, the one who would order the dissolution of the settlement and the dispersal—death, and slavery— of the surviving Langsarik pirates.

"Looks bad from Tyrell Yards, First Secretary." Specialist Vogel's tone of voice was mild and considering, almost neutral. Fisner was impressed at any man who could remain neutral after viewing the carnage at the Tyrell Yards. He hadn't seen it himself; but he'd heard Dalmoss's report. He could imagine.

"That tells me nothing, Vogel. I'm not exposing the Judge to public criticism on a 'looking bad.' What have you got that I can use?"

No, naturally the First Secretary would be sensitive about the Second Judge's position. There was the memory of the scandal at the Domitt Prison to take into account. Chilleau Judiciary would need persuasive evidence to show the media in order to justify the dissolution of the settlement; that was why those people at

Tyrell had been tortured. Why those people at Honangung were going to be tortured.

One documented atrocity was as good as eight indications of unrest or possible infraction of amnesty. If the atrocity were grim enough, it didn't even have to be clearly Langsariks to be convincing. That was how mob psychology worked; Fisner was counting on it.

"What we haven't got is a body, First Secretary. The staff listing names a Langsarik warehouseman on staff and on duty at the Tyrell Yards, and there's no Langsarik corpse. The implications are obvious."

Fisner glanced quickly to the floor, in case any hint of an internal smile of satisfaction should show in his eye. Precisely so. No Langsarik body. Conclusion, Langsarik raid. Negative evidence would do in the absence of eyewitness testimony. There was eyewitness testimony to the Okidan raid after all—his. Carefully qualified, so as to avoid being so obvious that it might raise questions in someone's mind by its very clarity.

"But you'll find the body, Bench specialist. Dead or alive. I'm sure of it."

Fisner wondered whether the note of grim amusement he thought he heard in the First Secretary's voice was really there, or just his imagination. Vogel bowed slightly toward the priority-access channel's portal on Factor Madlev's desk as he replied.

"We'll mount a quiet search, of course, First Secretary. There appears to be more than one body missing, so we have good hope of finding something."

Vexing. They'd noticed that Pettiche wasn't there.

Should he have done that differently? After all—to die in the service of the Angel of Destruction was to go to heavenly glory and eternal overlordship beneath the canopy of Heaven—

It was too late now. Pettiche had gone to Geraint in Dalmoss's place, with Dalmoss's identity papers— since Fisner needed Dalmoss to remain behind for the raid on Honan-gung. Pettiche had been gone for two days now. No, there was no profit in second-guessing himself; best simply to concentrate on the piece of the puzzle that he still held and leave the rest for later.

He held the Langsarik they'd taken off Tyrell.

Vogel continued. "The principal problem is that for all the talk of Langsariks, there's no hints as to how the Langsariks are supposed to have pulled things off. No missing crews. No unexplained affluence in settlement. We can't make it stick without some explanation, First Secretary."

Verlaine wanted Vogel to find the body, very well, Vogel would find the body; and if he didn't, it would have to be the result of determined avoidance, as cleverly as Fisner meant to arrange things. Somehow. He didn't know exactly how it was going to be yet, but the Holy Mother would guide him, as She had before.

"The public believes that the Langsariks can do magic, Vogel, evidence or no evidence. This is five within the year, and blood makes a strong impression on the minds of governments with merchants to look out for and collect taxes from. Things are warming up uncomfortably for the Second Judge. I'm promising a resolution soon, and doing my best not to define 'soon.' Any assistance you can offer will be greatly appreciated."

Fisner had assistance to offer, though nobody here could even guess.

If the First Secretary is getting pressure now, Fisner told himself with satisfaction, *just wait till the raid at Honan-gung.* That would put First Secretary Verlaine into a position such that he would have no choice but to revoke the Langsarik amnesty. He'd have all the evidence he needed to back him up. After that the Bench specialists could leave Port Charid and go on to bigger, better, more important issues than that of determining exactly who was actually responsible for commerce raiding in the Shawl of Rikavie.

"Understood, First Secretary. That's all I have. Bench specialist Garol Aphon Vogel, away, here."

He'd be away himself as soon as he could be.

Now that Vogel was back in Port Charid the Honangung raid could go forward, just as soon as Hilton Shires could be convinced that he had intercepted incriminating and important information.

"Chilleau Judiciary off transmit. Closing session, clear."

The Bench specialist terminated the transmit.

"Thank you, Factor Madlev, I'll be going. We have some investigations to conduct, but I have no information I can share with you at the present time."

"Just keep me posted as you can, Bench specialist, and thank you. Don't forget. Anything we can do to put your efforts forward. Anything at all."

Vogel nodded and left; Fisner prepared to continue the presentation he'd used to cover his presence here for Vogel's visit. It wouldn't be long; he was nearly done.

Then he had things that he could do to put Vogel's efforts forward.

And Vogel would never even know whom he really had to thank.

It was well past the end of his scheduled shift, but Hilton Shires had things to do before he could be comfortable leaving the day's report for the foreman in the morning. Floor manager Dalmoss had apparently spent as much of his time in administrative tasks as in supervision, and while this new warehouse complex was still far from finished, the foreman had started to move crates into the roughed-out warehouse on overflow.

They simply didn't have anyplace else to put the cargoes that were coming clear through to Port Charid now that they could no longer be accommodated at Okidan, at Tyrell, at the Combine Yards within the Shawl of Rikavie that had been absorbing the orphaned cargoes for months.

There were three freighter tenders on the airfield

just then, and one under cover in off-load; where were they going to put all of this merchandise?

It had to slow down.

It had to.

The Combine's cargo-handling facilities were already charging a significant premium for the service, in an attempt to bring demand into alignment with the increasingly limited supply of warehouse space and cargo-handling capability. Making money hand over fist, in Hilton's estimation, because he knew what the Factor was charging, and for amateur handlers in an unfinished warehouse—well.

The second shift on construction had gone off; third shift was at the far end of the facility trying to get the rest of the exterior walls up before the winter rains set in. Hilton was alone at his end of the warehouse, walking from cargo tower to cargo tower as he struggled to locate all of the lots his record showed as having been off-loaded on his shift.

It was quiet where he was.

The far end of the warehouse complex where third shift was at work was out of earshot; though Hilton could see movement down at the end of the facility, it was only in a vague and generalized fashion. Quiet, and he was tired; only three more columns of figures to locate and he'd be able to sign off on the receiving report and log his duty roster and go to bed.

The dormitory building was still under construction as well, but he could sleep there free of charge and be accounted for when the midnight tally report was done. He didn't relish the prospect of hiking all the way back out to the settlement at this hour. It was cold out there, and since the roads were not well lighted, it was a little difficult to navigate over the uneven terrain at the side of the transit track without mistaking a shadow for a rock or vice versa, with adverse consequences for one's flesh and clothing.

The dormitory would be warm and dry, and Factor Madlev made sure there was always hot soup in the communal kitchen for people coming off shift. So that was dinner, as well, and his wages on top of it—it was a good bargain all around.

If it hadn't been for the uncertainty that hung over the entire Langsarik settlement, life would be good. Factor Madlev firmly discounted the gossip, coming out very strongly against any loose anti-Langsarik talk on his work crews; but there would be no escaping it until the problem was solved somehow. Someone was raiding warehouses and murdering people. Langsariks had been very successful commerce raiders. Not all the public support Factor Madlev—and Foreman Feraltz, and floor manager Dalmoss, when he got back from Geraint—could give would change that fact.

Weaving his way through the towering stacks of off-loaded crates, Hilton checked crate markers against his list, filling out his tally sheet. Almost there. Less than two columns left to check, and he had hit a good grouping, the crates on this aisle seemed to have been stacked in order by accident. It didn't always turn out that way. Hilton had almost wondered if someone had jumbled the crates on him on purpose, earlier in the day, as part of a scheme of petty harassment or something—or maybe it was just a form of hazing, on the part of the crew.

Or maybe there was no intention to blame for the confusion at all, and that had just been the way the crates had stacked. It didn't matter. He was almost done. And he got paid for his overtime, so he had nothing to complain about.

He stopped at the end of one long row of crates to tilt his tally sheet to the light and check his figures; and then he heard something.

It was dead quiet in this part of the warehouse complex; there was no wind that night, and while the raw construction did creak and moan a bit while the temperature fell at sunset, what he thought he could hear was not the groaning of a growing building talking to itself but someone talking to himself.

Or at least someone talking.

Raising his head to cast about for the direction of the sound, Hilton thought quickly, his heart beating faster with involuntary excitement.

There was nobody there.

No one was on shift for cargo handling. He made up the shift roster himself in Dalmoss's absence. He knew. Not even he was scheduled to be there, but he was running late; on any normal day he would have left the area, hours ago.

Someone talking.

Hilton opened his mouth to give a hallo, then closed it again.

No one was supposed to be there; and the sound didn't quite seem like a normal conversation, somehow, it seemed to be near whispered. As though someone was telling secrets.

He couldn't see anything out of the ordinary down the long row of crates in either direction; but he thought he could get closer to the sound he heard. He had plenty of shadows to help him out. The lighting was still strictly minimal, and so far overhead that the cavernous deeps between rows of crates were almost as good as a shield against detection—so long as a man walked carefully, holding his tally board close so that any telltale glare off the document screen would remain hidden.

Whispering.

At the far end of the next row, at the back of the stacks, next to the rear wall that separated the warehouse from the back end of the administrative offices.

Hilton moved slowly and carefully through the shadows, keeping his breath quiet and his movement smooth.

He reached the far end of the back stacks, and when he bent his head—carefully, carefully—around the corner of the crates that ended the row, Hilton heard the voices quite distinctly.

Buyer at Kansin, especially the larger pieces. Guaranteed.

The speaker wasn't at the back of the row where Hilton was standing, but appeared to be at the back of the next row; so that only the width of the aisle and that of the row itself stood between them, and Hilton had the shadows in his favor.

Lost the better part of our last take. Boss isn't very happy about that. Not happen again.

He couldn't hear everything. Bits and pieces of the words were lost in the great hush of the warehouse, muffled by absorption by the bulk of the stacked crates. What he could hear electrified him.

Shut us down sooner or later. Honan-gung. While we can. The arrangements.

Hilton eased his body carefully around the corner of the stack of crates and peered into the darkness across the circle, hoping that the whites of his eyes would not catch the light. Two people. One of them talking. The outlines were indistinct, and the voice was oddly muted or muffled. He had to get closer to hear what they were talking about. To hear the details, because it was clear enough to Hilton what they were talking about.

He had to know who they were.

While we can still blame Langsariks. Can't have very much longer. One month, two months, tops.

Measuring the distance carefully in his mind, Hilton crouched down slowly to set the tally board on the ground. He could clear the space between them in four paces. He would have the advantage of surprise. He could get one of them, at least, and then they'd have a good chance of finding out what had been going on all of these weeks at Port Charid.

The tally board made no sound as he set it down.

But something alerted the whisperers regardless.

Hilton gathered up his energy to make his move, but one of them pushed the other suddenly.

Run.

He sprinted after them furiously, but they had a head start on him. They were both good runners. They had the darkness on their side.

Hilton followed the sound of footfalls as fast as he could run, spurred on by desperate fear of losing this chance; but the rows and rows of crates echoed the sound and confused the track, and Hilton had to stop at last and admit it to himself.

He'd lost them.

He'd had them within his grasp, and he had lost them, but he could go to the authorities and tell them . . .

Tell them what?

That he had heard someone plotting a raid, someone who took the blame for previous raids and exonerated the Langsariks by implication?

He couldn't even go to the authorities. Maybe they wouldn't laugh in his face, but there was no hope that they would take him seriously. He wouldn't take himself seriously, in their position.

He needed more information.

Slowly, Hilton worked his way back to where he'd been to find his tally sheet. He would come back with a light and check the area, but he didn't have much hope of finding anything.

He had the tally to complete.

If a raid was being plotted, and the conspirators had met among the stacks of cargo to confer, some one or more people who worked in the warehouse were in on it.

Not Langsariks. No Langsarik would have risked compromising the settlement by missing report in these troubled times.

There were other people on the various construction crews, and someone would give him a signal sooner or later. They didn't know how much he'd heard. They couldn't know. They'd think he'd just happened on them, and knew nothing.

He would be watching.

He wouldn't rest until he had information that would give the Bench specialist who had come to end the raids the hard facts he would need to find the damned pirates, and punish them for murderers.

Kazmer had no documentation to show; the Bench had everything that the freighter had been carrying when it had been impounded at Anglace.

He didn't need documentation.

"I was here not long before the raid on the Tyrell Yards," he explained to the man behind the counter. "I've shaved my beard since, but I was with my principal. Noman, his name was. We came for a freighter tender to move some grain out of atmosphere, do you remember? The freighter tender was just being released to service after maintenance."

The man behind the counter kept his face carefully expressionless. "I can't say that I do remember any such thing." No, of course he couldn't, especially not knowing exactly who Vogel—beside Kazmer, but ever so slightly in the background—might be. Vogel was not in uniform, but it wasn't a good time to trust strangers in Port Charid, especially not in seedy little third-rate freighter brokerages like this one.

"I'll tell you one thing, though," the man behind the counter said, turning and reaching behind him for a ledger portfolio. "All of our activity is fully documented. Correctly documented. Anything we do we get proper clearance for. See for yourself, maybe you can answer your own question."

Whatever that might be.

"I expect the records all got a pretty good going-over, after the last raid," Vogel said in a genial and conversational tone, stepping up to the counter. "More excitement than anyone really needs, if you ask me." Vogel had turned to the section in the portfolio where the hard-copy requisition documents were kept. The ones that showed original approvals for release of transport.

The man behind the counter was too suspicious to allow himself to be drawn into the complicity of complaint. "We have nothing to hide, and it's just what must be done. Our books are always open."

There it was—the release order Noman had brought to this broker to obtain the security keys to the freighter tender Kazmer had piloted through atmosphere to rendezvous with the freighter they'd taken to the Tyrell Yards.

Vogel pulled the document away from its secures and laid it on the counter, turning to the back of the portfolio where the receipts would be kept. "Nice release seal here," Vogel said, tapping the mark. "Combine Yards. Fisner Feraltz, that's his mark, isn't it? I suppose you've already had this run through authentication."

The man behind the counter was agitated, but still wary. "No, why should we? There's been no challenge. No question. What do you think you're doing?"

Vogel had completed the hand receipt and passed it across to the man behind the counter. "I'm taking this document. You'll initial, of course, as witnessing that all the information is correctly filled out? Thank you. Oh. Here. Have a look at this."

Kazmer couldn't tell exactly where Vogel got it, but Vogel was holding a little flat chop in his left hand. Could have been up his sleeve. On his chrono. Behind a button. Anything. "Bench special evidence sigil, there. This one's genuine." Vogel set chop to receipt, and the electronic traces of the microcircuitry it embedded in the fibers of the document's matrix glittered unnervingly in the flat light of the little front office.

Vogel folded the freighter-tender release and tucked it into an inner pocket somewhere. "If you're lucky, you'll never see another one like it. Thank you for your time."

So they were leaving.

The man behind the counter was holding the receipt up to the light, staring at the seal Vogel had set upon it. Kazmer closed the office door behind him quietly, reluctant to interrupt the man's awestruck concentration.

Vogel was standing with his arms folded, looking at people in the street. "That little courier," Vogel said. That was right; he'd told Vogel about the Langsariks' escape craft, the one with the contraband communications equipment. "Was that on the freighter tender? Or on the freighter you joined?"

"We transferred it with the grain," Kazmer replied promptly. "And carrying battle cannon, they said? The freighter tender's fuel burn did seem a little odd, now that I think of it. But I was thinking about other things."

Vogel nodded. "It'd have to be a sweet little piece of machinery to carry battle cannon. I wonder whose it is."

Kazmer knew.

But he'd almost reconciled himself to the fact that nobody would believe him.

It didn't matter so much in the end if they believed him about the Angel. Most of the rest of the Combine had never believed Sarvaw about the Angel anyway; it was hard for people to face the fact that such atrocities occurred. What mattered first and foremost was only convincing the authorities that whatever was going on in Port Charid was not the doing of Langsariks breaching the terms of their amnesty agreement. If only that point got through, the Angel could go diddle itself blind, with Kazmer's heartfelt blessing.

"Well, let's go see whether Feraltz has any insight on this. It appears to be his chop. Let's go visit the foreman, Daigule. Come on. Maybe could learn something."

But Vogel didn't start back toward the business district of Port Charid.

Vogel signaled for an auto-rent vehicle instead, and told the navigation unit—once he and Kazmer had gotten in—that he wanted to go out to the new con-

struction south of Port Charid, where the Combine
interests were building a new cargo-handling facility.

"Heard Feraltz was out on-site by default when I
ran into him yesterday at the Factor's office," Vogel
explained, once the vehicle was under way. "Lots of
activity out there. Probably best if we don't call him
away from his job."

Probably best if they caught him off guard and by
surprise, Kazmer decided. Vogel had no reason Kazmer
could imagine for suspecting Fisner Feraltz of anything; it was probably just second nature for Vogel to
plan to his advantage.

Kazmer had reasons to suspect Madlev's foreman,
whether or not anyone would countenance them.

Madlev's foreman was Dolgorukij, and the Angel of
Destruction was made up of Dolgorukij.

Madlev's foreman had been at the Okidan Yards
and lived to tell the tale, as well: surely that could be
suspicious in and of itself. The people who had done
the murders Kazmer had seen at Tyrell Yards were
not the kind to leave a man wounded but still alive
to call for help.

In fact it was suspicious.

Wasn't it?

Or was his dread and horror of the Angel of Destruction poisoning his mind, so that he saw the enemy
around every corner?

Fisner Feraltz struggled to his feet gamely as Garol
was announced at his office door in the administrative
area of the new warehouse facility. Garol could appreciate the effort it took; still, a man learned to work
with his bracing. So he'd been told. Wanting to get as
fresh a reaction as possible, Garol reached into his
jacket's inner pocket as he entered the room, shaking
the document free of its folds to set it down directly
on the foreman's desk.

"Good-greeting, nice to see you," Garol said
briskly, though he wasn't all that interested in being

polite. Feraltz's maneuvers to be present at Garol's report to First Secretary Verlaine yesterday had annoyed him; they had also raised questions in his mind. "Have a look at this for me. Your mark, here?"

There was no reason to suppose that Feraltz had anything against Langsariks, and every reason to suppose the contrary. Feraltz had certainly given an excellent impression of a man wishing to avoid the appearance of implicating the Langsariks for the Okidan raid. Too good an impression was suspicious in and of itself. Wasn't it just that touch too convenient that Fisner Feraltz had been Okidan's sole survivor—the sole survivor of any of these raids to date?

Precisely how had Feraltz survived the Okidan raid?

"It looks like my mark," Feraltz agreed, readily enough. "But here. For the record." He sat back down, carefully. Garol watched him sit back down. He didn't think Feraltz moved like a man fully accustomed to his bracing; and there was no possible reason Garol could think of for so ungracious a thought but sheer contrariness on his part.

Feraltz pulled out the chop that he wore on a chain around his neck and keyed its confirm mode before he held it to the chop mark on the document.

The chop jumped in Feraltz's hand, its static charge registering rejection of the chop mark on the document.

Feraltz frowned.

Pulling a ledger board from a side table, Feraltz leafed through the document originals until he found what he was looking for. Setting the open ledger board down on the desk beside the document Garol had brought, Feraltz keyed the confirm code on his chop again and held it to the chop mark on the document original in the ledger board.

The chop sang out its confirm code, shrill and self-confident. So Feraltz moved it over to the document Garol had brought once more, slowly, as if not to interrupt the microcomputer's concentration.

The chop shut up abruptly and bucked in Feraltz's hand.

"Interesting," Garol agreed, but he was not about to take Feraltz's word for it, and held out his hand for the chop. Feraltz passed it to him willingly, which told Garol all he needed to know; but he went through the motions anyway, comparing the chop to one or two other chop marks on document originals in the ledger board, then back to the one on the document he'd removed from the broker's office.

The chop mark on the document that had been on file in the broker's office was not genuine.

Forged.

"Any surrogate chops authorized?" Garol asked, passing Feraltz's chop back. He didn't have much hope of it, really, so it didn't disappoint him when Feraltz shook his head.

"None authorized, Bench specialist. I leave this one with Dalmoss whenever I leave Port Charid just so we don't get into that situation. Sorry. Is it important?"

Feraltz knew it was important.

Garol was increasingly convinced of that fact.

But he had nothing on which to base his suspicions. "Maybe. Hard to tell. Where is Dalmoss, by the way."

Dalmoss had the chop while Feraltz was away from Port Charid, so Dalmoss had it when the Tyrell raid was being planned. Maybe. Had Feraltz been back to Port Charid by then? He could find out—but he didn't feel like simply asking, he was frustrated and starting to feel like somebody was leading him on a merry chase.

Some Dolgorukij.

Feraltz?

Or the Malcontent?

Garol had already marked out a block of time in his mental scheduler for when this was all over, in which to become deeply disturbed about the Malcontent. People like Cousin Stanoczk didn't come up out of nowhere. If there were more like him at home, there was trouble in store for the Jurisdiction's Bench when the day came that the Dolgorukij Combine decided to flex its economic muscle.

"Gone to Geraint on a special assignment," Feraltz answered, sounding apologetic. "Sorry. We could call him back if you needed him, Bench specialist."

No, he'd have someone speak to Dalmoss at Geraint.

And he needed to get an analysis of the forged chop on the freighter tender's release document. Folding the document carefully, Garol tucked it away once more. "Quite all right. Thank you for your time, Foreman, I'll see myself out."

What was the wilder claim?

That some ancient secret terrorist society was resurgent at Port Charid for no better reason than to destroy the Langsarik settlement?

Or that a man who owed his life to the Langsariks should be involved in planning a frame so massive and ornate that it staggered the imagination—and was willing to countenance the torture killing of sixteen upon sixteen of souls just to pin the blame on his once-benefactors?

Garol had seen irrational behavior before in his life. But there was something going on here that was beyond irrational.

It was going to be that much more difficult to make sense of it; and if he could not make sense of it, the Langsariks were doomed.

Hilton Shires came across the corner of the administrative complex at one end of the new warehouse facility with his checklist in his hand, intent on getting through the morning's receipts by the end of his shift. He was tired, but he was beginning to feel as though he understood what he was doing and why he was doing it the way he'd been taught. That was a good feeling. If it hadn't been for the problems that faced his family—his immediate family, along with all of the rest of the Langsariks—he would have enjoyed the learning in its own right.

As it was he could not relax and concentrate on inventory management.

It had been three days since he'd overheard someone plotting an attack, and he had nothing to show for his after-hours sleuthing but frustration and anxiety.

Halfway into the administrative area Hilton happened to look up from the tally screen in his hand to check on his exact location, so as to avoid knocking into people, to be avoided if possible even when he was in a hurry. But there was someone there.

Looked familiar.

A man standing outside the doorway into the administrative offices where Hilton kept a desk just inside. Not wearing a warehouseman's coveralls; leaning up against the inner wall with his arms folded and his head bent in evident study of the industrial flooring and the unfinished trim.

Looking for a job?

Waiting for someone.

And it looked a lot like Kazmer Daigule, but it couldn't be. Kazmer had been captured off an impounded freighter at Anglace, and stolen cargo taken from Tyrell with him. So clearly Kazmer could not possibly be here, free and whole, and waiting for someone outside the administrative offices of the warehouse facility.

"Can I help you."

Hilton raised his voice and hailed the waiting man, closing the distance between them as he spoke. He got more, and not less, confused as he came closer; because the man looked up at the sound of Hilton's voice, and it kept on looking so much like Kazmer Daigule that Hilton was beginning to really puzzle how it could possibly not be.

"The Bench specialist. Said you had something to give to me, Hilton."

Sounded like Kazmer, or like what Kazmer might

sound like if his voice was being slowly strangled in the grip of some strong emotion or another. No, it made no sense. How did this person know Hilton's name? The reference to a Bench specialist was worrying—

"Sorry, help me out here."

It couldn't be Kazmer.

It was.

There couldn't be two people in the world with that exact same nose. Hilton stood and stared, stammering in his confusion. "Where did you come—how did you get—"

Kazmer looked awful: pale, worn, skinny. But it was Kazmer Daigule. "Long story," Kazmer said, his voice resonant with suppressed emotion. "Boring plot, though. I'm here with Specialist Vogel, you know him? He said."

Whatever it was that had happened to Kazmer it was terrible. The ferocious impact of Kazmer's fiercely contained grief was staggering.

Hilton thought fast.

Kazmer had been in Port Charid just before the Tyrell raid. Modice had been worried enough about what Kazmer might have been doing here that she'd used the Bench specialist to carry a message to Hilton, one that served as a warning. But something was wrong—if Kazmer actually had been compromised in the Tyrell raid, he would not be here now. But if he was free and clear of suspicion, what was the source of his evident anguish?

"Not on me, I'm afraid. The scarf. The sash. Whatever." He'd been afraid to carry it, for fear of genetic damage from corrosive radiation. A pattern like that was too perfectly awful to be truly harmless. "If you can tell me where you're lodging this time, I can bring it."

There had to be more at issue than the scarf. Kazmer seemed near tears; and while Kazmer was an emotional man, he'd never struck Hilton as maudlin.

"Perhaps it's best if you just destroyed it, then, Hilton. A Malcontent has no personal possessions. And as much as I owe Cousin Stanoczk already, the additional burden of dealing with that scarf might be too much."

What was this, "Malcontent"?

Who was Cousin Stanoczk, and what did Kazmer owe him?

"Then what would happen?" He had too many questions, and Kazmer was clearly not going to answer any of them. It made Hilton a little angry, but in a sad way. He'd thought Kazmer was his friend. "You brought the thing for my innocent little cousin. If it's really so toxic as all that, what possessed you to give her the wretched cloth in the first place?"

"It was a joke," Kazmer said, and the depth of sorrow that the simple phrase carried into Hilton's heart hit him like a fist. "Just for fun. And if I try Cousin Stanoczk's patience, he might just cancel his protection, I suppose. Then it would be back to Anglace for me, and Ship's Inquisitor Andrej Koscuisko asking questions about the Tyrell raid, and who did I see at Port Charid, and could Langsariks have been involved. And what were their names. And murder done, Hilton; I didn't really believe it till I saw it for myself, but what difference does it make?"

The words came almost too relentlessly once they started coming. Concerned already, Hilton felt his face drain white with the shock of what Kazmer was telling him as Kazmer continued.

"I know Langsariks would never do that. I know that now. Langsariks were never involved from the beginning. It was all a setup. But it doesn't make any difference, I'm telling you. I thought it would help if I cried for the Malcontent, if I didn't give evidence. It hasn't helped. Stanoczk would rather it was Langsariks than who it is. The fix is too good. Nobody believes me, Hilton, nobody believes us; gather everyone you can and get out of here—get out of here now—"

Someone was coming out of the administrative area, and Kazmer mastered himself with an obvious effort. Bench specialist. Hilton recognized him.

"Good-greeting." Vogel nodded cheerfully to Hilton; if he'd heard any of Kazmer's mad spate, he gave no sign. "Well. No help there, unless that's help. Let's go out to the settlement, Shires, I'd like a word with your aunt. Care to join us?"

He couldn't possibly. He wasn't finished with what he wanted to get done today, and he didn't know how the foreman felt about floor managers absenting themselves on personal business in the middle of the day— regardless of whose suggestion it had been. Trying to put some polite words together, Hilton shook his head.

"I'd really like to, Bench specialist, but there's inventory yet to log, and—"

Vogel took Hilton by the arm and started toward the nearest exit door. "Good, good. Glad to hear it. The scheduled inventory will still be here, won't it? No freighter tenders for load-out tonight? Just work with me here, Shires, I'm not in a very good mood."

Oh.

Well.

If that was the way Vogel wanted it.

There was a hired vehicle on standby outside the warehouse; Vogel took the lever to guide the vehicle off the grounds, scowling in deep concentration. Or simply scowling. Once they'd cleared the construction site Hilton spoke; he knew how to defer to authority, he knew Vogel had authority, but Vogel's rather high-handed behavior had got Hilton's Langsarik up.

"I have a job." Maybe Vogel didn't understand how unusual that was—for Hilton to admit it, anyway. "I have responsibilities. There's no cost objective supported by home visits on duty hours. I expect a note for my foreman, at the very least."

Vogel didn't answer him directly.

He pulled off the roadway instead and turned

around to face Daigule in the passenger compartment behind him.

"We have to figure out how to get it to make a difference."

What?

Kazmer just stared, and Hilton had no clue for his own part.

"I believe you, Daigule. I don't know about Cousin Stanoczk, but you convinced me. That means we have a serious problem, because the First Secretary can't take a hunch and a conviction to his Judge, and murder's been done. As you said."

Vogel had heard Kazmer, or at least enough of what Kazmer had been saying. Kazmer leaned forward and took the seat rail in his hands, as though to steady himself.

"They'll come for Hilton." What was Kazmer talking about? "They'll come for Modice. You know they will. We can't let it happen. We've got to do something."

As if Kazmer believed all the stories he'd ever heard about Bench specialists.

As if Kazmer believed that Vogel could set the Bench to rights by saying so.

"I don't know what we can do." It was too bad. Vogel didn't seem to have heard half the stories about Bench intelligence specialists that Kazmer seemed to have; he didn't sound the least bit confident.

Vogel being not confident was the worst thing Hilton could imagine there and then, with Kazmer Daigule in the car, once it was clear that Hilton understood what Kazmer was afraid of and how close they were to unimaginable disaster.

Kazmer was right.

They *would* come for Modice.

He would kill her first. Then at least it would be clean, and quick—

"Hilton's taking us home to visit with Agenis. I need you to go ask Cousin Stanoczk for a favor for

me, so say what you need to say to Modice; she's
worried you got mixed up in Tyrell, and you owe her
an explanation. Hilton. Kazmer says it's Dolgorukij
behind all this. I need to understand how it's managed,
where they're hiding the communications equipment,
what they're going to do next. We don't have much
time."

Should he tell Vogel about what he'd heard?

"No help from the foreman?" Kazmer asked. It was
as though there was so much to say, and so much to
think about, that he could only deal with the most
immediate issue. "You were hoping."

Vogel shook his head, steering the vehicle back out
into the roadway. There wasn't much traffic going out
to the settlement, mostly just the occasional delivery
truck with stock for the small convenience store. "The
chop was forged. Maybe Dalmoss knows about a du-
plicate, but Dalmoss has gone to Geraint, which is
why I need Cousin Stanoczk to get to Dalmoss as soon
as possible. Dead end. But I think he knows more
than he's saying."

"Forged chop?" Hilton asked, startled out of conservative silence. "What chop is that?" He had the
chop Dalmoss had left with him. He had it around his
neck, as a matter of fact.

Vogel drummed his fingers against the steering lever
thoughtfully. "Used to release the freighter tender to
leave Port Charid with Daigule as pilot," Vogel said.
"Right, Daigule? Claims to be Combine Yards. What,
do you know something?"

Hilton felt sick to his stomach. It couldn't be the
same one. Why would Dalmoss be connected with
warehouse invasions? That was like parricide, in a
way. Dalmoss was a floor manager. "Dalmoss gave it
to me before he left, said it was his backup document-
release marker, but he'd never gotten around to getting the authorizations all cleared. I didn't think the
Bench expected Langsariks to be handling such things,

but Dalmoss said it was all right so long as I didn't use it."

It had been a weak argument at the time, and it sounded weaker now. The outbuildings of the settlement were coming up fast; they were nearly there.

Slowing the vehicle to a crawl between residence buildings, Vogel frowned at the roadway, apparently considering what Hilton had to say.

"And we have only your word that you were given the chop." Vogel was thinking the grim equation through, from all appearances. "It's a setup ripe and rectified. Give me the chop, Hilton, and don't say anything to anybody. I've got to brief your aunt, I'll let her know."

Hilton pulled the chop out from beneath his inner shirt, jerking at the chain impatiently. "What does it mean, Bench specialist?"

"Until we find more real evidence, it means nothing." Vogel tucked the wretched thing away in a trouser pocket. Hilton could only hope Vogel's pockets were in better repair than his own tended to be. "Daigule, keep it short, I need you back to Port Charid before too much longer. Let's go."

The midnight meeting he might have mentioned to Vogel had gone out of his mind, the warehouse whispers drowned beneath the crushing impact of this horrible realization.

Set up.

They were using him.

And all this time he'd thought that he'd actually been doing rather well.

He needed some private time to wrestle his emotions to the ground; and then he had to get back to work.

Part of the job was being able to do it without getting emotionally involved, but Garol had given up on that almost as soon as this Langsarik trouble had started. It wasn't getting any easier as he went along.

"I've been to Tyrell, and I brought Daigule back with me." Garol realized that he was skipping the normal courtesy of a greeting; Hilton's news had rattled him more deeply than he'd realized. Or else it was just that feeling that he got with Walton Agenis, of never actually ending a conversation, just picking up the threads after a longer than usual pause. "Daigule and I know where some of the transport may have come from, but it isn't enough."

Walton Agenis eyed Daigule a little sourly, but stood aside to let Modice through from the back of the house. "Come into the parlor," she suggested. "You can tell me all about it." It wasn't so much an offer as a demand, but she had a right. Garol followed her into the house without argument, leaving Daigule to speak to Modice at the front door—or not-speak to Modice. Whatever. Garol didn't care. He had other problems.

"All of the markers keep pointing back at Langsariks." Once the door was closed behind him he couldn't keep his anxiety to himself any longer, talking to Walton's back as he followed her through the cramped hall into the tiny front room with its three chairs and its one small incidental table. No lamp. There was a fixture overhead, but the dim light was almost worse than no light at all, to someone coming in from the bright sunlight outside. "But Daigule was there. He says fourteen, sixteen people at least, and the raid covered more than half a day's time. So if it was Langsariks, how'd they make muster?"

There were chairs, but Walton didn't sit down; nor did she invite Garol to be seated—not because he was unwelcome, Garol sensed, so much as that she was thinking too hard about his question. So he stood. Walton Agenis faced the blank wall at the south side of the small room, talking to the paint.

"We could find a way, Garol. But we haven't. We agreed to the amnesty, we mean to honor it." It was good of her to use the present tense, Garol felt;

"mean," not "meant." The Langsariks hadn't given up on Jurisdiction. But he was almost ready to. "Is this the first time that any cargo has been intercepted?"

Garol nodded. "Right. There was an anonymous tip." Such things happened often enough; there was no reason to suspect it. Except that he was suspecting everything just now. "Jils has gone back to Anglace to run it down."

Someone had recruited Daigule, who knew Hilton. Maybe it had been a setup all along, and the cargo had been sacrificed to get Daigule's evidence of Langsarik involvement on Record—it wasn't the most valuable portion of the take that had been intercepted. Daigule's evidence was not on record; but Garol had the inside line on a forged seal, now, and Hilton had been holding it. The fix was so good.

"So, where's the other ship. They've got to be hiding those cannon somewhere. Probably illegal communications as well, for false positive identification." She'd spent a lot of time worrying that issue on her own, apparently. "But the traffic in and out of Port Charid is all freighter-driven. Very few craft as small as yours or that Dolgorukij's."

Few enough that Agenis had satisfied herself that the raider wasn't coming and going, apparently. "So the cannon are parked somewhere," Garol agreed. "We just need to find out where in the Shawl they are. Easy."

No, impossible. Locating something as small as a hardened courier with all of the space in the Shawl to cover would take a Fleet sweeps team a year or more, and Garol didn't have a year.

Walton shrugged, but it wasn't so much a gesture of dismissal as of frustrated despair. "Port Charid isn't staffed for long-term investigations, Garol. Everyone knows it's Langsariks. After a while that'll be all that matters. What are we going to do?"

She was not merely asking him to suggest a course of action. She was challenging him to make it right.

He'd promised her fair play, and she'd believed him; and based on his promise and her decision to trust his word, she had put the lives of five thousand Langsariks into the hands of the Bench here at Port Charid.

The Bench had other priorities than fair play.

The Bench could afford to sacrifice five thousand people to the rule of Law, especially if the public destruction of five thousand people would preserve civil order and prevent eventual disturbances that could easily cost far more lives over time.

The Langsariks were not very important lives when it came down to that. They had lived apart from their system of origin for more than fifteen years, they had become an embarrassment to the planetary government of Palaam. There would not even be much of an outcry.

Of course that was what the Bench had thought about the Nurail; and that had proved to be a miscalculation.

"We have another alternative."

It wasn't thinking of Nurail that gave Garol the idea. It was thinking of Langsariks

Walton turned around to face him. "I'm listening."

Garol spoke slowly, feeling his way. "If we can find a way to force the enemy out into the open, we don't need to find the cannon—they'll bring the cannon to us."

It wasn't a very good strategy, but it was all he had. As he spoke, however, Walton's eyes sparked with a sudden understanding that heartened him.

"Entrapment," Walton said, with a cheerful bloodlust in her voice. "I like it. It means holding out till frustration gets the better of the enemy, though, and he does something stupid. And if we can't straighten this out soon, the Bench will conclude that we've violated the amnesty, Garol."

He knew that.

"We'd better get it straightened out, then. I'll get a target analysis started. You get a list of places at Port

Charid where I could hide a hardened sixteen-soul scout with the spine to deploy battle cannon. We don't have very much time."

He didn't know how much time there was. He only knew there couldn't be much more of it. The fiasco at the Domitt Prison would only increase Chilleau Judiciary's conviction that a satisfactory ending to the predation at Port Charid had to be demonstrated in a timely manner—whether or not it had any necessary resemblance to reality.

"Not good enough."

Walton Agenis rejected his facile response. Garol didn't respect her less for it; she was Flag Captain Walton Agenis, and she was responsible for her people. "Solving the problem is all very well and good, Specialist Vogel, but you've been working on it for ten days now and you haven't solved it yet. I need a contingency plan. What are we going to do if the problem does not get solved? Your suggestions, please."

He didn't have any.

If he couldn't convince First Secretary Verlaine that the Langsariks were not in flagrant and egregious violation of the amnesty agreement, the Bench would send the fleet to collect the entire population for processing: penal servitude at best—a death sentence, for those members of the Langsarik fleet who were no longer young—and the Bond at worst.

He had no contingency plans to offer.

He hated having to admit that.

"What was your contingency plan if the amnesty negotiations had fallen through, back when?"

Why couldn't he admit it to her, and leave her to factors more powerful than the will of one man to resist them? The rule of Law was the cause to which he had dedicated his life, and the rule of Law was not always fair or just.

But she had trusted him.

The confidence of a leader of the caliber of Flag

Captain Walton Agenis was too precious to be allowed to slip away from him without a fight.

She made a show of thinking about it, and maybe she was calling some previously discarded alternative to mind. "Once the planetary government had denounced us we were running out of options fast. I'll grant you that."

That had been the death blow, though like many mortal blows its full impact had been felt only gradually.

In the beginning the Langsarik fleet had fought for recognition as a planetary defense fleet, in the face of the Bench's insistence that the existing fleet of Palaam's historical economic-competitor worlds be recognized as having lawful jurisdiction over. Palaamese commerce. As long as the Langsarik fleet could hope for recognition they could look forward to the day when their cause would be won and they could return home as lawful citizens.

But once the newly installed puppet government of Palaam had formally repudiated the Langsarik resistance, they had no basis for a claim to armed resistance against an unfair and unacceptable imposition.

What else could the Langsarik fleet have done but seek an amnesty?

Walton Agenis politely declined to state the obvious, out of respect for Garol's position; but Garol knew the answer.

The Langsarik fleet could have continued to operate as an outlawed gang of thieves, facing capture and death on all sides and slowly dying of attrition until they grew too weak to run and could be captured, tried, sentenced.

Or the Langsarik fleet could have made a break for Gonebeyond space and tried to escape from Jurisdiction entirely. Now they could not do even that, desperate though it was.

The Langsariks no longer commanded the transport they would need to escape.

Had it been some subtle form of cruelty to place them at Port Charid, with the Sillume Vector so close—and yet so absolutely inaccessible?

"We'll find the raiders. We've got to. Let me know if someone comes up with a line on anything, anything at all. There are a Langsarik and a Dolgorukij still missing."

The longer he stood here casting about him for solutions, the more depressingly clear it became that there simply weren't any.

Walton Agenis nodded. "I will if you will, Specialist Vogel."

Bowing to take his leave, Garol turned around and left the room.

He had to get back to Port Charid.

If he couldn't solve this problem, more than just Walton Agenis would have just cause to regret that they had ever trusted in his word.

The Bench specialist went into the house with Flag Captain Walton; Hilton made himself scarce. Kazmer stood to one side of the front door with Modice in the doorway, wondering what there was that he could possibly say.

There was no question in his mind that anything he had done to protect her was the right thing, and only what he would do again and again and again if he had to. But the price—which had been difficult enough to accept when he had faced impending disaster at Anglace—was almost intolerable to contemplate now that he stood face-to-face with Modice Agenis, and her looking up into his face with faith and trust and anxious concern in her beautiful dark eyes.

"Hello, Modice, how are you?"

He'd expected never to see her again. He'd reconciled himself to never seeing her again. He could think of nothing intelligent to say. There was so much he had to tell her, and so much more that he dared not so much as hint at.

"I've been worried about you, Kazmer. There was the Tyrell raid, and you hadn't said anything about your cargo."

Direct and straight to the point. He could hardly bear it; his nerves were already raw with emotion. "But then you heard that there was killing, right? And you knew I'd never do such a thing."

He was lying to her. To Modice. What did he think he was doing? He was trying anything to escape connection with the raid in her eyes. Coward that he was. He couldn't lie to Modice. What difference did it make? He belonged to the Malcontent now. Malcontents couldn't marry, and some of them liked boys. The thought of some trifling liaison with Modice was unthinkable. She was too precious to be anything but a first, an only, a sacred wife.

Modice frowned, but her gaze didn't waver. "I was afraid you'd gotten mixed up in something that would get you into trouble. Why did you come back to Port Charid, Kazmer?"

Yes, what difference did it make? Her good opinion of him was immaterial now; so what could be the use of trying to maintain that good opinion, by lying to her? Better if he told her the truth, and let her despise him. Maybe that was it. Let Modice despise him; and then it would not make so much difference that he could never marry.

"It's a long story. But I'll summarize. I thought Langsariks were hiring me to pilot a freighter with stolen goods. Yes. It was Tyrell. Only one thing, Modice, if you ever loved me. If you ever thought that you could have loved me maybe if I wasn't so big and clumsy and stupid, and not Langsarik."

She slapped him.

Hard, and across the face, and there was a surprising amount of force behind the flat of Modice's beautiful white hand. Her once-white hand, tanned from working in the garden. He caught her hand as she raised it against him for a second time, and stared at it dumbly. Her fingernails were worn from physical labor, her knuckles roughened from work. Modice. Work.

"How dare you say such a thing to me." She was so angry with him that she almost wept; he heard the quivering in her voice. "How dare you."

He was at fault for his impertinence. She was right. He could claim some measure of affection from her, as due an acquaintance who adored her; it was improper to even hint at anything more.

"I'm sorry." His face stung where she'd struck him. "It's only this, Modice. They were all alive when I left them. I swear it, Modice, by everything I ever loved. Those people. They were alive."

"All right," Modice said. "But take that back. About being clumsy and stupid. No, you're not Langsarik, but that's not a crime. Take it back, Kazmer."

How could she even speak of two such disparate things in one breath? "It's true. It's important to me. Please. Say that you believe me, Modice. I'll never see you again. Maybe." Kazmer added the qualification hastily; he didn't want to extract her word with an appeal for charity, as a sort of parting gift.

"I believe you about the Tyrell raid." She seemed almost bitterly unwilling to admit it; or else she was still angry at him about something. "You're not a liar, Kazmer. You're just wrong about some things. What are you going to do now?"

Did she really believe him?

What was she talking about, wrong about some things?

"I'm probably going to Azanry. I guess. I don't know, it isn't up to me anymore, I've—taken holy orders. Hilton can just throw the scarf away, it's okay."

Holy orders. Well, he guessed that technically speaking the election of the Malcontent was just that. He wore the crimson cord around his neck; he stood outside the reach of Combine common law and Jurisdiction civil prosecution alike. Because he was answerable to a much stricter rule of obedience and submission.

"Is that the reason you haven't been back? I told you. To the front door. And to bring a gift for my aunt."

If he thought hard, Kazmer could almost remember her telling him that. It seemed so long ago that he'd seen her last that he could hardly believe it had been weeks, instead of years.

"I've been in custody. And then once I got out I had to do as Cousin Stanoczk said. So I guess that's the reason. Yes."

"And you say you'll never see me again. That's the reason for that, too."

Yes. "I was part of it, Modice, even though I didn't know they would kill those people. I was the one that promised the others that it wasn't going to be like Okidan, that the people we were dealing with were Langsariks, and Langsariks didn't do things like that. I've done wrong. I have to make it up."

As Kazmer said it something lifted in his heart, and opened his eyes.

He had done wrong.

He was obliged for reparations.

All of this time he had been so shocked at how wrong the raid had gone, so worried that he would implicate innocent Langsariks by default, so set on insisting that he had not done murder that he had not faced the truth that his heart knew.

His heart knew that whether or not he had meant it, whether or not he had been duped, whether or not he had been lied to, he shared the guilt for Tyrell Yards.

He had not been the one to cause the horror, but he had been part of making it happen. He owed the dead a contrite reckoning for his role—howsoever indirect—in their atrocious deaths.

He had not thrown his life away for nothing.

If he hadn't called for Cousin Stanoczk, if the Inquisitor had taken his testimony, his evidence would have been used against Hilton and the Langsariks. He would not have seen what he had seen of the carnage at the Tyrell Yards. He would not have understood that he was guilty of a crime for which atonement was necessary and required; he might well have died in willful denial of any guilt for the murders done at Tyrell.

Then the reckoning that was to come would have taken place in some other form, in some other mode of existence, when he would no longer have any understanding of why it was appropriate for him to suffer punishment.

"Well, tell Hilton," Modice said, and Kazmer remembered where he was. "He can bring the scarf back to me. If it's the last I'm to see of you. If you were part of it, you did wrong, maybe, but not murder. Oh. I'll miss you, Kazmer."

She wasn't angry at him, Kazmer realized.

She was fond of him. And grieved.

Clutching the front of Kazmer's blouse to her, Modice wept. Kazmer put his arms around the priceless treasure of her body and rocked her gently, too confused by conflicting emotions to have anything to say.

She had it exactly right.

He had not done murder, but he had done wrong.

She was a genius. As well as beautiful.

It was a good thing he'd brought that night-courting gift after all, because as garish as it was, she would have to smile in rueful disgust every time she thought of it or him.

There were worse ways to be remembered.

Chapter Eight

"There are security monitors in place at the Honangung Yards, firstborn and eldest," Dalmoss said respectfully. "The evidence of atrocity will be that much more persuasive. But we will have to be sure that our performance is flawless."

It was very early in the morning. The administrative offices in the new warehouse facility were still deserted; that was the only reason that Fisner could afford to speak to Dalmoss in his office. Dalmoss would be safely hidden away again in the courier ship concealed within an off-lined freighter tender well before the shift change brought any incidental traffic into this part of the warehouse.

There wasn't anyone on the day crews who was likely to recognize Dalmoss anyway—they were all of them new hires, by and large, Langsarik to a man— but vigilance demanded Dalmoss be gone before any chance meeting could betray his presence. The enforced inactivity was wearing on his second-in-command, Fisner knew; but the Angel tolerated no inefficiency and brooked no unwise gambles.

"Do we have a coverage map? With planning, the surveillance could be made to see only what we want on record." Dalmoss had plenty of time in which to choreograph his raid. Not that there was so very much time before the raid would occur; but Dalmoss had nothing else to do, and nobody to keep him company but the Langsarik they'd brought with them from the Tyrell Yards. The Langsarik was safely drugged sense-

less, though, and sealed in a life-litter. He would probably have had little by way of interesting conversation
to offer under the best of circumstances.

"We have the security schematic, yes." So one of
Fisner's men had left it for Dalmoss to pick up at the
agreed-upon drop during the infrequent intervals
when they could afford for Dalmoss to be out and
about. "With respect, though, eldest and firstborn. It
could be too great a chance to try to use the record.
The more evidence there is on record, the more evidence there is for analysis, and perhaps discovery of
the secret. We should rather have Jevan disable the
entire system prior to our arrival, to be prudent."

Jevan was the Angel's man at Honan-gung, their
on-site saboteur.

Dalmoss was letting his nerves get the better of him.
"If there is analysis in the future, second eldest and
next born, what of it? It will be too late. The Langsariks will already have been dealt with, the raids will
have ceased, and what better evidence of Langsarik
guilt could there be than that once the Langsariks are
gone the thieving stops?"

Nor would the Bench be able to tolerate the public
scorn that would arise should they admit, even very
quietly, that they had moved too quickly against the
Langsariks, when they had evidence in hand to absolve them. So the Bench would not absolve them.
There was nothing to worry about.

Dalmoss bowed his head in token of submission to
Fisner's reasoning. After a moment he spoke.

"Your instructions for Honan-gung, then, eldest
and firstborn."

Fisner had given it some thought. "How long has it
been since Shires heard us talking, now? I have an
idea for using our friend to put the play forward. You
must stay well hidden, because he might recognize
you, but I think the result will be well worth the
effort."

Whether Shires had said anything to Vogel or not

was not something Fisner knew. But he'd thought the situation through carefully.

The whole plan from the beginning was to let Shires incriminate himself by drawing Vogel into an ambush at Honan-gung. So if Shires told Vogel, they were on course with that plan; but if Shires kept the information to himself, it could only be in order to take some dramatic action on his own part—action that could be used to implicate Shires either directly or indirectly in the raid when it occurred.

Either way the game was well worth the effort of setting it up.

"I have the documents prepared, eldest and first-born," Dalmoss said.

Good.

"Let's do the transfer tonight, then, second eldest and next born. That will leave a few days yet before Jevan will be ready for us at Honan-gung."

It would be good to be out of the bracing, even for just a little while. Dalmoss would be there to run interference in case Shires proved more fleet of foot than Fisner himself was, after spending so many hours of each day in self-imposed walking imprisonment.

It would not be long before the entire action would be completed. He could finally go back, then, back to his childhood home, and greet his surviving relatives, secure in the knowledge that the deaths of his family had been avenged.

Once he had accomplished the Angel's purpose in Port Charid he could go home an honorable and honored man, and be at peace at last.

He'd meant to get out early. Aunt Walton needed his help. It was frustrating to have to maintain the polite appearance of a normal day-to-day existence while others were working on exciting tasks. Maybe analyzing and cross-analyzing traffic patterns within and around the Shawl of Rikavie was not intrinsically exciting on the face of it; still, Aunt Walton believed that there was a murderer to be caught in just such a way.

Even his old folks were mobilized for the task.

So what was he doing here after dinnertime, yet again?

Running a cross-foot on some cargo on for the Okidan Yards, that was what, in response to the foreman's very distinctly expressed concern—a concern no less pressing for the fact that it had been transmitted to Hilton only third hand. Hilton had met Foreman Feraltz only the once; he knew what Feraltz looked like—bracing all over—but he hadn't really seen a very great deal of Feraltz since their first meeting.

Perhaps it was because of his junior and brevet status: all the more important that he not let the foreman down on recent cargo deliveries being held on behalf of the Okidan Yards. Okidan hadn't committed to rebuilding its warehouse facilities yet, but if trade was not to crash to a screeching halt for lack of a place to park the merchandise while it idled in search of a buyer, the inflated rates extorted by the Combine Yards had to be paid.

The least the Okidan Yards was entitled to in return for its payment of the premium on cargo handling in Port Charid these days was a careful and precise accounting for wastage and dwindling, as well as a reliable traffic report.

Hilton's stomach growled at him. He thought with longing of the hot soup that was waiting for him in the dormitory kitchen, but that only seemed to encourage his grumbling belly, so he put his hunger firmly to one side of his consciousness. Traffic report now; soup later.

It wasn't as though he was wasting his time there, not exactly. He was part of the vital playacting of normalcy, the critical window dressing in Aunt Walton's scheme to discover a raider while avoiding giving any advance warning before the troops arrived to make a spectacular raid. A legal raid. The raid that would provide evidence once and for all that the Langsariks were innocent of violating any part of the spirit of the amnesty settlement, and only very small and insignificant elements of the letter thereof.

Traffic report and reconciliation.

Yes.

But someone was singing outside the administrative offices. Hilton could hear the noise from his desk near the door—as far from the foreman's office as it was possible to get and still be in the administrative offices. Someone was out there in the warehouse singing a Langsarik love song too loudly and passionately for it to be a sober endeavor.

This was a problem on a number of levels. One, there was to be no liquor in the warehouse, and no coming into the warehouse under the influence of liquor—that was simple common sense. Whoever the singer was would lose his job if he was discovered, at least by anyone other than Hilton—quite apart from the potential curfew issues his presence there after hours presented.

Two, whoever it was could not carry a tune, and it was almost physically painful to hear such notes wrenched out of a perfectly harmless, basically innocuous, and certainly almost completely innocent tune. For the honor of the cultural heritage of the Langsarik fleet Hilton had to shut the drunkard up.

Then finally, whoever was out there singing was not inside trying to complete a traffic report and reconciliation. Was probably already fed and finished with the day's troubles. Had no business whatever being happy and relaxed and singing "Maid of the Forward Guns" while Hilton Shires was trying to get his work done so that he could get to bed.

Putting down his stylus and picking up a handbeam, Hilton opened up the door between the administrative offices and the warehouse proper, careful to avoid making any unnecessary noise. The handbeam was heavy and as long as his forearm and, apart from casting a bright focused beam of light, would serve as a satisfactory truncheon in case some drunk Langsarik wanted to fight. The longer Hilton had to listen to the murder of the song, the more he felt himself inclined to raise some welts on someone's head.

Where was that awful racket coming from?

The acoustics of the warehouse were unique; sound would either carry much farther than one would expect or not carry at all. That was why he'd lost those two men he'd heard talking in the warehouse the other night. He still hadn't quite made up his mind whether that incident had actually occurred, whether it meant what he'd thought at the time, and whether he should make an emergency trip to town to tell Garol Vogel all about it.

Setting off in a likely direction, Hilton stalked his prey, taking frequent stops to fix his direction in his mind. The topography of the warehouse changed on an almost daily basis as cargo moved in and out; that was why the traffic reconciliation was as complicated as it was, among other reasons. He didn't have any baseline mental grid to guide him.

But he was getting closer.

He could begin to make out words, and the occasional near miss of a melody.

Lovely maid that I adore. High-explosive rifled bore.

He'd learned the song as a child, well before he'd had much of any grasp of what the words actually meant. He had been just twelve or thirteen years old when the Langsarik fleet had taken its stand, and transformed itself by virtue of simple—and initially civil—disobedience from a commerce-administration fleet to a commerce raider. Pirates. Being raised on a pirate ship had disadvantages, but Hilton had had few complaints until now—when nothing in his personal history seemed quite so interesting and seductive as the idea of simply getting to bed before it was time to get up again.

Slinking down rows of cargo crates Hilton tracked

his quarry. *Recoil knocks me off my feet, let me prime your mortar sweet.*

He was getting closer.

Because he was beginning to hear words between music. Whoever it was, was talking to someone. Two of them? At least only one of them was singing.

Let me help your expert gunnery, promise I'll max your trajectory. It was a very rude song really. And Hilton could see who was singing it.

There was someone sitting on the floor halfway down a long row of cargo crates, half in the cone of light from the shelf spot, half-concealed in the shadows. Langsarik leggings. Very worn boots. Waving a sheaf of papers clutched in one hand as though keeping time, but not keeping any sort of time at all. His companion was more centrally seated, well within the light cast by the shelf spot; but Hilton couldn't see his face. Passed-out drunk, to judge by the body language.

How should he approach this?

He could rush them. They had no business being there if they weren't part of a normal work shift, and if they were part of a normal work shift, he'd know. They had no business being there drunk, either, but since they were drunk he could rush the one unconscious man all he liked without any effect whatever, while the singer was so drunk that the effect of being startled would probably only leave them all with a mess to clear up off the flooring.

People frequently got confrontational when they were drunk.

No, it would be best to approach these people calmly and slowly, and get them out before anyone else noticed them. Recriminations and lectures could wait till they were sober. First things first. He was going to need the cooperation of the singer to move the unconscious companion; a friendly approach was clearly the more productive of his options.

Switching on his handbeam, Hilton cleared his throat, sauntering slowly down the aisle as though he hadn't seen the two drunks in his warehouse. He could be the night watchman, except, of course, that they hadn't hired one yet. It didn't make much sense to pay for a guard in a warehouse that couldn't really be said to be secured anyway, especially as nobody really knew what was in which crate where.

"Haberdashery, convoy smashery, I'll show you some fancy danshery—"

Very drunk.

This called for more drastic measures. Hilton started to whistle as he walked, swinging his handbeam from side to side to create as much visual noise as possible.

It finally seemed to work.

"Hisst." The singer finally shut up—singing, at least. "Makile. We've got to shift. Come on, come on."

No reaction from friend Makile. Too drunk, maybe.

Hilton closed the distance, swinging his handbeam and whistling.

The singer continued to pound the inert body of his friend, his fistful of papers crumpling with every increasingly frantic blow. "Come on, Makile, let's get moving, now, you know we have curfew, mustn't violate the amnesty."

Nope.

No luck.

Hilton was close enough now to call out a friendly greeting. After all, who could really blame someone for taking shelter in the warehouse when he found himself at a temporary disadvantage? The man was right; there was a curfew. It was a pretty flexible curfew, but drunk and disorderly would emphatically violate it.

"All right! Company! Say. How about a sip of whatever it is you've been drinking? A man can get thirsty, walking night shift."

The singer pummeled his companion with one last desperate gesture, papers flying.

Then he took to his heels and fled, while Hilton watched him go with amused resignation.

Well, there was one down. One to go. It looked like he was going to handle the sleeper himself.

Hilton eased himself down to the ground next to the singer's silent partner, wondering what to do now. "So. What're you having."

No.

Something was wrong.

It was cold on the floor of the warehouse; and no warmth came from the inert body beside him. Hilton felt the hairs on the back of his neck prickle with dread and horror: and pushed himself away from the unbreathing body, hands to the floor.

Unbreathing?

He had to check.

Setting the handbeam down on the floor where it could illuminate some of the shadows, Hilton approached the still body that lay propped up against the crates.

No life.

No breathing.

Legs stiff, because he was dead; with the light shining on his face, the unnatural paleness of a countenance from which the normal blush of circulation had departed was too clear and too horribly unambiguous. Hilton had seen dead people before. There was no mistaking the chalk white putty of light-colored Langsarik skin when blood had ceased to color and warm it because the heart had stopped pumping.

Dead.

But there was no smell of liquor on him.

Perplexed as well as shocked, Hilton sat back on his heels to look at the dead man's face. Did he know this person? Langsarik by the looks of him, but no one Hilton thought he recognized.

He cast about behind him with his hands, meaning to shift his rump from his heels to the floor so that he could contemplate this situation more in depth and needing to set his palms to the floor behind him for bracing as he moved his center of gravity.

He set his right hand flat on a piece of paper that slid under the pressure, destroying any chance Hilton might have had of keeping his balance. He fell over backwards and knocked his head against the hard warehouse floor with enough force to jar the curse he meant to speak on the slipping of his hand out of his mouth entirely, unspoken.

Lying on his back, staring up into the blackness of the warehouse's rafters high above, Hilton caught his breath and composed himself. He was holding something in his right hand—he'd tightened his fist around the piece of paper, clutching for a handhold as he slipped. He brought his hand up in front of his face and turned the piece of paper front to back in his fingers.

Just a scrap of paper, really.

Poor quality, waxy finish, no wonder it had slid so easily. Marked in a fine bold hand. Trajectory calculations for a vector transit.

Hilton sat up slowly, his head spinning. What would any Langsarik be doing with a trajectory calculation?

There were other pieces of paper, fragments apparently abraded or torn while the drunken singer had beaten his friend in his unsuccessful attempt to rouse him. Hilton could read what was there, though. It was unquestionably a vector calculation of some sort, but it was maddeningly incomplete: the angle of approach was not specified, nor the point of departure. The only thing Hilton could tell with confidence was that the calculation was for an approach that started no closer to Port Charid than the Shawl of Rikavie.

Exactly where, in the Shawl of Rikavie?

A dead man, a drunk companion with a handful of notes. Too much celebration, perhaps. Celebrating what? Finalization of plans for the next "Langsarik" raid on warehouses in the Shawl of Rikavie?

This was not evidence which reflected well on Langsarik claims of innocence.

Until he had consulted his elders, he could not call in the Port Authority. It was too risky.

Hilton gathered the scraps of paper up and folded them into his blouse. The dead man could wait. Hilton dragged the corpse into a dark and very narrow space between cargo crates and marked his position with the handbeam so that he could be sure of finding it again.

His duty was clear: He needed to go see Aunt Walton and let her know. About the overheard conversation that he had happened to interrupt. About this.

Then she and he could go together to put these findings before Bench specialist Garol Vogel, in Port Charid.

Garol Vogel woke up in the middle of the night because there was someone at the window coming in, and it was cold.

Startled awake, his physical twitch was enough only to shake his brain into consciousness—not enough to alert the intruder, apparently. The window was still on its way open. Garol sat immobile, listening, watching; he'd fallen asleep in the room's one armchair, rather than lying down on the bed, so he was ahead of the game.

He heard whispers.

This is not a good idea, he's a Bench intelligence specialist, he can probably shoot to kill in his sleep and not even wake up until morning.

Garol thought he recognized the voice. He couldn't be quite certain; voices were different when a man was whispering. The window was open enough to admit a body, now, and the intruder angled himself through the gap awkwardly, a little too tall for a highbay bandit—or just unschooled in his art.

Vogel. Hey. Wake up. Don't shoot me. I'm friendly. Are you here?

The intruder was silhouetted against the ambient light from the night sky outside the rooming house. It wasn't bright, in the street, but there were clouds, and the airfield outside of town ran around the clock, so there was plenty of light hitting the clouds from the working beams on the airfield. It was enough. Garol knew his visitor, once he could put body and voice together. Hilton Shires. Walton Agenis's nephew and once-lieutenant.

And behind him?

Walton Agenis.

For a moment the idea of Flag Captain Walton Agenis breaking into his bedroom in the middle of the night was almost too poignant for Garol to bear, but he put the irrelevant fantasy away immediately. For future reference.

Maybe he's not even here, the bed doesn't look particularly occupied to me. Damn. We'll have to wait.

Walton Agenis, all right. Garol stirred where he sat slumped in his chair so that they would not be startled when he spoke. "That's just a rumor, about me shooting in my sleep. Bad idea, keeping loaded weapons under the pillow." If for no other reason than that was the first place people looked. "What can I do for you, Flag Captain?"

Shires had been visibly startled at the first sound of Garol's voice, his body language evident even in the low light of the darkened room. Agenis took it all in stride, however.

"First you can not turn on any lights; we'd rather stay secret till you've heard the news."

Fair enough. "No problem on this side. You might want to close the window. And the lightdrape, while you're at it."

She kept to the wall, where the shadows were deepest. Shires shut the window and closed the lightdrape carefully over it; Garol was happy to see that he used the drapes as his cover. Thinking every minute, that Shires. Agenis's nephew for a fact.

"Right," Walton said, once the room was safely shuttered against the night. "Have a seat, Shires. Talk to the Bench specialist. Tell him what we've been doing tonight."

Was this something he really wanted to hear? Garol wasn't sure.

But Walton hadn't asked him.

"You may remember that I've been filling in for my floor manager at the new warehouse, Specialist Vogel." Shires had sat down on Garol's bed; just as well it was still made up from the morning. Climbing up exterior walls in the middle of the night was frequently a messy business. "About five days ago I overheard an interesting conversation, or part of it. I hadn't told you because I hadn't told anybody."

He'd get to the details when the time came. Garol let him talk.

"Then tonight I heard a pair of drunks. Well, really only one drunk. There were two of them in the warehouse stacks, and one of them ran away. The other one was dead. There are incriminating but fragmentary documents. But the really interesting thing is that the body got up and walked off while I was briefing my aunt Agenis."

Quite a lot of information. Succinctly presented.

"I don't suppose there's any chance he wasn't exactly dead when you left him?"

Movement in the shadows, vague and ill defined. Garol turned his head away to let his peripheral vision work; Shires was shaking his head. "Body was cold, skin clammy to the touch, face and hands bloodless. Apart from that he wasn't breathing. And had no pulse. Nobody's gone missing tonight that we know of, Specialist Vogel, we checked."

Garol knew what he would think in Shires's place. At least approximately. "Your analysis, please, Lieutenant."

Shires took a moment to reply. Apparently he wasn't as sure of this next bit as he would have liked to be. "Well. You can call me paranoid, Specialist Vogel."

No, Garol had called him Lieutenant.

"But I'm clearly meant to think that I'm picking up intelligence by lucky chance. There's that other thing to consider, I already know I'm being set up." The forged chop, he meant, Garol supposed. "But they don't necessarily know that I know that I'm being set up. If whoever the enemy is was usually so clumsy as to let either incidents occur, they'd never have succeeded in staying unidentified for so long."

Garol had to agree. Shires's reasoning was sound; in retrospect, happening on the detail of the chop had put them ahead of the game—because Shires had trusted him enough to tell him about it, when Garol had mentioned the problem.

Suspicion was highly subjective. However, Hilton Shires could be expected to be highly motivated to believe that he was privy to evidence that might clear the Langsarik name and save the Langsarik settlement. He might be excused if he didn't examine the lucky chance that gave him such valuable information too closely.

"Let's hear some of the details of your experiences. It won't be sunup for hours, take your time."

Nobody would wonder if they heard noises coming from his room in the middle of the night. This was a decent rooming house, but it was a rooming house, and not all of its transient guests were reliable sober people or never wanted company at night. That was a part of the reason Garol was here, instead of insulated from the life of the port either on the Malcontent's courier or in one of the few more expensive lodgings Port Charid had to offer; he liked to be in the middle of life.

He was also much more easily approachable, here, if anyone needed to come and tell him something and didn't particularly care to be observed.

"All right. First. Days ago. I was working late, doing cargo reconciliation."

Still, Port Charid did have a curfew; it was a common tactic for a port with limited police resources. A curfew, and the bars were all closed; so who was making that racket, on the stairs? The bars closed well before curfew, so that people had time to get off the street. But whoever it was who was just coming home was very drunk indeed, to go by the shouts and exaggerated hushes Garol could hear coming through from the stairwell down the hall.

"Checking in the stacks. I started to hear voices. Nobody should have been in that part of the warehouse."

Oh good, the drunk was on this floor. And had a friend with him. Annoying; but no more than a petty irritation—the drunk would pass out, his friend would do the same, and things would be quiet again soon.

"I wanted to know who it was and what they were talking about. I snuck up on them. Two men, or two people anyway, talking. I wrote down the exact words I heard as well as I could remember them. But it was about fencing a cargo. Someone may have mentioned Honan-gung, but I'm not sure anymore about that."

No, the drunk wasn't in another room on this floor, the drunk was at his door. Hammering on the wall and calling to be let in. "Oh, let me in, friend, comrade, cousin, come on, I know you're in there."

Drunks made mistakes like that all the time.

But this drunk had a Dolgorukij accent; and—drunk as he seemed to be—he still spoke a dialect of High Aznir that was pure and sweet and beautiful.

Garol stood up.

"Company," Garol said. "Cousin Stanoczk. Malcontent. And, logically, Kazmer Daigule with him. What do you want me to do, Flag Captain?"

Walton Agenis spoke from the shadows, and her voice was clear and calm and confident.

"I want you to stop calling me Flag Captain, Garol; after all we've been through together it's insulting. Let the Dolgorukij in. All right, let the Sarvaw in, too."

Well, if she was going to be that way about it.

He'd better get Cousin Stanoczk out of the hall before he woke the entire hostelry.

Garol turned on the overhead light. It didn't shed all that much light, but it would be a noticeable anomaly if he opened the door with the lights still out. Out in the hallway Cousin Stanoczk was singing a song so purely obscene that it made Garol blush to hear it.

"Can't you quiet him down?" Garol hissed, checking the securities, opening the door. "People are trying to sleep."

Cousin Stanoczk fell against the door as Garol opened it, toppling into the room to fall flat on his face. He was carrying a full flask of something; Garol was grateful that it didn't break as Stanoczk fell—even while he registered suspicion in his mind over the fact that it didn't seem to so much as spill.

"Come on, come on." Hurrying Daigule into the room, Garol checked the hallway with a quick scan. No heads poked out of the other rooms. At least one door was ajar, though, signaling the interest of someone within who was listening—but reluctant to be caught at it. "Sorry about the noise," Garol said. "I'll take care of things from here. Thank you for your concern, good night."

He waited.

The door that was ajar fluttered, wavered, and finally closed; but with a very adept air of having been on the way to closed anyway, no thanks to you, sir or madam.

Cousin Stanoczk was sitting on the floor at the far end of the room with his back leaned up against the bed, his knees splayed widely in front of him and an expression of utter stupidity on his face. Walton Agenis had taken the chair, with Shires behind her for protection. *Who was protecting whom?* Garol wondered. Perhaps the point was simply that they wouldn't be visible from the street or across the street in that position, should there be any gap in the lightdrape across the window.

"To what do we owe the pleasure," Garol asked Stanoczk. Stanoczk waved the flask at him cheerfully.

"Little drink?" he asked. "Good clean stuff. Well. Stuff, anyway."

Speaking Standard. Garol raised an eyebrow at Kazmer Daigule, who had leaned his back up against the door after Garol had closed it. Daigule looked ready to collapse. "He sent me off on an errand to the Port Authority," Daigule said. "Some communications clearances he wanted. By the time I got back he was halfway into a bottle of wodac. That was hours ago. Now he decides it's time to come and see you, and I can't outwrestle him, he's drunk. I could hurt him."

If anybody could outwrestle a Combine hominid, it would be another. It would insult both men to suggest that Sarvaw and Aznir Dolgorukij were evenly matched, however. Daigule's point was perhaps simply that men who got too drunk didn't give the right cues when they were being pulled too far in the wrong direction; so a man could cause actual harm by accident. Stanoczk being too drunk to say "that hurts," for instance.

The truly interesting thing about Daigule's recitation, however, was that Stanoczk felt perfectly at ease sending him on errands without apparent concern that Daigule might not come back. Stanoczk had to be very sure of Daigule—one way or another. "Any idea what might have brought this on?"

Walton and Shires sat quietly, observing. Daigule shook his head, though.

" 'Pologies."

It was Cousin Stanoczk speaking. He was enunciating very very carefully. " 'Pologies all 'round. Especially you, Kazmer. I like you, you know? You'll make a lousy Malcontent. But I like you. Anyway."

Garol tried again. "Maybe there was a delivery while you were out. Maybe he wanted you out of the way for some reason. Where did he get the liquor, do we know?"

There were vague humming sounds from the Stanoczk direction of the room. Garol was beginning to worry. Stanoczk was speaking in plain Standard. If he started to sing that song in plain Standard, and in front of Walton Agenis—hell, in front of young Hilton Shires—

"Found your body," Stanoczk said.

He sounded very pleased with himself about it, too.

The reference was too apposite to be coincidental, surely. How could Cousin Stanoczk possibly know anything about that? Had he been visited by informers? But surely Daigule had been with him all evening, and Shires had only just arrived.

"Were we missing a body, Cousin?" Garol asked. He selected an appropriately respectful version of the word "cousin," out of common courtesy; but child of unknown birth order born to the eldest daughter of the younger brother of a mutual grandparent was as far as he was willing to go. The man was drunk.

Stanoczk nodded emphatically, his brown hair falling into his face as he rocked his head. "Terrible thing. Nothing to tell the parents. Aged mother. Infirm father. Um. Except that his father's dead and his mother's gone to work for a stables, but who are we to judge. A man must ride."

It was very good. But Garol was getting suspicious. "You are not as drunk as you seem," he said. "So stop playing games. What's this all about?"

Stanoczk raised his eyebrows, both of them, and stared at Garol owlishly. Then took a drink. "But I wish to be drunk." As though he believed that was a genuine explanation. "I very sincerely wish to be drunk. We have found the body, and he is not dead, and that the Angel might walk is a horror that no outlander can truly fathom."

"From the Tyrell Yards." Daigule broke in, sounding as confident as he was surprised. "There's been no identification from the forensic team, though, he sent me for results yesterday."

"Not from the forensic team." Stanoczk looked at the flask in his hand, and set it aside. Garol marked its location carefully. If it should spill, there was no telling what it might do to the floor—let alone anyone who might be sleeping in the room beneath this. "From Geraint. Going by Dalmoss. But he's not Dalmoss, which is why we noticed, you'd asked us to see about Dalmoss."

Garol decided to sit down. There was only one chair, and Walton Agenis was in it, watching and waiting for sense to begin to surface. There was a perfectly good floor, however; so Garol sank down to sit cross-legged on the modestly nondescript carpeting in the middle of the room, where he could engage Stanoczk one to one, at eye level.

"Interesting." It was at least that. "Tell me more."

"It's perfectly clear," Stanoczk said, sounding irritated. Petulant. Garol revised his working assessment: while he still felt that Stanoczk was not as drunk as he'd wished to appear to be, he was clearly more drunk than Garol had suspected, at first.

"We couldn't find him at Tyrell. Maybe he wasn't there. You asked after Dalmoss, we sent a trace to Geraint. Pettiche from the Tyrell Yards at Geraint. Going by Dalmoss. The foreman at the Combine Yards, and you would have heard about Feraltz by now."

Heard what? Feraltz's previous association with Langsariks? Whether or not Garol had "heard about" Feraltz, he would have expected Stanoczk to have told him if there was something Stanoczk thought Garol might need to know. Maybe there were allowances to be made for whatever twisted procedures Malcontents observed when dealing with Dolgorukij malefactors and offworld law enforcement, but Garol wasn't interested in cultural niceties when they started to jeopardize other people's lives. If Cousin Stanoczk could break the case for him, of course, he'd be inclined to let it go this once—

"So when do we get an interrogatory from Geraint?" He could be patient. At least until he got his interrogatory. "And where is Dalmoss?"

He didn't like the way Cousin Stanoczk had dropped his head to stare at the floor, though. It looked too much like the prelude to a plea for understanding in the case of a monumental mismanagement of resources.

"*Found* the body," Cousin Stanoczk said. "Didn't say we *had* the body." Reaching for his flask, Stanoczk took a deep pull from the lip, tilting the flask toward the ceiling. Emptying it, then flinging the flask against the far wall with a furious grimace of disgust.

Garol had been half-expecting such a gesture. He caught the flask out of its path, setting it down quietly beside him. Couldn't have people breaking flasks against the walls of rooming houses in the middle of the night. Tended to wake people up. Again.

"I explain," Stanoczk said. Garol was all in favor. "We were looking for Pettiche, and if Pettiche, who was not found at the Tyrell Yards, was on unplanned leave, he would logically only have gone in sixteen or twenty-four directions. So the description was circulated. Also we like to oblige Bench intelligence specialists whenever possible, so when Geraint received Dalmoss we went to see how he was looking and faring directly, but he was not Dalmoss, he was Pettiche."

Stanoczk was disgusted at him, now, but basically simply disgusted, and ready to take it out on the world. "Pettiche at Geraint, but traveling as Dalmoss, against which there is no law either beneath the Canopy or before the Bench. But between the time of confirming the identity of the man who was not Dalmoss, and matching him to Pettiche, he has gone. We cannot find him. We only knew that he was there, at Geraint, days after the Tyrell raid, as Dalmoss."

Garol gathered his knees to his chest and stared at the worn carpeting, thinking hard.

His feelings of intense frustration over the loss of

the interrogatory he could manage; since there was no way to tell whether Dalmoss would have provided useful information, there was no sense in worrying that bone.

He had thought that Cousin Stanoczk brought him hard evidence and a brief that would solve his problems at Port Charid, but Cousin Stanoczk had not brought him nothing, Cousin Stanoczk had brought him evidence that could be used—though it was indirect. Hearsay. It only meant that more steps would be required to transmute Cousin Stanoczk's information into salvation for the Langsariks.

"Found the body, lost the body, there is still no body, Cousin Stanoczk." Cousin Stanoczk knew that. The Malcontent was an irritation and had been nothing but an obstacle, but he was neither stupid nor willfully obstructionary. "So what's the point."

Cousin Stanoczk started to stand up. He didn't seem to be managing it very well; Daigule came forward to help him, and once Cousin Stanoczk was on his feet he faced Walton Agenis—of all people—and bowed very politely. But with apparent sincerity.

"It means that you are victimized by plots against you done by my countrymen, Flag Captain. Excuse me that I have not presented myself before now, my name is Stanoczk. I am a Malcontent, and responsible to the Saint my master for the good government of the children of the Holy Mother as they go out into the world. That you are wronged by Combine interests is no longer in dispute. We fear the worst. To Garol Vogel we ask: Can we be of any help at all, to make atonement on behalf of the Holy Mother's Church for wrong done you by Her own wayward children?"

Long speech. Unusually coherent, for a drunk; so maybe Stanoczk meant it. Walton Agenis shifted a little to one side in the chair; looking at Garol.

Oh, bloody hell.

"He's got resources we're going to need." He was already unhappy about his role in having brought the

Langsariks to Port Charid in the first place, worried and anxious about whether Walton Agenis's trust in him was ultimately to mean her destruction.

He didn't need to be reminded.

But he couldn't refuse Walton's implicit request either, just because it emphasized that she had not yet decided that it was time to begin to cease to trust him. "You're short access to computing power to run the traffic analysis. I've seen his comps. He can probably do things with them that I don't even want to know about." Because they were likely to be illegal, that was to say. "Send someone to the docks tomorrow as soon as you can. And assume that we're being watched at every moment."

Straightening up, Cousin Stanoczk spun drunkenly on his heel and staggered sideways, managing miraculously to land on his back on Garol's bed.

"One does assume so. Naturally," he said.

Daigule turned the light out, and Garol stood in the middle of his small room in the rooming house with Kazmer Daigule at the door, Cousin Stanoczk on the bed, Walton Agenis in his chair, and Hilton Shires standing calmly and quietly in a modified position of attention-rest behind her.

There was a way to get all of this sorted out, he knew it; but for a moment the insanity of the situation was almost too much.

"So, does anybody know any good jokes?" Hilton Shires asked. Garol shook his head vigorously, to clear it: He was losing his track.

"We'll probably have to wait for morning before we can disperse." They could take advantage of shift change, things got busy. "

Agenis and Shires, Garol trusted to have arrived unobserved, but getting away again was going to be a little different. Cousin Stanoczk's arrival had unfortunately probably focused the attention of the night watchman; if anyone was watching Stanoczk, they could be watching the window. "There are a few hours. Talk. Let's all get on the same vector transit. Shires. You first."

Maybe nobody was watching. It was probably a good idea to minimize any chance of their quarry noticing that they were getting closer . . . if they were getting closer.

"Funny that you should mention a vector transit, Bench specialist. I have these documents. And one of them may say 'Honan,' and another may say 'gung.' "

Garol stooped to the floor to retrieve the empty flask he'd intercepted on its journey to the far wall.

He was almost regretful to find it truly empty.

It was going to be a long wait, till morning.

Chapter Nine

Fisner Feraltz had come to work in the Combine offices in Port Charid proper this morning for two or three reasons. One of them was the desirability of being close to Factor Madlev's office, so that if the Bench specialist arrived to call through to Chilleau Judiciary he could find an immediate pretext to be there by the time Vogel was announced—or at least be on-site to talk to Factor Madlev immediately afterward, to see if he could get some hints on what had been said.

Another was to be away from the warehouse construction site in order to minimize chance contacts with Hilton Shires—in case some subconscious connection should be made in Shires's mind between the drunk in the warehouse the previous night and his foreman. There was no accounting for the leaps of comprehension that could occur at the most inopportune times even in the brain of the outlander; so it was prudent for Fisner to keep his distance more carefully while the experience was still fresh in Shires's mind.

But mostly Fisner came to work in Combine offices at Port Charid that morning because he had been out late last night helping Dalmoss with the body, and was too tired to force himself into his medical bracing fast enough to get out to his branch office in time.

The trick with the documents and the body had gone off beautifully: They had passed the information about a planned raid on Honan-gung to Shires, and escaped without being exposed as anyone other than Langsariks.

But had it worked?

Shires had gone; Shires had come back, with some of his Langsarik fellows. By that time Fisner and Dalmoss had moved the body, because if someone recognized the Langsarik as Parken from the Tyrell Yards, it would queer the setup.

The presence of the corpse had served its purpose in representing a genuine Langsarik to Shires while startling him out of any potential analysis and suspicions up front. With the corpse missing it was only Shires's word that there had been a dead man there at all, and Shires might well be distracted enough by that issue to neglect to think too deeply on any other aspect of the incident.

It was early yet for gossip to have gotten out. He'd be hearing all about it soon enough, Fisner was sure. The people on his crew—including his agents, of course, but even the balance of his crew, the majority of whom were innocent of any involvement with the Angel of Destruction—were encouraged to come to him with rumors. It was a management-communications issue. Open-door policy. Free intelligence.

It was with pleasant expectations that Fisner looked up as someone knocked at his open office door. Rather than a report from one of his people or a bit of tasty gossip, however, it was his receptionist Hariv at the door with a frown on his face, and a man behind him that Fisner thought he'd seen in town before.

"Excuse me, Foreman, a Malcontent to see you. Cousin Stanoczk."

Oh, this was interesting.

The Malcontent had been the Angel's bitter enemy from the birth of their holy Order. The opposition that the Malcontent had offered to the Angel at every step had traditionally been requited by the heartfelt hatred of the loyal sons of the Holy Mother for the degenerate offspring of bastard Saints. The Angel rejoiced in the grace and blessing of the Holy Mother; the Malcontent had to content itself with the patronage of a drunk, a failure, an irreligious and impotent man whose every action during his lifetime had ultimately failed to achieve its purpose.

With the arrogance characteristic of a Malcontent's inflated opinion of himself and his mission, Cousin Stanoczk hadn't even had the common courtesy to present himself to Factor Madlev—the senior Combine official at Port Charid, and surely a man worthy of respect—upon his arrival. His appearance here now would have some purpose behind it. Fisner was curious to know what that might be.

"Thank you, Hariv. Cousin. Come in. A very great honor." Fisner rose slowly to his feet, careful neither to exaggerate the difficulties the medical bracing placed in his way nor seem too comfortable with it. One was in no way obliged to rise for a Malcontent.

He was deliberately showing greater respect than the bastard Saint had any right to expect; but Cousin Stanoczk, true to the mindless and deluded misapprehensions common to the Malcontent, merely accepted the courtesy as due to him by right, and bowed with gracious condescension.

"Too kind, Foreman. Is it permitted to call you Feraltz? Yes, thank you, Foreman Feraltz. If I may be seated, by your kind permission."

Which Fisner had neither volunteered nor agreed to extend; that was the Malcontent to the life. Fisner sat back down. "How may I put the purpose of your patron forward, Cousin Stanoczk?" he asked politely. The Malcontent had brought Kazmer Daigule back to Port Charid with him. It could well be that Cousin Stanoczk would reveal some interesting information if his ego was stroked agreeably enough.

Cousin Stanoczk smiled in what he apparently believed to be an ingratiating fashion, though it merely turned Fisner's stomach. He was glad he'd not had time for firstmeal.

"You can do me very great service, in fact, Foreman. I have instructions to expedite handling of a freight cargo expected for Finiury, and we are particularly anxious that the freighter be processed as quickly as possible. It is awkward that I cannot say exactly when the freighter is expected, but our principal apparently has doubts about the security of the Finiury Yards in the Shawl and wishes us most particularly to shepherd the cargo ourselves through the Combine warehouses here at Port Charid."

Oh, this *was* interesting. Had the fish-eating Malcontent gone into trade in illegal armaments?

Did the Bench know?

"And in what way may we assist, Cousin Stanoczk," Fisner said, to remind the Malcontent that he had not answered the question.

The general outline of Cousin Stanoczk's request was clear enough: *I have an arms shipment coming in, it can't go to Finiury because there would be too much to explain to the Bench if Finiury were raided by Langsariks and the cargo discovered. I therefore need your help in getting the cargo hidden safely away as soon as possible at Port Charid.*

Maximizing the off-load in order to minimize the time that the freighter with its ever so emphatically illegal cargo would be tied up in the process, to minimize the window in which a representative of what passed for the Port Authority in Port Charid might ask to have a look at the cargo for routine spot check.

And relying upon the extralegal position of the Malcontent within the Dolgorukij church to ensure that the Combine Yards would gladly accept its role as transfer-man, without questioning Cousin Stanoczk's motives or cargo.

"Procure for me freighter tenders on standby," Cousin Stanoczk replied. He apparently did not feel as confident as he would have liked to be; he seemed to be choosing his words carefully, as though feeling his way. "To be ready to off-load on two hours' advance notice. I will, of course, pay a reasonable holding charge, but eight freighter tenders empty and fueled are most sincerely desired, and as soon as possible."

Fisner pushed himself away from his desk in the chair and out at an arm's length from the near edge, staring at the desk furniture as he thought.

Eight freighter tenders.

It was not a small favor to ask, what with the increasing traffic that was coming through Port Charid these days rather than off-loading in the Shawl, where the freighters could dock directly.

Eight freighter tenders?

But, oh, if he could only pull it off. To suck an extra premium out of the pocket of the hated Malcontent to fund the Angel's own agendas, and gain the leverage that having the secret knowledge would grant—Cousin Stanoczk had made no incriminating statements, but Fisner knew things about Finiury that Cousin Stanoczk could not imagine he knew—

There would be troops in Port Charid once the Angel wrought its final raid. The new warehouse would be searched for contraband; some pretext to examine the Malcontent's crates from Finiury could easily be arranged while Fleet was on-site. It would be a scandal of monumental proportions. It would discredit the Malcontent in the eyes of the Autocrat's court at least, if not Combine-wide; not for trafficking in illegal arms, but for having done so clumsily, for having permitted themselves to be caught at it.

Beautiful.

"It will not be easy to arrange. Or to explain." Making his decision, Fisner gave his consent to Cousin Stanoczk's proposal in such a way as to assure that the premium to be offered would be adequate to account for the trouble the requirement would entail. "I only have five tenders idle even now, and the lull is only temporary. I could come up with some excuse for off-lining the tenders, but nothing I can think of will be good for very long, and we will lose money if we have to leave goods in orbit waiting for off-load."

Cousin Stanoczk was frowning, in a servile and overanxious sort of way. "It is very distressing, Foreman, but we cannot permit any traffic to be made to wait. It would draw attention to the priority off-load of our Finiury cargo. That is contrary to the modest and public-spirited desire of our client."

Good point. Fisner hadn't thought about it, but it was obvious once Cousin Stanoczk brought it up. If traffic was on hold while a Finiury cargo got priority handling, it would only draw attention. People would naturally be interested in what the Finiury cargo was and why someone was willing to pay the clearly implied premiums to get the cargo unshipped.

Then Fisner had an idea.

There were to be no Combine freighters within the next two weeks; Factor Madlev had rerouted some of the Combine shipping to maximize the extra revenue available from other firms wishing to use the Combine facilities.

"Very well, Cousin Stanoczk." He would call the reserve ships in for maintenance. There were two of those; he had five on the ground in the normal course of the day's traffic, that made seven; he would only have to reserve his raid ship itself on standby. The conduct of the raid could occupy the freighter tender for a day and a half, with everything taken into account, but he would so shuffle his freighter tenders that normal traffic would cover it. Brilliant.

"You shall have eight freighter tenders, all empty, all fueled, all ready at your word. We will direct your cargo to the new facility. There will be no excess and burdensome oversight; you may confidently rely upon our discretion."

It would leave them without any emergency capacity, but he could do it without attracting any particular attention. If he scheduled things cleverly enough, he need not declare any of Cousin Stanoczk's offered premium to Factor Madlev. It would be additional income to fund the Angel's work, on top of the generous proceeds from the raids themselves.

Cousin Stanoczk bowed politely, but the reality of his relief was unquestionable. "Thank you, Foreman, I am very much in your debt. May the Holy Mother prosper all lawful purposes."

"Thank you, Cousin Stanoczk. It is our pleasure to oblige."

The Angel of Destruction was above the law of men, be it the Autocrat's code or the Jurisdiction's Bench.

What more telling evidence of the Holy Mother's blessing, than that She turned even the Malcontent to serve the Angel's purpose?

Suppressing a yawn, Hilton marked off another hull on his list and reset the temperature sensor. He hadn't been getting his beauty sleep. He hadn't gotten any sleep at all since early yesterday morning, but who was counting? He wouldn't have traded the all-night staff meeting Aunt Walton had held in Garol Vogel's bedroom for money.

"Three more and we're out." Kazmer's voice came quietly over the earpiece. Hilton was on receive, not transmit, because if he had been hiding battle cannon in a warehouse, he certainly would have a monitor on communications transmissions in the area. "Next."

Kazmer didn't have to say much on his end. Kazmer was eights away in a little closet on his Cousin Stanoczk's courier at Port Charid, tapped into the warehouse's employee-location grid. As acting floor manager, Hilton carried a trace so that the foreman could find him at any time; Kazmer knew exactly where Hilton was. Also that Hilton hadn't found anything yet, because he meant to do his superspecial secret version of the Hilton Happy Dance when he did, and there had been no dance activity on the warehouse floor so far that morning.

Someone had cannon hidden at Port Charid. If not cannon, at least a small courier hardened to take the deployment of battle cannon; when Kazmer had taken the freighter tender to rendezvous for the Tyrell raid, the courier had been on the freighter tender.

Hilton had a manifest list for each freighter tender at the warehouse, and the gross weights of each component part and total cargo were part of his records. Kazmer and Vogel had a rough estimate of weight for the courier Kazmer had helped to unload at Tyrell. Nothing on Hilton's docks would tip the scale at such a mass as that.

The warehouse floor was load-rated for freighter tenders with heavy ore cargoes. It flexed. There was a correlation between the thermal stress involved with flexing beneath the weight of the five freighter tenders currently parked at the new warehouse and the adjusted weight of the freighter tenders' cargoes, less fuel reserves. Hilton strolled casually down the line of parked freighter tenders with his tally screen and his thermal sensor, whistling to himself.

Let me help your expert gunnery, promise I'll max your trajectory.

The warehouse floor was warmer there than it had been beneath the prior freighter tender.

But was it because of the cargo load this freighter tender was carrying?

Or—Hilton asked himself with mounting excitement, strolling past the nose of the next freighter tender to scan the floor beneath the one after that from a distance—was it because there was something really, really heavy in the last freighter tender but one?

Frowning at his tally screen Hilton started down the pedestrian aisle between freighter tenders, his temperature probe casually aimed at the floor to his left.

Not the last in line, the first to be suspected, too easily moved in and out.

Not hidden in the middle of the line like a freighter

tender cleared and locked down and waiting to take on cargo. The last but one, the next to last, swarming with Langsarik work crews—forward only, of course— and in the process of clearing its cargo.

Hilton checked his tally.

The cargo was under quarantine for release of goods. As good as locked away, secured, no better place to hide a courier, and the weight in the aft cargo compartment of the last freighter tender but one stressed the floor that supported it with a thermal trace that showed orange and yellow on Hilton's readout.

It was heavy enough to be holding the battle cannon.

Hilton walked slowly all the way around the great beast, taking his time to master his emotions. This was it. They had the courier. Now all they had to do was find its crew, and this would all be over.

They'd be safe.

"Very good." Kazmer's voice was calm, but resonant with the excitement Hilton knew Kazmer was sharing. "Trace. Off-line now."

Now that they knew which one it was, the Langsariks could set a watch. Kazmer closed his transmission, careful to minimize any chance of interception. Hilton checked the last freighter tender as he passed under pretext of doing something with his tally screen; light as a feather. As freighter tenders went.

He didn't dare lay a tag on record, for fear of discovery. But Kazmer had the fix on his position; and Hilton had Langsarik maintenance crews up on the bare beams of the warehouse ceiling, keeping watch.

Cold up there. Drafty. Thankless duty, Hilton knew; but they had the enemy now. That knowledge alone was enough to warm a man body and soul, even one on watch far far overhead.

It was the end of a long day, and Garol Vogel was walking Walton Agenis home. It was about an hour and a half on foot from Port Charid to the Langsarik settlement; Garol felt the need to get out under the sky, and Walton hadn't argued.

They'd been in bed together all day.

At least that was the story, if anyone asked.

Once they'd cleared the outskirts of Port Charid and were well on their way toward the new warehouse construction site, Garol spoke.

"So you managed to obtain a false chop," Garol said, just to get the story out in the open once and for all. "Somehow. It doesn't really matter, someone will think of a way. You used the chop to authorize moving freighter tenders into orbit."

Hilton's find out on the warehouse floor that morning had been the final evidence. There was no longer any question about where the battle cannon were being hidden; now it remained only to decide where the battle cannon would be deployed next, and Hilton was in Port Charid with Cousin Stanoczk and Kazmer Daigule running the last of the contingency exercises even now.

"You hid your raid ship and its battle cannon on a freighter tender out at the new warehouse that the Combine started to build as soon as the Langsariks got here. Perfect timing."

Walton walked slowly, shredding the long leaf of a late-flourishing plant in her strong slender fingers. She was clearly in no particular hurry to get back; and if they'd been in bed together all day—Garol thought, almost despite himself—she might be moving a little slowly anyway. Muscular soreness.

He was ashamed of himself for having such a thought about Walton Agenis. It was ungallant in the extreme to impose on a lady to such an extent. If he ever actually did go to bed with her—

"Too bad we can't figure out a way for that to have been part of the plot, all along." Walton's comment interrupted Garol's train of thought, and not a moment too soon. The late-afternoon breeze ruffled her short red hair; it was cool, when the breeze blew, and she was wearing Garol's old campaign jacket.

"Right." Garol set his mind resolutely to the issue at hand. "Hilton's got the chop, says he got it from Dalmoss, what Dalmoss will say is predictable. The courier could have been in the warehouse all this time, for all we know."

The Langsariks had been scrupulous about observing the letter and intent of the amnesty agreement. No one had gone poking around cargo holds of freighter tenders without leave and authorization. Who knew how long that raid ship had been there? And since the warehouse-construction crews were almost all Langsarik, the setup was compromising by definition. Physical evidence of Langsarik involvement could always be come by later.

She was listening, and he was getting it all straight in his mind by talking it out. "You get into orbit, you rendezvous with a freighter, you make a raid. Your hired crew escapes, you rejoin your freighter tender, and return to base at Port Charid with no one any the wiser. We have the crew from the Tyrell raid, we can demonstrate how you did it."

She tossed the shredded leaf away from her with a gesture of disgust. "Leaving us with only two questions. Who's behind it. What to do about it."

"Cousin Stanoczk says the Angel of Destruction," Garol reminded her. "He may have that part covered."

"He hasn't come out and said, though. I don't need any Cousin Stanoczk to tell me who's behind it, if there is a Dolgorukij plot. It's Feraltz. It's almost got to be."

Garol considered this in silence for a moment or two, watching the shadows change across the hills far to the south. "Why Feraltz?" Granted that Garol himself had already decided that Feraltz was running a game; he still didn't understand why. "He's the one man in Port Charid with most owing."

That could be an answer of its own, of course, the ins and outs of gratitude and obligation being what they were.

Walton sighed. "Dalmoss is clearly part of it, if we believe Hilton abut the chop—and I do, needless to say. Feraltz very specifically wanted Hilton as assistant floor manager at the new warehouse construction site, so Feraltz arranged to put Hilton in his very compromised position. But there's more to it than that. I'd normally not want to say anything about it, but—"

There was a vehicle approaching on the track from Port Charid. Walton glanced behind her; Garol put his arm around her shoulder to draw her with him well off the track. Just in case.

"More to it, you said?"

She shook her head. "Wait. This one's coming for us. I've seen my nephew drive before."

All right.

The vehicle pulled over ahead of them on the side to the track and skidded to a stop, raising a cloud of dust and gravel. The door on the driver's side was open before the vehicle stopped moving, and Hilton Shires fell out.

Did a very creditable tuck and roll, too, scrambling to his feet and starting toward them almost without a break. His momentum carried him flat into Garol where Garol stood waiting, and Garol steadied him with an effort.

"Results," Shires said. "Analysis complete. It's got to be Honan-gung. It's got to be."

Cousin Stanoczk's people had been working the analysis all day. The documents Shires had picked up in the warehouse after hours the evening before. The historical pattern, available cargo readily converted into untraceable cash, potential body count, everything.

Garol pushed Shires away, hard enough to stagger him. "I'll keep company with your aunt if I damn please," Garol said, loud-voiced and angry. "Who do you think you are?"

Shires was smart, he picked right up on things. He didn't try to close the distance, he put one hand on his hip and shook his finger accusingly. "We know the target," Shires said, low-voiced, as if angry in response. Scowling. Lips drawn thin, body tense and hunched slightly forward, as if about to attack. "What do we do now?"

Walton stepped between them, and put her hands out to either side in the classic gesture of forcing a separation. "We can't prove anything on what we have," she said soothingly. "All the circumstantial evidence and hearsay in the world won't help us. We need to catch the raiders in the act for a positive identification. You know we do."

Dropping her arms, she turned her back to both of them and stared out across the road into the middle distance. Garol folded his arms across his chest. *Enraged senior male, challenged by immature younger male stepping outside his boundaries.* "I know what you're suggesting. But I can't risk the lives of the crew at Honan-gung without a really solid backup. It's just not acceptable."

Shires had both hands on his hips, now, but he'd straightened up a bit. *Younger male, not ready to back down, but feeling obviously intimidated and looking for a face-saving escape route.* "But we have no direct incontrovertible evidence. We've got to give the enemy the opportunity to betray himself, in order to convince the Bench."

Shires and his aunt were right.

Yet Garol couldn't see a way around it. Garol unfolded his arms and reached for Walton, drawing her by the elbow to stand by his side. *Senior male making his position absolutely clear, but softening marginally on aggressive response to challenge from younger male.*

"Not an option, Shires, I'm not risking lives on an ego thing. If we had police. A dockworkers' association. Reservists. Anything. But we don't." He couldn't call on the Port Authority for support. The Port Authority was dependent on the local mercantile authority for its enforcers: That meant Factor Madlev's people, Combine people.

The enemy would be tipped off, or worse—the enemy would have advance intelligence and would be able to forestall them, or even subvert the very people Garol might need to back him up. No. Hopeless.

Now Walton Agenis tucked herself very confidentially against him and raised her head to look up into his face. *Female offers conciliatory gesture to reconcile senior male and younger male.*

"You've got Langsariks," she said.

What?

What was that supposed to mean, "you've got Langsariks"? He already knew that he had responsibility for the Langsariks here at Port Charid, he'd brought them here, he'd negotiated the amnesty agreement, he'd promised them fair play. He hadn't told the truth. It wasn't for lack of goodwill on his part, but the Langsariks were not going to get fair play after all. The Langsariks were going to suffer for someone else's crime. There was nothing that Garol Vogel could see that he could do about it.

"It wasn't supposed to end this way, Flag Captain." He couldn't sidestep the issue. He owed it to Walton Agenis to tell her the truth, no matter how it would diminish him in her eyes. It was the only thing he had to offer by way of atonement for his role in the disaster that was almost upon the Langsariks. "Maybe we'll get a break. We could get lucky. But we've got to start preparing your people for the worst."

For all her submissive body language, Walton wasn't backing down a bit. "No, Bench specialist, we've got to start preparing for an ambush. They brought the raiders out as boxed cargo at Tyrell, Daigule said." The night before, during the marathon information-sharing session they'd held in Garol's bedroom, in fact. "We can use the same approach at Honan-gung."

All right, all right.

All right.

Garol caught her meaning, now. A seductive concept. But it would never work.

"I like it in theory," Garol said, and kissed the top of Walton's head on impulse—just to put the play forward, of course, for the benefit of whoever might be watching. "Don't get me wrong."

There was such a solid emotional satisfaction behind the proposal, and if the Langsariks couldn't pull it off, nobody could—or nobody within nine days' transit time of the Shawl of Rikavie, at any rate. But it wouldn't work. The Langsariks were prohibited any travel off Port Charid without strict supervision for a start, and forbidden to arm themselves without qualification—not even for self-defense.

Why wouldn't it work?

It was true what he'd just told himself: If the Langsariks couldn't do it, nobody could.

And Langsariks had pulled off more outrageous stunts still in their recent past, in their politely glossed-over but solidly successful careers as commerce raiders who had evaded the best efforts of the Fleet to pin them down and punish them for years.

"I've learned a lot about cargo-management systems, Specialist Vogel. I can make it work." Shires stepped forward with his shoulders rounded, his hands held out in front of him entreatingly. *Subordinate male yields, solicits forgiveness.* "Nobody needs to know that we've got troops on board. We can stay clear of the station monitors until we're needed."

Garol's head was spinning; he shook it several times, to try to clear his thoughts. *Senior male stands on his dignity, holds out for more abject apology in presence of female.*

"Lieutenant Shires. Hilton." It was so hard to reject, because it was so beautiful. He would enjoy it so much: to capture the raiders in the commission of a crime, to demonstrate the trustworthiness of the Langsariks, to keep the innocent civilians at Honan-gung safe from harm while giving him the data he needed to protect the Langsarik settlement.

He ached to embrace the idea.

He could not.

"It's been more than a year since any Langsarik has engaged in any action, at least that's the story I've heard. How are we going to keep someone in Port Charid from noticing? If you're discovered at Honan-gung before the raid, it will be the same as if you had been the raiders all along."

Shires was only smiling, his whole face full of such wolfish joy that Garol shuddered to see it. Pure. Brilliant. Savage in its certainty; and beautiful, as any perfect predator was beautiful. "That's one reason why we'll need you to come with us, Bench specialist. Legal authority. The apprehension won't be lawful without duly constituted Bench representation. You'll have to deputize us to cover for it. Besides, you'll want to be there."

Shires was right.

About both things.

"Puts the entire community at risk," Garol said, to Walton. *Senior male solicits option of female; should peace be made with subordinate male? Will his status suffer if he yields too easily?* "Are you sure about this, Flag Captain?"

She nodded with vigorous self-confidence. "It's my best alternative. And the other alternatives aren't worth considering."

It was not a brilliant idea, necessarily; merely a reasonable one—but the emotional payoff that it offered was almost irresistible.

"So let's get on with it. Hilton. Aren't you supposed to be on shift? Vogel and I will take the vehicle, you walk it off."

Female offers face-saving extrication to both males,

*trading temporary inconvenience of walking to work
for easy escape of young male from injudiciously in-
voked confrontation.* Garol straightened his shirtfront
with an exaggerated glare at Shires and followed Walton Agenis to the for-hire that Shires had brought
from Port Charid.

Garol remembered what it was like to burn with
the pure joy of approaching battle, hungry to starving
for the chance to take action at last against a despised
and cowardly opponent.

After all these years, did he have the moral courage
to resist the temptation and deny Shires his chance to
clear his name?

Or was he going to find himself agreeing to make
use of the offered Langsarik resources, just because
he'd never been able to forget what it had been like
when he'd been twenty?

Midnight in Port Charid. The previous night had
been absorbed in an ad hoc strategy session in Garol's
bedroom; Shires had located the battle cannon—or at
least the freighter tender on which the battle cannon
were presumed to be—that morning. Cousin Stanoczk
and his people had completed the target analysis hours
ago, and Garol had seen Walton Agenis safely returned to the Langsarik settlement himself.

He had everything he needed now, target, location
of enemy resources, plan of attack.

He was almost ready to call it a plan and get going.

"I agree that the analysis factors all point to Honan-
gung," Jils admitted, closing the portfolio containing the
scraps of paper that Shires had picked up on the warehouse floor last night. "What is less obvious is whose
target it is."

Garol Vogel sat in the small aft cabin of the courier
he'd had sent from Anglace to Port Charid on
freighter to meet him. Now that his own transport
was there, he had less excuse for using that of Cousin
Stanoczk, which was a shame in a sense—the Malcon-

tent's courier was significantly more luxurious than his own, even if the technology standard was not all that different.

"It's Langsariks or it's not." He knew what she was getting at, but there was no reason to make it easy on her. "Let's assume for one moment that it's Langsariks. Why would they tip us off?"

"Because the Langsarik target isn't Honan-gung, Garol. Get you all excited about Honan-gung and you leave them time and opportunity to make one last hit somewhere else. Maybe Finiury. There are indications that arms shipments may be going through Finiury, Garol. The Bench is finalizing its case."

He knew that. He'd just been thinking about other things. He'd had other problems on his mind.

Jils continued. "But if there are arms at Finiury and the Langsariks raid, we could have a takeover situation on our hands. You've got to let Verlaine set Fleet on alert."

He hated it when Jils made too much good sense. Hated it. He pushed himself up out of his chair and covered his frustration with a quest for a cup of bean tea. You couldn't get bean tea on the Malcontent's courier, not unless you asked for it. Rhyti. Weak as water by comparison, even if rhyti's mix of naturally occurring and mood-altering chemical substances were seductive enough in its own right.

"We're saying it's Honan-gung if it's not Langsariks, and I'm dead on for Honan-gung because I believe it's not Langsariks," Garol said with his back to Jils, from the bean tea brewer. Basically, that was what she was telling him. "And there's still a chance that it is Langsariks, and my own emotional investment in the settlement has created a blind spot in my analysis."

"Our emotional investment," Jils said quietly, and Garol bowed his head in gratitude to her. "Yes. And if we've called it wrong, we've potentially endangered many more souls than just the warehouse crew at Finiury. If we're badly mistaken, it could be Tyrell all over again, but at Port Charid—with plenty of frustration on the Langsariks' part to work out. It's more than we can risk, and what's the harm of calling for Fleet for backup?"

But she knew the answer to that one already. "I don't know. That's the problem. You never know with Fleet. For all we know they'd send us the *Ragnarok*, and we all know that'd just mean a lot of unnecessary interrogations. I don't want Fleet involved if I can avoid it. I don't like the uncertainties."

Fleet was there for muscle, though. Fleet was the only enforcement muscle a Bench intelligence specialist had. Fleet was the police arm of the Bench. He was supposed to call for Fleet when he could no longer control the situation himself.

He wasn't willing to admit that the situation wasn't under control; and yet Jils was right. If he was wrong about the Langsariks . . .

"You're the man on the ground on this one, Garol." She'd given him her evaluation; she thought it was Honan-gung. She'd reminded him of the alternatives, too. Bench intelligence specialists didn't dice with the lives of innocent people. "It's your call."

It *was* his call.

He was responsible to the Bench for the success or failure of his solution to the problem Chilleau Judiciary faced at Port Charid, the apparent resurgence of Langsarik piracy, the contempt for the amnesty, the disruption of trade, the retardation of the economic development of the site.

He would put Port Charid on notice that a Fleet detachment was coming. That would force someone's hand; the only question remaining would be which someone, exactly, it would turn out to be.

If it was a raid on Honan-gung, he would be ready for them.

If it was a Langsarik raid on Finiury, there would be a bloodbath in Port Charid with Garol Aphon

Vogel written all over it: and if that happened, he wanted to be the only one responsible.

"If that's the way you feel about it." On all levels. "I think you should leave, Jils."

She looked a little surprised, eyeing him sharply as if to judge whether he had taken offense or not. Her expression smoothed as he continued, however.

"Go back to Chilleau Judiciary and tell Verlaine all about it. Take me with you. I'll let them know we're coming."

Jils knew his mind. He didn't have to explain.

"We leave tomorrow, then. Good enough."

There were times when Garol wondered whether working with Jils was becoming dangerous. They knew each other almost too well. That could lead to a failure to detect a developing irregularity in the other's conduct, potentially injurious to the Judicial order and the maintenance of the rule of Law.

So long as justice was served, was that a problem?

It was for Jils; and Garol knew that.

For Jils Ivers it was only justice if the rule of Law was served. If the Judicial order was violated, it could not be just or judicious, no matter what the surrounding circumstances might be. There was no point in exploring the issue with her, though, so Garol simply stood up, giving her a bow of formal thanks for her support and her acuity.

"I'll go make our call to Chilleau Judiciary."

If he was right about the Langsariks, it would work out.

If he was wrong?

Would he be able to live with himself if he unleashed the beast that had ravaged the Tyrell Yards on an undefended population at Port Charid?

There was only one way left to find out.

Time enough to ask himself that question once this was all over.

*   *   *

"There may be some irregularities in the cargo manifests at the development site," Fisner Feraltz admitted, generously. "But with Dalmoss away at Geraint, we're using a temporary floor manager. A man with experience and reliability, who was once an officer in the Langsarik fleet."

It was the morning of the second day after he and Dalmoss had played coy with the corpse of the murdered Langsarik from the Tyrell Yards. Fisner stood in Factor Madlev's office reviewing the morning reports, which were presenting some problems—some carefully constructed problems. Fisner had yet to see any real development from the seeds they had planted that night; so he had initiated further measures of his own, to be in place in case they should prove to be required.

Factor Madlev frowned. "But there are irregularities? Trusting to gain trust is all very well, Fisner, but we can't take chances with other people's cargo. It's our honor. As well as our duty."

Chewing on his lip, Fisner took a moment before he replied. As a matter of fact Shires was doing quite a good job at receiving reconciliation, by and large; but Fisner had reasons for planting the doubts in Factor Madlev's mind. "I'm sure it's just the learning curve, Factor. But I am concerned. I felt it should be laid before you, if only as an informational item."

Fisner heard footsteps approach the open doorway behind him; when he heard the Bench specialist's voice he closed his eyes, saying a silent prayer of submissive thanks.

"Good-greeting, Factor, thank you for seeing me. Foreman."

Bench intelligence specialist Garol Vogel.

Factor Madlev stood up politely, lowering his head in greeting. "At your disposal entirely, Specialist Vogel. Ah . . . Fisner, should you perhaps go?"

"Of course." Fisner could afford a prompt response.

The Holy Mother would not have placed him here so fortuitously had She not arranged for him to remain.

"Not necessary, Factor, thank you for your concern." Vogel was but the tool of the Holy Mother's purpose. To that extent Fisner was Vogel's master; and Factor Madlev's, too. "I'm leaving Port Charid, and I'd like you both to be fully briefed. In strictest confidence, of course."

Fisner already knew part of what Vogel had to say. In general, if not in detail.

Vogel had apparently been expected, the link to Chilleau Judiciary set up in advance; Fisner stepped back to close the door to Factor Madlev's office—and efface himself, as well—as the communications link cleared.

First Secretary Verlaine came on over the line.

"This is Verlaine. Your status, Bench specialist?"

Was it his imagination—Fisner asked himself—or did Vogel actually hesitate? He certainly seemed to pause to take a breath before he spoke.

"Beg leave to inform you, leaving Port Charid for Chilleau Judiciary with evidence to lay before the Bench as to the precise identity of parties responsible for recent predation at Port Charid."

Very formal indeed. Factor Madlev had sat back down, staring at Vogel with wide-eyed wonder. Perhaps Vogel's certainty of phrase did seem like the result of some wonderful feat of Bench specialist ferret work, to Factor Madlev. Fisner knew exactly what Vogel thought he knew. Vogel was like warm dough in his hands; he had but to supply the yeast, and Vogel would puff the tale up to twice and three times its original size.

"Good news, Specialist Vogel. Here's mine."

The First Secretary's voice was so clear from the voice port on Factor Madlev's desk that Fisner almost believed he could see the skeptical expression on the First Secretary's face. He didn't even know what First Secretary Verlaine looked like. He had to be a big

man, though, probably bearded, a Factor Madlev of a
man; because his voice was of the depth and timbre
that only resulted from great chests and substantial
bulk.

"News, that is, not good," the First Secretary continued. "I have a Fleet Interrogations Group on
alert." This news came as an obvious shock to Vogel;
but not so much as Fisner might have thought. So
perhaps Vogel was further along than even Fisner
had hoped?

Verlaine was still talking. "We cannot justify an
abeyance of sanctions for very much longer. As you
know, the Second Judge's trust in your judgment is
considerable, Specialist Vogel. She and I therefore
both hope that you will be able to resolve the difficulties at Port Charid in an expeditious manner without resort to the expense of a Fleet Interrogations
Group."

A Fleet Interrogations Group on alert?

What was its charter to be?

He could use this—it would be brilliant.

"I was going to suggest a Fleet detachment, First
Secretary. There will be no need for a Fleet Interrogations Group, but I am asking that police resources be
detailed immediately." Vogel sounded only reasonable
and mild; but the First Secretary—Fisner was de-
lighted to hear—was not having any of it.

"I have already made promises to representatives
of the planetary governments concerned, Specialist
Vogel. Pending a satisfactory resolution to the situation at Port Charid, the Third Fleet Interrogations
Group at Dobe has been placed on standby alert to
travel to Port Charid and investigate allegations of
violation of the amnesty agreement on the part of the
Langsarik settlement. If proved these violations will
be construed as nullifying the amnesty, and the full
range of Bench sanctions will be implemented
immediately."

Beautiful.

Unleash a Fleet Interrogations Group with such a Brief, and they would find evidence of organized violation of the amnesty among the Langsariks. There was no question about it. That was what a Fleet Interrogations Group did. They would go through the Langsariks until they had collected enough by way of confessions to validate whatever measures the Bench could want to take. Given enough bodies to process, they would get what they were looking for, with certainty.

"I'm sorry to hear that, First Secretary," Vogel said; concerned, yes, but still confident. "Fleet Interrogations Groups so frequently generate their own momentum. I trust to satisfy the Second Judge as to the complete irrelevance of any such requirement. Leaving Port Charid today, expect arrival at Chilleau Judiciary in three days' time."

Yet until the Second Judge had reviewed Vogel's evidence, the Fleet Interrogations Group would logically remain on standby. Having been driven to the point of putting the Fleet Interrogations Group on standby in the first place, they would have to wait for dramatic news before they could issue a stand-down without losing credibility. Fisner knew exactly how he could get that Fleet Interrogations Group on its way to execute the vengeance of the Angel of Destruction against the Langsariks—before Vogel even got to Chilleau Judiciary.

By the time Vogel even knew what was happening it would be too late. The Fleet Interrogations Group would be on-site, at work, and Langsariks would confess to everything. Anything the Fleet Interrogations Group asked them.

"We'll wait." The First Secretary didn't sound convinced; the battle was half-won already. Soon it would be academic. "But not for very long. Priority call as soon as you arrive, Specialist Vogel. We're very anxious to review your findings."

Fisner had to stifle his grin of glee. It was an effort, but he managed.

Vogel bowed to the voice port on Factor Madlev's desk, saluting the Bench in the person of the Second Judge's principal administrator. "Leaving very soon, First Secretary. Vogel away, here."

"Looking forward to it. Chilleau Judiciary, way."

The First Secretary spoke for the Second Judge, and Vogel answered to the Bench. If the Bench decided not to wait any longer for Vogel's solution to its problem at Port Charid, that was the Bench's right and prerogative.

"So, we'll be having an end to all this, soon," Factor Madlev said. It was obviously as much as he dared say but so much less than he wanted to know.

Vogel nodded confidently. "That's right, Factor Madlev. The information I have for the Second Judge is conclusive. Once she but sees what I have to show her, it will be all over but the deliberations."

Vogel would never know; but the Angel of Destruction had bested even a Bench intelligence specialist and shaped Vogel to its will in the pursuit of its special mission.

Once the Fleet Interrogations Group arrived, with its Brief in full effect—

The Langsariks would die horribly, and he would be revenged.

Midmorning, the day after Hilton had located the battle cannon on the floor of the new warehouse, Kazmer Daigule sat before the console in the wheelhouse of the Malcontent's shuttle, watching as Garol Vogel's courier tracked for the Shawl of Rikavie and the Sillume vector.

"Good riddance," Cousin Stanoczk said, from behind him. "Nothing but trouble, Bench intelligence specialists. Now perhaps we can all get on about our business here, without the interference of persons impertinently trying to interest themselves in other people's affairs."

It was a pretty little thing, Vogel's courier. In his previous life Kazmer had dreamed of some year owning something like that. Now he owned nothing—but if he was to face a lifetime of service as pilot on craft such as the one Cousin Stanoczk had taken from Anglace, had he really lost? Since realistically speaking his chances of ever affording anything in either class were slim indeed—

· "That's the idea, anyway," Garol Vogel said, from where he stood at Stanoczk's side. There was no hint of resentment in his voice, though Stanoczk could be unpleasantly sharp when it suited him. "Has the freighter tender we want moved yet, Daigule?"

No, it hadn't. In fact the freighter tender that Hilton had identified as the one to watch was the only one that Fisner Feraltz had not released to unload and stand by in response to Cousin Stanoczk's request, made a day ago, for eight freighter tenders to be made available.

Kazmer keyed his window on the warehouse's traffic monitors, just to be sure. "Stasis," Kazmer said, pointing to the screen with satisfaction. "Going nowhere. So we can be sure that it's the one."

Vogel nodded with grim satisfaction, then looked to Cousin Stanoczk. "How are we doing on the cargo for Honan-gung?"

Cousin Stanoczk bowed in polite response. "In final preparation even now, Specialist Vogel. The carpenters have been working without rest at the airfield, building a transfer case for the large refrigeration unit we hypothetically expect at Honan-gung. We can load for departure by evening."

Vogel nodded approvingly. "Fast workers, those Langsariks. I'm sorry, Daigule, but we can't take you with us."

Kazmer looked up over his shoulder at Cousin Stanoczk, surprised.

"Kazmer understands that he will be needed here," Cousin Stanoczk said firmly, but Kazmer imagined that his voice was not completely unsympathetic. "If for no other reason than to be seen. Were he to drop out of sight while I remained bustling about in Port Charid, the quarry might become suspicious. We do not love each other. We are always eager to expect the worst of each other."

The Malcontent, and the Angel of Destruction. Stanoczk was talking about the Angel. It was perhaps true that Kazmer and Cousin Stanoczk did not love each other; but love had nothing to do with the relationship. Kazmer was genuinely obliged to Cousin Stanoczk. And Cousin Stanoczk had treated him fairly enough, at least thus far.

"Also, Hilton Shires is leaving," Stanoczk said. "Kazmer will be waiting for opportunities to slip away, while I am not watching. So that he can go and make love to the cousin."

His role was to be that of the go-between, then, carrying messages between Cousin Stanoczk and Walton Agenis.

It was a good plan. But it meant talking to Modice. That was unkind of Stanoczk, to send him to talk to Modice, because it hurt.

He was resigned now to what he had done and what he had to do to make up for it. It was going to make him feel much better to see the murderers punished for their crimes, that was true enough. Still, the sooner he was away from Port Charid—the sooner he could start to pretend to forget Modice Agenis—the easier it would be for him to wear the red halter of the Malcontent.

"Well thought." Garol Vogel approved, but could hardly guess at what the arrangement was going to cost Kazmer in wear and tear on his emotions. Not that it mattered. As far as Garol Vogel was concerned, Kazmer was a criminal anyway, escaped from lawful punishment by stealth and worthily deserving any punishment that came his way by way of substitution. "I'll be seeing you, then, Cousin Stanoczk."

"Kazmer. I am going to go visit with Factor Madlev. Would this not be a good time for you to fetch a for-hire and go out to the airfield to see if Modice is there?"

He would be the package man, then. Vogel would hide in the for-hire that Kazmer would take from the docks in Port Charid out to the airfield, and when Kazmer got to the airfield—to ask around for Modice—Vogel could slip away, unseen, undetected, to join the Langsarik ambush party loading for transport to Honan-gung.

"You know Sarvaw, Cousin Stanoczk. We are completely untrustworthy. Ruled by our passions utterly."

He meant it to sound like an agreement, playful, entering into the spirit of the deception; but he had not fully mastered his bitterness. He could hear it in his own voice. Cousin Stanoczk surprised him; stepping forward, putting one hand on his shoulder, Cousin Stanoczk leaned over him and kissed his forehead with grave and absolute reverence.

"You are as good man as any and better than most, Kazmer Daigule. You will see vindication, it is my sacred duty to you. —Now I am leaving, I will see you later."

Kazmer didn't see what vindication had to do with Malcontents. But he was irrationally comforted by Cousin Stanoczk's gesture, nonetheless.

Chapter Ten

After his meeting that morning with Factor Madlev—
with its bonus of seeing Specialist Vogel—Fisner had
come back to his office in the new warehouse, taking
Hariv with him to provide administrative support. He
had some catching up to do, and plenty of work to
keep Hariv busy; so it came as no surprise when Hariv
knocked at the door to Fisner's office for instruction.

"Yes?"

Hariv looked a little unsure of himself.

"The floor manager to see you, Foreman. The Langsarik. Shires. Asks for a word."

Fisner thought fast. The office was well lighted;
Shires had seen him in the warehouse only under conditions of low light and was less likely to make the
connection accordingly. He had laid aside his overblouse, sitting at his desk in his shirtsleeves; Shires
had seen him in the warehouse only fully clothed and
wearing warm clothing for going out at night, so there
would not be any hinted connection there either.

Since he was seated Shires was likely not to notice
that he had finally laid aside his medical bracing. So
as far as Shires was concerned Fisner would still present the appearance of impaired physical performance—with the unconscious assumptions of limited
mobility suggested by that.

He was probably as safe from exposure by Shires
as it was possible for him to be. It would only attract
unwelcome attention if he rejected a normal request
during the normal course of the day's events without

an obvious and self-evident excuse. Which he did not have.

"Thank you, Hariv, of course. Now?"

What would it matter if Shires did start to suspect something, at this advanced point in the campaign? To whom could Shires bring a half-formed suspicion? The Bench intelligence specialists had left. It was only a matter of hours before their courier would reach the Sillume entry vector. Once that happened they were as good as neutralized for three days, the time it took to travel on Sillume from Charid to Chilleau Judiciary via Garsite.

As Hariv opened the office door more widely to admit Shires, Fisner made another quick calculation. Shires had heard him whispering to Dalmoss in the warehouse. He would be sure to speak loudly and confidently.

"Foreman Feraltz. Thank you for seeing me, sir."

Shires came only part of the way across the room, stopping at a polite distance in the middle of the rug. Discomfort and uncertainty seemed to discourage him from seeking eye contact; Fisner relaxed a bit, but only internally, careful to maintain his formal posture.

"Something's come up, Foreman," Shires said. "This is awkward. I very much appreciate the trust you've reposed in me, opportunity to learn, and so forth. But it's a family matter."

Quitting?

"I'm afraid I don't understand, Shires, what's on your mind?"

Raising his eyes to Fisner's face for one quick glance, Shires seemed almost to blush, dropping his gaze again immediately. "There's a man working out in the Shawl at the Honan-gung Yards, not really my relative, but I am related to his sister. There's a situation. His family needs him, but there's the employment contract with Honan-gung. Hand for hand. I've got to get to Honan-gung so that Willet can get back to his family, I don't know how long I'm going to have to cover for him. I'm very sorry, Foreman."

Oh. Was that it? Or did Shires actually have something more subtle on his mind?

Disappointed understanding was clearly what was called for in this situation; Fisner frowned, to demonstrate concern. "I feel sure you wouldn't come asking if it weren't a real problem, Shires. But I have to note that this puts us in a very difficult situation, with Dalmoss not back from Geraint."

Now Shires took a deep breath and threw back his head, staring up at the ceiling for a moment—as though getting his thoughts together—before he met Fisner's gaze, very frankly. Utterly honest. "To be brutally explicit, Foreman, there's a certain sort of irregularity involved. Personal behavior. It can be put right if an intimate friend can be identified before much more time elapses, but timing is critical. For the family's sake."

That was a lot of inventing to do.

If it was inventing.

Maybe Shires had thought the clues through and arrived at Honan-gung; why not? There was the question of what exact evidence Bench specialist Vogel thought he had, to present to First Secretary Verlaine at Chilleau Judiciary.

It was at least possible that Shires actually had no other motive than to address a family problem. Somebody was pregnant, without benefit of prior family negotiation and agreement. It happened. It even happened to Dolgorukij.

Shires at Honan-gung . . .

Shires could not be hoping to rescue Honan-gung from a raid single-handedly; that would be insane. Perhaps Vogel had not believed him, and now he sought to put himself in a position to be an eyewitness for the Langsarik defense; but if that was what Shires had in mind, he was self-deluded. Who would take Shires's evidence on behalf of his people seriously?

There was more.

If Flag Captain Walton Agenis's own nephew and lieutenant should be at Honan-gung when it was raided, his presence—especially under such irregular circumstances as those represented by this sudden excuse to get out to the Shawl—would be powerful circumstantial evidence of Langsarik guilt.

"When must you go?" Fisner asked, careful to sound as reluctant as possible. Shires let his breath out in an audible sigh, as of relief.

"Willet can come back on an inbound that's scheduled to load at Honan-gung. I can get passage on outbound freighter *Sarihelt* stopping at Honan-gung to take on cargo tonight. Thank you, Foreman."

He *was* in a hurry.

When his body was discovered at Honan-gung—a casualty of the firefight, overlooked by mischance—what would the Bench make of his eagerness to get to Honan-gung as soon as the Bench specialists had left, to be in place in time for the raid that was to come?

And Shires had Dalmoss's undocumented chop, the one they had used to obtain the freighter tender's release for the Tyrell raid; better and better.

"It can't be helped." Shires had apparently correctly guessed at Fisner's permission, so he wouldn't push that any further. "I can't promise that your place will be held for you. But you've done very well, Shires, I hope you'll give us a chance to employ you again once these domestic entanglements have been resolved. Good-greeting, then."

Fisner turned his attention back to the administrative details of his daily tasks, smiling.

It was a matter of hours from Port Charid to the Shawl of Rikavie. Once the freighter came up to speed, there was little for Hilton to do but brood about how the freedom that had been their natural right had been denied them as part of the terms of the amnesty agreement. Life at Port Charid had not been torture: It was knowing that he was trapped there that had shadowed his psyche, for more than a year now.

He didn't want to dock at Honan-gung.

He wanted to steal the freighter, hit the Sillume vector, and fly forever—or until his air ran out. It would be worth it, to die in space. It would be a good death. Satisfying. Fit. Appropriate.

He couldn't afford the distraction.

He had work to do.

The freighter docked at Honan-gung, but nobody came out of the dockmaster's office to greet them. Hilton had his instructions. The freighter crew let down the loading ramp, and Hilton stepped down out from the belly of the beast to the docking bay's loading apron. Hilton walked by himself across the empty and unpeopled warehouse floor with his documents board in his hand to pay his respects to the dockmaster, who was waiting for him in her office. He could see her standing at the office's observation port, watching him come, and someone behind her with a jelly-stick. Nasty.

What, didn't they trust him?

Just because he was Langsarik—

He was on camera, too. He knew it; Vogel had clipped into the communications braid as the freighter neared the Honan-gung Yards, checking to be sure they knew where the eyes were. Parking an access slip in the information stream, to be ready when the time came. Hilton stopped short of the dockmaster's office and called out.

"Hilton Shires come from Charid to relieve Willet, Dockmaster. We have your permission. May I come in?"

He had no intention of quarreling with a man with a jelly-stick. Get hit with a fist, and bruise your face; get hit with a jelly-stick and smash all the bones at the side of your face into a pulp. Hilton was not interested.

He did his best to look defenseless.

After a moment's consideration the man with the jelly-stick opened the door to the dockmaster's office to let Hilton through. Hilton went, but only because he knew Vogel was watching. He hoped that someone would intervene if the dockmaster decided that she didn't like his looks.

Marching up to the dockmaster, Hilton bowed politely, holding his documents board in front of him so that she could read what was there. "Thank you for your confidence. My credentials, ma'am."

A personal request that she play along with the charade that was required to get the ambush in place without alerting the quarry; one signed by Garol Aphon Vogel, Bench intelligence specialist. Identity chops could be forged; the raiders who had vandalized Tyrell would hardly be deterred from attempted forgery of Jurisdiction chops by the relatively insignificant penalty of death for doing so.

But it was such a beautiful chop mark, crisp and sparkling and ornate and complicated, that it was convincing in and of itself. Hilton was sure the dockmaster couldn't help but be impressed. He was impressed, but he already knew that the chop mark was the genuine article.

"Are they, really?"

The station's surveillance was focused in other directions than within the dockmaster's office, but Hilton knew he couldn't afford anyone glimpsing any anomalous behavior. They'd start to wonder. The presence of the man with the jelly-stick was enough of a problem. If Jelly-stick turned out to be the enemy's inside man, they would have a piece of work to do to get him taken off line without alerting his principals either directly or indirectly. Jelly-stick didn't look Dolgorukij to Hilton, though, so maybe they were all right.

As though any seven people with jelly-sticks would present serious difficulties to people with Langsarik battle cannon tucked casually into their hip pockets, if Hilton actually had been a raider.

The Bench requests your cooperation in investigating a serious crime. Please take your cues from the bearer, Hilton Shires.

Signed and sealed.

The dockmaster seemed undecided for a long and trepidatious moment.

Then she made up her mind, handing the documents board back to him with a nod of acquiescence.

"All right, Shires, what can I do for you?"

That was two.

One had been getting out of Port Charid with their cargo undetected. That left only three—getting set up here, while staying out of sight—and four.

Four.

Ambushing a raiding party, capturing the killers who had done their best to ruin the Langsarik settlement, and returning in vindicated triumph to Port Charid.

Maybe it was a little more than four, maybe that was actually four through eight, but there was no question about two, which meant four was coming.

"If you would care to accompany me, ma'am, to inspect the cargo seals in place prior to off load. With your escort, of course."

Garol Vogel was waiting on the freighter, out of sight. In safe concealment. The man with the jelly-stick would have to be included, because though he might not have seen the text on the documents board with its impressive official chop mark, he certainly knew by now that something was going on.

There was a lot to do.

They had to locate the raiders' inside man, going on information from Kazmer Daigule and that Cousin Stanoczk of his. They had to get cargo into place.

They had to find Willet and send him back to Port Charid. And then they had to wait.

"Lead on, then," the dockmaster said, beckoning the man with the jelly-stick with a wave of her hand to let him know that he should come with them.

Soon, soon, soon he would have revenge for the dead and the honor of the Langsarik fleet; and he was eager for it.

From where she knelt in the garden pulling the weeds, Walton Agenis could see the dust on the vehicle track, someone approaching the settlement—in a transport van, rather than in a for-hire or on a speed machine. It was that size of a cloud. The vehicle track was graded and paved, but the autumn rains had yet to set in; the dust on the road was as good as an advance warning signal.

Who would it be?

Midweek. That explained it. Walton watched the dust cloud for a moment, evaluating its dimensions and its rate of travel; then bent her head to her weeding once again. Yes. Midweek. It would be the supply van from Port Charid coming out to stock the little concession store that the Fleet had put out here to serve the community's miscellaneous requirements for notions, sundries, small amounts of luxury foods. The supply van from Port Charid.

It was early for the concession truck to arrive, though, didn't that usually show up after midday? The morning was early yet. The first shift at the construction site down the road was no more than two hours old. Traveling a little quickly for the concession van, maybe. The driver of the concession van was usually in no particular hurry to get here, and in no particular hurry to leave.

She was not liking this.

She was not liking this more and more, moment by moment.

She sat back once again, watching the dust on the

vehicle track. There were more than one of them approaching.

The settlement was as deserted as it ever got. Many of the Langsariks with physical labor left in them were at the construction site. Others were in Port Charid doing entry-level administrative or custodial jobs, oiling the machinery of commerce with their low-cost labor.

If someone was going to raid the settlement—

This was not the time to do it, not with most of the Langsariks population dispersed to one job or another.

Or was it?

Had someone decided to accept the added task of tracking down each and every one of her crew, as an acceptable price for avoiding any potential resistance in mass that might have threatened had they chosen another time? There were more Langsariks than police or Port Authority employees in Port Charid. There were almost more Langsariks than able-bodied others; where would the resources to take them all at once come from?

Pushing herself up off the ground, Walton stood up. She could see Modice at the side of the house, watching the road. The vehicles were turning off the main vehicle track, making for the settlement proper.

Three transport vans, not supply trucks; still, they were headed for the concession store.

What was going on?

Nobody pulled up to her door to require her presence, though she was one of the senior members on the municipal board of the settlement.

Modice was looking in her direction, now. Walton couldn't see the expression on Modice's face from where she stood, but Modice's body language was sufficiently eloquent to communicate concern and uncertainty.

All right, if they didn't come for her, she'd go to them. Tucking her gardening trowel into her belt loop, Walton stepped across the rows of ripening root vegetables to go see what this was all about.

Modice started moving, too.

Other people in the settlement had seen the transport vans arrive or heard them pass through the settlement on the way to the concession store, alerted by the unusual speed at which the vehicles were traveling. A small crowd had gathered by the time Walton arrived; but there didn't seem to be anybody near the store itself.

As Walton Agenis got closer she saw the reason why.

Troops.

There was a cordon of people between the small crowd and the concession store, drawn up in formal array. They weren't in uniform, and they weren't in very good position, but they were all carrying weapons; so troops it was.

What was this all about?

Walton pushed through to the front of the crowd of people, looking past the cordon now to see if there was anybody she recognized.

"Factor Madlev!"

He started when she called out to him, as though she'd frightened him. It *was* Factor Madlev, and someone she thought she vaguely recognized with him: her nephew's foreman from the new construction site, Fisner Feraltz.

That was why he was familiar, then.

She remembered Fisner Feraltz. He'd been much younger, but he hadn't changed so much; and nothing she had ever heard had hinted that he had yet dealt with the traumatic event that had made him an orphan.

Factor Madlev was a decent man, if unsure of the wisdom of placing Langsariks in positions of trust.

But Fisner Feraltz was the enemy.

Turning, Factor Madlev started toward her; Feraltz put out a hand to detain him, saying something in a low voice. There were people she didn't recognize in the store, going in and out with boxes through the back. Whatever Feraltz said was apparently convincing, because Factor Madlev stopped; but then Madlev waved her forward to come and join him, so the armed men had to let her pass.

Feraltz stepped back and away from Factor Madlev, but Walton didn't care if he heard what she had to say or not. "Factor Madlev. A surprise. What's going on here? The store won't be opening for another hour or two yet."

Some kind of a search, that seemed obvious enough now that she was close enough to get an unobstructed view. What, did someone think you could hide Langsarik battle cannon in flour boxes? It was ludicrous on the face of it—but she couldn't deny her uneasiness.

Maybe it wasn't battle cannon they were looking for.

Maybe it was some other kind of contraband, and contraband could be planted.

The people who ran the supply transport between the concession store in the settlement and Port Charid were all Madlev's people, so at least some of them could be Fisner Feraltz's people. She didn't think the people who watched the store broke open every case when it came out, not until it was needed. It would be so easy . . .

Madlev was visibly uncomfortable. He nodded to her in greeting with a look of genuine concern on his face. "Good-greeting, Dame Agenis. My apologies for this unannounced visit, but. Well, frankly. There was a tip. An anonymous tip. My clear duty, to see what might be at the heart of it."

Tension knotted in Walton's stomach like a muscle spasm; but she managed to keep her voice steady. "Tip. What was the nature of this tip, Factor Madlev?"

It was obvious, wasn't it?

Uncomfortable as he clearly was with his role, Factor Madlev was also determined not to shirk his duty as he saw it. "To be quite clear, a claim that evidence relating to raids within the Shawl of Rikavie could be recovered from the storage room here. We can't not test the claim."

Of course they couldn't.

Walton watched the searchers work with dread and with anticipation that was equal parts of apprehension and eagerness for the play to run out. They would search until they found what they were looking for. They would find something; the enemy would not have risked an anonymous tip unless they had their prize in place.

Vogel had gone to ground at Honan-gung to wait for the next raid, and was not available to help.

Did this development mean there wouldn't be a raid at Honan-gung? Had the complicated setup Hilton had witnessed been abandoned, for whatever reason, for this unexpected—unheralded—approach?

No, that didn't made sense.

Discovery of contraband was still strictly circumstantial, clearly ambiguous by virtue of its location. More than just Langsariks had access to the stores.

Two men came out through the back door to the concession store sideways, carrying a small crate between them. They set it down at Factor Madlev's feet, grim satisfaction clear in their determined expressions.

Walton didn't even need to look to know. If she didn't even look, though, it could be taken as evidence that she already knew quite well what was in the crate. So she stared with wide-eyed wonder at the contents of the crate: a nest of padding that surrounded a beautiful little clutch of crystal gems for energy arrays, the smallheavies that warehouses kept for emergencies.

The wrappings were all marked with the sigil that identified them to the Okidan Yards.

Smallheavies were the single most valuable commodity—in market price to mass ratio—in known Space: portable, untraceable, and very easily convertible into other forms of laundered cash besides.

"Your people broke the seals," Walton noted,

pointing. "How are we going to be able to prove who hid these here?"

It didn't have to be a strong argument; all it had to be was strong enough.

Evidence recovered on an anonymous tip was purely circumstantial, suspect by its very nature. No matter how strongly implicated the Langsarik settlement was by this discovery, they could not be convicted on this evidence alone.

"It looks bad, though, Dame Agenis," Factor Madlev said. The regretful sorrow in his voice was genuine; Walton could respect his desire to put the best construction on things. "We'll have to make a report. To Chilleau Judiciary, with Garol Vogel gone."

More than that, Feraltz would have to carry out the raid on Honan-gung in order to put visual evidence of atrocities on the record.

She hoped that Feraltz's raid was at Honan-gung.

If it was anywhere but Honan-gung, they could be lost, despite the best efforts of Vogel and Hilton and Modice's Daigule combined.

He had coordinated the raid, arranged for an escort for Agenis afterward, and otherwise made himself so much a part of the day's work that Factor Madlev had no apparent questions in his mind about Fisner's right to be here for this one.

"Urgent news from Port Charid, First Secretary." Factor Madlev had been a silent witness during previous interviews between Specialist Vogel and the Second Judge's First Secretary; he seemed a little intimidated, now, but he knew his ground and field, growing more confident as he spoke. "I am of course not privy to what information the Bench specialist may have to present to you when he arrives. But I am fully familiar with the outrages we have suffered here at Port Charid over the past months."

Factor Madlev paused for a moment, glancing at Walton Agenis's impassive face. Madlev's misplaced sense of decency was to blame for her presence here. Fisner felt it unnecessary, but she could do no harm. Factor Madlev seemed finally to be convinced—so much was clear from his determined tone, as he continued.

"Now there is additional evidence linking terrorist acts to the Langsariks settled here at Port Charid. Dame Agenis herself will admit to what we all saw earlier today, plunder from Okidan, recovered from a hiding place within the Langsarik settlement."

Terrorist acts. It was a word choice that Fisner could appreciate; all the more so since Fisner had not had to take any hand in guiding Madlev to the right phrase.

"Recovered, yes," Walton Agenis said. She hadn't asked permission to speak; she was only here on sufferance—but her boldness won her the attention of the First Secretary, because Factor Madlev seemed too startled to rebuke her. "But on an anonymous tip, from an area to which other than Langsariks have had continuous and uncontrolled access since the very first days of the settlement. We have not violated the terms of our agreement with the Bench, First Secretary. I assert our complete innocence of any involvement with theft and violence in system."

Well, what else could she say?

And Factor Madlev, for once, insisted on his right as the acting governor and Bench proxy at Port Charid.

"Dame Agenis's position is reasonable and honorable, but there is cause to believe that she no longer speaks for the Langsariks. We have been patient, First Secretary. We have appealed to the Bench for help after the raid on Penyff. After the raid on Sonder. After the raid on Tershid. Okidan. Tyrell. You sent us Bench specialists. They have gone, and told us nothing."

Madlev warmed to his subject as he spoke. He was right. Absolutely right. Completely right. Unchallengeably right. "We are responsible citizens of the Bench, First Secretary. We have a right to security in the conduct of trade. Would the Bench tolerate these pirates if they were anyone else but Langsariks?"

There was silence from Chilleau Judiciary, as the First Secretary apparently took a moment to digest Factor Madlev's assertion.

"What do you want me to do, Madlev?"

Fisner caught his breath and held it, almost despite himself. This was crucial. If Madlev backed down now—

Madlev didn't back down. "I say it's time to admit that the Langsariks are our primary suspects, First Secretary, with respect. It may seem disrespectful to mention such a thing in this regard, but we have all heard a great deal about recent and regrettable failures within the Second Judge's administration to execute good governance and observe the rule of Law. At the Domitt Prison."

Far from backing down, Madlev pressed forward more strongly than Fisner would ever have imagined. He had not realized that Factor Madlev had such strong feelings about this—but perhaps Madlev took the Bench's inaction as a personal reflection. If not on him personally, than on the Bench's respect and consideration for his position here. Yes. Perhaps.

There was a sound from the communications link, as of clucking one's tongue. A sound of exasperation, or of warning. "You put your case very strongly, Factor Madlev."

Should he not?

Did Verlaine mean that Factor Madlev should comport himself with more submissive meekness in the presence of the First Secretary?

"I state only the facts as we see them, First Secretary. The firms who have invested in Port Charid did not expect to put lives as well as capital into the enterprise. Those lives deserve consideration. If Port Charid is truly important to the Bench for the development of trade routes across the Sillume vector, it is high time the Bench showed some evidence of its respect. Sending Vogel was a good first step. But Vogel's gone, we have heard nothing, the dead are unavenged, there is physical evidence here. I appeal to you."

No, Fisner realized, with satisfaction. Madlev did not appeal to Verlaine. Madlev demanded. "Send troops, if nothing else, to secure the Shawl. Do something."

There was no answer for several moments, but there were voices in the background. One of them Verlaine's.

When Verlaine came back at full volume he sounded both angry and resigned. "Very well, Factor Madlev," Verlaine said; and Fisner felt his heart leap in exultation. "I have spoken to Specialist Vogel. You are right, you deserve nourishment. Here's what I've decided to do."

Glancing at Agenis quickly, Fisner saw her face pale, dread evident in her eyes—no matter how resolute her expression. She was right to dread, Fisner told himself, guarding his fierce joy carefully to prevent any hint of his delight from escaping. This was the beginning of the end for the Langsariks.

"I will release the Third Fleet Interrogations Group to depart for Rikavie immediately, with a fully endorsed schedule of inquiry—pending final authorization, which I will issue or cancel once I have reviewed the evidence Garol Vogel promises. You have been asked to be patient for too long. There will be an end to it."

An end to the Langsariks.

A Fleet Interrogations Group would generate confessions, to be claimed as evidence; there would be more evidence on record after the Honan-gung raid. Walton Agenis's very own nephew was at Honan-gung. Hilton Shires would be easy to identify on Honan-gung's record scans; and there was reasonable hope that he had the forged chop with him. On his body.

There would be no claiming ignorance for the Lang-

sariks after that; Verlaine would have to issue the final
authorization. The Fleet Interrogations Group would
already be on hand, ready and waiting. It would all
be an accomplished fact before Vogel could hope to
return to Port Charid, even if he turned around the
moment he reached Chilleau Judiciary.

After that Vogel could raise concerns all he liked.
Once the Bench had evidence on Record, the truth
behind that evidence would be no longer relevant. The
rule of Law and the upholding of the Judicial order
would demand that the Bench proceed against a
proven enemy, prosecuting the case against the Langsariks to the fullest extent of the Law.

"It can't come too soon, First Secretary. With respect." Factor Madlev had gained his point. He could
step back, lower his head, bow politely to the communications port on the desk. "Thank you."

Agenis stood and stared at the far wall, and Chilleau
Judiciary closed the communications link between
them.

Madlev sighed deeply.

Then he walked over to his desk and sat down.

"Escort Dame Agenis back to the settlement,"
Madlev said, to Fisner. "No contact with other Langsariks. The household is under quarantine."

Fisner understood.

He knew there was nothing the Langsariks could
do. But if they knew there was a Fleet Interrogations
Group coming for them, they would unquestionably
try something.

"Of course, Factor Madlev. Dame Agenis. If you'll
come with me, ma'am, and please don't try to speak
to anybody. We'll keep things as liberal as we can."

Everything was perfect. It had all added up, and
now it was playing out beautifully.

Had Madlev published the coming of the Fleet Interrogations Group, Fisner might have had to recon-
sider the wisdom of the planned Honan-gung raid. It
might be taken as anomalous behavior on the part of

people expecting to be taken to task for their evil deeds in the near future. This way was much better. He could have his raid, his booty from Honan-gung, and his Fleet Interrogations Group, too.

Agenis looked at him, and for a moment Fisner imagined that there was something in her eyes that he did not like—wild contempt, and scorn, and challenging defiance.

It was only a flash, and only a moment.

"Very well, Foreman. Let's go. I don't need to make any trouble. We'll be vindicated by due legal process soon enough."

He had imagined it. Obviously.

Agenis turned toward the door in response to his gesture, and Fisner followed her out, to escort her back to the Langsarik settlement and place her under house arrest.

The Holy Mother smoothed the way of those who worked Her will in the world.

And the Angel of Destruction was invincible.

The Langsarik troops Garol had brought with him had been carefully dispersed quietly, surreptitiously, well out of the way of observation by either the station's monitors or any of the station's personnel—except for the dockmaster herself, and the man who had met poor Shires with jelly-stick in hand and a threatening expression on his face. The maintenance chief. Garol's pod had been wheeled into the dockmaster's safe room, where he had easy access to every incoming communication without the awkward complication of relays that could be noticed or misdirected.

The chime that went off to rouse him from his meditation was no signal incoming to Honan-gung, however.

It was Jils Ivers, in transit for Chilleau Judiciary.

Garol frowned, and toggled in.

"Vogel here." He spoke quietly. The pod was

soundproof, but there was no sense in pushing his limits. "Go ahead."

She didn't sound happy, but there was no reason for her to call him unless there was a problem. "Verlaine. Trouble at Port Charid, a raid on the settlement, hot cargo. Stand by."

All right.

He was securely webbed into his station in the pod, so he didn't more than frown to prepare himself for a confrontation. He heard the signal tone that let him know Jils had braided into skein, and spoke. "First Secretary. Vogel here, sir."

Verlaine wasted no words: clearly under pressure. "I have Port Charid on my neck, Vogel. They raided the Langsarik settlement and found loot from Okidan. I need a convincing story if I'm going to hold action on this."

A raid. Garol thought fast. Such a ploy was a natural part of a conspiracy; maybe he should have expected it. But if it got the conspirators what they wanted—would the Honan-gung raid be abandoned?

"This is not totally unexpected, First Secretary." Not predicted, perhaps, but absolutely in character once it had happened. "I hold my point. My evidence will be definitive."

He just didn't have it yet; but he couldn't tell Verlaine that. Verlaine was on the line with Port Charid. Garol didn't know with certainty whether or not his quarry was listening in—one reason for the charade Jils put forward, the play that he was actually on the courier with her in transit to Chilleau Judiciary.

He could not afford to compromise his chances for the clear and undeniable proof of Langsarik innocence that he needed now more than ever.

"Reluctantly unable to accept as read, Vogel. I've got to think of the Second Judge's reputation. I don't like to override, it's your mission, but I'm running out of time. Give me something to hold Port Charid off. Please."

Garol had to respect the First Secretary's frustration.

But he couldn't say anything more, not and hope to complete the mission he had embarked upon. "I appreciate the delicacy of your situation, First Secretary. Anything you can do to suspend further decisions until I can show you the evidence will be very deeply appreciated."

Awkwardly phrased, but with luck his sincerity would come through. The only question was whether Verlaine felt he could afford to stand behind Garol, with mounting political pressure to take action.

There was a moment's silence; then Verlaine spoke.

"I'm sorry, Bench specialist. I have my Judge to think of. I accept as given your assertion that you can identify the guilty parties. However, I have perceptions to manage as well."

Lost.

"Understood, First Secretary."

Because, unfortunately, Garol did understand. Verlaine had been backed into a corner. The Second Judge had come under widespread criticism from political enemies for her failure to more aggressively detect and deter abuses of the Judicial order injurious to the rights of accused parties in detention at the Domitt Prison.

With publication of the incriminating results of a raid on the Langsarik settlement, Verlaine almost had to take action; it was either that or suffer a storm of criticism such that no responsible First Secretary could be asked to endure on behalf of the Judicial order.

Verlaine didn't even sign off.

The signal didn't drop; Garol listened in on Port Charid.

The Third Fleet Interrogations Group.

It was bad; but it was not over yet. He needed something to ensure that the Honan-gung raid would go off on schedule, whenever that was, and the Third Fleet Interrogations Group would have to do. They did not yet have lawful authority to make Port Charid their playground. If he got evidence before Verlaine released the Brief . . .

Now more than ever he needed the proof that only capture of the guilty during the active commission of a violent crime could provide him.

Jils came back on the line. "Garol. What do you want me to do?"

He didn't know yet. He needed to think things through. He had to have that raid; he didn't dare try to transmit from here to Chilleau Judiciary for fear of detection by the sophisticated communications equipment Daigule had indicated was at the enemy's disposal.

So long as the raid came quickly enough, he could still get his proof to Chilleau Judiciary in time to prevent the release of Brief to the Fleet Interrogations Group. Once they had their Brief, they would not abort their mission for any Bench directive until they were finished—on their own terms.

Politics.

"Track that Fleet Interrogations Group for me, Jils. Let me know when they clear the exit vector at Sillume."

And thanks.

But she knew that.

Extra words were dangerous when communications were on redirect.

Jils was off; Chilleau Judiciary was off. He was alone with his thoughts.

If there was to be a raid at Honan-gung at all, it had to happen soon, before the Fleet Interrogations Group arrived.

Could he rely on the greed of this so-called "Angel of Destruction" of Cousin Stanoczk's to try for one last payout?

How long would the Angel keep him waiting—and how long could he afford to wait before he would be forced to admit defeat?

He was already defeated.

If he could not take prisoners in a raid at Honan-gung, there would be no proving to Chilleau Judiciary that the Langsariks were innocent victims of conspiracy.

He would hold where he was, and wait.

He had no acceptable alternatives to hope for.

Kazmer Daigule parked his for-hire well clear of the little house where Walton Agenis sat under house arrest. The lights that the guards had trained on the building cast shadows in sharp relief, so the scene took on an air of unreality, strange and oppressive in the darkness of the settlement. Was it some variety of harassment? Kazmer wondered. Or was it just un-thinking cruelty, the sort of blind impersonal brutality that was that much the more difficult to bear for being so completely thoughtless?

The guards were warehousemen from the Combine Yards in Port Charid proper—Dolgorukij. Uncomfortable with their role as security, they gathered at the front of the house as Kazmer approached, frowning and doing their best to look stern, bulked up with cold-weather gear in the crisp night air.

When he was within easy hailing distance one of them spoke. "You, what's your business here? You can't go in, you know."

The awkwardness they clearly felt in their performance of their task was eased by their quick recognition of what, if not who, he was. Dolgorukij knew Sarwaw as Sarwaw knew Dolgorukij, and honest warehousemen were naturally put at ease by their inbred knowledge of their racial superiority.

It was a useful trick of the blood, something the Holy Mother had ordained to give Her Sarwaw children an edge even in adversity against their opponents. Kazmer knew how to deal with Dolgorukij bullies. It was nothing personal, not really.

"There should be no problem, cousin, surely." In

the shadows cast by the bright lights against the
greater darkness Kazmer could see eyes narrow in disdain and suspicion at his choice of words. But even a
Sarvaw could lay claim to a privileged position, without blushing, when it was a Malcontent who spoke.
"I'd just like to go and see Modice. She's at home?
With her aunt?"

The guards were not receptive to his powers of persuasion, however. Kazmer fingered the neckline of his
blouse nervously, pulling at the fabric next to his skin
as though his collar were too tight—taking care that
the red ribbon that he wore next to his skin showed
clearly.

The guards relaxed.

"Sorry, cousin, no offense," the spokesman said.
Kazmer was amused to note that he ranked greater
kinship as a Malcontent than he could ever have been
granted as a Sarvaw. "Don't bring us shame before
the foreman, though. Go on in."

He was a Malcontent. He could go anywhere, do
anything, and be bowed on his way by people who
would never dream of granting such a privilege to anyone else. It *was* funny.

Crossing the brilliantly illuminated space between
the cordon and the house, knocking softly at the door.
"Is Modice home?"

They knew that he was there, of course. They'd seen
him coming. It was almost as bright inside as if the
lights had been on, and the lights weren't on, though
the windows had been only partially screened over.
Frugal. Saving of energy. Why turn on the lights when
Port Charid provided such ample illumination at no
charge?

Modice let him in and closed the door behind him.

Walton Agenis sat in the tiny living room watching
him come. The effect of the shadows on the wall from
the lights outside was ghastly.

"You're looking well, Modice," Kazmer said. Modice had gone out to fetch the gelsheets that she'd been

preparing in the kitchen, but they wouldn't know that, outside. They could be listening. He had to assume that someone might be listening. But whoever might be listening could only guess at the potential meaning of whatever they might hear. "Are you getting enough rest?"

Modice was back with gelsheets in a pan, paper-thin sheets of gelatin made opaque with starch. And a stylus. "Not very well, Kazmer, I'm afraid. These lights."

Kazmer wrote on the top gelsheet and passed the pan to Walton Agenis. *FIG clears vector w/in 24 hrs. Must raid before pursuit possible.*

It was a form of freehand code; he couldn't afford to arouse suspicion by concentrating so long on what he needed to write that there was a break in the conversation. "Do you have something you could use as a compress, to cover your eyes? A scarf might do it. If the colors weren't too bright, of course."

Agenis lifted the gelsheet from the pan and folded it up neatly. "Would you get me something to drink, girl." Writing on the next gelsheet in the pan. "I don't want you coming around to court Modice, Daigule. I've told you before. You're not fit to husband a Langsarik."

Progress of organization. Contingency plan?

"Modice could do worse than take a Sarvaw sweetheart," Kazmer protested, mildly. Even a Malcontent lover would be a better fate than the Bond, after all. "I might be able to protect her. Things don't look very promising, you must know that."

Quiet, no alarm. Good progress. Vogel returns PC if raid delayed.

If the Angel cut the margin for its raid too fine, Vogel would be forced to abandon the ambush; Vogel was adamant on the subject. He would be at Port Charid before the Fleet Interrogations Group arrived, one way or the other.

Kazmer had his doubts about that.

Vogel was clearly all but desperate to prevent the

Fleet Interrogations Group from settling in to do its work; but without the evidence that ambushing the raid would produce, how did Vogel hope to prevent it?

"Better pure and falsely accused than soiled and safe, Daigule," Agenis insisted, inflexibly. "Modice."

Modice had returned with a tray and a pitcher of water, three glasses.

"Modice, I don't want you seeing this person again. You are not to let him in, if he has the audacity to return to my house to insult me with his importunity. And in our hour of vulnerability, Daigule, you should be ashamed."

"Aunt Walton, please. You're just upsetting yourself. Here. I brought us all a nice glass of cold water." Three gelsheets from the stack in the pan had been discarded; that was one for each glass. It would be a moment before the gelsheet in his glass dissolved, however.

If anything goes wrong, Aunt Agenis wrote on the next gelsheet in the pan. *Get Modice out of here.*

It was a firm hand, though written on a gelsheet. The tension and the waiting, the uncertainty and the anxiety, were taking their toll on Walton Agenis; but she saw as clearly and as far as ever she had. Kazmer could only bow in her direction. It was not for nothing that she had been called the Deep-Minded.

"I'd better not, Modice, your aunt wants me out of the house. But if there's anything I can do, you send for me, all right? You don't have to toady to this harridan; she'd rather see you dead than with me. And I could make you happy."

He kept his tone very reasonable and calm, he thought. All things considered. Walton Agenis straightened up in her chair so abruptly that she spilled half the water in her glass, her face suddenly transfused with mirth despite it all, and mouthed the words back at him with a look of exaggerated outrage. *Harridan?*

"You can't talk about my aunt that way." Modice's

voice trembled as she fought to keep her composure. "Perhaps you'd better leave, Kazmer."

The gelsheet in his glass had dissolved; Modice would take the unused sheets back to the kitchen, to make cellophane dumplings. It took a steady hand to make Langsarik cellophane dumplings under the best of circumstances. That she could pretend to do so convincingly under these was a measure of her nerve.

"Well. I'm sorry you feel that way." He could express all the resentment he had a right to feel, without holding back. Modice made wonderful cellophane dumplings. He wouldn't be there to help eat them. "You'll be sorry. I wouldn't wait too long to change my mind if I were you, though. I've got my pride, you know."

And she could buy it for three dumplings and a smile. She had. Or rather she could have, in the past, because it was no good anymore, no matter how good a cook she was.

Take care of Modice, Walton Agenis had said.

Now that it was too late, she would trust him.

Kazmer paused on the threshold of Agenis's house to let the resentful anguish in his heart paint his countenance an appropriate shade of outrage and insulted fury; and left them there together in the surreal shadows of the floodlit house.

"The Third Fleet Interrogations Group is due off the Sillume exit vector in twenty hours." They would be able to stage from the new airfield at the construction site; Dalmoss was in no danger of an accidental meeting with any Malcontents, Sarvaw or otherwise, out here. Those people were in Port Charid proper, where they belonged.

No, they belonged in Hell, but it was not Fisner Feraltz's mission to see them escorted safely to their destination—he knew where his special duty lay. "You must be near enough to the entrance vector to make pursuit a clear waste of energy."

"How do I know that, eldest and firstborn?" Dalmoss asked, and there was just the slightest trace of insubordinate challenge in his voice. His long days of seclusion had worn upon him; the proximity of the Langsarik corpse had made him nervous. It would be all right. After this Dalmoss would be able to rest and recreate himself in the bosom of his family, at home, on Arakcheyek. "In order to time my raid. Must I have special knowledge?"

Good question. Fisner thought for a moment. "The Langsarik leader was present when we talked to Chilleau Judiciary. She passed on the information somehow. If you set your margin carefully enough, it will seem clear that you miscalculated, you didn't expect the Fleet Interrogations Group in system so soon, you flee in disarray—leaving the body of at least one of your people behind."

Hilton Shires.

How beautifully it all fit together, when the Holy Mother smiled upon the enterprise.

"Twenty hours. Ten hours from the exit vector to Port Charid." Dalmoss was talking it through, out loud. Fisner could bear the trivial details of it patiently: It would serve as a useful check on the soundness of Dalmoss's reasoning, tipping Fisner off if he needed to retire his raid leader. "Four hours from Port Charid to Honan-gung, at this time of year. So if we leave in panic and disarray as soon as the Fleet Interrogations Group clears the vector, there is no point in pursuing us."

Dalmoss would hit Honan-gung; there would be a raid in process as the Fleet Interrogations Group came off the Sillume exit vector. The raiders would escape, but they would not be able to save their families. The Bench's punishment would be stern and swift—though after the Fleet Interrogations Group had done its work, the Bench sanctions would be perhaps something of an afterthought.

"You must prepare," Fisner urged Dalmoss to energize him, get him going. "You must be away from Honan-gung inside of thirty-four hours. There is much to do. This is our finest moment, second eldest and next born."

Dalmoss bowed, his expression determined and joyful. "Sweet indeed is Holy ordinance, firstborn and eldest. With your blessing we triumph."

With the Holy Mother Herself on their side they were invincible.

Before two days had passed it would be over for the Langsariks at Port Charid.

Chapter Eleven

Hilton lay flat on his back on a scootplank on the floor beneath the crane's trolley with a probe in one hand and a gleam in the other. "What exactly am I looking for, Jevan?" he asked, trying to make sense of the bewildering array of nozzles and blind access bits on the underside of the crane's power box. "Hydraulic scan? Flux regulation coupling?"

Silence.

Hilton wondered if he'd lost his work partner. That was more serious than not knowing what to do with the problem at hand. Jevan was the only Dolgorukij on the crew here, the man the Malcontent had identified as a probable agent for the Angel of Destruction. Hilton needed Jevan where he could keep an eye on him, figuratively if not literally. If Jevan had some means of sending a covert signal to warn the raiders away, Hilton needed to know immediately.

So where had Jevan gone?

Footsteps approached the crane trolley where Hilton lay; Jevan. Maybe. "Sorry, Shires." Yes, that was Jevan. "Maybe we should hold off on this for now. I just heard, there's a freighter coming in. They might need help loading-out."

Hilton thought for a moment. Jevan could have heard, yes, if he'd been chatting with someone in the dockmaster's office when contact was made.

"Maybe we should all go get sticks," Hilton suggested, not moving. "Can't be too careful. Might be Langsariks."

Jevan laughed, crouching on his heels to stick his face into the gap between the bottom of the crane's trolley and the floor.

"You're a funny man."

Jevan could well laugh, Hilton told himself, excitement building within him. If Kazmer's Cousin Stanoczk was right, Jevan already knew that they weren't Langsarik raiders.

"Come out from there, Hilton, we'll be wanted."

Yes, he'd wager on it. Shutting off his gleam, arms straight to his sides, Hilton pushed himself out from underneath the crane's trolley on his scootplank, using his feet for propulsion. "No arguments from me, friend. I'd much rather load than muck around with this stuff."

He felt a tingling sensation, in the sole of his work boot.

Vibration from the movement of the scootplank?

No.

Vogel's signal.

Jevan was holding out a hand to help him up. Hilton took the welcome assistance in the spirit in which it was offered. It was nothing personal. Jevan was a perfectly amiable person; but he was in league with the enemy of the Langsariks, plotting the ruin of the Langsariks. There was blood to balance between them besides.

Maybe it was personal after all—at least on Hilton's part.

"Ready?" Jevan asked. "I should probably go and find the others. In case we're needed."

What made Jevan so sure that they would be?

Still, it might just be common practice on warehouse crews to minimize work effort. "I know," Hilton suggested, to enter into the spirit of the game. "I'll go help find people. I think Teller and Ames are on remote."

The hesitation in Jevan's eyes was very quickly masked. "Well. Sure. Why not? I'll get out to interim stores, then." But it was there; and Hilton could have smiled out loud to see it, except that he might be misinterpreted. Or tip Jevan off.

The signal buzzed twice more in his work boot and was still.

Hilton waited until Jevan was out of sight; then turned, heading toward the corridors that led to the maintenance tunnels for the remote sites where the solar arrays were generating the station's power.

Where he had a raiding party that needed to get to the docking bay.

They had been on alert for two days. They were ready for some action.

Garol Vogel stood behind the dockmaster in her office with his back to the windows in the wall, watching as she engaged the incoming craft.

"All right, *Melrick*, your credentials clear. Permission to dock, transmit your manifest."

It claimed to be the freighter *Melrick* from the Bortic Yards, outbound from Charid for Lorton and scheduled to carry a consignment of cultural artifacts for the cultural institute there as well as licensed replicas for sale on the open market.

"Freighter *Melrick* here, thank you, dockmaster. Initiating transmit." Was it his imagination—Garol wondered—or did he recognize that voice? Had he heard it somewhere before? One thing was for certain—the accent was good. Garol knew it wasn't really Langsariks. He believed and hoped it wasn't Langsariks. But the freighter's captain sounded Langsarik to Garol.

The freighter claimed to have off-loaded at Port Charid and taken on cargo at the Combine Yards before paying a visit to Honan-gung as its next-to-last stop before it made the Sillume entry vector. The next-to-last part was a good touch, Garol felt. Subtle. These people were good.

Garol watched the freighter on approach as its manifest scrolled over the receiver. Shires was with the Dolgorukij, but not so close that the man had no opportunity to send the all clear for the raid to his headquarters. There had been no signal that Garol had intercepted: yet the freighter was here. Garol could only hope that meant that the signal would only have been sent if there had been a problem.

Kazmer Daigule had been tracking the freighter *Melrick* without pause since it had made rendezvous earlier today with a freighter tender from Port Charid— *that* freighter tender, the one whose weight indicated that it was carrying battle cannon or something equivalently and anomalously heavy.

This was what they had been waiting for.

The hardest part of this mission was about to start. He had to keep the raiders distracted while the Langsariks did their thing.

All he really wanted to do was to borrow someone's weapon and shoot them all, simply shoot them all, for the trouble they had caused and the people they had killed, for the hazard they'd created for a people trying to integrate peacefully into Jurisdiction, for the shockingly insolent disregard they showed toward civil society and the common right of common people to live free from fear in an ordered society.

And he couldn't.

He had a duty to the Bench to uphold the rule of Law. That meant not just doing the right thing, but doing it the right way.

"Pretty exhaustive," the dockmaster said to the freighter on the communications line, as Garol tracked the progress of the docking sequence on the monitors. "This could take some putting together."

He had people in position, but if the freighter simply blew in, they would do him no good. He had to trust to the basic mercantile instinct of the Dolgorukij hominid. There was good loot to be had at Honangung. Even with its provenance destroyed or forged, the cargo that the freighter was requisitioning would generate a lot of free cash flow. Secret terrorist societies were almost always short of cash for funding.

"Yes, I know, dockmaster." The freighter captain's voice was regretful and a little diffident over the communications line. "Unfortunately for me, I'm already on deficit time. Any chance of putting a rush on? I've got ten casks of something here. I can't say it's drinking alcohol because it's on my manifest as syrup. We somehow didn't quite manage to obtain any tariff seals, either, so you know I have to get rid of it somehow before I reach the Port Authority in Lorton. Just in case."

So far it conformed to the pattern Daigule had described. There had to be a way to collect the crew all in one place, and it had to be something relatively unremarkable and ordinary, something that wouldn't arouse any suspicion. The raiders knew that Daigule was at Port Charid; but by the same token—if their intelligence was as good as their historical successes indicated—they also knew that Daigule's evidence had not been published. No one had been warned; at least not so far as the raiders knew.

"Well. In that case," the dockmaster said, giving Garol a wink that went by too quickly for him to be sure he'd actually seen it. "I'll let the crew know. Pressurization sequence initiating. Stand by."

This was crucial.

The outer bay pressurized; the blast curtain rolled back, and the freighter tracked forward slowly into position with its cargo bays accessible.

The freighter captain's voice came back across the communications link. "We'll be doing some cargo shift while we're here," the captain said. "Won't be able to start load immediately. Should be ready by the time cargo's assembled, hope you understand."

Garol nodded to the dockmaster. Perfect.

They didn't seem to be planning on moving troops onto the floor concealed in cargo cases this time. It was all to the good if the raiders stayed in the freighter until they thought it was time to make their move, though it complicated the task of Shires's commando. Garol wanted to minimize any potential shooting.

But there were no cameras, no motion detectors, no surveillance in the murky deeps of the docking bay on the other side of the freighter; there was no way to be sure that Shires and his team could pull it off.

"No problem," the dockmaster said. "It'll give us a chance to get organized ourselves. We'll be ready when you are."

Garol hoped so.

It was all up to Shires now.

And Shires had even more to lose than he did.

Crouched behind the waist-tall roll of ground cloth at the far end of the docking bay, Hilton listened to the feed from the dockmaster's office, scanning the freighter with an assessing eye. Late-model Corense shipyards, deep-space cruiser, fit for live and other perishable cargo; the perfect vehicle for transport of luxury goods, and if it carried cannon, what of it? A freighter had a right to self-defense. There were pirates to contend with.

"So. How's the weather in port?" the dockmaster asked, her voice casual in Hilton's ear over the communications feed from the docking bay on the other side of the freighter. Making conversation. Keeping the freighter engaged.

People were starting to filter into the docking bay; the first cargo crates were arriving. He thought he could see Jevan among the workers.

Hilton looked down the line to his left. Leaning forward slightly, Ousel met his eyes. Hilton looked to the flank of the freighter and back to Ousel; Ousel nodded.

Hilton slid to the right over the rough flooring to clear space for Ousel's people to exit. Four of them, keeping low but not crawling, careful to stay in the shadows that the freighter cast. There would be no sensor net that would pick up a hominid. Corense freighters carried damage control for space debris, but the ship's comps knew better than to irritate their master by sounding an alarm every time a maintenance crew came belly under in docks.

"Oh, about the same, dockmaster." The freighter captain didn't sound all that interested in the weather, though. "Say. We'll be ready to start loading soon. We'd sure appreciate any help you can provide."

Jevan would be counting, probably, but there was no way Hilton could see that Jevan could communicate directly with the ship. Maybe the freighter captain was counting as well.

Filappe next.

The external accesses on Corense freighters were usually distributed evenly across three intervals aft, midships, and forward. Filappe had the spanners. There were no pressure alarms to fear, since the bay was pressurized. They had all studied the layout. If this wasn't the ship Kazmer had fingered, they were all in potential trouble—so Hilton wanted to find out as soon as possible.

"And we'll really appreciate your discards." The dockmaster's voice was clear and carried well over the feed from the dockmaster's office that Hilton was carrying. "Got one or two more people yet to notify, but cargo's coming together beautifully. You'll see."

He got the middle access.

Three of his team beside him, Hilton crept stealthily to the side of the freighter, anxious to identify his point of entry. He was off by some lengths, but it was all right, because Vogel had worked it with the dockmaster. The lighting was on their side as much as possible. He could move down the flank of the freighter safe from observation.

But get in?

The bolts on the access port were clean and freshly coated. Hilton felt a moment's panic as he ran his hand around the outline of the access panel. It was too fresh. Had someone bolted it from inside?

Shilla had the wrench.

Torbe slid the cutting edge of a flexible knife around the edges of the bolts where they met the freighter's skin, then stepped back.

Shilla fit the tool to bolt and leaned on it, but nothing moved. Backing away, Shilla stared at the bolt with what looked like horror on her face, in the dim light. Then she leaned into the bolt again: It moved this time, it gave against her weight, and going by the grateful glance she flashed at Hilton—grateful for success, and sharing her emotion—it had been sheer anxiety, and not horror, that he'd seen before.

There were nine bolts.

Torbe and Vilner held the panel as Shilla pulled the last bolt, easing the panel away from the side of the freighter as it came down. Hilton gave Shilla a hand up into the freighter's outside maintenance passage. Once he and Shilla were both inside, Torbe and Vilner passed the outer panel through, so that they could lean it up against the wall of the passageway on the inside. No sense in putting it on the ground, where some ill chance might lead to premature discovery.

Holding up his hand for absolute stillness, Hilton listened for alarms that the ship might send if its hull was breached. There was a good reason to be confident that there would be none; most such alarms depended upon a sudden catastrophic loss of atmosphere, or some anomalous decline in the air pressure within the passageways closest to the hull.

He didn't hear any alarms.

He heard some sounds coming through the open hull, indistinct noises that bounced off the far wall of the docking bay from the opposite side of the ship. He heard—or thought he heard—the stealthy whisper of fabric against fabric from far down the corridors, on his right, on his left, as the other teams worked.

Satisfied, he gave his team the nod.

There were access portals between the maintenance passageways in the ship's hull and the ship's interior. Any such access portal was required by common practice and common sense to have an external override. People got trapped against the hull. It happened. They had to be able to get back into the ship whether or not the portal had been locked off from inside.

There would be a system alert this time, Hilton was sure of it. There were supposed to be system alerts any time a portal was opened between the maintenance hull and the ship's interior.

They had three things in their favor.

One was the possibility that no one on board would notice the visual alert; that was what the Corense lines used on hull access.

Then, since their commando attack had been carefully planned to come while the crew was busy, if anybody did notice the telltale alert they might just ignore it—assuming it to be some mechanical malfunction— until the excitement was over and there was slack time to investigate.

And, finally, they could hope that if anybody noticed, whoever on board went to check on the alert would come alone or in pairs, to be easily overpowered by Langsariks. Real ones.

Shilla cracked the seal on the access to the opening edge of the hatch to judge the potential air-pressure differential between the outer hull and the interior of the ship, to get an advance warning on whether or not the interior doors on the freighter were open or closed. Hilton didn't hear any hiss or sigh of air moving as she pushed the hatch open; so either the ship was open inside—or someone unsympathetic had opened the connecting door to whatever room this hatch led to and was waiting for them with a weapon at the ready.

They flattened themselves against the inner wall of the maintenance passageway, hiding themselves as best they could to be ready for an attack if one should come. Shilla pushed the hatch cover full open, with her body blocking anyone's view of the passage behind her. Hilton was impressed by her courage—it took nerve to expose yourself to enemy fire in order to win time for your team to respond.

Nobody shot Shilla.

Sticking her head through the open access port quickly, she checked left, then right, then left again; and then climbed through.

After a moment she was back. "All clear," she said, but quietly. A mere gesture might have been coerced at weapons point; this way they knew that she was her own woman and could follow her through with confidence.

Storeroom, and almost filled with crates except for the safety requirement of the clearway to the door.

The crates all carried Combine markings; but in the low light Hilton thought he could see the ghost of other seals, altered but not entirely obliterated.

So this was where at least some of the contraband was stored. On a freighter, in orbit. There would be little chance of the stores being discovered under Combine seal—and the foreman, Fisner Feraltz, had the chop. Ingenious. He would have to remember that. He had to complete his mission first and foremost, though, so Hilton went to the doorway, to listen.

All of the doorways would be open, if the evidence of this one could be taken as a measure. Freighters habitually opened all their doors when they were docked, to get the maximum benefit of free air circulation and replenishment. Trading old air for new.

He heard someone moving, but the sound was indistinct; he couldn't quite make it out. He was going to have to get closer. Hilton slipped out into the corridor, with his people behind him concealing themselves within open doorways and following as they could.

Somebody spoke.

"Well, that's done, then."

Hilton knew the voice.

"Come on, let's go tell the boss. Wonder if he's got all the cargo ready, yet."

It was Ippolit, from the warehouse construction site at Port Charid.

Hilton looked back over his shoulder at Vilner and Shilla, who were closest, and gave the sign. *At least two. Probably not more than three.* They had a small advantage of number if there were three. The advantage of surprise more than covered any potential difference.

Hilton straightened up and stepped across the threshold, a glad expression on his face.

"Hey! Ippolit! I didn't know you were here, friend, it's good to see you. What are you doing here?"

They could well know that he was at Honan-gung Yards, he'd gotten leave from Feraltz in person after all. He could almost see the calculation in Ippolit's face, the swift assessment of risk factors leading to a conclusion and a plan for action.

"Shires. Well. As I live and breathe. Have you met Berd, Shires?"

Reaching out for him to put a hand to Hilton's shoulder in friendly greeting, Ippolit advanced on Hilton. Hilton knew he couldn't let Ippolit lay hands on him, and retreated into the corridor. "I thought this was a Bortic ship. Second job, Ippolit?"

Ippolit followed; Hilton gave him no other choice. This was going to be tricky. Berd was still inside the storeroom, watching. Hilton needed to dislodge Berd from his defensive position in order to control the situation.

Ippolit helped.

"Well, it's a little more complicated than that, I'll tell you all about it. Berd! Berd, this is Hilton Shires from the warehouse. Langsariks. I've told you about him, come out and shake his hand."

The others on his team were nowhere in sight. Hilton didn't know which nearby open doorway might be sheltering whom. He certainly hoped that they were nearby.

"Oh. Yeah. Right, Shires, from the warehouse." Shifting himself out from behind the cargo crates that he'd been rearranging, Berd followed Ippolit out into the corridor. Hilton retreated from Ippolit's advance, hoping he wasn't too obvious, wondering where his people were.

"Say. Guys. What's this all about? You should be at Port Charid. Why were those crates marked Combine, if this is a Bortic ship?" Hilton asked nervously, backing down the corridor. Ippolit and Berd came on with steady confidence, as if secure that Hilton couldn't get away. He was backing up toward the front of the ship. There would be more of the raiding party waiting there, clearly.

"It's very simple, really," Ippolit assured him. "You see, Shires—"

Ippolit charged.

Right past an open doorway that let into a darkened storage room.

Torbe was there.

Stepping out swiftly from his concealment, Torbe clubbed Ippolit as he went past. As soon as Torbe made his move, Vilner and Shilla made theirs; they had Berd restrained and silenced before Berd had time to react.

Maintenance tape, three times around the wrists behind the back, twice between, and the tag end pressed down firmly on the outside of the hand. The same thing again around the ankles, to control movement of the feet and prevent bolting or kicking.

Maintenance tape again in a broad patch over the lower part of the face, to cover the mouth. It could be worked loose over time, of course, with determination and enough spit. But it would do for as long as they needed to keep the two men from giving an alarm by calling out.

Two down.

How many to go?

They had to hurry.

Vogel would stall on the outside for as long as he could. They had to be ready to finish the act before the raid leader realized he was discovered and took some desperate measure to avoid capture.

Hilton wanted all of these people alive.

He would settle for nothing less than complete exoneration.

When the *Melrick*'s captain finally deigned to make an appearance Garol retreated from the dockmaster's office into her secured room and pulled a detail scan up on screen. The dockmaster herself went out to talk to the freighter captain.

The freighter captain was not someone Garol recognized—he looked vaguely familiar in form, perhaps, but no more than that, and even that could just be his ethnicity—but there was no sense in making the false assumption that the freighter captain would not recognize him after he'd been in Port Charid for days.

Listening in on the conversation between the dockmaster and the freighter captain, Garol waited.

"Ah, I'd hate to come across as ungrateful for your help," the freighter captain was saying. "Is it me, or is this taking a little longer than we'd hoped?"

Garol knew what the problem was: Shires hadn't shown up. They would particularly want Shires's presence on the record, as well as being sure to collect him for general purposes of leaving no survivors. The load-out was going as well as anyone could wish, the cargo manifest almost made up and ready to load. The raiders would want to quarantine the warehouse crew as soon as the work of fetching the booty had been completed.

"I think everybody's here," the dockmaster replied, reassuringly. "You've got their full cooperation, no question about that."

Garol got the signal from Shires.

The freighter was secure.

It was time.

He pulsed the dockmaster in turn; and she made a suggestion to the freighter captain, as if it was an afterthought.

"I'm not sure I see one of my people, though, you're quite right about that. Maybe Jevan knows, he and Shires were teaming on maintenance earlier. Hey! Jevan!"

Garol watched on the internal monitor, inside the dockmaster's inner room. Jevan came into view on the screens, trotting across the floor to join the freighter captain and the dockmaster. He wanted Jevan to be with the freighter captain, so that he would be able to take them together. The freighter captain would be relying on Jevan to know where everybody was.

"Jevan. Where's Shires? I don't see him."

Jevan looked from the dockmaster to the freighter captain, but the picture was too small for Garol to decide on his exact expression. "He said he was going to go call up the people in the remote tunnels. Ames and Teller. They're here, he must have said something to them."

The dockmaster nodded. "Well, I'll just go find out. No, you stay here, Jevan, entertain the captain, I'll be right back."

Garol had warned her to get clear of the freighter captain when the time came for him to make his move, to avoid any unpleasantness with hostage-taking. Turning around, the dockmaster moved toward her work crew, calling for the people Jevan had identified. "Hey. You two. Over here, I need to ask you something."

That was his cue.

Garol left the dockmaster's inner office, checking the transmits as he passed. He wanted this on record. He'd promised the First Secretary something to look at.

He opened the door of the dockmaster's office and stepped out into the docking bay. The two people that the dockmaster had called didn't pay much attention to him. As far as they were concerned he was probably someone from the freighter, which explained why they didn't know him.

The freighter captain stared, though, and Garol greeted him with a cheerful wave.

"Hello there," Garol called. "My name is Garol Vogel. Bench specialist. And you're under arrest."

The shock on the freighter captain's face was quickly replaced with an expression of satisfied vindication. The freighter captain clearly could hear the people leaving the freighter, behind him. He didn't have to look to know that they were his men and they were armed.

"I don't think so," the freighter captain—the raid leader—said. "Specialist Vogel. The man we Langsariks have to thank for our vacation here at Port Charid, and all of this lovely loot. Really very much indebted to you, sir."

It was too bad for the raid leader that the people he heard coming out of the freighter were not his troops with weapons. They were Langsariks with weapons. Jevan was looking behind the freighter captain at the people coming out of the freighter, and there was horror clearly evident on Jevan's face. He probably recognized Shires right off. He might not recognize Shires's commando, but he wouldn't have to know them by name to realize who they were.

"You're not Langsariks, and it hasn't been a vacation, but I will accept responsibility for the arrest. You're Dalmoss, I expect."

The raid leader's confidence seemed to falter for the first time. None of the assembled warehouse workers was staring in shocked alarm at the armed men he clearly believed he had at his back. The dockmaster had clued them in by now, and they were watching with keen interest, but no fear. The raid leader did not go so far as to look over his shoulder to see what was there: not yet. He glanced with almost perfectly concealed nervousness up toward one of the docking bay's security monitors, instead.

"My name is Noman," he said.

Well behind the raid leader, Shires had stepped clear of the captured crew of the freighter, unshipping a peculiar set of small stones or spheres that hung at the end of multiple strands of cord that looked to be about as long as he was tall.

"Just as well." It took Garol a moment to realize what Shires was doing. Once he grasped Shires's plan, Garol did what he could to put it forward. This was a dangerous and determined enemy, one they had been lucky to manage as well as they had done so far. They could not afford to risk any uncontrolled events so close to a complete triumph. "Dalmoss went to Geraint, after all. Funny thing, though. How do you suppose he turned from Pettiche into Dalmoss? And rose from the dead, because there were no survivors at the Tyrell Yards, were there? Especially not Dolgorukij ones."

Out behind the raid leader Shires had started his ropes spinning. All of the spheres were tethered to a common ring; he put them into motion one by one, over his head.

When he had them all moving together he started to walk forward. Garol imagined he could hear the sound that the heavy spheres made whistling through the air, straining at the ends of the ropes. A rotor. A windmill. A wheel of a theoretical sort, but deployed hub to rim by wrist action rather than rim to hub by friction.

"I don't know anything about Dolgorukij." The raid leader seemed determined to carry his course through. "But I am grateful to that fat old Madlev. His warehouse is a great hiding place. You could tell him I said so—if you weren't going to Hell—"

There it was, the telltale twitch of the hand toward the blouse, the reach into a pocket. For a bomb. Garol braced himself to spring, aiming low, knowing he had to cross the distance between them before the raid leader had a chance to arm his suicide device.

A whistling sound of thrown spheres sliced through the air like knives, the rope-wheel wrapping itself around the raid leader with a ferocious impact that pinned his arms and dropped him to the floor of the loading bay in one swift movement. The raid leader shouted once in pain as the spheres took him, then once again as his head hit the ground; it happened too quickly for Garol to be able to reach him in time to break his fall.

Garol was with him in an instant, however, checking the pocket first before he dared check for breathing or a pulse. There would be a suicide device, and he'd seen evidence of an implosion grenade at Tyrell. Dying now would leave him with a definite sense of anticlimax. Garol expected to enjoy the denouement; for that he had to manage to live through to it.

The bomb was a tidy one, flat and innocuous in appearance. Garol sat back on his heels to examine it, turning it over and over in his hands and thanking the blind gods of fortunate happenstance for Dolgorukij arrogance. The suicide device had not been primed, or it would have been much easier to detonate. The raid leader—and Garol believed it probably *was* Dalmoss—had not been truly prepared to die, and Garol knew he might well owe his life, and those of everybody else nearby, to that one lapse in discipline.

Dalmoss stirred on the ground, coughing painfully as he regained consciousness. Shires came up to retrieve his spheres, grinning in enjoyment of his catch. "Don't move, floor manager," Shires warned, cheerfully. "Cracked ribs. Maybe fractured arms. You'll do yourself an injury, lie still. Hardly recognized you. New beard?"

The Dolgorukij, Jevan, had suffered himself to be bound by the dockmaster herself, staring down at Dalmoss in a clear state of shock. "I don't understand,"

Jevan said. "I don't have the first idea who these people are. I've never seen them before in my life."

Which people?

The false Langsariks that Shires's people were marching out of the freighter under guard?

Or the Langsariks themselves?

"I'd like to believe you," Garol assured him. "Don't worry. Everything will be sorted out soon enough. All we need from you now is a little patience."

Some of the warehouse crew was bringing a stretcher for Dalmoss, one with stout straps to secure an unconscious patient. Another of the warehouse crew walked behind, towing the medical cart—the emergency medical technician, clearly enough. "Dockmaster. We need help securing these people for transport. Can you hold them here for a few hours, while I arrange for an armed escort?"

He didn't want them under Langsarik guard. There were limits to the amount of temptation one could put before the best of people before they lost their sense of proportion in a rage for vengeance.

"We have a very nice transfer case for a refrigeration unit," the dockmaster pointed out, agreeably. "You may remember having seen it. Easily modified for adequate segregation of belligerent parties. It'll be our pleasure."

Transfer case for a refrigeration unit?

Transfer case.

"Quite so. If you'd just be so kind as to secure these people, then, dockmaster, being mindful of Shires's very useful warning in handling the raid leader. His name is Dalmoss. We hope he'll be in adequate condition to answer several questions of extreme interest."

He liked this dockmaster; she stood for no nonsense, but she knew the value of a good joke. He had brought his Langsariks in a transfer case for a large refrigeration unit. What more poetic prison could there be?

"Oh, we'll be much more careful with them than

they were with any of our warehouse people. My word on it, Specialist Vogel."

And he believed her.

Which was good: Because he had to get to Port Charid as quickly as possible, now, to lay his evidence before First Secretary Verlaine and get that Fleet Interrogations Group turned around.

With this raid timed the way it had been, he hadn't a moment to waste. The Fleet Interrogations Group would be coming off the vector within four hours from now. And it was four hours from Honan-gung to Port Charid.

He could try for a contact with Chilleau Judiciary from here, from his station in the pod within the dockmaster's inner room; but he needed Feraltz in hand before he published any bulletins. Try as he had, he hadn't quite convinced himself to trust that task to Cousin Stanoczk. Religious rivalry, the honor of the Dolgorukij Combine, saving face for the Autocrat— no. It was too risky. Hc had to do it himself.

"Thank you, ma'am, you're a gentlewoman and a scholar. Shires. Let's get out of here."

They would take the freighter back to Port Charid and park it off in orbit; Cousin Stanoczk would come aboard to ferry them down to Port Charid, as soon as they could get there.

Composing his message to the First Secretary in his mind, Garol followed the Langsariks up into the freighter for its preflight checks, happy to note a team doubling back to the opposite flank of the ship to close up the access portals in its side.

He was almost ready to relax and look forward to the confrontation with Feraltz yet to come.

Fisner Feraltz sat at his desk in the administration area of the warehouse construction site after the day shift had gone to their dinners, reviewing the daily work sheets and smiling to himself.

All over but the shouting.

The Fleet Interrogations Group was due within nine scant hours. The freighter—with all the riches that the Holy Mother had bestowed upon Her faithful servants—would be leaving for the Sillume vector at any moment.

The distress call had been sent more than five hours ago now.

Not from Honan-gung itself, not really; from the freighter, but through the Honan-gung dispatch, so that there was no telling any difference. The port was even then preparing what relief ships it could muster, but it would be too little and too late.

Just like the Tyrell raid.

Just like Okidan, and the raids before; the earlier—less sophisticated—raids, when they had still been learning their role. It almost made one admire Langsariks. Learning to raid had been a useful measure of the caliber of the opponent that they faced; and the absolute requirement for the ruthless extirpation of any such challenge to Combine primacy at Port Charid.

All of the progress that the work crews had made, really, it was an admirable effort. These people had organization. Self-discipline. A good work ethic. How pleasant it was to know that he was not even going to have to pay for their work. He was free and clear of a good two weeks' wages for the entire construction effort.

Was there a way to paper that fact over and take the additional tithe for the Angel's use?

And his.

There was a good proportion of this wealth due him, not as a reward, but so that he could show what influence and luxury a man could earn in the service of the Holy Mother. Recruitment. As he had been recruited; and yet he had needed no such appeal to venal motives to gain his allegiance, but only this, position and authority and trust.

There was someone in the outer office but Fisner paid them no mind, absorbed in happy calculation.

Until Hariv knocked almost in a panic at the door, opening it—before Fisner had a chance to agree to be seen or refuse to be bothered—to reveal the very unwelcome apparition of Bench Specialist Garol Aphon Vogel and Factor Madlev behind him.

Fisner sprang to his feet. He had an escape route, there was a washroom adjoining his office with an extra door that let on to an adjacent office whose exit was at the back of the administrative area. But why should he flee?

He bowed to Factor Madlev instead and remained on his feet to show deference to his superior. Factor Madlev would encourage him to be seated, he had been badly wounded scant months ago, after all.

Factor Madlev did not invite him to sit.

"Good to see you," Vogel said. "I was hoping we'd find you in. I've just come from Honan-gung, Feraltz, and it shouldn't surprise you to hear that the things I found out there make me very interested in your answers to some questions of Bench interest."

Behind Vogel, Madlev frowned, clearly unhappy. Factor Madlev had brought the Port Authority with him; none of the Angel's own people. All of the Angel's people were at Honan-gung, all except him. What did Vogel mean, he'd just come from Honan-gung? Vogel had gone to Chilleau Judiciary. Vogel was days away from Rikavie.

Unless it had been a ruse from the beginning . . .

Fisner sat down. If this was to be a confrontation, it would be on his own terms. "I can't imagine what you mean, Bench specialist." He could draw Vogel out, find out what Vogel knew. Then he'd know what Vogel didn't know. That would be a start on a strategy. "I had thought you were at Chilleau Judiciary."

It was true that Vogel hadn't been with the First Secretary when Factor Madlev had called just hours ago, though. After Factor Madlev had received the distress call from Honan-gung. The First Secretary had done the only thing he could have done; Fisner had taken care to leave him no choice. Did Vogel know that?

What did Vogel know?

Vogel wasn't saying. "As I have been, and expect to be in the future. These people will escort you to detention, Feraltz, to wait for the Fleet Interrogations Group arriving from Dobe. If you'd be so kind."

Factor Madlev's discomfort would permit him to endure in silence no longer. "But the Bench warrant was issued against Langsariks, Bench specialist," Madlev said, as Fisner watched Vogel's face avidly. "Not four hours gone past. When we told the First Secretary at Chilleau Judiciary about the distress call from Honan-gung."

Fascinating, Fisner thought. *Vogel had to be exhausted: there was no other possible explanation for the nakedness of the dismay in his face.*

"Honan-gung sent no distress calls, Factor Madlev," Vogel said, flatly. "I was there. I know."

Vogel's emphatic insistence seemed to put Madlev on the defensive. "Nevertheless, Specialist Vogel, Port Charid received a distress call from Honan-gung five hours ago. We were unable to get a response from Honan-gung on any frequency. We had to put it before the First Secretary."

Fisner closed his eyes and bowed his head as his heart sang.

It was so clear, so perfect, and so beautiful.

Vogel had set a trap at Honan-gung, but Vogel hadn't stopped the distress call—perhaps he hadn't realized that Dalmoss's freighter would be sending one.

Vogel had put Honan-gung on transmission silence while he returned from Honan-gung to Port Charid to make his crowning arrest, that of Fisner himself.

And even as Vogel had made his triumphant pilgrimage from Honan-gung to Port Charid, the Holy Mother had put out Her hand to turn his purpose to Her service. Factor Madlev had done what any decent honest man would do on receipt of such a distress call, he'd called for help, and Chilleau Judiciary had had no grounds to deny him—because the First Secretary was as much in the dark about Vogel's actual whereabouts and activities as Fisner himself had been.

Vogel had come from Honan-gung in triumph, to arrest him.

But the Angel of Destruction had triumphed over all.

"Well," Vogel said, and the word seemed all too inadequate for the worlds upon worlds of emotion that it bore. "We'll have to contact the First Secretary immediately, then. Nothing is changed, Feraltz, you are still under arrest, and there will be a reckoning in time. Factor Madlev. If you'll have your people take charge of the prisoner, I'd like to get back to Port Charid to contact the Bench at Chilleau Judiciary."

Vogel was wrong about that, too. There would be no reckoning. After all the Holy Mother had shown him of her power, how could he doubt for so much as a moment that she would bring him out of threatened captivity to honor and glory?

He would be looking forward to witnessing Vogel's discomfiture, on that day. It was uncharitable of him, yes, perhaps.

He owed Vogel no charity.

Vogel had done his utmost to thwart the sacred Will of the Holy Mother. Vogel deserved to suffer humiliation in return for his misguided meddling, if not worse.

"It's all right, Factor Madlev," Fisner declared firmly, as though Factor Madlev had hesitated to do as Vogel directed. Factor Madlev had not perhaps moved very quickly to put Fisner under arrest, but he seemed to cherish no reservations whatever beyond the reflection on his own pride to have his foreman accused, and looked a little puzzled, as Fisner continued.

"I have nothing to hide. Take me into custody. I'll be fully exonerated of whatever it is the Bench specialist means to accuse me"—which Vogel had neglected to divulge, which was a disappointment, he could have started to work on his story— "whatever that is. Shall we go? Guards?"

He would be out of custody again before daybreak. Perhaps before supper.

Vogel would realize that he was powerless against a far more formidable opponent than he could possibly imagine; and Fisner would go free, to watch the painful and appropriate conclusion to Vogel's misguided Langsarik experiment with amnesty at Port Charid.

Chapter Twelve

Shutting the door behind him, Garol Vogel turned to pace in Factor Madlev's now-empty office, where the secured-communications portal was kept. He didn't want any witnesses. He had no confidence in his own discretion at this point, and he was not willing to berate the First Secretary in front of any local authorities that might lose respect for the Bench because of it.

Keying the transmit, Garol sat down at Factor Madlev's desk and engaged the privacy nets in the walls, mechanically, not really thinking about it. This was a disaster. He had worked so hard to prevent it. What was he going to do?

"Bench specialist Garol Vogel. For First Secretary Verlaine, priority transmit, urgency immediate."

He couldn't sit still.

He lunged to his feet from the chair in a convulsive movement, snatching his worn campaign hat off his head and crumpling it in his hands, stretching it and twisting it in a fury of agonized self-reproachful emotion before he jammed it back down at the back of his head as though it were a personal enemy whose ultimate despite was to be worn on the head of a Bench specialist—all the while pacing, quartering the room in precise measure left to right, front to back, on the diagonal.

In the middle of the second or third such transit his signal cleared; Garol heard the concerned voice of the First Secretary. "Specialist Vogel. What news?"

What news. What news? How dare he ask what

news? Garol couldn't stop moving. He would explode. He needed the physical stress of sustained if low-impact exertion to hone the wild edge off of his despair and free his mind for calculating evaluation. He was a Bench intelligence specialist. Calculating evaluation was what he was all about.

"I've just come from the Honan-gung Yards in the Shawl of Rikavie, where I and a properly deputized party of Langsarik commandos successfully interrupted a warehouse-invasion raid."

Striding without ceasing from wall to wall, from corner to corner, the placing of his feet somehow seemed to help him place his words with concise care.

"Returning to Port Charid under communications silence, I have just placed the ringleader under arrest. I can demonstrate with complete confidence that a group of Dolgorukij from the Combine Yards is responsible for staging the so-called Langsarik raids, including the torture and murder of warehouse crew."

Verlaine was listening, hearing him out. Maybe Verlaine was beginning to have a bad feeling about where Garol was going. Garol hoped so.

"It was never Langsariks, First Secretary, not since the real trouble began. Factor Madlev tells me that the Third Fleet Interrogations Group has received its charter activation orders. They'll be here inside of eight hours."

Then Verlaine spoke, since Garol's statement was as good as an accusation after all. "We were unable to make contact with you, and Ivers could share little by way of evidence, Specialist Vogel. I have been doing my best to win time for you to work, but even had I been aware of your plans—which I was not—"

It was mild enough, as an implicit criticism. It was also fair. Perhaps he could have approached this mission differently. Perhaps he could have laid it all out for the First Secretary, without risking compromise. But he'd had his reasons. He didn't know how sophisticated the abilities of his opponent might be. He still didn't know with certainty whether this secure line was actually secure.

"—I could no longer deny the right of the Port Authority to demand action and see sanctions levied. There was a distress call, Vogel, under the very nose of the Fleet Interrogations Group another raid. What would you have had me do?"

Anything but what he had done. Verlaine was not denying it. He had activated the mission of the Third Fleet Interrogations Group, and now it was functionally autonomous from the Bench until such time as it decided to declare its mission completed. Fleet was jealous of its Bench prerogatives. Politics had twisted the knife in the heart of the Langsarik settlement the final crucial fractions of a measure between a grave wound and a mortal one.

"The Langsariks are innocent." It was all Garol could think of to say. "I've had every cooperation from them. They've honored the terms of the amnesty, First Secretary. To see them destroyed by a Fleet Interrogations Group despite their best efforts to uphold the rule of Law is bitterly offensive."

"What difference does it make?"

Verlaine asked it with meditative gravity that weighted the flippant phrase, so that it came out a genuine request for a reply. "I'm not sure we're left with any other possible outcome, Bench specialist. The settlement has been too badly compromised. You may well have identified the true culprits, but can the Langsariks be said to have any real hope of a life at Port Charid yet before them?"

Three-eighths of the way from one corner of Factor Madlev's office to the other, Garol stopped and bowed his head. A genuine question deserved a genuine answer. It took him a moment to get one out, however.

"That's a true statement. As far as it goes."

The criminals, the Dolgorukij terrorists, this supposed "Angel of Destruction" had done too good a job of pretending to be Langsariks. Port Charid had

learned over a period of months to blame the Langsariks, and not for mere piracy and theft but for murder
and atrocity as well. He had failed in his mission. He
could not salvage the amnesty agreement.

Nor could he accept that as a reason to abandon
innocent people to a Fleet Interrogations Group. The
Second Judge would be amply vindicated by the Fleet
Interrogations Group's findings, that was almost certain—given the nature of its Brief.

And yet—if Fleet really wanted to play politics—

"But it doesn't mean we can sell the Langsariks out
to the Fleet. And I see a potential problem."

There was no hope of simply canceling the activation order. It was one of the basic rules that governed
the uneasy relationship between the Fleet and the
Bench: The Fleet was subordinate to the civil authority, but once chartered was free to ignore the civil
authority until the mission laid on it by the civil authority had been accomplished. And it was Fleet that
decided when that was.

"I'm listening," the First Secretary said. But Garol
thought that Verlaine was thinking, too.

"We can't afford another scandal along the lines of
the recent unpleasantness at Port Rudistal." Where the
Domitt Prison had stood. "And once Fleet realizes, as
it must, that there is no true Brief at Port Charid—it
could easily be used against Chilleau Judiciary, First
Secretary."

Torture enough Langsariks to assure themselves
that the confessions were all just the pain talking,
something even the average Inquisitor could discern.
Then torture another fifty or sixty more just for the
sake of the argument.

Run a series of inquiries on drug-assist alone, and
end up with proof of innocence.

Go public with the fact that an innocent and unarmed population had been foully betrayed by the
Bench officers that had promised to protect them. It
could get ugly.

It could even force the Second Judge into retire-
ment—especially if Fleet chanced to discover that
Garol had had the real criminals in custody before
the Fleet Interrogations Group had even arrived at
Port Charid.

Or the Fleet Interrogations Group might just do the
job it had been sent to do and issue no challenge to
the Second Judge's public image.

Was it worth the risk that Fleet would use its Brief
to the discredit of the Second Judge?

Now that Verlaine knew that Garol had the truth,
and that the Langsariks weren't to blame—

"I am at a loss to understand what you think the
alternative might be." Garol thought he heard frustration there, in the First Secretary's voice. He hadn't
been entirely fair to Verlaine, maybe. But Garol had
no particular reason to trust anybody, First Secretaries
emphatically included. "If you could keep the two of
them apart, your Langsariks and the Fleet Interrogations Group. If you could wave the scepter of wonder,
and transport the settlement intact to cloud-cuckoo
land through lands of mist and magic. I might be able
to work a nullification of Bench instruction, in a
month or so. Maybe. If."

An impossible task.

But the First Secretary had suggested it.

With all other situational elements taken into consideration, Garol knew exactly what he had to do.

It went against nearly everything he had fought for
during most of his adult life. But it was unquestionably
the lesser of two evils.

"Yes. If the Langsarik settlement simply disappeared, there would in that case be no risk of negative
public reaction consequent to a misplaced accusation
of crimes against the Judicial order. I understand, First
Secretary. I will do my utmost to protect the honor
of the Second Judge and Chilleau Judiciary, in the
service of the rule of Law. Vogel away, here."

He had only one escape route open to him now;

and no time to lose if he was to hope to make it free and clear.

"Aunt Walton. Aunt Walton, please, wake up, something is wrong."

Walton Agenis struggled into consciousness, unable to parse Modice's frantic pleas into coherence but knowing by tone of voice that it was serious.

"Modice. I'm awake. You can stop shaking me now."

She was stiff and sore from sleeping in the chair in the front room; how did Vogel manage? She couldn't sleep at all in her bed, though, too unwilling to be caught at so much of a disadvantage when the soldiers came for her.

If she was going to die, she would do so with as much dignity as she could manage, for as long as the torturers of the Fleet Interrogations Group would permit.

"Unusual changes in pattern, Aunt Walton. There are transport trucks out there, and more coming, you can hear them from the roof." Where Modice had made an observation station for herself, in the unfinished attic space up beneath the eaves. "Something's coming."

And it didn't sound friendly.

"Do we have something to eat?" Walton asked, gathering her strength to stand up. "High-fat, we may need it. I'm going to go wash my face."

They'd be coming to the door soon enough.

She couldn't be looking very formidable, with her face dead pale and her hair in wild disarray, her clothing wrinkled from having been slept in. She was the Flag Captain, the representative of the Langsarik fleet before the world. She wanted to maintain appearances.

Modice brought breakfast as Walton tidied her person, combing her hair between bites of fried fat-meat and toast dripping with butter. There was a small ventilation window in the washroom; Walton could hear the roar of the trucks that Modice was worried about.

She could hear it when the noise of the engines stopped.

This was it, then.

She went to the door and stood behind it, waiting for the knock.

It was a knock that seemed somehow familiar, when it came. Walton waited for a suitable interval to pass—to make it clear that her response was a considered action, not mere reaction to the demand for her attention—and nodded at Modice to open the door.

It was Garol Vogel, standing there.

"Ma'am," Vogel said, touching his fingertips to the brim of his dilapidated old campaign cap in some peculiar form of a salute. "I'm bringing an evacuation order. Langsariks to be removed from settlement at Port Charid immediately, by express direction from Chilleau Judiciary. If I could ask you to step outside."

He stepped back.

Walton could only stare.

There was her nephew, Hilton, behind Vogel; so they were back from Honan-gung—but if they were back from Honan-gung, why were the Langsariks evacuating?

Had they failed to acquire the evidence that they had hoped for?

Or was it even more simple than that?

Walton followed Vogel out of the house. There were transports lining the roadway into the settlement, dozens of transports, and at least some of the drivers were Langsariks by their body language. She didn't recognize anybody at the distance, her eyes were still half-asleep; but she knew her people. Those were Langsariks.

Factor Madlev stood several paces removed, with an armed escort; the people who had secured the perimeter around her house were formed up in a detachment to one side. It was not an impressive one, either, but these were not professional soldiers.

. Once she was well clear of the doorway, Vogel stopped and stood with his back to her, assuming an approximation of a position of command attention that was too precise to result from imperfect learning—it was the gradual relaxation over time, rather, of a once-perfect discipline. Not for the first time Walton wondered about Vogel's past: But there was her own future to worry about, and she could not spare Vogel the energy.

"Factor Madlev," Vogel said, pitching his voice to carry to as many of the people who were there as possible, "as I have mentioned briefly to you on our way here, I have received instruction from First Secretary Verlaine at Chilleau Judiciary on behalf of the Second Judge. The amnesty agreement between the Langsariks and the Bench has been declared compromised, and I am to ensure that the Langsarik population at Port Charid vacates the settlement as quickly as possible. The Bench will pay commercial rates for every freighter and other appropriate transport that can be made available for this purpose."

She could hardly believe what she was hearing.

Nor did she seem to be alone.

"Specialist Vogel." Factor Madlev's reply was in a cautious tone of voice that only carried as far as Walton's doorstep. "Wouldn't it be just as efficient to leave these people here and let the Fleet Interrogations Group take over?"

Vogel shook his head. "I can't argue with you on the point, Factor Madlev. My instructions were to remove the Langsarik settlement from Port Charid as a failed enterprise. It is too much to expect the decent citizens of this port to tolerate the presence of persons suspected of crimes both mercantile and murderous for a moment longer. Do I have your support, Factor Madlev?"

Factor Madlev didn't really care. Walton could see

it in the shrug of his shoulders, hear it in the tone of his voice.

"Of course we will fully support any Bench initiative, Specialist Vogel."

Madlev knew that Vogel meant to get them off-world before the Fleet Interrogations Group arrived. And Madlev was perfectly willing to go along with that.

It was too much to believe that Madlev would turn a blind eye to their escape, still believing that they were responsible for the raids—so Factor Madlev knew better, now.

That meant that Hilton and Vogel had succeeded at Honan-gung and brought back evidence that the Langsariks were innocent. What happened to the Langsariks now was not apparently an issue of keen concern to Factor Madlev, except that Factor Madlev would share a common understanding that vulnerability to a Fleet Interrogations Group was not something to be wished on innocent people.

Bowing crisply, Vogel turned away any lingering doubts or questions with a call for immediate action. "Thank you for your understanding, Factor Madlev. There are eight freighter tenders off-lined at the new airfield, you'll make them available? Very kind. Lieutenant Shires."

Hilton, looking very tired, looking very tense, but looking also absolutely energized by the activity to come. "Yes, Bench specialist."

"Lieutenant, you will go with Factor Madlev to identify and select suitable shipping, please. I want to begin to load within the hour."

Vogel didn't wait for acknowledgment; in the manner of a superior officer supremely confident of a subordinate's ability, he turned back to her directly. "Flag Captain."

Her turn now, to receive her orders. The idea appealed to her sense of the absurd, though her emotions were generally too stunned by what was happening and how fast it was happening to really enjoy the sensation. "Bench specialist?"

"If you would muster your command, ma'am, and be out at the new airfield absolutely as soon as possible. Because any Langsarik who is still at Port Charid when the Fleet gets here is as good as dead. But not quickly enough. If you know what I mean."

She understood him completely. The Langsarik fleet had lost people to interrogation before.

"Eight freighter tenders." She was impressed, and didn't mind him knowing. "I'd like to know how you managed that. But I don't see what good it does without transport, and it takes a few hours to bring freighters on-line, once they've been parked out in geostationary orbit."

He knew that as well as she did. She was just making sure he knew that she knew. Did he mean to cram them all into a warehouse somewhere out in the Shawl of Rikavie? Because that was the maximum range of most freighter tenders, under ordinary conditions.

"Which is exactly why we're so lucky that Madlev got a distress call from Honan-gung. Even though it precipitated the danger from the Fleet Interrogations Group." Vogel spoke softly, for her ears only. Well, hers and those of Modice, behind her. "There are seven freighters up there coming on-line for a rescue mission. Some of them are even armed for pursuit. We brought an eighth back with us from Honan-gung. It's borderline workable. But it'll be enough."

She knew she'd been asleep. She knew she'd been under horrific stress, waiting to see her people condemned. She couldn't think. That had to be the reason that she thought what was happening, was happening. "You're taking a risk, Bench specialist. We could overpower the crew on the way into the Shawl. You'd never see your freighters again; think of the expense, not to mention the embarrassment."

Vogel had started to shift his weight, doing a species of dance on his feet. Impatient. "Nothing compared

to the potential damage that another scandal like the
Domitt Prison could create for the Second Judge. The
First Judge is old. Verlaine wants his Judge to be in
a good position when the post comes up vacant. We
don't have much time, Flag Captain, let's get moving."

He meant for them to take the Sillume vector for
Gonebeyond space. He really did.

"Modice," Walton said, and her niece stepped up
smartly and nodded her head.

"Yes, Aunt Walton."

"You heard the Bench specialist, Modice, issue the
assembly order, evacuation plan in effect, timing critical. Mark and move."

Modice had only been waiting for assurance that
she was truly to send up the flags. As it were.

Vogel followed Modice into the house and came
out again carrying a chair from the living room, setting
it down in the pathway before the front door so that
it faced the road.

Walton sat down, and Vogel posted himself behind
her, doing his peculiar version of command wait.

Just as well.

She had too many things to ask and to tell and to
say to him to be able to say a single word right now.

Standing in the dock's loading bay behind Cousin
Stanoczk, Kazmer Daigule ached to be going with
the Langsariks.

"I'm afraid I cannot in good conscience offer the
use of this courier," Cousin Stanoczk said with polite
firmness to Hilton Shires. "It is not mine, and I am
responsible for my husbandry of the Malcontent's resources. What I can do is release some stores to you.
I have a list."

Kazmer had put it together himself. He hadn't understood why Stanoczk had wanted it, but it was complete: foodstuffs, clothing, and replacement parts, all
held in Combine warehouses here at Port Charid.
Kazmer was already serenely confident that the Lang-

sariks had loaded all the contraband they'd been able to find out at the new warehouse construction site, where Feraltz had apparently been stashing it. Langsariks could move very quickly when they needed to.

"How about your comps, then?" Hilton suggested. "I could steal them at gunpoint. If it would help."

Cousin Stanoczk raised his hands in a gesture of mock-horror; he was holding something in one hand. "Oh, the Saints forbid that such a thing should come to pass, Shires. You'll need the secure codes. Be gone when we get back, I've got an errand to run."

Stanoczk glanced back at Kazmer expectantly, glancing from him to whatever it was in his left hand. So Kazmer reached out and took it. The master code unit for the courier's communications equipment. Top-of-the-line. Beautiful stuff.

Stanoczk walked away toward the door at the back of the docking bay that would lead out to the receiving area and then out onto the street. Hilton stepped up to take the master code unit, but Kazmer could not quite bear to let go of it.

"So you're getting away?"

Hilton looked confused, but his small frown of concern gave way almost at once to one of sympathy. He let his hand drop back to his side. "Yeah, Kaz. We're out of here. Never thought it would end like this."

Kazmer had been part of the ending of it. But Hilton knew all about that; that wasn't the problem. The problem was that Kazmer wanted to go too.

"Probably for the best." He had caused so much trouble for the Langsariks, directly and indirectly, and it had all been because he had wanted to help. He could hardly stand the idea that they were leaving; and for Gonebeyond space. Kazmer had always wondered what was out there. Hilton would get to find out, but Kazmer had given his life away to the Malcontent, and there was no going back on the bargain.

"And we've got to hurry." Hilton's gentle reminder called Kazmer out of his self-pitying grief, his keen

regret over the fact of Hilton's going away. He liked
Hilton. He wanted the best for him. Cousin Stanoczk's
comps were the best.

Kazmer pressed the master code unit into Hilton's
waiting hand, and was almost ready to say good-bye
with a willing heart; but he was interrupted before he
could say anything more.

"Sometime this octave, Daigule, if you please."

Cousin Stanoczk called out to him in a firm voice,
not needing to put any venom into the rebuke for
Kazmer to recognize it for what it was. Kazmer was
the slave of the Malcontent. Cousin Stanoczk was his
master. Kazmer blushed in vexation to be publicly
called to heel, and ducked his head—unwilling to let
Hilton know how hard it was to see him go.

"You heard the boss. Don't scratch the furniture,
Hilton, it's a nice ship."

He had to turn hastily and walk away, or he was
going to say something he'd regret. Something stupid.
Something like *tell Modice I love her with all of my
heart*, or *I would to all Saints I was going with you.*

He didn't look back. He didn't dare. Cousin Stanoczk was waiting for him impatiently, and he had no
right to keep Cousin Stanoczk waiting. If it hadn't
been for Cousin Stanoczk, none of this might have
happened. The Inquisitor would have questioned him,
it would have gotten ugly, he would have said Hilton's
name. It would have been over, instead of just beginning, so how could he grieve just because he was not
going to be allowed to be a part of it?

"I'm sorry, Cousin Stanoczk." *Forgive me.* "I didn't
mean." *To keep you waiting.* Cousin Stanoczk didn't
seem interested in Kazmer's incoherent attempts at an
apology. Cousin Stanoczk took him firmly by the
elbow and drew him out bodily into the receiving area.

"Enough talk, Kazmer. We have work to do, and
not much time."

The other members of Stanoczk's crew were already
waiting at the street entrance. They had a transport,

and one of them was carrying a security hood. Kazmer wondered, dully, what Cousin Stanoczk had in mind. Over the past few hours, he hadn't been paying much attention to anything outside the problem of the Langsariks. Stanoczk had kept him busy.

They were six in all, with Kazmer himself and Cousin Stanoczk. The hired transport took them to the administrative headquarters of the Combine Yards in Port Charid and stopped outside one of the side entrances.

"We won't be long," Cousin Stanoczk said to the man he had driving. "Stay alert. I don't want any unnecessary complications."

Kazmer began to have an idea.

Into the building and through the corridors—Cousin Stanoczk had clearly been studying a schematic. Kazmer had to hurry to keep up with the others. It was the storage vaults Cousin Stanoczk wanted; when they got there, there was a guard posted, but Cousin Stanoczk did not seem to be surprised.

Kazmer stopped and stood waiting with the rest of them while Stanoczk went forward to speak to the guards.

"I've come for your prisoner," Cousin Stanoczk said. "Will you need a receipt? I have clearance."

They were just warehouse security, and they looked uncomfortable. By now every Dolgorukij in Port Charid knew who Cousin Stanoczk was. Dolgorukij noticed Malcontents, though they pretended to ignore their existence most of the time.

The guards—there were two of them—traded glances. "I'm not sure about that, Cousin," one of them said. Kazmer could tell by the degree of relationship that the guard was willing to grant to Stanoczk that he was feeling very uncertain indeed. "We weren't told. We'd better wait for the Bench specialist."

"Normally I would agree with you," Cousin Stanoczk assured the guards, speaker and silent alike. "But not this time. It is the honor of the Holy Mother herself that is at stake. The Malcontent requires the attendance of your prisoner at an inquest to be held in his honor. I take full responsibility."

An inquest, in the old and formal sense. An inquiry. A debriefing.

Interrogation, but under the control of the Malcontent, and no Fleet Inquisitor to share the shameful secrets of the Combine's sordid past—Kazmer could almost sympathize. The Bench would have Dalmoss and the other men being held even now at the Honangung Yards, for its interrogation. The Bench would naturally confine its questions to topics which interested the Bench; but the Malcontent would want the Angel of Destruction itself, and of all these prisoners only Fisner Feraltz—the apparent ringleader, chieftain, head—was likely to have any real information on the organization and operation of a terrorist society thought dead.

The one guard looked at the other, then shrugged. "I'm sure it's best for all of us," he said. "I can't imagine our Feraltz preferring to go to Fleet. But we have custody, Cousin. How can we in honor cede it to you?"

The guards clearly did not know the extent of the problem. Vogel had obviously said nothing about Angels, or else the guard would have known quite well that Feraltz would almost certainly rather anything than to fall into the hands of the Malcontent.

On the other hand—depending on what the guards themselves remembered of the horror stories of their youth—they might well be more, and not less, willing to see Feraltz in Stanoczk's hands if they did know. They might feel more guilty about it, though, if personal malice came into play, so it was best that Cousin Stanoczk made no such appeal.

"I can promise you absolutely that if you but tell the Bench specialist that I have assumed personal custody, he will understand." Kazmer had to agree. Vogel might not hold the guards blameless, but he would

reserve his wrath for the man who really deserved it—
Cousin Stanoczk.

The Malcontent was proof against the displeasure
of even a Bench intelligence specialist, or his name
wasn't Kazmer Daigule.

The guard shrugged again. "Very well, Cousin, but
I will have a receipt. Yes. Thank you."

Cousin Stanoczk had one already prepared.

The guards opened the door to the storeroom they
were using as a cell. Kazmer could see clear through
to the back—it was a small room. Fisner Feraltz sat
on a low cot with a strongbelt around his waist and
his wrists shackled; when he saw Cousin Stanoczk
standing in the doorway he stood up and took a step
forward, his face full of alarm.

"What's he doing here, you can't—I won't—"

Feraltz had not accounted for the hobbles he wore.
He fell flat on his face, full-length on the floor, and
two of Cousin Stanoczk's crew hurried forward with
the security hood.

Feraltz was imprisoned in the walking cage of the
security hood before he found his voice. The heavy
fabric covered him from head to mid-thigh; as Kazmer
watched in bemused wonder at the efficiency of the
operation, Stanoczk's crew pulled Feraltz's shackled
hands deftly through a panel to the outside of the
hood, sealing the panel up again so that Feraltz's
hands were isolated outside the hood.

There was a mesh panel in the thick and imperme-
able material of the hood where Feraltz's face would
be, so that he could breathe; but Kazmer heard nothing but incoherent noises from beneath the hood.

So they'd brought the gag as well.

Kazmer thought of the bodies he'd seen at the Tyrell Yards, the look on the face of the dockmaster; a
woman who had been alive when he'd left her, a
woman who had offered no threat to the raiders.

He found that his instinctive sympathy for any man

in Feraltz's position—in the hood, and the gag—was absent.

"Thank you, gentlemen," Cousin Stanoczk said. "We'll be leaving. Should you be rebuked by the Factor or by the Bench specialist for transferring the prisoner just be in touch, and the Malcontent will see that all is made right for you."

The crewmen who had hooded Feraltz were already moving him down the hall and toward the exit as Stanoczk spoke. Feraltz couldn't walk very quickly with his ankles hobbled; but there were straps on the outside of the security hood, so the crewmen simply dragged Feraltz along with them. Kazmer hurried after them, while Cousin Stanoczk stayed behind for a moment to soothe any doubts that the two guards might have.

It took no time at all to reach the waiting transport. They loaded Feraltz into the passenger compartment, secured between two crewmen; but there was a problem.

It was a six-man transport, and Feraltz made seven.

Cousin Stanoczk stood beside the transport with Kazmer, scratching his head behind one ear as if in confusion.

"Well," Cousin Stanoczk said. "Kazmer, this won't do. I don't have room for you. You'd better see if you can get a berth with your Langsarik friends, and you'd better hurry, too, if you don't want to be left behind."

Kazmer frowned. What was Stanoczk saying? "Get a berth, Cousin Stanoczk, I don't understand. Oughtn't I be coming with you? I'll get a for-hire and meet you."

Stanoczk shook his head with impatient disgust. "I don't want you, Kazmer; I can't use you, and the Langsariks need you. You're a good pilot. You're none of mine, though, so give me your halter and get out to the airfield."

Give him his halter?

Was Stanoczk even speaking plain Standard?

Kazmer stood and stared. Stanoczk reached out for him with a short sharp obscenity, pulling Kazmer's collar open at the throat to snap off the red leash of the Malcontent in one quick and almost savage gesture.

"We made a contract so that you could protect your friends, Kazmer, and your friends have not been protected. There is no contract. What part of 'get out of my sight' did you not understand?"

This couldn't be happening.

It was too much to grasp.

Kazmer seized Cousin Stanoczk by the shoulders and kissed him passionately, first on one cheek and then on the other. Free. That was what Cousin Stanoczk was saying. He was free.

"Your for-hire is waiting," Stanoczk pointed out. "Stupid Sarvaw."

Free to court Modice like an honest man.

Kazmer fled from the street to the for-hire that Cousin Stanoczk had pointed out, the one Cousin Stanoczk had readied, waiting for him.

He had to get out to the airfield. Now.

Once he was away with the Langsarik fleet, he would see what the books said about how a man should honor the Malcontent, to give thanks for a miracle unsought but even so granted.

It was four hours till dawn, and the Fleet Interrogations Group had cleared the Sillume exit vector hours ago. It would reach Port Charid soon. Unless the Langsariks left local orbit at Port Charid within the hour, they would have no chance of outrunning a predictable attempt on the part of the Fleet Interrogations Group to stop them short of the entrance vector.

It was going to be complicated enough to move so many ships of so many sizes through the Sillume vector at something approaching one and the same time as it was.

Shires had mustered ten freighters in all, with the

one they'd confiscated from Fisner Feraltz's people added in. There was loot on that ship that the Bench might want to have, to build its case against Feraltz's cabal; but the Langsariks were going to need capital.

Garol was sending them out into Gonebeyond space, and who knew exactly what they would find there?

"You can come back, of course," Garol said diffidently to Walton Agenis, standing beside her at the airfield. Watching the last of the Langsariks load. "Once the uproar's settled down. We could try to work a rehabilitation. Think about it."

She shook her head. "I don't think so. But I won't rule it out. Hadn't you better come with us, Garol? To, oh, preserve contact between the Bench and the Langsariks, maybe gain insight into the political situation in Gonebeyond. To the extent that there may be one."

Garol kept his voice even with a terrible effort. She couldn't know how much he wanted to. "I have enough explaining to do at Chilleau Judiciary to keep me busy. Thanks for the offer, though."

He wanted to go.

He liked the Langsariks. And Walton Agenis was in his heart, a woman of courage and wisdom and beauty and grace. A friend.

She said nothing. Garol watched a for-hire pull up to the bottom of the loading ramp, deployed on the tarmac before them. Kazmer Daigule stumbled out, almost tripping over his own feet in his eagerness to clasp Modice Agenis to his heart and spin around three times with her in his arms before disappearing with her up the ramp and into the ship.

Cousin Stanoczk had warned him; sending word that since the Langsarik fleet was short on current experience at vector transits, having been land-based for more than a year, he was sending Daigule out on loan. So he said.

Garol had his doubts about the "loan" part.

"Come with *me*, then, Garol," Walton Agenis said quietly. "Or I'll miss your company. We could be good for each other, I think. I don't want it to be that I'll never see you again."

Passionate words, but she said them so calmly that it was too clear that it was the mere truth.

It tore a hole in his heart and let all of his anguish out, all of his pain, all of his grief at what had become of the Langsarik settlement, all of his hopeless certainty that he was condemned forever to walk through the world and never be part of it, to see joy and love and never have any.

He couldn't handle it.

Drawing her to him with a carefully controlled gesture Garol folded her to himself, standing for a long moment heart to heart with the Flag Captain of the Langsarik fleet, Agenis the Deep-Minded. Walton. Maybe not the only woman he had ever loved, but unquestionably the one he loved more deeply than any before her.

She'd be all right.

He'd be all right.

He had to hold on to knowing she would be out there, somewhere, in Gonebeyond space, and that if he ever saw her again, she would greet him with a bowl of her niece's grain soup and pick up the threads of their conversation as though they'd never been apart from each other.

"Not just yet." He couldn't let go of her. And he had to. Shires was waiting at a polite distance to escort his commander on board her flagship. It was the last to ferry Langsariks to the freighters that waited in orbit. They had to get away. "But I appreciate the offer. Maybe later, Walton, you'd better go."

He didn't dare kiss her, nor did he need to.

She stepped away from him and took a deep breath. "Very well. Not good-bye, Garol. See you later."

Sometime, someplace.

She walked away from him past Shires, to the base

of the loading ramp; and Garol knew that he had to say something, or hate himself for it for the rest of his life.

So he waved.

"Have a good!"

Have a good trip. Have a good transit. Have a good escape. Have a good life.

Apparently startled, she paused halfway up the ramp, looking back over her shoulder, then broke into a broad grin and waved back.

It was just what he needed, no more and no less, and he turned his back on the freighter transport as the airfield's leftover Dolgorukij ground crew closed up the ship, walking almost calmly off the scorched tarmac to take shelter in the control room, and watch her leave.

They would make the vector. They would be gone before the Fleet Interrogations Group could intercept them, and the Fleet Interrogations Group had no Brief to try to do so—he intended to make that point very clear. As soon as the Langsarik fleet was safely away.

He'd given up too much to let any six Fleet Interrogations Groups stand in the way of a successful escape.

Standing in the traffic controller's map room at Combine headquarters, Garol Vogel watched the Third Fleet Interrogations Group on its way to Port Charid, and the ragtag Langsarik fleet nearing the Sillume entrance vector at the far end of the vector aisle.

It was going to be close.

The lead ships in the Fleet Interrogations Group convoy—three ships, out of twenty—were altering trajectory, but not on approach to Port Charid: on a course to bypass Rikavie entirely and head for some target as yet unidentified. In the Shawl of Rikavie, perhaps.

Garol knew better.

"Hail the Fleet convoy, please." The communications master was on his boards; by the swiftness of his reply he had anticipated Garol's request.

"Your channel is open, Bench specialist, skein in braid. Stand by for the commander, Third Fleet Interrogations Group, coming on-line. Now."

Garol meant to leave no doubt in the commander's mind as to who was in charge at Port Charid. So he spoke first. "This is Bench intelligence specialist Garol Vogel, on detail by instruction from Chilleau Judiciary. Why have your leaders changed course, please."

It annoyed Fleet when they were in the position of answering, rather than asking, the questions. That was all right. Garol didn't need them cooperative. He just needed them at Port Charid, rather than chasing out after ships on their way to the entrance of the Sillume vector.

The leading edges of the Langsarik fleet had begun their vector spins, their sensor traces distorting with the activity.

"Third Fleet Interrogations Group commander Minrodie, Bench specialist. We see a suspicious population movement in flight from Port Charid for the Sillume vector. The possibility exists that they are Langsariks. There is no response to lawful requests to stand down and return to Port Charid for interview. Pursuit is required to resolve questions about identity and motivation."

Yes, as he'd thought. Minrodie had done the analysis; Garol couldn't fault her reasoning. He was just going to have to be unreasonable. "Commander Minrodie. Does your Brief extend to conduct of search and seizure of commercial shipping? Abort your pursuit and make your scheduled orbitals at Port Charid. Acknowledge compliance."

No, her Brief did not authorize any such interference with trade. It was a formality, perhaps. But it was all Garol had to go on.

At the plotter scan to the right of the map wall

Garol thought he saw the first of the Langsarik ships drop off the scope.

But the three ships from the Fleet convoy were making good progress and gaining on the tail end of the escaping Langsariks. A ship pursued by another of similar size accelerating in too-near pursuit could not make a vector transit; the perturbation in trajectory created by such pursuit made a correct calculation impossible. He had to call the Fleet convoy ships off.

"Request your confirmation that subject ships are civil transports engaged in the lawful conduct of Bench-sanctioned trade, Bench specialist."

Minrodie wasn't giving in. Garol didn't blame her for it, though he had to force her compliance any way he could.

"I affirm that to my personal knowledge subject ships are all commercial hulls en route to the Sillume vector, so directed by me in response to instruction received from First Secretary Verlaine, Chilleau Judiciary. Abort your pursuit. You are exceeding the terms of your Brief."

Not as if that ever stopped Fleet.

But Minrodie's conviction did seem to falter. The three pursuit ships had not swerved from their intercept course, but none of the other ships in the convoy showed any signs of joining the chase. Yet.

Three more of the Langsarik ships were gone, including the first of the freighters. Some Langsariks had escaped, then, but Garol needed them all to be out of there, because the Langsariks were going to need each other in order to survive. Not only that—but the last of the freighters, the last of the ships, the freighter that had been the last to clear Port Charid, that was the ship carrying Walton Agenis.

"Failure to respond to a lawful request to stand to is a violation of Bench commercial procedure and within Fleet's Brief to enforce," Minrodie insisted.

Her three pursuit ships were gaining on the Langsarik fleet.

"And when a Fleet commerce-control group is posted at Port Charid it will duly enforce the commercial codes, that will be its charter. It is not your charter. You are not a Fleet commerce-control group, and you have been ordered to Port Charid. You will proceed to Port Charid. Any harassment on your part of commercial hulls can be expected to generate adverse notice at the highest level of authority."

He was beginning to sound desperate.

He was afraid it wasn't going to work after all. Agenis's freighter might be able to outrun the Fleet ships, but he couldn't risk finding out. If the Fleet ships got really annoyed, they could fire on the freighter. The Langsarik fleet needed its Flag Captain. Garol could not afford to contemplate what it would mean if Agenis were taken—Agenis, and her beautiful niece Modice, and her very capable nephew Shires, and even Kazmer Daigule, a basically decent man even if his grasp of Bench commercial codes was a little on the questionable side.

One of the ships among the fleeing Langsariks faltered.

It was a very small craft, the smallest on scan, so small in fact that it might well have escaped attention had it not started to transmit. A courier. A bomb ship? A decoy?

The acerbic tones of Cousin Stanoczk's strongly accented voice cracked over the comms, and Garol had to rub his chin briskly with his hand to cover a smile of relief and gratitude. Cousin Stanoczk. Intervening just as things were near critical, to hold the Fleet pursuit up just enough.

"This is a privately registered courier ship with diplomatic papers for the Dolgorukij Combine, what is the meaning of this outrage?"

Cousin Stanoczk, Garol noted, could do "outrage" with the best of them. There was a confused babble of circuit overrides and half-finished questions from the Fleet side of the communications; then Commander Minrodie was back.

"Transmit your clear codes, if you please. Confirmation of identity in progress."

The three pursuit ships slowed. The last Langsarik freighter was almost close enough to start its vector spin. Garol had to pay conscious attention to not holding his breath.

"Clear codes on transmit. You have not explained. The Combine will protest this arbitrary intervention in private business in the strongest possible terms unless we are permitted to continue on our way unmolested. Immediately."

Half the Langsarik fleet was away.

If Stanoczk could hold those three pursuit ships for just a while longer, it would be too late for them to ever catch up—and a pure waste of energy to even try. Not to mention the associated loss of face to go all-out in pursuit of a ship and not catch it. Fleet hated that. Bad for their image.

"We confirm identity and diplomatic immunity." Commander Minrodie sounded clearly reluctant to admit the fact, though. "On behalf of my command I apologize for the pursuit my ships executed on my direct orders. You are clear to go. —Abort pursuit."

It had to be difficult to see an enemy running away and not give chase; but Stanoczk had successfully interrupted the momentum of the pursuit, and Minrodie apparently knew when the balance of situational factors turned against her.

"Specialist Vogel," Commander Minrodie said, "I look forward to seeing you on our arrival. I'll want to hear all about the instructions of First Secretary Verlaine. I didn't know Combine diplomatic ships took direction from Chilleau Judiciary."

Or anywhere. She was quite right. She knew very well that something was wrong with the picture that she was seeing.

"At your convenience, Commander. Vogel away, here."

The communications line cut out, but the message on the scanning screens told him everything he needed to know.

Langsarik ships vanishing into the Sillume vector. The last of the ships just about ready to start vector spins; the Fleet convoy still steady for Port Charid, the three ships that had gone forward in pursuit turning back to rejoin their formation.

And then there was the tiny blip, the almost invisible trace, the surprising presence of Cousin Stanoczk in the train of the Langsarik fleet.

What was the Malcontent doing on his way to the Sillume vector?

Garol sat down.

Feraltz.

He'd been too busy worrying about Langsariks to check in on the ringleader of the false Langsariks. Stanoczk had to have left Port Charid in a hurry, in order to have gotten to where he was now. He'd sent Daigule to the freighter with the Langsariks. But had it been simply because of sympathy for Daigule's situation?

Or had there been something else going on as well?

"Son of a bitch," Garol said to himself. Half-infuriated; half-admiring.

If Stanoczk had taken Fisner Feraltz out from under the very nose of a Bench specialist—there would be merry Hell to pay at Chilleau Judiciary when the First Secretary found out that Garol had mislaid his most valuable prisoner.

It didn't matter.

Stanoczk had been where Garol needed him, when Garol had needed him there—to protect the rear guard of the Langsarik fleet and see Walton Agenis safe to the vector.

So long as the Langsarik fleet was safely away, he

could face even Stanoczk's underhanded dealing with forbearance and equanimity.

They had done it.

The Langsariks were free.

He had actively aided and abetted the successful escape of the Langsariks from the custody of the Bench and the orderly conduct of the Judicial process. He had willfully and deliberately sent the Langsariks out from under Jurisdiction altogether, in flagrant violation of the rule of Law.

It was the first time he had ever acknowledged any higher priority than that to which he had dedicated his life since he had left his home system and sworn his oath of service to the Bench.

But if the rule of Law was not the greatest good, after all that he had done in his life to uphold it—

If he had not done right to have discarded a lifetime's devotion to the rule of Law, there was no future for him anywhere.

Afterword

Garol Vogel sat quietly in the midmorning light of a streetside café in a small port halfway between one Judiciary's administrative center and another's, watching the steam rise from a cup of pressure-extracted bean tea.

Life was good, at least for a moment.

Nobody knew where he was or how to reach him; he was as close to off duty as he could remember ever being. The air was crisp and cool; the spicy fragrance rising from his cup was a pleasure no less intense for being simple.

A dark shape passed across the face of the morning sun, a shape that brought with it a fragrance that Garol seemed to remember. The Malcontent Cousin Stanoczk had laundered his clothing with soap mixed with powdered piros resin, from the scent of it; at least that was the most likely explanation for it, in Garol's mind.

"You're blocking my light," Garol said.

Nobody was supposed to know where he was.

But since his experiences at Port Charid, Garol knew better than to believe that this was a coincidence.

"Yes, thank you." Cousin Stanoczk pulled a wire chair clear of an adjacent table and sat down. "I don't mind if I *do* join you. What are you drinking?"

And wasn't Cousin Stanoczk in a good mood. Garol was still making up his mind whether he was going to yield to irritation or decline to give Stanoczk even so much honor as that.

"It's good." Tossing off his cup of bean tea—a little too hot, but pain helped him focus—Garol waved for the server. "You should try it. It'll put hair on your chest."

The server was prompt with two servings. Cousin Stanoczk recoiled with exaggerated timidity from the cup that the server set down in front of him. "I didn't know you cared. But you're not my type."

Garol had taken one hit of bean tea already; this would be his second. Three was his limit, when it was pressure-extracted. He had to give himself time to sneak up on this next one. "Shut up. You're disgusting."

Stanoczk laughed and took up his cup of bean tea with a gesture too absentminded to be that of a man who was unused to the beverage. "While you, on the other hand, are the man of the octave. Single-handedly clearing the vermin out of Port Charid. Elderly people safe to carry large sums of cash money, children frolic in the streets, grown men sleep more easily at night."

If only it had been that simple.

First Secretary Verlaine was still trying to decide whether he was more relieved than outraged, or the other way around.

As far as public relations went, it had come off. The Langsarik settlement had been removed from Port Charid, and it was really nobody's business where the Langsariks had actually gone. The raids had stopped, after all; that was all that people really cared about.

As far as the private man was concerned, though, Garol was resigned to waiting for a while before the First Secretary came around to Garol's way of looking at things.

"I've been meaning to speak to you about that." It hadn't been very high on his list of priorities, no. But it had unquestionably been in the back of Garol's mind. "You took something I wanted. I don't want it back. But I do want its evidence."

Stanoczk breathed deeply of his bean tea, his dark eyes hooded. Playing for time, obviously.

"Fisner has been badly damaged for a very long time."

Garol could take that in several ways. But Stanoczk seemed perfectly serious.

"It takes time to build trust, and he will be most useful to us when he grows willing to share the information he possesses. But there is something I am free to tell you."

It wasn't as if Garol had honestly expected any different.

He supposed it was petty of him to grudge Cousin Stanoczk his one source, when the Bench held ten. There was probably nothing he could really do about it anyway; unless he wanted to make an issue out of it—and Garol was fresh out of the energy required to take on ancient and entrenched secret services one-handed.

Maybe next year.

"Let's hear it."

Stanoczk had finished his bean tea and was running his ring finger around the rim to pick up the last traces of his drink. Disgusting. "Yes. I'm to invite you to a handfasting. It is not to be a traditional ceremony, because it is a mixed marriage. The bride is Langsariks, and her accepted suitor is Sarvaw."

Stanoczk had heard news?

"Where do we send our heartfelt expressions of goodwill?"

Stanoczk shook his head. "The happy couple haven't quite settled on a permanent address. But I'm to assure you that you'll always be welcome with the family."

Cousin Stanoczk had heard from Walton Agenis. Or at least from someone who had heard from Walton Agenis. Garol took a moment to observe the pain in his heart, mildly surprised at its intensity. He was usually better than this at losing people that he loved, but maybe that was the problem. She wasn't lost. She was waiting for him in Gonebeyond space . . . or if she wasn't waiting, she was there, and he could go.

But would not.

"Lost your new man, then." That'd be more than one of them with explaining to do. Not as if it was any of his business.

Stanoczk just shrugged. "Him? He'd never have worked out. No. I undervalue him. He could have been brilliant, but he would have been miserable. That's not the way we do business."

This was interesting. "Exactly how is it that you do, er, business, then?" Garol had been a little unclear on that, from the beginning.

"Simple exchange of absolutes." Stanoczk had waved for the server to come back and bring more bean tea. Two more. Both of which he gathered to himself; Garol hadn't touched his second cup yet. "You give me everything. I give you anything."

Well, that told Garol exactly nothing. "So what did you get?"

Stanoczk flashed him a quick look, and for a moment Garol wondered if he'd actually managed to take Cousin Stanoczk by surprise. It was hard to tell. Maybe Stanoczk was just offended.

"It is myself and the Saint between, Garol Aphon."

If not actually offended, emphatically standing on his dignity and his Dolgorukij syntax. So much for that.

"Thanks for stopping anyway," Garol said, as graciously as possible. "We'll do it again. Feel free to drop in any old time."

It was good to know that the Langsarik fleet had survived at least this long on the other side. They were resilient. They would make it work.

Kazmer Daigule and Modice Agenis. Like wedding a heavy mover to a racing shallop; but they had history between them, from what little Garol had ever been able to observe. Daigule had a good heart and strong will to carry it forward. Modice could do worse.

Garol couldn't imagine it could get any better for Daigule, marrying the spectacular beauty that he adored—smart and strong and brave, as well as beautiful. Almost too much for any one man.

Stanoczk slurped his bean tea hastily, one cup after the other, as he rose. "Right, Vogel. Same to you. Feel free to call on us if you need us. Any consular post or higher. Tell them that Cousin Stanoczk is looking for you, and they'll do the rest."

Shouldn't it be the other way around?

And surely there was more than one man named Stanoczk in service to the Malcontent. It was a relatively common name. At least among Dolgorukij.

"Thanks. I'll remember that."

Stanoczk left without paying.

But that was a signal, from someone like Cousin Stanoczk. He'd meant it when he'd said that Garol could call on him. And the price of a few cups of bean tea was as nothing compared to the value of the news that Cousin Stanoczk had brought him.

Langsariks safe, Modice to be married, and there was communication taking place between Gone-beyond space and worlds under Jurisdiction, however private and secretive.

Agenis had escaped.

The Bench had been saved from a shameful stain in its honor, a corrosive miscarriage of justice that could only have contributed to the increasing instability that bedeviled all of Jurisdiction space.

The First Secretary would come around, or he wouldn't.

It was only rarely that Garol had a chance to take pride in having made a decision, without it being tempered with regret for the consequences, the outcome of his actions.

Conflict and compromise, politics, propaganda—

Once in a great while he got a chance to act on his fundamental sense of fairness and equity, and have it come out right. Instead of just less wrong.

With that knowledge in his heart, and Cousin Stanoczk's message in his thoughts, Garol sat in the increasing warmth of the late morning; and for a small but sufficient space of time, he was happy.

Classic Science Fiction & Fantasy from